Praise for the novels of Nina Bruhns

Three-time overall winner of the Daphne du Maurier Award for Excellence in Mystery/Suspense

If Looks Could Chill

"A thrill ride of fast action and hot sex in the steamy Louisiana bayous, Nina Bruhns's latest delivers it all!"

—CJ Lyons, bestselling author of *Warning Signs*

"An exhilarating romantic suspense . . . Fans will not be able to put the thriller down until finished."

—*Genre Go Round Reviews*

Shoot to Thrill

"Suspense just got a whole lot hotter with Nina Bruhns's dynamite romantic thriller. A hero to die for and a heroine to cheer for . . . An awesome, sexy story."

—*New York Times* bestselling author Allison Brennan

"Intense pacing . . . powerful characters . . . searing emotions and explosive sexual tension! Once I started reading *Shoot to Thrill*, I couldn't stop! Nina Bruhns writes high-action suspense at its very best!" —Bestselling author Debra Webb

"Sexy, suspenseful, and so gritty you'll taste the desert sand. A thrill ride start to finish!"

—*USA Today* bestselling author Rebecca York

continued . . .

"A provocative, sexy thriller that will get your adrenaline pumping on all levels. A riveting breakout novel that will shoot Ms. Bruhns straight to bestsellerdom. Move over, boys, and see how it's really done!"

—Award-winning mystery author Tamar Myers

"Nina Bruhns's book will thrill readers who love action and romance in their stories. *Shoot to Thrill* is a wild ride, full of spec ops adventure and fun!"

—Award-winning author Gennita Low

Praise for the other novels of Nina Bruhns

"The stuff legends are made out of."

—*Midwest Book Review*

"Shocking discoveries, revenge, humor, and passion fill the pages . . . An interesting and exciting story with twists and turns."

—*Joyfully Reviewed*

"[A] delightfully whimsical tale that enchants the reader from beginning to end. Yo ho ho and a bottle of fun!"

—Award-winning author Deborah MacGillivray

"This is one you will definitely not want to miss!"

—*In the Library Reviews*

"Nina Bruhns . . . imbues complex characters with a great sense of setting in a fast-paced suspense story overladen with steamy sex." —*The Romance Reader*

"Gifted new author Nina Bruhns makes quite a splash in her debut . . . Ms. Bruhns's keen eye for vivid, unforgettable scenes and a wonderful romantic sensibility bode well for a long and successful career."

—*Romantic Times* (4 stars)

"The intricate and believable plots crafted by Nina Bruhns prove she is a master of any genre. Her talent shines from every word of her books." —CataRomance.com

"The kind of story that really gets your adrenaline flowing. It's action-packed and sizzling hot, with some intensely emotional moments." —*Romance Junkies*

"Nina Bruhns writes beautifully and poetically and made me a complete believer." —*Once Upon A Romance*

"Tells a very rich tale of love . . . A book you are going to want to add to your collection." —*Romance at Heart*

Berkley Sensation Titles by Nina Bruhns

SHOOT TO THRILL

IF LOOKS COULD CHILL

A KISS TO KILL

A Kiss to KILL

NINA BRUHNS

BERKLEY SENSATION, NEW YORK

THE BERKLEY PUBLISHING GROUP
Published by the Penguin Group
Penguin Group (USA) Inc.
375 Hudson Street, New York, New York 10014, USA
Penguin Group (Canada), 90 Eglinton Avenue East, Suite 700, Toronto, Ontario M4P 2Y3, Canada
(a division of Pearson Penguin Canada Inc.)
Penguin Books Ltd., 80 Strand, London WC2R 0RL, England
Penguin Group Ireland, 25 St. Stephen's Green, Dublin 2, Ireland (a division of Penguin Books Ltd.)
Penguin Group (Australia), 250 Camberwell Road, Camberwell, Victoria 3124, Australia
(a division of Pearson Australia Group Pty. Ltd.)
Penguin Books India Pvt. Ltd., 11 Community Centre, Panchsheel Park, New Delhi—110 017, India
Penguin Group (NZ), 67 Apollo Drive, Rosedale, North Shore 0632, New Zealand
(a division of Pearson New Zealand Ltd.)
Penguin Books (South Africa) (Pty.) Ltd., 24 Sturdee Avenue, Rosebank, Johannesburg 2196,
South Africa

Penguin Books Ltd., Registered Offices: 80 Strand, London WC2R 0RL, England

A KISS TO KILL

A Berkley Sensation Book / published by arrangement with the author

PRINTING HISTORY
Berkley Sensation mass-market edition / April 2010

Cover art by Craig White.
Cover design by Rita Frangie.
Interior text design by Kristin del Rosario.

For information, address: The Berkley Publishing Group,
a division of Penguin Group (USA) Inc.,
375 Hudson Street, New York, New York 10014.

ISBN: 978-0-425-23383-2

BERKLEY® SENSATION
Berkley Sensation Books are published by The Berkley Publishing Group,
a division of Penguin Group (USA) Inc.,
375 Hudson Street, New York, New York 10014.

PRINTED IN THE UNITED STATES OF AMERICA

10 9 8 7 6 5 4 3 2 1

To Mary Alice, Tamar, Judy, Dorothy, and Vicki,
the best friends anyone could ever have.
Love you all!

ONE

Manhattan
April, present day

THEY *were using her as bait.*

Dr. Gina Cappozi could feel them following her. All day she'd had that peculiar sensation of eyes on her back, the spill of goose bumps on her flesh for no reason, a tingle in the hairs on her neck . . . obviously the STORM Corps special ops guys must be doing what they did best—lurking in the shadows, watching her from doorways and alleys, scanning the busy Manhattan streets for danger. Always there for her. Always watching her back. Waiting patiently for their mutual enemy to appear.

She wished they would just go away and leave her the hell alone.

Their constant presence was meant to be reassuring. It should be a comfort knowing they were there watching out for her. But it wasn't. Because even though STORM Corps had once heroically saved her life, and now supposedly had her under protective surveillance, she also knew those spec ops guys had an agenda—to get their hands on *him*, their hidden enemy, any way they could.

And she was their Judas goat.

Well, too bad. They'd have to wait their turn at the bastard. Because she wanted him even more than they did.

Her nemesis. *Captain Gregg van Halen.*

Gina glanced around as she quickly took the steps down into the black maw of the Lexington Avenue subway tunnel. No familiar faces lingered in the crowd as the crush of mindless, homebound humanity carried her along in its wake. Would she be able to give her babysitters the slip this time?

Or maybe they'd decided she really was paranoid, that her pursuer was just a figment of her PTSD-induced overactive imagination, and had already gone away and left her on her own. Maybe it was van Halen she could feel stalking her.

Good. Let the bastard come.

Just let him try and hurt her. She was ready. Her body was healed. And her mind . . . well, her mind was as healed as it was going to get. For now.

She was armed, of course. She never left her Upper East Side brownstone without her weapon of choice. Hell, even inside her home, she was never without her knife. Nowhere was safe for her, indoors or out. Not as long as van Halen still drew breath.

She wrapped her fingers firmly around the handle of the razor-sharp KA-BAR knife tucked in her coat pocket. Oh, yes. She'd been practicing, all right. Lunging and plunging it into the heart of a straw target, over and over, until little piles of cut straw lay scattered on the ground all around and its cloth covering was sliced to ribbons. Day after day, week after week. She'd decimated a hundred targets or more, much to the chagrin of her STORM self-defense instructor.

She was confident now, no longer terrified of the mere thought of coming face-to-face with the man who'd haunted her nightmares for the past six months. The man who had sold her to terrorists and walked away without a backward glance.

Really, what could he do to her that she hadn't already endured? Nothing. He couldn't hurt her. Not this time. Not her body. Not her heart. He wouldn't take her by surprise again. He wouldn't get the chance.

No one would. Because Gina Cappozi was taking her life back.

And Gregg van Halen was going to die.

That was for damn sure. The very hand that had lovingly stroked his skin and caressed his body to fevered arousal was going to be the same hand that ended his miserable life for good.

And if she was very, very lucky, it would happen tonight.

FUCKING *hell, not again.*

STORM operator Alex Zane struggled to take a breath. Frantically, he fought against the menacing desert mirage as Afghanistan closed in all around him, binding him in a breathless straitjacket of horror. Desperately, he tried to block the piercing screams.

"No!" he cried. "Get the fuck away!"

Too late. No way out of the nightmare now.

He hugged his rifle to his body and burrowed his back into the rocky hillside above the Afghan village where he'd been sitting for hours, waiting for the signal to attack. Screams of pain echoed through the heat-shimmering air like sirens of death.

His comm crackled and his team leader's urgent voice broke over the headset. "Zero Alpha X-ray, this is Zero

Alpha Six, do you read me?" Kick Jackson sounded urgent. But competent. In control. *Unlike Alex.*

He grasped at Kick's voice, clinging to it like a shipwrecked sailor. "What's going on out there, Alpha Six?" Alex asked, fighting the panic. *Fucking breathe, soldier!*

Kick's voice barked out, "Do not move in! It's a trap. Repeat, do not— God*damn* it! Drew! Get back here!" Kick swore again, and Alex could hear his sharp breaths, like he'd taken off at a dead run. In the background, the terrible screams grew louder. "Abort and withdraw!" Kick yelled, cursing. Then the comm went dead.

Suddenly, an explosion ricocheted off the mud walls of the village below. Alex flung his rifle onto his back and scrabbled up the rocky hillside to take a look. No way was he retreating, leaving Kick and the others to—

A dozen village men surged over the ridge just above him, pointing their weapons at his head and shouting. His pulse rocketed out of control. *Sonofa fucking bitch!* He spun in the dirt and launched himself down the slope. He hit the comm. "X-ray under attack!"

His assailants swarmed after him. He had to lead them away from the rest of the team.

No! Don't do it! his mind cried out. *Don't—*

Gunfire erupted all around. More screams.

Fire scorched across his temple and pain burst through his shoulder. He jerked and stumbled. The world tilted, then went black. But miraculously, he was still conscious. Terror crushed his chest. He scrambled up again and ran. Blind. *My God, he was blind!*

He ran straight into a human hornet's nest. Vicious hands grabbed his arms, fingers yanked painfully at his hair, gun butts slammed into the soft organs of his body. He cried out in agony, striking back, kicking with all his blind fury.

His captors just laughed. And beat him until his flesh turned to red oatmeal.

Then they bound a rope around his ankles and threw him to the ground.

A raw sob escaped his throat. Fuck, no! No. No. *Fuck no!*

"Alex?" Kick's reassuring voice floated in on a cool breeze.

He tried to yell an answer. But his throat had strangled closed on a mute cry. He knew all too well what came next. And there was nothing to do but endure it. *Again.*

Or go completely insane.

Which he might do anyway. *Again.*

"Alex?" Kick called from far away. *Too far.* He'd never reach him in time.

The motor of a Jeep roared and gears ground. He thrashed against his bonds. *Fucking damn it to hell!*

The rope around his ankles yanked taut. *Oh, God, this was really happening.* He tensed his body. Prepared himself for the hideous pain.

"Alex!"

The Jeep jerked forward. So did he. A bloody layer of skin stayed behind on the ground.

He screamed.

"Alex! Wake up!" The order was firm and clear, like the voice of God. It would not be disobeyed.

Alex surged out of his nightmare, wrenched upright with a lurch, and hit his head on the solid roof liner of an SUV.

Jesus!

He looked around frantically as he shook off the dregs of an illusion so real it made him doubt his own sanity. Tall buildings crowded around the vehicle. Horns blared on the busy street. Men in suits chatted on their Bluetooths.

He was back in Manhattan.

"Shit!" he gritted out, gulping down a painful gasp of much-needed air. *"Shit."* He grabbed the steering wheel and gripped it to steady his throbbing, reeling head. Harsh breaths stung his lungs as he forced himself to calm his raging insides.

Just another damn flashback . . .

Today was his first op for STORM Corps, and he'd spent all day sitting in an SUV on a stakeout—not on some godforsaken A-stan mountaintop fighting insurgents. *Thank God.*

All too slowly, the debilitating panic and adrenaline subsided. Until, finally, he was able to unclench his fingers and stomach. *Fuck.* He'd never been claustrophobic before. But then again, he had never been a lot of things before . . . until the events of the past two years had taken their heavy toll. He shouldn't have been particularly surprised when the insidious panic swept over him, stealing the air from his lungs and thrusting him into a living nightmare of hallucination. But he always was.

"You okay, bro?" Kick asked at length.

Alex exhaled heavily. Looked up into the worried face of his best friend, who was white-knuckling the edge of the open SUV window, leaning in. Not touching or reaching for him. Just observing, at the ready. He'd been through this before, the debilitating flashbacks. They both had.

"Fuck," Alex said aloud, shaking like a goddamn leaf. "Fucking hell."

"Yup," Kick said. Perfect understanding weighted his intense gaze. That day in A-stan when Alex was captured, Kick had been half blown up by a land mine and left for dead. It had been a long, long road back for both of them.

And it wasn't over yet. Not by a long shot.

But *hell.* Alex had really thought he was ready to go back to work. After all, the injury-induced blindness was gone, his body weight was back up to where it had been before the tender loving care of his al Sayika terrorist captors had starved it in half, his muscles were again firm and rippling . . . if under a web of angry red scars. He no longer flinched at sudden sounds or movements.

Much.

It was just the fucking claustrophobia that still got to him. Who'd have thought simply sitting in a closed vehicle would trigger it? He sighed. More damn fodder for his damn shrink.

He steadied his fingers and slashed them through his hair. "I don't know how long I've been out. Did I screw up? Is she home? Did I miss her?"

Her being Dr. Gina Cappozi, the object of the surveillance he may just have goatfucked all to hell. Gina Cappozi had also been a captive of al Sayika for three months, but here in the States, and for entirely different reasons than Alex. They'd brazenly captured her, beaten her, and compelled her to produce a horrific biological weapon to use against her own country, hoping to kill millions in an attack on U.S. soil. But she'd outsmarted them and foiled their plans.

After her rescue, the decimated terrorist organization was out for vengeance and had put a price on her head. A big one. Double the price they'd put on his and Kick's after his own rescue. Everyone, including Alex—hell, especially Alex—was expecting some fanatic *jihadi* to show up and collect on it any minute.

Thus Gina's protective detail, of which he and Kick were a part of. The operation was being run by STORM Corps—Strategic Technical Operations and Rescue Missions Corporation—Alex's and Kick's relatively new employer. STORM had been contracted for the mission by the U.S. Department of Homeland Security.

Initially, Alex had been on Gina's tag team, but he'd kept jumping at shadows, absolutely certain she was being followed by someone other than STORM. But no one else on the team had spotted any kind of tail, or danger, or anything suspicious at all. It was just him being paranoid.

Big fucking shock.

So he'd been reassigned to watch her brownstone—a throwaway job no one had thought he could possibly fuck up . . . though no one had actually said it aloud.

How wrong they all had been.

"No worries," Kick told him now. "Dr. Cappozi's fine. She just got on the subway to come home."

It suddenly dawned on Alex that Kick was supposed to be on tag duty today with Kowalski. "Then what are you doing here?" he asked. "Are you sure nothing's happened?"

"Gina's safe," Kick reassured him. "But there's been a development. NSA picked up some interesting chatter overnight."

Alex was instantly alert. "What kind of chatter? About al Sayika?"

Kick nodded.

Alex narrowed his eyes. For many years both he and Kick had worked as operators for an outfit called Zero Unit, which was an ultra-covert black ops unit run from the deepest bowels of the U.S. Central Intelligence Agency. But after the deadly disaster in A-stan, and another near-debacle six months ago in the Sudan, Kick was convinced al Sayika must have a mole working for them—either within Zero Unit itself, or someone higher up, maybe in another government agency with close ties to ZU. How else could the terrorists have obtained such accurate details of both ill-fated operations? Details solid enough to sabotage the missions and leave most of the teams dead.

When Gina had been taken right from under their noses at Zero Unit headquarters, there had been an investigation. Sure, everyone had been cleared. But Kick still had his doubts. *Someone* had betrayed them. Alex agreed. They were dealing with an inside traitor of the worst ilk.

So they'd both quit Zero Unit and joined STORM, a similar but non-governmental spec ops outfit. They were fairly certain that STORM had not been infiltrated by the terrorists. Last year, the organization had staged Dr. Cappozi's rescue in Louisiana, as well as Kick's retrieval of Alex over in the Sudan—all without leaks from their side.

Dr. Cappozi's current protection detail was just part of a bigger mission: to find and eliminate the scumfuck traitor working as a mole in the U.S. government for the al Sayika terrorists. Dr. Cappozi was convinced the man they were looking for was her former lover, Captain Gregg van Halen, a Zero Unit operator who'd gone rogue shortly after her capture. The evidence supported her belief.

If she was right, this van Halen prick was directly responsible for Alex's imprisonment and torture, Kick's terrible injuries, and the hideous deaths of their teammates.

For Alex and Kick, the mission was one of pure revenge. God help van Halen when the two of them got hold of him.

And they would. That was a goddamn fucking promise.

Kick finally opened the SUV's door and got in. "Quinn called a meeting," he said. "He wants us back at HQ, ASAP."

"What about the Cappozi place?" Alex asked, glancing uneasily at the three-story brownstone before hesitantly reaching for the vehicle's ignition. "What if I'm *not* being paranoid and—"

"Johnson has her six on the subway. And they're bringing in Miles to finish your shift here," Kick told him. "She'll be in good hands until Marc and Tara take over their regular watch at nine tonight."

Alex pushed out a breath. "All right." He checked the dashboard clock. It was just after five. "I guess that works."

Kick raised a brow as he put the SUV in gear. "You good to drive, bro?"

Alex gave a humorless chuckle. "Worried about my mental health?"

"Hell, yeah. I need to stay alive. Newlywed and all, remember?"

"Like I could forget," he muttered with a wry curl of his lip. Kick had been relentlessly happy since tying the knot. Not that Alex begrudged his friend. He was glad *one* of them was happy, at least.

He gunned the engine to life. "And damn, Kick. In case you hadn't noticed, *every*one behind the wheel in this town is a fucking lunatic. Trust me, I'll blend right in."

GREGG van Halen followed Gina Cappozi onto the subway car at the last possible second, making sure she didn't dart out again just before the doors closed.

She didn't. Didn't even try.

Not that it surprised him. For the past week, since returning home to Manhattan after her lengthy convalescence upstate, his lover had done nothing to avoid being found. Nothing to escape the menace that lurked in the corners of the darkness, seeking to hunt her down.

It was almost like she was taunting him. Or fate. Except for the occasional furtive, hollow-eyed glances she gave her surroundings, you'd never know she was in a constant state of terror.

Avoiding the vigilant observation of the STORM agent tailing her, Gregg casually grabbed the center pole of the subway car along with the horde of commuters anxious to get home for the night. The sliding doors slammed shut and the wheels lurched forward with the distinctive rattle and squeal of the New York subway.

He turned his back on Gina. He didn't need to face her. In fact, he preferred watching her in the flickering reflection of the grimy window. Better to keep the rage from showing in his face and giving him away.

Her dark green eyes went to and fro as she clung to an overhead strap, her gaze alighting for a quick perusal of each passenger before shifting to the next. Always moving. Always searching.

For him.

He allowed himself a grim inward smile. *So nice to be wanted.*

She'd never see him, though. Yeah, she'd see a man, a tall man, his head and shoulders obscured by a baggy hoodie. But not *him*, not Gregg van Halen. Not until he chose to show himself. Which he wouldn't. Not with those STORM clowns following her every move. But he could be patient when he needed to be.

Gregg had been invisible for so much of his life, it took no effort at all to remain so. Even in plain sight, in broad daylight, he was a true shadow-dweller. A ghost.

A spook.

His lips flicked up. An apt description. For it went far deeper than his job. The shadows themselves drew him. Dark obscurity spoke to him. Even now, it whispered in his ear, beckoned to him from the pitch-black void just beyond the strobing flash of the subway window where he watched his own reflection, and that of his woman.

Alas, he could not answer the call and slip back into the void. There was something he must do before returning to the sheltering comfort of anonymity. He must deal with the overwhelming wrath in his heart. And take care of this woman. His lover.

In the mirrored film noir frames of the moving window, he searched her face for any sign of recognition. Or of alarm. And found none. Her eyes passed quickly over him.

But within himself, crouching right next to the anger that simmered and roiled in his chest, he felt a bone-deep physical recognition of her. And had a sudden, overwhelming need to put his hands on her. A need so potent and visceral it nearly sucked the breath from him.

He *knew* this woman, intimately. Knew her flesh and her fears. He had plunged deep inside her and felt her quake with the pleasure his presence there had brought her. And had felt her tremble with the fear of his absolute power over her.

He wanted to feel her quake and tremble again.

But she would never allow it. Never accept him again as she once had.

Because he had betrayed her.

He had betrayed everything.

He battled back a surge of sick fury. Steeled his insides and beat back the clot of unwanted emotion. Anger would not help. Emotions would not help. Only action would.

As the train screeched around a curve, he released the pole, letting his body wedge into the clutch of commuters surrounding her. No need to hold on. His balance was perfect, honed through years of hard physicality on his job as a mercenary for Uncle. Bit by bit, inch by inch, he eased closer to her—the backward bump always accidental, the sideways step seemingly unintentional. Until his back was at her front. Not quite touching.

But oh so close.

Close enough to catch the familiar, tempting scent of the woman he'd once tied to his bed and taken in ways that had both thrilled her . . . and frightened her to the marrow.

He'd always frightened her. From their first wary, agenda-filled meeting, he'd scared the pants off her. Literally and figuratively. It was part of his attraction. And hers. She had once loved the edgy thrill of it. But now . . . she hated him. Hated him with a depth that nearly matched his own.

While she'd been at the sanatorium up north, from hidden vantage points on the grounds he had watched her body slowly heal from the terrible trauma she'd gone through. But in her mind the terror still loomed as large as when she'd been a captive of al Sayika. She'd learned to defend herself, studying deadly moves, plunging her knife into the center of a man-shaped target over and over. Imagining it to be his own black heart, he was sure.

During the months he'd observed her and covertly listened in on her debriefs and conversations via the device he'd planted in her room at Haven Oaks, one thing had become abundantly clear: Gina Cappozi wanted him dead. And *she* wanted to be the one to kill him.

Too bad he couldn't let that happen.

The train sliced through the black tunnel, lights flashing to the cacophony of the steel rails. He cocked his head to the side and inhaled, picking out his lover's unique fragrance from the potent olfactory brew of refuse, burning brakes, and the perfumed sweat of a thousand bodies.

She glanced around uneasily. Nervous. Instinctively sensing a predator close by.

Impassively, he read an ad sign hanging on the wall, keeping his face hidden. She anxiously caught the eye of the STORM agent across the car from her, who shook his head reassuringly. She shuddered out a breath and tightened her grip on the strap above her again as wheels screamed and the train pulled to a herky-jerky stop at the next station.

Passengers all around disgorged, jostling them so her body was wrenched away from his. New people crowded around. He steered closer. The doors slammed shut again.

Heedless to the danger, he turned and deliberately stepped up right behind her, this time his front to her back. She was tall, especially in her work heels, but he was taller. Much taller. Heartbeat accelerating, he spread his feet and grabbed the strap next to hers.

He hovered over her. *Close. So close.* Silky strands of

her long black hair tickled his nose . . . smelling of the woman he had stripped naked and taught to pleasure him as no other woman ever had.

His body remembered those nights. Achingly well. He could still hear the echoes of her groaned sighs and throaty moans as he took her. Could still feel the touch of her fingers and the tip of her tongue as she explored his body to their mutual, shivering delight.

His cock grew thick and hard, remembering.

Again the brakes squealed, the car slowed; people shifted in readiness to exit.

He nearly vibrated with the urge to touch her. To step into her. To press his body right up against hers and feel her succulent curves fitted against his unyielding muscle. Just for a fleeting moment.

But he didn't dare.

She must have felt the air around them quicken. Must have sensed the taut, electric thrum of lust, which pulsed through his whole body for want of her. Must have inhaled his eager male pheromones as they sought a way to lure her to his bed again. Suddenly, she went rigid. Her knuckles turned white on the strap she clung to. Her head whipped around and she raked his features with a fear-sharpened glare.

But he had already looked away. Averted his hooded face so she couldn't see the hunger prowling in it like a trapped tiger. Or read the intent lying there, in wait. Waiting for the right moment.

To take her.

The train jerked to a halt and she stumbled backward into him. She gasped. He didn't move. But she felt it—the long, thick ridge that the memories had raised between his thighs. Her breath sucked in. Her hand dropped. To touch him?

He knew better. She was reaching for her knife.

But too late.
He was already out the door.
It wasn't time. Not quite yet.
But soon he would have her.
Very soon.

TWO

THE rest of the team was waiting for Alex and Kick in the penthouse of the classy Park Avenue hotel they were using as their Manhattan base of operations.

One thing about STORM Corps, they didn't scrimp on amenities for their operators. STORM Commander Kurt Bridger always said as long as the team was INCONUS—inside the United States—they should be enjoying life's luxuries. Because you never knew what fetid armpit of the world they'd be sent to tomorrow, expected to lay down their lives for the client. Nice digs were the least the company could do in return, Bridger said.

Alex had become all too familiar with fetid armpits during his dozen years with Zero Unit—not to mention his sixteen long months at al Sayika's Club Torture. Even now, he'd sometimes wake up as the sun peeked over the horizon and find himself shivering on the cold marble floor of some gilded hallway or crammed into the deepest, darkest corner of a closet in whichever lavish rooms he was occupying, stinking of fear.

Old habits died hard. Especially when they'd been formed at gunpoint. Or worse.

But on the nights he actually remained in his bed, it was nice to wake at dawn, nose-deep in feathered comfort, five-hundred-count cotton soothing the savage itch of his still-tender scars. So, yeah. Alex appreciated STORM's generosity more than he could say.

This evening, the penthouse serving as the Cappozi op HQ carried the scent of old roses, sweet coffee, and . . . lasagna? In the white stone foyer, Alex paused for a second to inhale the welcoming scents before following Kick into the suite. They headed for the situation room—the kitchen—where Bobby Lee Quinn always held his team meetings.

Quinn was the op leader this go-round. He'd recently been promoted out of the field onto STORM Command, but because he'd led the ground team that had rescued Dr. Cappozi four months ago in Louisiana, at his request Bridger had reassembled most of that team and put Quinn back in charge of it. Alex had heard all about the Louisiana op from Kick, who'd been an integral part of it, and from Dr. Cappozi herself. Despite some major setbacks, the team had successfully saved the hostage, foiled a biological attack on U.S. soil, and shut down the entire al Sayika sleeper cell that had kidnapped her. The tangos were now all either dead or in jail.

Alex, of course, had been flat on his back at that time, recovering from his captivity and totally useless up at Haven Oaks, a STORM-owned sanatorium in central New York. Which was also where Gina Cappozi had gone to recuperate from her horrific experience, and where he'd gotten to know her.

It helped that she had met and trusted the people protecting her now—and that everyone on the team had a very personal stake in the outcome. Hell, Kick had even married Gina's best friend, Rainie, who was now working as a nurse at Haven Oaks.

There were eight on the Cappozi protection detail, rotating in shifts: Kick Jackson, Commander Bobby Lee Quinn, Darcy Zimmerman, Marc Lafayette, and Tara Reeves, all of whom had been on the Louisiana op, plus Dez Johnson, Miles Cavanaugh, and Alex himself.

As he strode with Kick through the penthouse to the kitchen, Darcy Zimmerman, the team's whiz of a computer specialist, glanced up. She was sitting at a polished wood desk covered by a conglomeration of high-tech monitors and towers. Darcy was tall, blond, and model-gorgeous. Oh, yeah, and she could kill you seven different ways before you even knew she'd moved.

She rose to tag along. "Hey guys. Anything new on the surveillance?" Darcy wasn't on the watch team. Her assignment was to work her electronic magic and get a bead on the enemy through cyberspace.

"Same ole same ole," Kick answered, thankfully keeping mute about the flashback incident. "But Alex still thinks Gina's being followed by someone besides us."

Darcy flicked Alex a glance. "See anyone today?" She actually took his paranoia seriously. Sweet.

He shook his head, torn between gratitude and embarrassment. "Just the usual demons."

Darcy gave him a sympathetic smile, hooked her arm through his, and gave his cheek a sisterly peck as they entered the kitchen. "Don't worry, Zane"—Darcy always addressed everyone by their last name—"it'll all get better with time."

"Hey!" Quinn feigned a protest at her intimate gesture. The commander and Darcy were an item. Well, more than an item, actually. They'd gotten engaged and moved in together a few months back.

She went into Quinn's arms and they shared a soft kiss. *Not* a sisterly one. "You know I only love you, babe."

Alex turned away with a grimace. Excuse him while he puked. Like it wasn't bad enough with newlyweds Kick and Rainie mooning over each other every chance they got, via the phone or otherwise.

Alex *so* did not want to be reminded of love, or anything remotely close to it. Unfortunately, the affliction seemed to be epidemic on the team of late.

Kick caught his eye and gave him an impertinent wink.

Alex scowled back, pretending to have no idea what his friend was alluding to. Or rather, *who*. As fucking if.

Kick had been there through the whole sordid mess Alex laughingly referred to as his love life, since his return from captivity. Kick believed he had soured on women because his longtime fiancée, the perfect, flawless, Southern belle society deb Helena Middleton, had dumped his ass the day before their wedding, effectively leaving him at the altar. And by the way, yes, that would be the *same* fiancée who had reportedly remained faithful to Alex's memory the *entire* sixteen months he'd been at Club Torture and presumed dead.

Alex snorted. *Soured?* Kick didn't know the half of it.

Fuck, he didn't know the *quarter* of it . . .

Not that Alex would ever tell. There were some things a gentleman just did not divulge about a lady, no matter how poorly he'd been treated. Nor how intensely relieved over her unexpected but welcome change of heart . . .

"Heard from Special Agent Haywood lately?" Kick asked him with a smart-ass glint in his eyes.

Special Agent Rebel Haywood. The name hit Alex like a fucking jackboot in the teeth.

Followed closely by vivid images of the delectable Agent

Haywood that still haunted him from countless captive dreams. His angel, he'd called her then, back when he'd been trapped in hell. Because at the time he'd had no memory of her name, or who she was. Or, for that matter, who *he* was. Those amazing dreams of Rebel Haywood had gotten him through much of the horror of his imprisonment.

His angel smiling. His angel teasing.

His angel *naked*.

Totally, wonderfully, titillatingly naked.

Pure fantasy, of course. In real life he'd never seen her naked. Ever. Not that he hadn't *want*ed to. It was just all that other stuff that came with *being* naked he hadn't ever wanted. Or rather, hadn't ever wanted to deal with again. He'd learned his lesson on that score, thankyouverymuch. Which was how he'd landed in that huge marriage mess with Helena Middleton in the *first* place. And why, since meeting Rebel several years ago, he'd always avoided the uncomfortable knowledge that she'd been crushing on him the whole time.

Way too heavy for the old pre-capture Alex. He didn't need or want the emotional responsibility for another human being's happiness. Not with his job. Or all his other issues . . . He was gone half the time, in dangerous situations that could turn deadly at any given moment. And when he was INCONUS . . . well, let's just say he wasn't planning a family anytime soon.

Rebel Haywood was strictly picket fence material. She wanted a husband, kids, and Sunday barbeques. She'd hinted at it often enough. No. He could never have made a woman like her happy.

But what about the new Alex? Post-rescue?

True, being tortured for sixteen months changed a man's perspective. And priorities. But some things never changed. Well, unless they got worse, of course.

Thank Jesus the pretense with Helena had come to a

screeching halt. She was far better off without him, and she obviously knew it.

But the tempting Rebel Haywood and her enduring crush? God. What would he do if the opportunity to have her—really have her—ever presented itself? After experiencing the sweet torture of those dreams, he'd be a saint not to act on it. But as much as he wished it were otherwise, he could never be the man she wanted him to be. Hell, *needed* him to be. Not in the long term, anyway. Not in the happily-ever-after picket-fence-two-kids-and-a-dog sense she wanted with him. Not then. Not now.

So it was just as well that was no longer an option. She'd made sure of it by transferring to the FBI field office in Norfolk, Virginia.

Oh, yeah. And by fucking her brains out with some other guy.

Alex ground his teeth. *His own damn fault.* Yeah, and Helena's—but thankfully, that whole screwed up relationship was over and done now. And so was he. With women. Christopher Alexander Zane had learned his lesson. Yes, indeed.

Kick winked again. Alex ground his teeth harder. All right, fine. Maybe Kick *did* know the half of it.

He sent his friend a warning growl. *Drop it, dawg.*

Unperturbed, Kick chuckled, and went over to the counter and poured himself a cup of coffee. *Fucking joker.*

"Evenin' all." The greeting came from the doorway. Marc Lafayette yawned as he strolled into the kitchen with Tara Reeves tucked under his arm. Tara looked as fragile on the outside as Alex felt on the inside. She'd been through a monthlong hospital stay recently, also thanks to al Sayika. But unlike Alex, her outward appearance was deceptive. On the inside she was strong . . . thanks to the support of her new husband, Marc.

The pair looked like they'd just rolled out of bed. Which

they no doubt had. Alex glanced at the clock. Almost 6:15 p.m. *Rise and shine*. Marc and Tara had the night shift surveillance.

Alex stifled a groan as they, too, kissed tenderly before accepting mugs of coffee from Kick.

Jesus, please, just take me now. That flashback was looking better and better.

"Pass me one of those," Alex grumbled, holding out his hand for a steaming mug, which Kick gave him along with an unrepentant grin. Alex gave *him* the finger, much to Kick's amusement.

They all took seats around the large granite-topped table. Thankfully, Commander Quinn got right down to business by sliding a single page of computer printout onto the center of it.

"This is the communiqué NSA intercepted," Quinn said. "The origin of the e-mail was somewhere in Washington, D.C. They believe it was sent out by al Sayika. What do y'all think?"

Somberly, everyone read it. If NSA was right, this was bad news. The next attack was coming faster than expected.

When the paper got to him, Alex skipped over the source logistics and just read the translation of the original short Arabic message.

> *Zero hour approaches! The garden of paradise beckons. The trigger will arrive tomorrow. Praise God and do His will!*

As he read, Alex's blood ran cold.

Normally he was a skeptic when it came to intelligence gathered from unsourced, intercepted e-mails. Hell, it could be some ten-year-old punk hacker in Poughkeepsie who'd sent it to his buddies as a joke. Even the zero-hour thing, a deliberate allusion to the infamous 9-11 chatter, was by now a cliché, used by every terrorist wannabe in the world. But Alex had to admit, this message had a certain ring of authenticity.

"Let's assume NSA's right and it is real," Quinn began grimly. "Then it looks like their next target is D.C. Not terribly surprising. The question is—"

"—what is this trigger they're talking about?" Alex finished.

Darcy gave voice to what they all were thinking. "A *nuclear* trigger?"

"Do these assholes never give up?"

Three months ago, the al Sayika cell that kidnapped Dr. Cappozi had attempted to release a horrific Armageddon virus in several U.S. cities, planning to kill millions of people in retaliation for one of their leaders being martyred in the Sudan. Quinn's team had managed to stop the massacre in the nick of time.

"A dirty bomb?" Kick suggested.

A chorus of curses sounded around the table.

Quinn said, "NSA's working on tracking down the e-mail's exact place of origin within the District, and the FBI and CIA are digging into possible missing nuclear triggers around the world. State Department and Homeland Security have raised the national threat advisory level to red at all U.S. points of entry for the next forty-eight hours. *Everyone* coming into the entire country is going to be searched."

Marc pointed to the e-mail's text. "Any idea where this garden of paradise is?"

"Or *what* it is," Tara amended. "I doubt al Sayika's raising marigolds."

Everyone made noises of agreement. Tara was new to special ops, but as a former cop she had good instincts.

"There is one possibility," Commander Quinn said. "The Coast Guard got a tip about a yacht moored out in the Chesapeake Bay, called *Allah's Paradise*. It's been anchored there for a few days, though, so the timing isn't exactly right."

"Still." Marc's brows beetled. "The names are too similar to ignore. Who's following up?"

"Coast Guard and FBI. A joint team will board the yacht tomorrow morning," Quinn informed them.

"That's it? No other clues?" Darcy asked. "E-mails? Wiretaps? Kidnappings?"

"A marked increase in chatter, nothing more specific than this," Quinn said. "But NSA believes the threat is real. They've been monitoring al Sayika closely since December, when we took down the Abbas Tawhid cell in Louisiana."

Alex's body instinctively recoiled at the hated name. Tawhid had been one of the two terrorist leaders personally responsible for his own suffering at Club Torture. Tawhid had been a savage brute, and his co-leader's nickname said it all: the Sultan of Pain. Alex still had screaming nightmares about both men.

Thank God they were now dead and buried.

He rallied before a flashback beset him for the second time that day, and turned determinedly back to what Quinn was saying.

"—with the FBI?"

Which had apparently been addressed to him, because everyone at the table turned to gaze at him expectantly. Except for Kick, whose expression had frozen somewhere between horror and vast amusement.

WTF?

Alex cleared his throat and tried not to look like a complete idiot. "Um, what? Sorry, I was, uh—"

Everyone at the table carried his own share of personal demons, and Alex's were no big secret. *Well, most of them.* Quinn breezed right over the momentary lapse. "I was just saying that Commander Bridger suggested we get with the FBI and Coast Guard on this ASAP."

"The e-mail?" Alex clarified, momentarily puzzled as to why he'd been picked to deal with computer stuff. Had he missed something? "Isn't that Darcy's area of expertise?"

Quinn shifted in his seat. "Not the e-mail. The yacht."

"Ah. Right," Alex said, hastening to cover his inattention. "Sure, no problem," he agreed.

Quinn blinked. Then he smiled. "Great. You leave first thing in the morning. Darcy'll book you a seat on the—"

Whoa. *What?* Alex's stomach sank on pure, raw instinct. "Leave?" He *had* missed something. Something important. "Leave for where?"

"The FBI's field office on the Chesapeake Bay, of course. In Norfolk."

Norfolk? As in Norfolk, *Virginia*?

Then it hit him right between the eyes. The FBI. Norfolk . . .

Oh, sweet baby Jesus.

Quinn wanted him to—

Alex lurched to his feet. "*Hell*, no. I can't *pos*sibly—"

"*Some*body on the team has got to go down there and check out the yacht," Commander Quinn refuted in a tone that brooked no argument. "The *Allah's Paradise* could be our best lead yet."

"Please don't ask me to do th—"

"You know her best, Zane." Quinn didn't need to use her name; everyone at that table knew exactly which "her" he was referring to. He threw up his hands. "Hell, Alex, she was going to be a damn bridesmaid at your—"

Darcy's elbow jabbed Quinn in the ribs and he halted mid-word. He glanced uncertainly at her, then rolled his eyes and turned back to Alex. "Look. I know she reminds you of a rough time in your life, but I trust you're not some dewy-eyed virgin who needs to be tiptoed around. And if you are, you've got no place on my team. Or in

STORM Corps, for that matter. Be in Norfolk by oh-nine-hundred, Zane, and that's a goddamn order." The commander's eyes narrowed. "You got a problem with that?"

Alex swallowed down the tirade of protest he wanted to let loose. Goddamn *right* he had a goddamn problem with it. *Fuck*ing hell.

"No, sir," he answered the team leader tightly, and dropped back onto his chair. "No problem at all."

But behind his forced smile of concession, his innards were in free fall.

Rebel fucking Haywood.

Please, God. Just fucking kill him now.

THREE

Washington, D.C.
Later that night

METRO Police Detective Sarah McPhee peered over the edge of a stinking back-alley Dumpster in northeast Washington, D.C., careful not to touch the foul metal container. The Dumpster was lit up like the Lincoln Memorial, the surrounding brick walls of the alley painted with a grotesque mosaic of distorted shadows and light caused by people moving around in the circle of illumination. Beyond that circle, the brightness quickly faded to midnight blackness.

Inside the Dumpster, sprawled on top of the rank contents, was the body of the vic, her long black hair spread around her head like a dark halo. Her once-olive complexion glowed pasty white in the harsh crime scene lights. The woman had once been really beautiful, Sarah noted. Nice clothes. Good body. Healthy skin. Definitely did not belong in this part of town.

Dump job, she thought. "Damn shame," she murmured aloud before she could stop herself.

The conglomeration of uniforms, techs, and coroner staff

working around the Dumpster studiously ignored her comment, continuing on with their respective pursuits. Clipped footsteps echoed through the alley, and newly promoted Lieutenant Gus Harding marched up, late as usual.

"What have we got here?" he demanded importantly of no one in particular. The LT was fond of TV crime shows and imitated the brusque demeanor of the prime-time actors whenever possible. Like it made him seem more qualified for the job, or tougher. *Or taller.*

Predictably, Jonesy—Detective Jonas Louden, whose nickname was Detective Loudmouth due to his annoying tendency to boom at the top of his lungs—jumped in to answer, flicking out his well-worn leather notepad before Sarah could even open her mouth to speak. "Female, twenty-five to thirty-five. With that black hair, prob'ly Italian," Jonesy pronounced in a definitive statement.

"Or Hispanic, or Middle Eastern, or Indian . . ." Sarah mumbled. Or heck, any number of other nationalities or combination thereof. This was America, land of the melting pot. But Detective Jones was nearing retirement, and tended to dwell in a past when "ethnic" still meant Irish, Italian, or Jewish.

Lieutenant Harding flicked Sarah a dismissive glance. She was *not* close to retirement—for reasons of age anyhow, having recently tipped the scales at forty-five—but she had a good ten years on the rookie lieutenant. And that made him nervous. Like he knew *she* should be the one with the lieutenant's shield. Which she should. Everyone knew it. And she would have had it, too, if not for that unfortunate incident . . .

But she wasn't going there.

Harding turned back to Jonesy. "Any ID?"

Nope," he said. "Nothing. No effects of any kind. Just the clothes on her back."

Harding again glanced over the grody rim of the Dumpster, this time peering down at the assistant medical examiner, who'd donned a blue disposable jumpsuit and booties to keep his designer duds and elegant leather shoes clean as he went Dumpster-diving. To his credit, the man hadn't uttered a peep of protest when he'd climbed in.

"COD?" Harding asked him.

"Nothing obvious," the A.M.E., Dr. John Stroud said, looking up from the muck with youthful blue eyes. Gawd. He couldn't be more than twelve. How was it everyone on the planet was suddenly younger than she was? "No blood. No wounds," he reported. "No outward signs of internal trauma."

Sarah forced her mind back on track. Okay, *that* was interesting. When a body was dumped like this, cause of death was usually pretty obvious. Gunshot. Knife wound. Beating. Rape.

"What about TOD?" the LT asked.

She averted her gaze back to the alley as Dr. Stroud pulled his temp instrument out of the vic's liver, read it, and mentally calculated. "Recently. About two to four hours ago, I'd say preliminarily."

Sarah twisted her wrist to look at her watch. 10:06 p.m. Which put TOD sometime between six and eight o'clock that evening.

The LT grunted. "When can you get me the autopsy report?"

"We're a bit backed up," Stroud said. "Tomorrow afternoon's the earliest I can manage."

Harding turned to Sarah and, arranging his rotund face in pleasant insincerity, said, "McPhee, I'd like you to attend."

Nausea stroked through her stomach. It was a dare, she knew that. No. More like a nasty, condescending barb in the guise of a routine assignment. She shoved back the impulse to tell him no. Everyone around them was surreptitiously watching her. They could all go screw themselves.

"Sure," she told him. "Meanwhile," she added, keeping her voice even, "you should probably have CSI collect that." She jabbed a finger at the grimy brick building behind the Dumpster. Specifically at the rotting sill of a broken window where the very corner of a small black cell phone stuck out, blending into the dirt and mottled shadows so well it was nearly invisible. Unless you were actually looking.

The CSIs all turned as one, scanning from the ground up to the lone window that no one had inspected yet. She knew someone would have gotten around to it eventually—the geek squad was nothing if not thorough, and the scene had not been released yet, after all—but it was gratifying to show them all she was still a damn good detective, despite recent evidence to the contrary.

The LT marched over and squinted at the cell phone, mouth thinning in irritation. He jetted a breath through his nose and barked at the closest tech to do his goddamn job, then spun and marched away again, right out of the alley.

Okay, then. Sarah dug into her jacket pocket for her own notebook, and focused her attention on the clutch of seedy-looking individuals gathered on the other side of the yellow taped-off perimeter at the mouth of the alley.

"Guess I'll go interview the witnesses," she said to anyone who might give a damn.

"Hang on, McPhee," Jonesy boomed loudly. "I'll come with you."

Sarah sighed. Oh, goodie.

Chesapeake Bay outside Norfolk, Virginia
The next morning

FBI Special Agent Rebel Haywood stood in the prow of a United States Coast Guard RB-M response boat, enjoying the early morning calm before the storm of the coming operation. A cool spray of salt water misted her face, contrasting with the cozy warmth of the spring sun on her skin. It had been a while since she'd been out on the water, and she was loving every minute of it. Even under these circumstances.

"Approaching target vessel," the voice in her headset comm squawked. "Take your positions, people."

Just ahead, the object of the joint USCG/FBI operation, a small but elegant yacht called *Allah's Paradise*, lay anchored in a picturesque inlet on the western shore of the Chesapeake Bay.

Rebel's cell phone suddenly vibrated in her pocket. She did a mental wince, quickly pulling it out to check the screen. And almost groaned aloud. *Helena Middleton*. Figured. Helena *would* phone at the worst possible moment.

For a nanosecond, Rebel debated turning off the thing. But she was working, and her SAC needed to be able to get ahold of her at all times. He insisted on it. Especially this morning. This op was high profile and he wanted constant updates.

The phone vibrated again.

On the other hand, Captain Montgomery, the USCG operation commander, and ensigns Chet and Sampson, the two other über-macho Coast Guard mopes who rounded out today's detail, were already disgusted enough that the FBI had sent a *girl* to do what they considered a man's job. Best not to lower herself even further in their estimation by taking a personal call while on duty. She let it go to voice mail.

"Stand ready, people," Captain Montgomery ordered over the comm.

The RB-M slowed. Overhead, the boat's loudspeaker crackled. "This is the United States Coast Guard. Please prepare to be boarded for inspection," Montgomery's voice called.

Her cell vibrated again. *Bother.* Helena Middleton had the tenacity of a junkyard dog.

Seriously. No sane person would pick up right now. On the other hand, Rebel figured she had a good forty-five seconds until the real action started. If she answered now, at least she'd have a great excuse to hang up quickly and stop it from ringing at an even worse time.

With an impatient sigh, she muted her comm headset, made sure no one was looking, and tapped her discreet Bluetooth earpiece. "I'm in the middle of something, Helena."

"Good lord, sweetie, about time you answered!" Helena's sweet-as-honey South Carolina accent held just the slightest hint of rebuke. She and Rebel had been friends—well, their parents had been, anyway—growing up among the old-money, South-of-Broad Charleston aristocrats, then coincidentally both of them had moved to Manhattan four years ago, resulting in their being roommates for the first couple of years in New York. Their ultra-conservative Southern parents had been pleased neither girl had been subjected to the corrupting influence of a Yankee roommate. It was mortifying enough Rebel had joined the FBI instead of marrying a good old Southern boy from a good old Southern family. *That* had nearly killed them. As for Helena's parents, well, God help her if they ever found out she'd quit that Cordon Bleu cooking school long ago.

The Coast Guard RB-M eased about to approach the yacht. Ensigns Chet and Sampson tossed lines across, securing the two vessels together for boarding.

Rebel tried to cut her phone call short. "I'm sorry, Helena, but I really have to—"

"Why, Rebel Haywood," Helena scolded cheerfully. A perfect Southern belle, Helena did *every*thing cheerfully. Rebel could take lessons. "Do you have any earthly idea how many times I've tried calling you lately?"

Actually, she did. Fourteen. Fifteen, if you counted the last voice mail. Her relationship with Helena was . . . complicated. Which was why she'd been routinely ducking the other woman's calls for the past month. Okay. Maybe two.

Montgomery strode past Rebel to the railing and yelled across the gap to the swarthy, bearded captain of *Allah's Paradise*. "Captain Brett Montgomery, here. Permission to come aboard, sir?"

"Yes, sure. Come ahead," the man answered in heavily accented English.

"Seriously, I can't talk now," Rebel told Helena under her breath, reaching up for the off button behind her ear.

"Keep weapons secured unless provoked, people." Montgomery's quiet order sounded over her comm headset. "On my order."

"Oh, this'll just take a second," Helena's drawl insisted stubbornly in the other ear. "I promise."

Sweet goodnight. "Talk fast. There may be gunplay," Rebel warned dryly, giving up. Not that she really expected any, but one could always hope. It wasn't Helena's fault she was clueless and obstinate as the day was long. She'd been brought up that way. Her parents were even more myopic than Rebel's. A difficult feat.

"Bless your heart," her friend said with a perfectly modulated laugh. *Every*thing Helena did was always perfect. "Keeping the country safe as usual, I presume?"

At Montgomery's signal, Chet and Sampson vaulted easily over the rail onto the other vessel and came to attention, followed by the captain, who flicked a withering look back at Rebel. Well, more precisely at her outfit.

She returned his smile through her teeth.

She'd drawn this assignment *after* arriving at NFO—the FBI's Norfolk Field Office—for work this morning, and therefore had of necessity reported to the USCG dock located in the neighboring harbor of Portsmouth wearing a sea-foam green skirted linen suit and strappy heels.

Yeah. *That* had gone over well.

Montgomery had issued a long-suffering sigh, thrust a pair of chum-riddled puke-yellow sneaks two sizes too large at her, snorted at her inappropriate pencil skirt, and wordlessly led her onto the waiting Coast Guard RB-M response boat.

She now unhooked the latch of the gangway gate and swung it open, hiked her skirt up and jumped inelegantly across onto the rolling deck of the yacht. "What do you *need*, Helena?" she asked, fixing to hang up.

"Oh, it's not me who needs you," Helena said blithely. "It's Alex."

At the smug pronouncement, Rebel almost tripped over one too-big sneaker. She grabbed the rail for balance, missed, and nearly went down again as the gate smacked closed on her behind. "What?"

Until six weeks ago, Alex Zane had been Helena's fiancé. He had also been Rebel's best friend. Operative phrase: *had* been. Talk about complicated. She'd been ducking *his* calls even longer than two months. Including twice just last night. Seriously. Like she was going to talk to him before bedtime? So she could dream of him all night? Again? She might have it bad, but she wasn't *that* nuts.

And oh, yeah. For the record? Her avoidance had *nothing* to do with that steamy almost-kiss she and Alex had shared in a very weak moment last December. Nor had her hasty move to Norfolk within days of that weak moment. Because of that weak moment.

She slammed her eyes shut. Okay, what. Ever. So maybe it had.

"What's wrong with Alex?" she asked Helena, those two phone calls yesterday suddenly changing character. "Is he okay?"

All at once, the air was rent by machine-gun fire.

Whoa! Two men burst out from the bridge of the yacht, yelling in guttural Arabic as bullets sprayed the deck wildly. Instantly, Chet and Sampson returned fire. The swarthy yacht captain went down with a bloodcurdling scream.

"Take them, people!" Captain Montgomery yelled.

"Gotta go," Rebel told Helena as she rolled for cover and whipped out her Glock 23. Bullets splintered the wooden deck where she'd stood just seconds before.

Another burst of gunfire had Ensign Sampson staggering backward, his pristine white uniform blossoming red. He fell with a crash. Rebel quickly ducked out from her cover, returning fire as she grabbed Sampson's collar and dragged him behind a tubalike vent.

Pock-pock-pock came Chet's covering fire. Followed by a howl from one of the assailants. With an ugly sneer and an uglier curse, the third Arab shooter spun and ran straight toward Rebel.

"I don't think so," she muttered and took aim. But before she could pull the trigger, he screamed and grabbed his side. His gun skittered across the deck, along with streamers of blood. For a second, all was silent.

Montgomery ran and turned him onto his back. He appeared dead. Ensign Chet tackled the first man with a set of handcuffs. Rebel checked Sampson's pulse. It was weak but steady, thank God.

After gingerly scooping up and pocketing the dead man's gun in case he wasn't as dead as he looked, she cautiously crept forward and glanced around. Something moved, a flash of black in her peripheral vision. She whirled. *Nothing there*. Was that a splash? Or just the slap of the waves trapped between the two vessels . . . ?

She crouch-ran to the yacht's main salon door, which stood wide open, waving back and forth with the rise and fall of the ocean swells. Hmm. Maybe she *had* seen someone running past. She peeked into the salon. *Clear*. She ducked down and crept through the salon door, halting to listen carefully.

"Rebel?" Helena's hesitant voice sounded in her ear.

She jumped, startled. *Sweet goodnight*. She had totally forgotten about the phone call. Heart pounding, she reached for her earpiece. "Not now, Helena."

"Alex needs to speak with you," the other woman said before she could hit the off button. "Right away."

"He's got my number," Rebel bit out, hating that she couldn't make herself just hang up on her friend. She squinted and peered deeper into the salon. Not that she and Helena had ever been genuinely close friends. Especially after she and Alex had become engaged. That had killed any chance of a real friendship.

"I have your number, too," Helena returned with an edge of accusation. "You never answer either of our calls."

A small thread of guilt tightened around Rebel's heart, then twanged painfully. She *had* been close with Alex. But he was the one who'd ended their friendship when she'd attempted to move on by finding herself another man. Admittedly, she had not chosen wisely—the man being Wade Montana, her boss. *Former* boss. But that really wasn't Alex's concern. Or relevant at the moment.

She eased out a measured breath. "Fine. Tell Alex I'll answer next time."

"Tell him yourself," Helena said. "He's not really speaking to me."

"Leaving a man at the altar will do that," Rebel muttered, tilting her head at a strange sound.

But other than a huff on the phone, all she heard was the *tick tick ticking* of the door waving back and forth.

She frowned. Or was the ticking noise on her phone? It sounded more electronic than— It *was* coming from her phone. But—

"Rebel, there's really something you should know about Alex and me—"

With a sudden start she recognized the sound.

Oh, no. No, no, *no.*

She hit the off button for real this time, and sprinted out of the salon.

"Abandon ship!" she yelled, rushing toward Chet and Montgomery as they led the shooter who was still alive toward the Coast Guard vessel. *"Bomb!"*

The two ensigns halted for a nanosecond, then sprang into action. They shoved the injured prisoner through the gate onto the RB-M, and Montgomery secured him to the rail with a Flexicuff. Rebel did a sliding dive to grab Sampson's collar again, hauling him furiously toward the gangway opening.

Chet rushed to untie the lines while Montgomery made a dash for the RB-M's bridge. Sampson groaned as the engines roared to life. Chet grabbed his torso, helping her hoist him over the final barrier.

"Everyone onboard?" Captain Montgomery yelled from behind the wheel.

"We're good!" Chet yelled back. There was no time to go back for the two dead men. "Go!"

She and Chet both landed on their butts and collided hard with the injured Sampson as the boat shot forward with a jerk and a spinning turn to run full out. Water sprayed in a rooster tail, drenching everyone in the frigid wake. But they'd gotten away.

Not a moment too soon.

With a deep rumble, *Allah's Paradise* lit up in a ball of flame and a deafening ka-*boom.*

Rebel covered her ears and threw herself over Sampson just as Chet did the same. She ended up sandwiched between the two men. A second explosion ripped through the air. Flaming debris rained down around them.

Then just as quickly, the early morning air went deathly still.

"Jesus on a freakin' fork," Chet swore after a few tense heartbeats.

"Language, ensign."

He deftly lifted himself off her and Sampson. "Sorry, ma'am. You hurt?"

At least she was pretty sure that's what he said. Her ears were ringing and her hearing was muffled like when she used to wear those fluffy earmuffs on ski trips to Switzerland as a kid. She gave him a wobbly smile. "Just my dignity," she answered, then turned to Sampson to check on his injury. She peeled off her jacket and pressed it to his bleeding gunshot wound as Chet reeled off to check on the prisoner. "And my suit," she added resignedly, meeting Ensign Sampson's grateful eyes. "Donna Karan," she told him philosophically. "My favorite." Now covered in blood, guts, and black ash. At least it matched the rest of her. But Sampson was alive, and that's all that really mattered.

"I'll buy you . . . another damn suit," the ensign wheezed out with a cough. Then he grinned painfully. "But with . . . a shorter skirt."

She laughed and made a face at him. "In your dreams, sailor."

"Oh . . . yeah." His eyes fluttered closed.

She glanced back at the burning remains of the rapidly sinking yacht. They were lucky to be having any more dreams at all. If her Bluetooth hadn't picked up the static from that bomb's timing mechanism, they'd all be dead now. Blown to little, tiny bits.

A long shiver traced down her spine.

That's when she noticed the *whop-whop-whop* of an approaching Coast Guard helicopter.

"Hang in there," she told Sampson, who was barely

clinging to consciousness. "Help is already here. You Coastie boys are fast."

"Always ready," he croaked proudly, which turned into a groan.

The helo roared overhead, circled once, then spit out four guys in black wet suits from the open side doors. Within seconds they'd splashed down in a perfect formation alongside the RB-M, which Montgomery had pulled up just out of range of the sinking yacht, and swiftly climbed on board.

The helo circled again and another guy dropped out of its door, this time on a line, along with a stretcher basket for Sampson. They both zoomed down at breakneck speed toward the RB-M's rolling deck. Rebel cringed, hoping they didn't hit a bad swell so the guy went splat.

Just then her cell phone rang again.

"You have got to be kidding me," she muttered, and mashed the Bluetooth's on button. "I *really* can't talk right now," she yelled over the deafening *whop-whop* of the rotors.

"Goddamn it, Rebel!" a man yelled back over the phone, shocking her senseless with the familiar sound of his voice. "Where the *hell* are you? Are you hurt?"

She froze, her reflexive language admonition sticking in her throat. Impossible. *It couldn't be*. How could he possibly know—

"Fucking hell, *answer* me, goddamn it! Is this stretcher for *you*?" he bellowed.

She peered closer at the man descending on the line from the helo. He hit the deck, spotted her standing there, scowled ferociously at her blood-covered clothes, then took off running toward her at full tilt.

Broad, tall, golden, and beautiful as an avenging Viking warrior-god.

"Angel! *Talk* to me!"

Lord help her.

It was Alex Zane.

Before she knew what was happening, he swept her off her feet, cradling her body to his chest as he did a running U-turn and sprinted back toward the stretcher.

She finally found her tongue. "Alex, I'm fine! Put me down!"

He skidded and swept a glance at her clothes with a doubtful frown. "You're soaked in blood."

"Ensign Sampson's." She flung a hand back at the wounded man. "The stretcher is for him. You need to—"

Alex came to a halt, blinked down at her, and finally seemed to realize what he was doing. For a split second he hesitated. Then in a single motion, he cursed and dropped her feet to the deck. But instead of releasing her, he cursed again, pulled her into a bruising embrace, and crushed his lips to hers.

Rebel's world stopped dead in its tracks.

Her breath stalled in her lungs. Her heart ceased to beat. Instantly her mind emptied of all thought.

There was only Alex. Alex kissing her. Finally, finally, *finally* kissing her!

How long had she waited for this exact moment? A lifetime . . .

Her soul leapt for joy, her legs turned to liquid. She gasped, and for a heartbeat he paused to look down at her, his shocked expression that of a man who hadn't expected this reaction from her. Or himself.

"Oh, Alex," she breathed.

That was all it took. His mouth swooped down to cover hers again. His tongue pushed demandingly between her lips and the taste of him burst through her senses. Senses that had wondered a thousand, no, a million, times what

Alex Zane's kiss would taste like. What *Alex Zane* would taste like.

She surrendered completely to the wonderful, amazing moment. She couldn't begin to process the myriad emotions and sensations exploding through her as he murmured, "Thank God, you're okay," whispering it over and over into her mouth as he kissed her greedily.

She was dimly aware that she should stop this. Stop *him.* But there wasn't a prayer that she would. That she *could.* After waiting for so long, for so many lonely, frustrated, wishful years for this very moment to happen, nothing short of death could make her pull away. And probably not even that.

So she let him kiss her, and let the incredible kiss go on and on and on. Nothing else mattered. Nothing was more important than this stunning turn of—

Someone cleared his throat loudly behind her.

Very loudly.

Which was at least enough to make Alex come to his senses. His lips jerked away from hers and his gaze skittered over her shoulder.

A wry smile then creased his beautiful mouth, a mouth reddened and wet from kisses. *Her* kisses. "Sorry, sir. We're, um"—an indulgently masculine expression crossed his face—"friends."

Friends?

Okay . . .

She followed his gaze to the last vestiges of the burning *Allah's Paradise* as it sank below the surface of the bay, then moved back to Captain Montgomery, who must be standing right behind her. She attempted to ease away from Alex, but he wouldn't loosen his grip on her. It was like trying to pry herself away from the Terminator.

"Glad to see everyone made it," Alex said. He continued glancing at the crew but held on to her like he'd never let her go. Her heart did a funny little dance. She was so confused! Last time they talked—and she used the term loosely—he'd made it clear he didn't even want to be friends anymore. And now this . . .

He looked over at Sampson, who was being strapped into the mummy basket by the frogmen. "How's the injured man?"

"He'll be fine," Montgomery said. "Thanks to your . . . *friend.* Special Agent Haywood, thank you," he added from behind her with such sincerity that finally she came to her senses.

She muscled out of Alex's arms and turned to the Coastie commander with a blush. "Trust me, my pleasure, sir. I owed you for the sneaks anyway." She stuck out a foot and wiggled the ugly yellow shoe, crossing her arms in front of her as she did so.

Montgomery grinned. "Next time, I may even spring for a Coast Guard cap." He touched the brim of his own in a semi-salute and headed for the wheelhouse, stopping en route to supervise the helo's takeoff with Ensign Sampson and two of the frogmen. The other two frogs were just climbing back on board after having placed several red buoys out to mark the spot where the yacht had sunk.

The commander called orders to the crew, fired up the RB-M, and pointed the prow toward Portsmouth harbor and home.

Rebel turned back to Alex. He mirrored her gaze with such naked desire in his eyes that her heart fluttered madly. But funny dance or not, that "friends" remark had reminded her all too vividly of the rockiness of their relationship. Besides, the Coasties were openly staring.

"Alex, why are you here?" she asked, pressing her banded arms into her abdomen to keep her chaotic emotions from spilling out like a broken gumball machine.

"To rescue you," he said, stepping into her again. His breath was warm compared to the sudden chilly wind that whipped over them as the vessel scudded along.

"Very funny." He was kidding. Well, she assumed he was kidding. Rebel didn't need rescuing and he knew it. What she needed was—

He put his arms around her once more and pulled her close.

She sighed and relented, returning his embrace. Heaven only knew what she really needed. But *this* . . . this was far too tempting. The arms of the man she loved around her, the promise of more in his eyes . . .

But there were too many unresolved issues hanging over them. Too much history. Too many burnt bridges. "Why are you really here?"

"Same reason you are," he murmured into her hair. "To check out the yacht that just blew up. STORM sent me."

Surprise flitted through her. "Is this about the suspicious e-mail intercepted by the NSA?" That was the reason she'd been sent, too.

He nodded. "The Department of Homeland Security has extended our contract to work on the al Sayika traitor case."

"They think *Allah's Paradise* is somehow tied in with that?"

He nodded again. "I'm supposed to liaise with the Coast Guard and the FBI on the investigation." His lips grazed her temple, setting off sunbursts of heat in her body and melting her willpower a little bit more. "It's off to an explosive start, I must say," he murmured

She wasn't exactly sure if he meant the yacht . . . or their kiss. Both, she supposed. Which for some reason alarmed her.

"Looks like we'll be working together for a few days," he casually added.

That alarmed her even more. In the half-dozen years

she'd known Alex in a professional capacity—she'd been the FBI liaison to Zero Unit when they met—they'd only *talked* about investigations and operations. They'd never actually worked together on anything.

Not a good idea.

In fact, now that she was thinking straight again, *none* of this was a good idea.

He tilted her chin up with an index finger. His golden lashes dipped to a sexy half-mast. "So, angel . . ." he murmured huskily. Her stomach zinged in dreadful anticipation of what he might say next. Which turned out to be the worst possible thing she could imagine, under the circumstances.

He leaned down and his deep voice rumbled in her ear. "So, tonight. Mind if I stay at your place?"

FOUR

"TAKE care. Love you," Gina said with a smile for her best friend, Rainie, though they were miles apart, and flipped her cell phone closed. Rainie had relocated upstate to work as a nurse for STORM Corps at Haven Oaks Sanatorium, but they talked every day by phone. Sometimes more than once.

Her friend worried about her, Gina knew, and wished she could be here in New York to help her reacclimatize to "normal life." Yeah, Rainie was no one's fool. She suspected there was something Gina was not telling her. She knew about Gregg, of course—*every*one knew about Gregg after Gina's paranoid delusional outbursts at Haven Oaks, seeing him lurking behind every tree and even ducking behind doorways in the heavily guarded and top secret recovery wing for wounded operators. Gina's friend was worried she intended to do something foolish.

Like kill the bastard.

Smart lady.

Rainie kept asking her why she thought Gregg was after her. Why would he possibly want to kill her? Gina didn't know why. All she knew was he *was* after her. Every cell in her body had felt his dogged pursuit from the day of her rescue until this very minute. She was in mortal danger. And she wouldn't—couldn't—rest until he was no longer a threat. Which meant dead.

But unfortunately, Gina couldn't kill him unless she could find him.

It had been a whole week since she'd been released from Haven Oaks and moved back to her Manhattan brownstone, and she hadn't caught sight of him yet. Though, yesterday she'd had a close call. Riding the subway home, she'd felt his menacing presence so thickly she'd pulled her knife and nearly stabbed a perfectly innocent man who'd only had the misfortune of standing behind her on the train. Gregg had vanished like the ill wind he was.

But she hadn't imagined him. She *hadn't.* Not this time. He'd been there. She'd smelled him in the air—that powerful, arousing distillate of sage and gun grease and hard, relentless male. She'd felt him, too. It had been impossible to miss the fleeting press of him, stiff against her backside. A challenge . . . A warning . . . *A promise.*

She pocketed her phone. Glanced around. Someone different sat in the STORM surveillance SUV on the street this morning, she noted, not Alex Zane as usual. The new guy was pretending to talk on his own cell phone, gesticulating wildly in a perfect pantomime of a frustrated New Yorker. The tag team was nowhere in sight, but that was to be expected. She rarely saw them outside of a crowd, only felt their presence.

This morning, she was out on a contrived errand to pick up fresh flowers for her apartment. Maybe today would be the day she lured van Halen from the shadows. So she could put an end to this terrifying game of cat and mouse, one way or another.

As she strolled the two blocks from her home to the neighborhood florist, the morning sun sparkled gaily off the newly washed windows of a bookstore up ahead. Puffy clouds floated across the sky. The delectable fragrance of coffee and pastry wafted out from the open windows of a café as she walked past. There, at an outside table, a man and woman held hands over the checkered tablecloth, giving each other smiles in a sweet vignette of normalcy.

Everything was just as it should be. Quiet. Ordinary. Unthreatening.

Still, a charge of adrenaline coursed through Gina's limbs.

He was close by.

She felt in her pocket for her knife. Its smooth, solid handle answered her fingertips reassuringly. *Could this be it?* Taking a steadying breath, she opened the door to the flower shop. As always, a string of bells tinkled welcomingly overhead. She went in. Five minutes should be plenty of time for van Halen to set up whatever ambush he had in mind. But she'd be ready for him.

When she came out ten minutes later, in her right hand she carried a small bunch of yellow rosebuds mixed with blue forget-me-nots—symbolic, if not particularly subtle—and her black KA-BAR knife held rigidly behind it.

Suddenly, there was a commotion at the café across the street. The woman at the outside table screamed and jumped up. The man shouted, rushing to shield her. Another man lay bleeding on the sidewalk in a pool of crimson. Gina gasped when she recognized him as one of the STORM agents.

Sweet Jesus. Why did Gregg *kill* the man? It was *her* he wanted! She'd made it easy enough for him to get to her.

A noise cracked behind her. She whirled. Her pulse exploded. *A gun was pointed right at her forehead.*

But she was prepared. She didn't flee. She raised her

knife, ready to lunge at her attacker, just as she'd practiced over and over. But for one heart-pounding nanosecond, she hesitated.

Omigod. *She couldn't do it.*

Suddenly, the knife was whisked from her hand. Before she could even scream, it plunged deep and true, straight into the false heart of her betrayer. Thank God for the other STORM agent!

Nevertheless, the sickening *slurk* of blade piercing flesh, the *whoosh* of the air and strangled gasp bursting from his lungs, and the instant slick of blood that sprayed her whole front made her want to vomit. But the gag froze in her throat as her attacker sank to his knees, a look of shocked horror sweeping across his dark face. A look that no doubt mirrored her own.

The man wasn't Gregg.

She spun in panic.

Rough hands reached out and grasped at her. *Oh, God!* But her knife was still in the other guy. It had never occurred to her to retrieve it. She jumped away from the second attacker. Directly backward into the grip of a third man. She struggled fiercely, but he seized her arms from behind and yanked at them, pulling her savagely into his grasp. There was no getting loose. Where was the STORM agent now? In a flash, the second man pulled a long, curved dagger from under his Windbreaker and raised it with a sneer.

She screamed.

But just as he was about to thrust the dagger into her, he stopped in mid-motion, eyes widening, his arm poised in the air like a cartoon character in freeze-frame. He, too, crumpled to the sidewalk, someone else's knife lodged in his throat. There was a dark blur, and suddenly the grip on her arms fell away. It was immediately replaced by a strong handful of fingers with a viselike grip on her upper arm.

"Come," came the growled command from behind her back.

A command that her body knew so well. Delivered in a deep, powerful voice that still managed to instantly arouse, even as her insides quailed in terror.

Gregg!

She cried out in panicked denial, struggling to escape from her nemesis. *"No!"* This wasn't right! Not how she'd practiced!

"Gina. Stop."

"Bastard! Leave me alone!"

He didn't argue. Didn't say a word. Simply held her fast, and suddenly a sharp prick stabbed her in the arm. A million tingles rushed through her body. *Oh, God. She was dead.* He caught her when she crumpled.

His grim, handsome, hated face was the last thing she saw.

"SOMEONE flag down a cab!" Gregg van Halen shouted at the crowd that had quickly gathered around. He had to get out of there pronto. He lifted his lover's limp body into his arms. "This woman's hurt! I need to get her to a hospital!"

People generally thought New Yorkers were rude and uncaring, but the fact was, they were pretty damn good in an emergency; 9/11 had probably taught them that. Or perhaps the profound tragedy had reminded them of their all-too-vulnerable humanity. So he'd barely had time to gather Gina up before a cab was waiting by the curb and someone had opened its door for him. At the last second, he bent down and scooped up the yellow-and-blue bouquet lying next to one of her assailants—the second of Gina's three attackers he'd killed.

Her protective detail was toast. One STORM operator lay dead across the street. Where the hell was the other guy?

"Tell the cops I've taken her to Bellevue," he called as he climbed into the cab and the door was slammed behind him. He told the driver, "There's a fifty for you if you get me there in less than five minutes."

Naturally, Gregg had no intention of taking Gina to the emergency room. He'd left a rented car at the parking garage next to the hospital in anticipation of just such a scenario. He'd been following her since her release from Haven Oaks, expecting an attack on her of some kind—because someone else had been following her besides him. Someone other than her STORM detail. Whoever it was wanted her dead, that was for damned sure. This attack proved it beyond a shadow of a doubt.

Of course, STORM would soon know it was Gregg who took her. It would have appeared too suspicious to the witnesses to keep his face hidden as he whisked her away, and they might have stopped him. So now STORM and DHS and everyone else in the world looking for him would be even more convinced he was involved with the terrorists. His name was already at the top of everyone's suspect list for being the government traitor working as a mole for al Sayika. They'd all assume he was in on the attack just now, and that Gina's capture was part of some big plot.

Whatever. He'd deal with repercussions later.

For now, he thanked God he'd gotten to her in time. She'd be fine. The dose of ketamine he'd administered to render her unconscious was effective but not dangerous.

At the hospital, he paid the cabbie his promised fifty plus another twenty for good measure, thanked him, lifted Gina from the backseat, and carried her swiftly toward Bellevue's double glass doors. After the taxi pulled away, he veered off in the opposite direction.

Taking the parking garage stairs two at a time to the second level, he nodded somberly to those who stared, mur-

muring, "Chemo. It always knocks her out." The gazes quickly turned from suspicion to pity.

During the half-hour drive back to his apartment, he took the opportunity to call Tommy Cantor.

Despite being hunted by every law enforcement officer and federal agent on the planet, Gregg had maintained contact with a handful of his former confidential informants—the ones he was sure wouldn't rat him out to his enemies. Three of the CIs he paid very, very well. The other two were loyal to him personally.

Tommy was firmly in the latter category. A third-year Zero Unit recruit, Gregg had saved Tommy's life on two different missions his rookie year. The kid came from a poor, rough background and lacked respect for authority. Tommy wasn't a bad operator, he just sometimes let his baggage and bitter emotions get in the way of the job. At least, he used to. After the last occasion, Gregg had taken him under his wing and taught him how to survive—by mastering control. Of everything—his life, his surroundings, his unrelenting desire to make good, but most of all his runaway emotions. The kid had been grateful for the tutelage. Thanks to Gregg, Tommy was still alive today, and did not believe for a minute what everyone was saying about him. Nice that somebody didn't.

"Can you talk?"

"Yep. What's up, Cap?" Tommy asked. Being a Zero Unit operator with full access to their vast resources, the kid had been helping Gregg with research and intel, as well as keeping him informed regarding Zero Unit's manhunt so he could stay one step ahead of his pursuers.

"I have her." He didn't need to say who. Tommy knew all about the explosive situation with Gina.

"Jesus. Really?" Tommy said. "Is that wise?"

"Probably not." Gregg glanced in the rearview mirror at the woman lying slack on the backseat. "Hell, definitely not. But I had no choice. There was an attack on her just now. In Manhattan." He quickly outlined what had happened.

"What can I do?"

"Where are you?"

"Um . . ." Tommy hesitated.

"Never mind. Not important." Gregg was always careful not to compromise Tommy's mission secrets. Helping him was more than enough. Technically, the kid was committing treason by doing so.

"Dr. Cappozi, is she hurt?"

"She's okay. But I want you to find out what Blair knows about the attack." Colonel Frank Blair was Gregg's former commander—well, current commander if you didn't count the fact that he'd been AWOL from the unit for seven months. Blair was also Gregg's number one suspect for being the al Sayika mole. It was Colonel Blair who had ordered him to bring Gina to the place where she'd been kidnapped by the terorists, and Blair who'd sent Gregg OCONUS—out of the U.S.—so he hadn't found out about it for three critical weeks, leaving the trail stone cold. Unsurprisingly, Blair was the Zero Unit commander most determined to hunt Gregg down. "And contact the police, too. I want to know everything anyone even thinks they know about the attack."

"Sure thing, Cap. What about Dr. Cappozi? You need help? I could—"

"No, I'm good. I'll take care of her."

"Copy that. I'll get back to you."

Gregg hung up and drove around in a pattern for a few minutes to make sure he was not being followed. He wasn't.

When he got back to his apartment, he carried Gina into the bedroom and laid her out on his bed. He gazed down at her. At the tempting sight of her lying there so vulnerable and helpless, his pulse quickened and his body grew heavy with want. God, she was so damned beautiful.

And *fuck*. Was he ever a bastard for thinking those kind of thoughts.

He ignored his physical need and sat down next to her. Gently, he brushed aside a lock of hair that had fallen across her face. She stirred, and he moved his fingertips to trace along her jaw. At his touch, a whispered moan slipped past her lips.

A smile tipped the corners of his mouth. She might hate him, but she still wanted him.

Good. That would make this much easier.

He picked up a silver chain curled on the nightstand. At one end of the chain, a fur-lined cuff was fastened. The other end was attached to his bed's heavy wrought-iron headboard.

For a moment he was tempted to buckle the cuff around her wrist and snap the padlock closed, as he'd done so many times before.

But this wasn't about bondage and pleasure.

Setting aside the restraint, he opened the nightstand's drawer and lifted from it a much more delicate silver chain. From it dangled a small silver heart. Much better. Reaching down, he looped the bracelet around her trim ankle, and fastened it there.

Then he straightened. And slowly began to peel off her clothes.

AT NFO—the Norfolk, Virginia, FBI field office—Rebel dropped a hastily assembled file in front of Alex, and gave him a smile she hoped didn't betray her nervousness . . . or her massive confusion.

A medic had checked over their cuts and bruises at the Coast Guard facility in Portsmouth, then Rebel and the Coasties from the RB-M had endured a meticulous two-hour debrief by Homeland Security on what exactly had happened on the *Allah's Paradise.*

The Coast Guard was part of the Department of Homeland Security, and DHS had apparently contracted STORM to track down some kind of "trigger" referenced in an e-mail intercepted from an al Sayika operative. Well, didn't it just *figure* they'd send the one STORM agent on the planet who could tie her in knots and blow her world to smithereens?

After their debrief, Alex had driven her back to NFO, just over the bridge. The two of them now sat side-by-side squished into her postage stamp–sized work cubicle, attempting to come up with some kind of plan for how to proceed with the case of the exploding yacht. Which, somehow, they had ended up working on together.

Not that anyone had asked *her*.

But unfortunately, she'd already used up her daily quota of Divine Intervention mere seconds after Alex had dropped that unnerving bomb.

Mind if I stay at your place?

She'd been struck into dumbfounded silence at his total departure from their long-established platonic—their maddeningly, frustratingly, and no doubt very *wisely* platonic—relationship, after which she'd stammered out some nonsense about working late while she frantically tried to sort out her reaction to that bolt out of the blue.

Luckily, she'd been saved from an actual coherent verbal response when Lieutenant Montgomery had summoned him to a conference call between the Coast Guard and STORM Command regarding how to go about reaching the sunken yacht to search it for the unknown "trigger." They believed the terrorists had blown up the yacht either to destroy it, or to conceal evidence that would lead them to it.

Alex was to lead the search. Which meant there was no way possible for her to avoid working with him.

For the rest of the morning, every time she felt he was on the verge of bringing up the whole can-I-stay-with-you subject again, she'd managed to head it off at the pass. But she knew her moment of reckoning would soon be nigh and he would demand an answer, whether she was ready to give it or not.

Did she mind his presence in her apartment? Possibly in her bed? Was she really ready for this?

What on earth should she say? More importantly, what on earth should she *do*?

Meanwhile, she was stuck sitting thigh to thigh with the man in the tight confines of her cubicle, feeling embarrassment creep up her neck at his deliberate study of the pictures and other personal items she had pinned to her partition walls. Thankfully, she hadn't put up her favorite photo of him—determined to have a fresh start and all that—which she'd had prominently displayed in her New York cubicle before transferring south four months ago. How mortifying would *that* have been?

Mentally she steeled herself and sat down in the chair crammed next to him, indicating the file she'd just plopped onto the desk. "This is everything we've been able to dig up on the owners of *Allah's Paradise* and her ports of call over the last ten weeks." Perhaps not surprisingly, her last stop had been in Louisiana. The state seemed to be a favorite of al Sayika for some reason. "No reports of a missing nuclear trigger in the U.S. or anywhere else," Rebel told him. Despite two other agents plus herself working diligently on information-gathering for the past few hours, the jacket was depressingly thin. "How 'bout your people? Any luck?"

Alex picked up the file but didn't open it. "A bit. Nothing on a missing trigger, either. But Darcy was able to run the fingerprints from the dead guy's gun you picked up, as well as our wounded prisoner's. Found matches." He slid a pair of printouts over to her. "Their names are Hassan Mina and Gibran Allawi Bakreen."

She looked at the reports in surprise. "But we ran both those sets of prints here at the Bureau, and nothing came up. Not from AFIS, the military, or NCVIC." The usual fingerprint databases.

"STORM has other resources," he said.

"Like what?" She'd dealt with STORM Corps briefly during the Gina Cappozi rescue back in December, but everyone associated with the outfit had been pretty tight-lipped. Especially Darcy Zimmerman. Her respect for the woman's abilities rose considerably.

He regarded her for a moment, as though even he was weighing how much to say. "STORM Corps is one of the best PMCs—private military contractors—in existence. We've been hired by nearly every major international company at one time or another, and a couple dozen foreign governments. Rescue and retrieval missions, mostly, but also sensitive strategic operations that possibly corrupt local military or law enforcement can't be trusted to carry out. Part of our contract is a clause that gives us absolute access to all clients' intelligence databases."

Wow. "And these companies and governments trust a PMC enough to allow that?"

"They have no choice. STORM Corps isn't just any random PMC. We're in big demand worldwide and can pick and choose our jobs. It's a deal-breaker clause."

Incredible. Her bosses would kill to have access to that level of information. No wonder he'd hesitated before telling her. "Don't your clients cut you off after the mission is over?"

He smiled. "Darcy is really good at her job. So are all our other comp specs."

"I'm beginning to see that." But better she didn't. "And

what else has Darcy found out about our unsubs? Are they al Sayika?"

"Suspected," he said. "France had the dead guy on a terrorist watch list, and the wounded one in custody is wanted for questioning in Sweden in conjunction with the foiled kidnapping of a member of parliament."

She gave a low whistle. "So the yacht being in Chesapeake Bay so close to Washington, D.C., that's probably no coincidence."

"Definitely not. The bay gives ready access to the Potomac River, which runs practically straight to the White House. I think it's a pretty safe bet our boys were planning something nasty, with D.C. as the target."

"And possibly involving a nuclear trigger." The thought raised the hair on the back of her neck. "But what, exactly?"

"That," he said determinedly, "is what you and I are going to find out."

"How do you propose we do that?" she asked, ever practical. Even with the two men's names, they had precious little to go on. And their only living suspect was in surgery for his gunshot wound and wouldn't be available for questioning for hours, if not days.

Alex leaned back in his chair. "First thing is to search the yacht. If we're lucky, we'll find the trigger somewhere onboard."

"Unless that blur of movement I saw before the ship exploded really was another terrorist jumping overboard, and he took it with him," she said with a frown.

"We should be able to tell from our search how many men were on the boat."

"True. Except for one minor detail," she reminded him. "That yacht is now at the bottom of the bay."

"Not an obstacle," he said evenly. "Ready to go diving?"

She hiked her brows. "Excuse me?"

He gave her what might have passed for an impish smile, except it didn't quite reach his half-lidded eyes. "You and me. Sexy wet suits. Sharing oxygen. Finding booty . . ."

The double meaning was a little too obvious to miss, but she pretended anyway. "Alex, you know very well I haven't been scuba diving in years." They'd always talked about her getting recertified so they could dive together, but it had never happened.

The curve of his smile didn't alter, but something distinctly unhumorous dimmed the sexual glitter in his eyes. The air shifted like quicksilver. "That's not what I heard."

For a second she was confused. Then she realized what he must be alluding to: the trip to the Caribbean she'd taken in January with SAC Wade Montana. Someone must have told him about it. Helena most likely, since she and Alex had still been happily engaged at the time. Or maybe Gina or Rainie. Rebel had stayed in touch with both women after Gina's rescue last December.

She looked Alex in the eye. "You heard wrong," she said.

He shrugged but didn't look away. "Doesn't matter anyway. I can recertify you myself."

"Since when?" she asked, surprised. This was new.

"Since I got bored at Haven Oaks and did the full instructor course there. Commander Quinn can fax your recert to the boat if you pass. Which you will."

She straightened at the part he'd glossed over. "What boat?"

This time, his lips curved for real. "STORM has arranged a cabin cruiser for us."

The man was just full of surprises today. She arched her brows again. "What, the Coast Guard's ships aren't good enough?"

"Let's just say we have some specialized equipment." As he said it, he finally broke eye contact and looked down at the file he still held in his hand.

She was getting a little tired of hearing how great STORM's resources were. What was the FBI? Chopped liver? "Such as . . . ?" she asked.

"Besides," he said, adroitly sidestepping her question, "I don't like being dependent on other agencies." He opened the file and began to peruse it. Completely avoiding her gaze.

A curl of suspicion threaded through her. "Alex, what are you not telling me?"

At that, he did look up. Aloud, he said nothing, but in his expression she could read the answer perfectly. *Plenty.*

Just then, Special Agent in Charge Carballosa came around the corner of her cubicle. "Made any headway yet?" he asked.

Alex switched focus to the SAC. "Still too early to tell," he said with a straight face.

Her boss held out an envelope to him. "This was delivered for you."

"Thanks." Alex took it, ripped it open at the end, and shook out the contents. A set of keys dropped onto his palm. "Excellent. Our transpo." He shot her an unreadable glance.

Carballosa made to leave. "You good to go, Haywood? Clear on your orders?"

Hold on. "What orders, sir?"

The SAC's gaze flicked between Alex and her. "Mr. Zane didn't fill you in?"

A desperate feeling tightened her gut. "Apparently not, sir."

"A task force will be up and running by end of day to deal with this situation," he informed her. "STORM Corps is working with DHS and the Coast Guard. You've been assigned to coordinate exchange of info between the Bureau and STORM Corps."

Relief spiraled through her. Was that all? "Be happy to, sir."

"Good," he said, and made to leave. "Call me personally with an update at least twice a day."

Wait. "Where will you be?" she asked.

"Right here," he said. "Mr. Zane said you'd be out of the office for a few days."

Out of . . . ? Her stomach dropped. "Why would I—"

"You're on loan to STORM for the duration, Haywood. From now on, you'll take your orders from them"—Carballosa gestured at Alex—"through Mr. Zane, here."

Her jaw dropped in consternation. "But—"

"And Special Agent Haywood?"

She stifled her cry of protest. "Yes, sir?"

"You make *damn* sure we find that trigger before whatever shit these fuckers've got planned for this country hits the fan. Understood?" With that, SAC Carballosa turned on a toe and disappeared around the corner of the cubicle.

Good thing, because she couldn't have squeezed a word past her blossoming outrage to save her life.

And she *really* didn't want any witnesses to the homicide she was about to commit.

She rounded on Alex. "Under your command?" she ground out.

He regarded her with glittering eyes. "Has a certain ring to it, I must say."

She clamped her jaw. "Look. I don't know what's gotten into you about . . ." She stopped, unable to say it.

One golden brow quirked in blatant challenge.

She felt her face flame, but lowered her voice and gritted out, "I don't know where you got the idea I would just fall into bed with you now that you're free, but—"

"No?" He snorted, anger hardening his expression. "Really?"

"What's that supposed to mean?" she demanded.

"You'll fuck an asswipe like Wade Montana five minutes after you meet him, but not the man you've been in love with for five years?"

Indignation surged through her. "How dare you—" She broke off, infuriated not so much because it wasn't true . . . but because it was, and they both knew it. "Wade is a good man."

But she still chastised herself for her weakness in getting involved with Wade in the first place, and had done so since succumbing to his whirlwind seduction at the precise moment when she'd been at her most vulnerable—right after Alex and Helena had set a date for their wedding.

How could she have known their engagement would be called off less than two months later and they'd break up for good?

Not that *that* should make a difference. Alex had made his choice of women *very* clear long ago, and only a desperate fool would allow herself to accept second place in his heart.

No matter how much she loved him.

A woman had her pride.

Of course, no one in this conversation, least of all Alex Zane, had mentioned *any*thing about hearts. Or heaven forbid, love.

"How *dare* you?" she repeated, anger at herself fueling her outrage.

He leaned into her space. "Our *kiss* this morning, that's how."

She leaned backward, dashed by the cold truth of that, too. "Y-you caught me off guard."

Again, he gave a derisive snort. "Fucking bullshit."

"Language, Zane," she admonished.

"Pretend all you like, angel, but I know you want me. Dump the bastard." He leaned closer and murmured coaxingly, "Be with me."

How long had she wished and prayed to hear him say those three little words? Well. Or three little words to that effect.

"You're not being fair," she murmured.

"How so?" He reached for her. He curled his fingers behind her neck and pulled her face toward his. "You don't love him. You can't possibly love him."

That's not what she'd meant. She and Wade had decided to keep things casual and non-exclusive after that disastrous trip to the Caribbean, and had since drifted apart pretty much permanently. No, she didn't love him. How could she? "That's not the point," she said.

"I'm not asking for a commitment, Rebel."

Yeah. *That* was the point. Alex didn't want *her*, he only wanted sex.

As though sensing the direction of her thoughts, he brushed his lips tantalizingly over hers, and said, "I'll be with you for as long as you want me, angel. I promise."

Her heart gave a stutter. Could he really mean that?

Why not? Alex Zane was the most loyal person she knew. When he gave his word, he kept it. He'd proven that over and over again in the past. With Helena, for instance.

But could Rebel really trust him *now*? Being a virtual prisoner of war, going through such unspeakable horrors for so long, it must have changed him. How could it not have?

Was he still the same man he'd been before his ordeal? And even if he was, could she live with the knowledge that she was his second choice and always would be?

He pressed his lips more firmly to hers. Warm. *Persuasive.*

"Trust me," he urged softly.

Could she?

She swallowed heavily. Torn as never before. *She needed time*. “Let me think about it,” she said.

He gave her a masculine, satisfied smile, as though her answer were already a given. “Take all the time you need.” He kissed her one last time. “Now let’s go pack you an overnight bag. We’re moving onto the boat.”

FIVE

"MCPHEE."

Sarah punched the blinking line on her desk phone, hoping against hope it was the coroner calling to let her know the autopsy of the Dumpster vic had been postponed indefinitely. Or better yet, had been moved up unexpectedly and, oh, hell, she'd missed it.

"Detective McPhee, this is FBI Special Agent in Charge Wade Montana."

Sarah picked up a pen in surprise. "Yes?" she said cautiously, glanced at the clock, then quickly scribbled down his name, the date and time. "What can I do for you, SAC Montana?"

"You ran a fingerprint search last night, on a woman named Asha Mahmood."

Speak of the devil. Sarah'd gotten back to the station late last night after interviewing witnesses—none of whom had seen anything, surprise, surprise. But someone in the medical examiner's office had also been burning the midnight oil and e-mailed over a clean set of the vic's prints. So she'd run them, and come up with the name, an address that upon investigation this morning turned out to be fake, and not much else.

"Yes, I ran her prints," she said. One thing she'd learned in her varied encounters with the agents of Uncle Sam: never volunteer anything to a feeb. Always make them ask.

"May I ask what it was about?"

She smiled wryly. At least he was polite. Nice voice, too. Smooth. Cultured. She could just picture him in his natty blue suit and red-striped tie. Or was he more of a Men in Black with reflecto sunglasses guy?

"May I ask why you want to know?" she returned just as politely.

There was a pause. *Yeah, here it comes.* She didn't know what, but federal interest in a case or a vic always spelled trouble, no matter how nice the guy's voice.

"I'm afraid I can't tell you that," he said.

She was shocked, *shocked.* "Oh. Well. What a coincidence," she said pleasantly. "I can't, either."

"Detective McPhee," he said with studied patience, "I would sincerely appreciate your cooperation in this matter."

"And what matter is that, SAC Montana?"

He sighed. And to her surprise, chuckled. "Okay. I surrender. Tell you what. Why don't we meet and discuss this over lunch? My treat."

Uh-oh.

"No pressure," he added. "Just a friendly exchange of information."

Ri-ight. Still. Against her better judgment, she was intrigued. What had this vic been into? Knowing that could help in her murder investigation.

She checked her day planner. Four hours until she had to be at the M.E.'s. "All right. How's fifteen minutes? Where would you like to—" The buzzer on her intercom sounded. "Hang on." She pushed the button. "Yeah?"

"You up?" came the voice of the dispatcher.

"Yep." She grabbed her notebook. Because Jonesy and another detective were testifying in court today and two others were out at another call, she was up in the duty rotation again.

"DB reported at Kenilworth Aquatic Gardens on Anacostia Ave." The dispatcher rattled off the relevant information.

Ah, well. So much for lunch.

"Got it." She pushed the line for the feeb. "Sorry, duty calls," she told Montana. "I've got a homicide."

Montana promptly said, "Where? I'll meet you at the scene."

Okay. "Look, I don't—"

"I'll bring lunch with me."

All sorts of alarm bells went off in her cop brain. Definitely Men in Black. She better watch herself if she didn't want to be turned into an alien. Or worse, have the FBI horn in on her case.

"How 'bout I call you when I get back?" she suggested. "Good talking to you, SAC Montana." She hung up. Without getting his number. If it was important, he'd call back. Which would give her a chance to be better prepared. But meanwhile, she had a case, and with any luck she'd be away from her desk for the rest of the day.

Kenilworth Gardens, eh? The little-known national park situated along the Anacostia River was dedicated solely to water plants. An unusual place for a murder.

She grabbed her things and made the fifteen-minute drive, pulling up just as the assistant M.E. did. He got out of his BMW and gave her a smile and a wave. "Detective McPhee. Busy day, huh?"

She smiled back. "Thanks for the quick turnaround on those prints last night, Dr. Stroud."

"No problem. And please, if we're going to be cutting up dead bodies together later, call me Johnny."

She tried not to choke. On either count. "All right. And I'm Sarah."

They walked through the ugly gate that led into the park, and followed the dirt path down to the ponds where the new vic had been found. The thick smell of standing water and wet earth filled the air, along with the buzz of awakening spring insects.

Since the murder scene hadn't been released by the CSI team yet, she halted when they hit the outer edge of the built-up maze of man-made ponds. With a wave, Dr. Stroud—Johnny—kept walking onto a narrow levee between them. "Give me five minutes."

A handful of gardeners in muddy hip waders and the park ranger in a Smokey hat milled about, observing the police activity from a roped-off section of the path where they'd been herded. She joined them.

The shallow green ponds themselves were for the most part bare of vegetation, save for a glutinous haze of slime and algae. She didn't know much about plants in general or water plants in particular, but her mom had kept a pretty pink tropical water lily in a half-whisky barrel on the back deck growing up, and it had to be taken in each winter and set out again in spring.

The official last frost date in D.C. was just a few days away—although Sarah never put her tomato plants out on her apartment's microscopic balcony before Mother's Day. So she wasn't surprised to observe big white buckets filled with rotting plant detritus sitting along the water's edge, evidence that the staff must be cleaning out the ponds in anticipation of spring planting. Which must be how the DB had been discovered. She wondered idly how long the victim had been in the slimy water. Yuck. And how it had gotten there.

Pulling out her notebook, she turned to the gardeners and ranger and started asking her questions. She was just finishing up with the last witness when a tall, good-looking, fortyish man in a dark blue suit strolled up holding a Burger King bag.

He peered at her over the rims of amber-colored reflecto-aviators. "Detective McPhee?"

She did a double-take.

Oh. My. God.

Probably a few years her junior, the guy was at that stage of forty-something that made a man look affluent, sexy, and in his prime—fit, tanned, tailored, and financially sound.

Well, except for the Burger King part. Lunch? Really?

"SAC Montana, I presume," she drawled, torn between irritation and annoyance.

"I brought lunch," he said with a bad-boy smile that had doubtless captured the heart of many a hapless rookie straight from the Academy who didn't know any better.

"Seriously? Burger King?" she said dryly.

"Angry Whoppers," he said, and waggled his eyebrows.

Okay, you had to give the man points for a sense of humor. Unwillingly, she felt her lips form a half smile. "How perceptive of you," she said.

"That's why they pay me the big bucks. So"—he looked around—"where can we sit and chat?"

She snapped her notebook closed and started back toward the parking lot without bothering to check if he was following. "I can't believe they let you onto an active crime scene. Somebody's gonna wish he didn't get up this morning." Referring to the guard at the gate.

"Not his fault," Montana said from behind her. "He got a call from your lieutenant to let me in."

She jetted out a breath, halted and spun, hands on hips. She should have *known* Harding would—

Montana ran right into her.

For a split second the front of their bodies pressed together intimately. No longer than an instant, but long enough to feel the hardness of his muscles and the broadness of his chest against her breasts. Not to mention a few other things she *def*initely should not be feeling.

Like a crazy zing of sexual attraction in the pit of her stomach.

Whoa.

She stepped back. He stood still. He cocked his head, gazing at her over those impenetrable glasses again. His eyes were blue as the spring sky. "I'm hungry," he said, his voice suddenly pitched low. "How 'bout you?"

God, had he felt it, too? Was that an invitation for more than Angry Whoppers . . . ? Or had her overactive imagination just skipped from too-fertile to plain-old-stupid, due to being without a man for so long?

"Um, look—"

"No strings," he said. "You don't have to give me anything you don't want to."

She blinked. What exactly *were* they talking about here? "That's good. Because I don't have much to give."

His lips tilted up—mobile lips, no doubt brimming with experience. "I'll be the judge of that."

Holy. Jesus.

She swiped the bag from his hand. "We can eat in my car." *In full view of the officer guarding the gate*, she reprimanded herself sternly. With that, she strode off down the path.

And wondered what the bloody hell he *really* wanted.

GINA awoke with a peculiar feeling in the pit of her stomach. Something was—

Omigod.

Then she remembered. The attack! She let out a cry of

despair. Visions of blood flew through her mind. Along with the feel of powerful hands gripping her and . . .

Gregg.

Bolting upright, she looked around frantically. *Mother of God.* She was in his apartment!

And in his bed.

She would recognize that heavy wrought-iron headboard anywhere. Its unusual custom features had figured prominently in their lovemaking on the occasions he'd brought her here . . . and in her fantasies ever since.

But those fantasies were about to turn into nightmares.

Her hands flew to her mouth, stifling a cry of panic.

That's when she noticed her arms were bare. She looked down at the rest of her body. A desperate whimper escaped.

She was naked!

What had he done to her?

"Hello, Gina," his deep voice said from nearby.

She whipped around, and saw him.

He was sprawled casually in a chair by the window, fingering a bottle of beer clasped between his hands. His faded jeans had holes at the knees; his signature black T-shirt hugged a torso that was still ripped from granite. Short-cropped sandy hair; hard, sculpted features; and a shoulder-holstered gun tucked under his armpit completed the picture of the consummate badass. Despite his slack pose with one motorcycle booted–foot resting negligently on the other knee, his whole body oozed strength and power.

Her throat went painfully dry. She recognized, almost viscerally, that tall, broad, hard-as-nails body. Felt the power of its impact at such a primal level she nearly cried out in protest.

But she managed to swallow down the sensation and ask, "Why am I here? What do you want from me, Gregg?"

His sensual lips curved downward. The movement made

the hollowed angles of his ultra-masculine face even more harsh than usual.

She should be terrified. She *was* terrified! And yet . . .

A spill of goose bumps washed up her arms and over her chest. Against her will, a coil of sexual desire tightened in her center. *Lord help her.* Why did the bastard have to look so damn amazing? She didn't understand why her body steadfastly refused to acknowledge her fear of him.

"Why am I naked?" she demanded, gaining strength from her inner mortification. She clutched the bedsheet to her tightly, pulling it up to her neck. "What are you going to do, rape me before you kill me?"

A muscle ticked in his cheek but his expression didn't alter. "Your clothes were covered in blood."

She quickly touched her face, flashing a glance at her hands again. Both clean. He'd washed her, too.

He dropped his boot to the floor and rose catlike from the chair. Her heart pounded erratically. But he just walked to a dresser and from the top picked up a pair of neatly folded black sweatpants and a black T-shirt.

In a vase sitting next to where the clothes had been stacked, she suddenly noticed a bouquet of yellow roses and blue forget-me-nots. The flowers she'd dropped? She was so surprised, she didn't sense him approach until he tossed the clothes down on the bed in front of her.

She started badly, panic zinging through her like an electric shock. He halted, watching her with narrowed eyes as she frantically scrambled backward.

They stared at each other for an endless moment. At length he said tightly, "Gina. I'm not going to rape you. I didn't dress you because after cleaning the blood off your body, I didn't trust myself to touch you for one second longer. Yes, we have history, and it's pretty damn clear I still want you. But I wouldn't take you by force. And I'm *not* going to kill you."

An uncontrollable tremble went through her. She didn't believe him! The man was heartless; he'd sold her to terrorists! They'd beaten her, drugged her, and forced her to use her expertise in genetic research to weaponize a horrible biological agent. If not kill her, then what could he possibly want with her? Why was he doing this?

She let out a squeak of horror as an unacceptable thought hit her. *Surely, he didn't intend to give her back to them?* Please, God, no! She couldn't go through that again!

As the squeak morphed to a scream, he was on the bed in a flash. One powerful hand clamped over her mouth, his arm banded around her body. "Shhh," he sussed in her ear as the frantic sound fought in vain to explode from her. "There's no need to scream, sweet thing. No one will hear you anyway. Please stop."

No!

She struggled against his hold. Against his hand. Against the worst fate imaginable. She fought him as tears blinded her and sobs clogged her throat. She scratched and clawed and pounded him. And all the while he held her fast, not giving an inch.

"Hush, now," he murmured.

The words triggered an irrationally calming memory of a similar deep voice.

Hush now.

During the worst of her torture at the hands of her captors, when she'd been beaten nearly blind and to the brink of death, the man she'd called the Voice had come to her once, with soothing words and drugs to dull the pain.

But *he* hadn't let her go, either.

"It's okay," Gregg said.

No! It wasn't okay!

Thanks to him, it would never be okay again.

She fought and fought, until she exhausted her strength and ran out of tears. And still he just held her. It wasn't a soothing embrace. Nor was it cruel. It was more like . . . awkward.

"Hush, sweet girl."

If she didn't know better, she might think he was actually trying to comfort her. The idea of *that* stunned her into stillness, broken only by a long, hiccup-punctuated exhale.

He bunched his hand in the hem of his T-shirt and tried to raise it to wipe the tears from her face. But because of his broad chest, the shirt wouldn't stretch up past her chin. So he pulled it over his head, then used it as a big, soft hankie, daubing the wetness from her cheeks, eyes, and nose.

Shock swept through her, as did the scent of him from the shirt that caressed her face. His naked chest brushed against her bare breasts as he moved, sending her nipples into tight spirals. She held her breath, resisting the irrational urge to pillow them up against her abductor.

He paused. His focus slipped down to her breasts then up again, hesitating for a heartbeat at her lips. For a split second she thought he might actually try to kiss her.

Her stomach clenched. She turned away.

His hands dropped abruptly. "I'm sorry," he said, and she wondered bitterly to what he was referring—touching her naked breasts, making her cry, selling her to terrorists . . . What?

She shuddered out her choked breath and closed her stinging eyes. "Go to hell."

He gave a soft, sardonic laugh. "Sure. Now, why don't you lie down and get some sleep." He went to the dresser, swiped up a new black T-shirt, and yanked it on. Thank God.

She pressed her mouth into a quavering line. "I want to go home." The trembling statement came out sounding so pathetic she scarcely recognized herself in it. That had been happening a lot lately. The pathetic part.

"Sorry. Not going to happen," he said.

Anger finally overran her fear. "Haven't I suffered enough for you?" she demanded.

He gazed over at her impassively, but the tic in his cheek twitched again. "There's no phone. The door is locked and all the windows are barred. There's no way out of here, so you might as well make yourself comfortable. The good news is, no one else can get in, either."

He turned to leave the bedroom.

"Gregg?"

At his name on her lips, he halted at the door. The shadows of the other room touched him like gray fingers reaching out to caress him. He didn't turn around.

"Why?" she asked. Her voice cracked on a roil of surfacing emotion. "Why did you do it, Gregg? Why did you give me to those animals? For money? Al Sayika blood diamonds? How much did they pay you? How much was my life worth to you?"

Even under the T-shirt she could see the muscles in his broad back coil and tighten. Like he wanted to turn and beat the crap out of her. Or someone. But he just walked out, his body quickly swallowed by the dimness of the curtained room beyond.

"Tell me!" she yelled after him, desperate to know the worst. He halted again. This time he did turn. A shaft of light from the closed drapes painted over his face. Her own tears welled anew and brimmed over onto her cheeks. "I loved you!" she cried. "Why did you betray me?"

He flinched visibly. His hands balled into silent fists.

At the gesture, horrible memories seared through her of the many beatings she'd taken at the hands of her terrorist captors. Pain razored across her heart at the idea that this man whom she'd once thought she loved could do such evil. To her.

As if it took a great effort, he swallowed and met her gaze. His blue eyes burned like the fires of Hell.

He said very carefully and deliberately, "I did not give you to them, Gina. It wasn't me."

SIX

IN his logical mind, Gregg knew Gina really believed he was the one responsible for her kidnapping by al Sayika, and therefore for all the suffering she'd endured. For months he'd known that.

But hearing the accusation spoken so forcefully from her own lips nearly gutted him. It was all he could do to respond without putting his fist through a wall or smashing some piece of furniture into a million pieces—which would only serve to terrify her even more.

She didn't believe him. He could see that clearly in her eyes. In her whole body.

It didn't matter. He didn't need her to believe him—or to like him—to do what needed to be done.

"If it wasn't you who betrayed me," she accused, flinging a hand around her, "then why this? Why are you holding me against my will?"

He took a step toward the bed. She was still huddled on the far side of the mattress, clutching the sheet to her chest.

But it had slipped, and he could see her breasts again, ripe and sensual, their tips dark and beaded with excitement.

In special ops, one of the first things a man learns is that fear produces the same physical reactions in a body as sexual arousal. It was a lesson he had taught Gina with painstaking care in their relationship as lovers. She had always been turned on by being just a little afraid of him. She'd liked his penchant for domination, responded hotly to his physical control over her. And he in turn had been incredibly aroused by having that power over her.

But that was before.

Now? Her eyes held a different kind of fear. One he wanted no part in arousing.

"I have to keep you here," he said, forcing his gaze away from her bare body. "For your own protection."

Her lips parted. "Protection? Are you kidding? *You're* the one I need protecting from!"

"No," he said flatly. "I'm not."

But he *would* be if she didn't cover herself. Her feelings for him might have changed, but his hadn't. He still wanted her with a craving that gnawed at him like a wolverine. It had been pure torture stripping off her bloody clothes and washing her smooth skin of blood earlier and not awakening her by joining their bodies together as he'd always done when they'd shared a bed. He'd left her naked instead of dressing her, terrified of doing something they'd both have bitterly regretted. Just as he would now if she didn't put on those damned clothes.

"Get dressed," he ordered gruffly, mastering his need. Just as he'd mastered everything else in his life. "I'll make you some lunch."

He didn't wait for her response, but went to the galley-style kitchen and opened a can of soup. French bread, a hunk of cheese, and steaming, fragrant tea completed the meal. He set it on his small kitchen table. When he looked up, he saw she'd dressed in the clothes he'd given her, and was clinging to the bedroom door frame, watching him.

"Come and eat," he said.

She shook her head. She put out her bare foot and raised the hem of one leg of her sweatpants to show the silver heart and chain he'd fastened around her ankle. "What is this?"

"A gift," he said after a short hesitation. How could he explain the complicated feeling behind the gesture? The powerful surge of possessiveness that had rushed through his veins, the protectiveness he'd felt as he'd locked the chain around her limb and claimed her with his talisman? And the sense of relief knowing that within the curve of the silver heart nestled a tracking device that he could activate if he ever needed to—providing she didn't take a hacksaw to the thing and throw it out the window. "A symbol of my good intentions."

She gazed at it suspiciously. "It doesn't have a clasp."

"No," he said. "Let it be a reminder that I'll always be with you. Not to hurt you. To *protect* you." He didn't add "even if you don't want me there," but it was clear in her face that she understood that much. But it was a pretty trinket, one he'd known she would like, and he could also see her uncertainty about its ultimate meaning.

She lowered the pant leg. "There's a tracking device in it, isn't there?"

"What do you think?"

"I don't want it."

"I know. But do you really want to take a chance on no one finding you when the bad guys show up next time?"

She just glared.

"Now come and eat," he repeated.

"I don't think so," she said without moving.

He controlled the annoyance that wanted to rise. "What? You think I'm going to drug you? Poison you?"

She gnawed on her lower lip, silently eyeing the food. Obviously, she did.

"Fine." He bent to spoon up a mouthful of soup. Then another. He swallowed it down and tore a hunk of bread onto which he sliced a sliver of cheese, and ate that, too. He drank half the mug of tea, then refilled it from the same pot. "Convinced?"

"Protection from whom?" she asked, avoiding the question.

He regarded her. "Come over here and sit down and I'll tell you." He backed away from the table, all the way to the kitchen counter, and leaned his butt against it, folding his arms over his chest so he wouldn't reach out for her.

She still didn't move.

"Sweet thing, if I'd wanted to hurt you, I'd already have done so," he said reasonably.

Her eyes cut up to him from the table. "Don't call me that."

He stifled a sting in his heart. She used to like it when he called her sweet thing. So did he. Because she was. Incredibly sweet. Sweet sounding, sweet tasting, sweet smelling, sweet looking. She was the sweet and soft to everything hard and bitter inside him.

Even now, with her beautiful dark eyes filled with such loathing and suspicion, she was still the sweetest thing he'd ever seen.

"Whatever you want," he said dispassionately, and pointed to the meal. "Now, eat."

"When you've answered my question."

Even though she still clung to the door frame, in her refusal he saw a glimmer of the old, strong, and stubborn Gina, and was gratified. He wanted her fighting, not cowering.

"All right," he conceded, rewarding her. "Protection from the al Sayika thugs who tried to kill you this morning, and all the others that will follow, now that you're out of Haven Oaks. They must think you can identify them. And they'll keep sending assassins until you're dead. I have to protect you."

She shook her head. "Don't even try. I know you're al Sayika's paid dog. You were there with them this morning! Besides, STORM is protecting me."

He ground his jaw at the insult. Controlled his anger. "And a first-rate job they did, too."

She worried her bottom lip with her teeth, dismay crossing her face. "You killed him. Dez Johnson, one of the STORM agents. You only wanted me. Why did you have to kill him?"

He stared at her. Told himself it didn't matter that she believed he was firmly on the side of evil. The truth was, her would-be assassins had distracted the more seasoned STORM guy and set a trap for Johnson, who'd been just new enough at this game to fall for it. Gregg hadn't gotten to him in time.

"I didn't kill him," he said evenly. "But I did kill the terrorists. If I hadn't, you'd be dead now, too."

She stared back at him, then turned away with a shiver. She couldn't very well deny the truth of it. She'd been there. Seen the attacker's gun pointed at her forehead. And her own knife planted in his chest.

Which apparently convinced her Gregg wasn't out to kill her. Not yet, anyway. Evidently, he had to rape her first.

She edged toward the table and warily sat down. He held himself very still, though God knew why he bothered.

"You've been following me," she said, hesitantly picking up the spoon. There was only one, and they both realized in the same instant that he'd already eaten from it. She set it down again.

Clenching his jaw, he pulled a new one from the drawer. "Yeah. Ever since you were rescued in Louisiana," he said, holding it out to her.

He held it steady as she regarded him, comprehension slowly dawning in her eyes. "Ever since . . . then you *were* at Haven Oaks."

He nodded. "Got a job there as a groundskeeper."

"But how? STORM security is . . ."

He gave her a patient look. "I worked CIA undercover black ops for over a decade, Gina. I wouldn't be very good at my job if I couldn't get past a little security check."

She paled, looked from him to the spoon in his hand. "I wasn't hallucinating. I *knew* I'd seen you."

He gave up and set it on the table for her, then returned to his spot against the counter. "Yeah, I let you see my face a couple times, hoping . . ." He pressed his lips together, remembering the look of abject terror on hers each time he had. *Fuck.*

She picked up the spoon, put it down. Picked up the bread instead. Put that down, too. "Why? Why watch me?"

"I told you. To protect you."

Her eyes filled again as she shook her head. "That doesn't make any sense. Why sell me out and then protect me? Out of guilt?"

"I told you, Gina. It wasn't me who sold you to those monsters."

He could see her struggle desperately against the assertion, unable to reconcile his denial with what she thought she knew.

A tear trickled down her cheek. "You drove me there, Gregg—to the place the terrorists kidnapped me. You said it was Zero Unit's northeastern headquarters, but how do I know it wasn't a complete setup? That you weren't part of the plan all along?"

Thinking about that day sent liquid rage streaking through his veins. She was right; he *had* driven her to ZU-NE on the back of his motorcycle that afternoon, at the request of his commanding officer, Colonel Frank Blair, ostensibly to identify the body of a missing friend she'd been searching for. When they'd arrived, Blair had immediately handed him marching orders, sending him OCONUS on a three-week mission to Kurdistan. It wasn't until Gregg returned that he'd learned Gina had vanished. And another week until he'd put all the pieces together. And realized he'd been used.

Blair had denied it, of course. Even after some fairly persuasive questioning.

And that's when Gregg had gone AWOL. From Zero Unit, its handlers within CIA, and the whole damn world. It *had* been a setup, no doubt about it. But *he'd* been the one set up, to take the fall if Zero Unit's involvement in a prominent American scientist's kidnapping was ever discovered. If caught, there was no doubt in his mind that he'd fall victim to CIA's usual tactic for ridding itself of an inconvenient operator—he'd disappear without a trace, to rot his life away in some stinking foreign political prison without the benefit of a trial. He'd seen it happen before, and it wasn't pretty.

He must figure out who was really behind this. And soon.

"I guess you can't be sure I wasn't involved," he admitted. "But I'd hoped you knew me better than to believe it."

He'd spent the entire three remaining months she was missing trying to find her. Which hadn't been easy. He'd been branded a deserter—though technically he wasn't, because Zero Unit was not part of the military—and worse, the terrorists' accomplice. Even now his face was plastered across every MP and law enforcement office's Most Wanted board, not to mention every ZU operator, CIA officer, and Interpol agent in the world was looking for him. Tough to move around under those circumstances, even with Tommy and his other CIs helping him.

In the end, when he'd finally found a solid lead on who might have taken Gina and where she was being held, he'd been forced to phone it in anonymously to DHS because his own hands had been so severely tied. He hadn't wanted her to spend one more minute with those al Sayika scumsuckers because of his own inability to mount a rescue.

Head bowed, she studied the bowl of soup before her. "How can I believe anything you say?" she quietly asked. "You've lied to me about everything—*everything*—from the moment we met."

His heart squeezed. He opened his mouth to deny it, then snapped it shut. Lying was a way of life when you worked for the Agency. They'd met because she'd been his assignment. He'd been sent to stop her asking some very inconvenient questions about a woman who'd disappeared in conjunction with one of their covert operations. But once he'd seen her, talked to her, kissed her, made love to her . . .

"Our intimate relationship was not a lie," he denied tightly.

She looked up. Accusation again swam in her big brown eyes. "Wasn't it?"

"No."

He pushed off the counter angrily, and she jumped, knocking her chair over as she surged to her feet and backed away from him in fear.

Fuck it. He couldn't take this another minute.

He stopped, exhaled, and said, "Eat your soup before it gets cold, then get some rest. I'm going out for a while."

He felt her eyes on his back as he retrieved his spare weapon—a Beretta with the serial numbers filed off—from the bedroom and tucked it into an ankle holster. His SIG Sauer P226 Elite was already in its usual spot—in the front of his waistband under his T-shirt. Sliding on his black leather jacket, he grabbed his keys and went to the door. "I'm locking this from the outside," he said. "There isn't another key, so don't bother tearing the place apart searching. But help yourself to whatever else you want."

With that, he left the apartment, turning the key in the lock behind him with a firm *snick.*

Christ.

It took him all four flights of stairs going down to the street to master his anger. Not anger at her. Anger at himself. That he'd gotten into this ludicrous situation in the first place. If he'd only just done his job—seduced her to shut her up as ordered, then walked away when the deed was done—and not gotten emotionally involved. Not let himself fall for her body and grow dependent on her adoration, not start to think maybe, just maybe, he'd finally met a woman whose warmth and love could banish the perpetual coldness in his heart . . .

Fuck it.

None of that mattered now. His foolish, uncontrolled foray into the realm of emotions was over. All that mattered was keeping Gina safe from those who would harm her.

Hell, he should have brought her here days ago. With her safely hidden at his place, he wouldn't have to follow her 24/7, trying vainly to protect her while she left herself ridiculously exposed to attack just to lure him out in the open. He'd been stupid, stupid, stupid, letting meaningless emotion influence his decisions. He knew better. *Knew* better. He'd spent his whole life ridding himself of those irrational impulses.

It wasn't going to happen again.

But now he had to work fast. Everyone involved thought he was a traitor. Gina'd just confirmed that. Thanks to the witnesses after the attack, they'd know he was the one holding her now. No stone would be left unturned in the search for her—and him. If the *real* traitor found him and he disappeared, she'd be left out there all on her own.

He knew very well that STORM Corps was only using

her as bait to bring down the al Sayika mole. He'd listened to enough of their conversations back at Haven Oaks to leave no doubt of their strategy. So if they believed the traitor had been caught, they'd assume she was safe, and cease their surveillance.

Gregg didn't want to think what might happen to Gina without him to protect her.

He *had* to find the traitor before he found them.

Both their lives depended on it.

"SO, I'll see you later tonight, Detective McPhee?"

"Looking forward to it, SAC Montana."

Sarah watched the disturbingly sexy FBI agent walk purposefully to his car and climb in. It was a late-model BMW. Dark blue, of course, God forbid he break the FBI dress code even in his choice of vehicle color. Though it was a convertible. A peek of rebellion . . . or vanity?

Okay, that was weird.

Not the car. The dinner invitation.

The whole setup had Sarah's internal red flags whipping back and forth, doing tricks worthy of her niece's high school color guard.

Still. The guy was totally gorgeous. Who was she to turn down a date with the most attractive man she'd met in years just because there were probably more strings attached than in her grandpa's tackle box? This wasn't a date, it was a fishing expedition. That much was pretty obvious.

She started up her ancient Chevy with a grin. Yeah, well, two could play at *that* particular game. She couldn't wait to see how far he'd actually go to get what he wanted from her.

Whatever the hell that was.

For the past half hour they'd sat in her car eating the Angry Whoppers he'd brought, sipping Cokes, and making small talk . . . while he'd danced around the real topic of his interest—the dead woman in the alley. He'd asked what Sarah knew about her, nodding politely when she'd told him she knew pretty much diddly.

"Why are you so interested in this victim?" she'd asked.

"Sorry, can't tell you," he'd cited with that smug FBI twinkle in his honest blue eyes. "Ongoing investigation."

God, she hated that. She'd really wished she had something she could hold out on him with. Unfortunately, she really did know diddly.

So they'd moved on to other subjects, including the murdered guy in the lily pond, about whom she knew even less since they hadn't run his prints yet. That's when Montana had surprised her with the dinner invitation. Good grief. You couldn't get much more blatant than that. Which was why it shocked the hell out of both of them when she'd accepted.

His blue eyes had fought not to grow speculative, but slowly he'd smiled. She'd smiled back. With the confidence of a woman having years of experience dealing with this sort of Neanderthal chauvinism. She could work these guys in her sleep, with one hand tied. Hell, sometimes with *both* hands tied.

Wade Montana was nuts if he thought he could manipulate information out of her by using sex. She'd tell him what she wanted, when she wanted, if she wanted. And if he didn't like it, well, he could just go twinkle those sexy blue eyes at someone else.

ALEX Zane stared pensively across the water as he steered the *Stormy Lady*, the cabin cruiser that STORM had provided for him and Rebel, out of Norfolk harbor and onto the Chesapeake Bay.

God*damn* it.

He couldn't believe Dez Johnson was dead. Murdered in cold blood, his throat slit from behind while defending Gina Cappozi from an assassination attempt—Gina, who had once *again* been kidnapped. This time not by the terrorists themselves, but by the traitor who worked for them. The man they were now all hunting—Zero Unit operator-gone-rogue Gregg van Halen.

For the first time in months, van Halen had actually been spotted, his identity confirmed beyond a shadow of a doubt. From what STORM had been able to piece together from the clutch of frightened-out-of-their-wits witnesses, after Gina and Dez had managed to neutralize three of the would-be assassins, van Halen had killed Dez, swooped down and knocked out Gina, then made off with her unconscious body—in a *taxi*, of all fucking absurdities.

God, what a fucking clusterfuck.

Alex had heard that Kick was in a lethal rage. Kick had been Dez's partner this morning. While Gina was buying flowers, Kick had gone to check out a suspicious individual who'd ducked into the building next door. When he'd come back, Dez and three others lay dead on the street and Gina was gone.

Kick blamed himself big-time for falling for the decoy. Which was bullshit, of course. If the threat had been real and he *hadn't* investigated, the outcome would have been just as bad. It was a no-win situation, either way.

Now the team was galvanized. Out for blood. And Alex desperately wanted to be back up in New York with them, helping to run van Halen to ground. But Commander Quinn insisted someone had to investigate the sunken yacht, and that someone was Alex. The yacht might hold evidence about the rumored attack on Washington, D.C., Quinn had argued, and possibly clues as to where van Halen was holding Gina. Not to mention the illusive "trigger."

Alex slashed his hand through his hair. He *hated* being

the invalid, deliberately kept away from the action. He needed to *do* something. Tackle someone. Shoot someone. Hell, *any*thing.

"You okay?" Rebel asked, coming up beside the captain's chair where he sat white-knuckling the cabin cruiser's wheel.

"No! I'm not fucking okay," he snapped. Then squeezed his eyes shut to compose himself. *Hell.*

"Language, Zane," she said, but with such compassion that it made him even more furious.

His temper had gone totally haywire since returning from captivity in the Sudan. His therapist said it was probably a reaction to having to hold in his rage for so long under so much duress. But Alex thought it was just that his whole fucking life had gone to shit since coming back from the dead. There were days when he actually yearned for the basic simplicity of his imprisonment.

And not having anyone nag him about his goddamn language.

"I'll stop swearing when you start fucking me," he gritted out.

She just gazed at him with her big, sympathetic green eyes. "They found the bodies of the two dead men from the yacht this morning," she said, ignoring his outburst. "They were floating half out of the water onshore farther up the bay." Then she sighed and walked away.

Shit.

"Angel, wait." He swiftly slowed the craft, threw it onto autopilot, and went after her, catching her by the wrist before she could escape below. She didn't want to come, but he pulled her into his arms and held her. "I'm a fucking bastard," he murmured. "No wonder you don't want any part of me."

If he'd hoped she'd deny the notion, he was sorely disappointed. "Yeah. You are," she said. "When you want to have a clean, civil conversation, let me know." She tried to pull away.

He held her tighter. "I do want to," he said. "I'm a goddamn mess, I admit it. But I need you, Rebel. Even if it's just to talk, I need you with me." He grazed his lips over her springy red hair, kissing her temple. "You're my rock, baby. The only one I can tell what I'm really feeling. You do know that, don't you?"

It had always been that way between them. Since the first time he'd met her. One of her first assignments as a new FBI agent had been as liaison to CIA's Zero Unit, where he'd already been an operator for a half-dozen years at the time. They'd talked endlessly in those days, sometimes right through the night. They'd never so much as kissed; it hadn't been a sexual thing between them. Not that he hadn't been incredibly attracted.

But that was exactly why he *hadn't* let himself feel that way about her. Not consciously, at any rate. To a woman like Rebel Haywood, sex meant commitment. Long-term, picket fence, baby-making commitment. None of which he'd been willing or able to take on. Not with a woman he actually loved. Because of the job, he'd told himself. Yeah, and then there was that other not-so-little issue.

But that was five years ago. A lot had changed in five years. *He'd* definitely changed. And now he was free of that ill-conceived marriage of convenience to Helena . . .

Hell, Alex had always been a one-woman man. For better or worse. He could commit to being true to Rebel, no problem.

Sexually. If nothing else. Because he couldn't give her anything else.

Not that she'd *want* any more than good sex from Alex Zane, once she'd seen the real him. Not if she was remotely sane. Or like any other woman he'd ever been involved with. Rebel wanted marriage and children. And Alex was a fucking wreck of a man. She'd get that soon enough.

"I've been miserable without you to talk to," he confessed. Meaning it.

She remained silent. But at his reminder of their former closeness, her unyielding stance softened a little.

"Please, Rebel," he whispered. He trailed kisses down the side of her face, blazing a path toward her mouth. God, there had been times in his al Sayika prison hell when he would have sacrificed a whole goddamn year of his wretched life to hold and kiss her like this. He'd wanted her comfort, and her body, so damn badly. He still did.

Screw talking.

His own body grew hard as he pulled her up against it, showing her graphically just how much he wanted to be with her. He sought her lips.

She shied away. "Alex," she groaned softly. "You have to stop."

His gut twisted. And now he was too late. *Fuck.* "So you do love him, then . . ."

"Who?"

"Your lover. Montana."

She shook her head against his chest. "No."

She'd told him once before it was only sex between her and her former SAC. No strings, just a good time. Not that he'd actually believed her. She wasn't the kind of woman to sleep with a man she didn't have feelings for. She'd practically thrown the affair in Alex's face. Understandable. He'd still been engaged to her friend at the time, yet had callously confessed to wanting to sleep with Rebel. Had nearly kissed her, too, overwhelmed by *his* feelings of frustration.

God, what a fucking complicated mess.

"If you don't love him, then why should I stop?" he asked, sounding petulant even to himself.

Hell, he was close to getting down on his knees and begging. He hadn't had sex with anyone but himself in over two years. *Her* fault. He hadn't wanted to be with anyone but her. Not for ages. Helena, he'd never had sex with—though to be fair, his own sadly misguided and sex-starved hormones were not even a factor in *that* whole fiasco. But after the wedding fell through and he was set free, he'd seen Rebel's face in every woman he'd started to pick up and walked away from in disgust—because it wasn't the woman he really wanted. And believe him, he'd tried more than once.

"Why stop, Rebel?" he asked again, pushing it. Pushing her to do what they both wanted.

"You know why," she said, and he stifled the urge to scream like a little girl.

His hands were still on her ass. He coaxed her a fraction of an inch closer, so her mound pressed into his aching arousal. For a moment she let her body melt against his, all the way from her cheek down to her toes. God-*damn*, she felt good.

"Let's say I don't know why," he murmured, on the verge of imploding from frustration. "Tell me."

She let out a long exhale against his neck. "Because," she said, "you're going to hurt me."

"Never," he refuted hotly. Of all the things she might have said, that was the easiest to deny. Hell, women hurt *him*, they left *him*, not the other way around. "How can you say that?" he asked, bewildered.

"Because," she said simply, "you already have."

He felt shame. Okay, it was probably true. He'd always suspected he'd hurt her terribly by choosing Helena over her. Rebel had been sure there was something lacking in her body or her personality that kept him away, something in her character he couldn't live with, that made him prefer the other woman to her. But she had no clue. The lack was purely within himself; the fatal flaw *his*. The person he could not live with if he misled her with promises he couldn't keep was himself alone.

"I'm so sorry, angel," he murmured. "I'll make it up to you, I swear. Tell me what I need to do and I'll do it."

Anything but tell her the truth. That would drive her away for sure.

Rebel tipped her head and gazed up at him, the look in her eyes more heartrending than anything he'd ever seen.

"All I've ever wanted was for you to love me best, Alex. But you never did. And it's much too late to change your mind now."

And *that* broke his heart completely. Because she was *so* damned wrong.

He had always loved her best. And *that* was why he could never give her any more than just sex.

SEVEN

REBEL couldn't believe she'd actually had the courage to say those words aloud. At least now her wounded feelings were out in the open, no longer bottled up in that dark, empty space in her aching heart. She felt better. Not much. But a little.

Until Alex choked out, "Fuck it. You're *wrong*, Rebel. God, you are so very wrong."

He swept her up into a crushing embrace. Before she knew what was happening, he'd thumbed her chin down and wrapped his fingers around her jaw, dragging her up on her toes for a deep, drowning kiss.

She meant to wriggle away, honestly she did, but she just couldn't resist stealing a long drink of him. He felt too good, tasted too sinfully seductive, smelled too arousingly male—and far too much like the man she knew she would love forever . . . even if he didn't love her back.

Around Alex Zane, she had no will of her own.

He lifted her farther off her feet and she instinctively

wrapped her legs around his hips. Her arms curled around his neck, bringing her body so close to his she could almost melt over him, like warm chocolate on an ice cream cone.

"Oh, angel," he murmured as his mouth moved over hers. "I want you so much." His tongue slid between her teeth and this time she opened willingly, eagerly, to its wet thrust. Her senses spun, dizzy from the onslaught of him. Of all she had wanted for so very long. *Even if he didn't love her.*

"Alex, please," she groaned. Afraid that instead of begging him to stop, she was begging for something entirely different. But needing it so badly she thought she might die.

"I'm here," he told her. "God, I'm here for you."

She clung to him as he took one swift look around to make sure they were near shore and well outside the shipping lanes, then he spun to the *Stormy Lady*'s controls. Seconds later the anchor dropped and the engine shut off. He swept her up and in three strides had carried her to the steep stair-ladder that led belowdecks.

She held him tight. "I don't want to let you go," she murmured, knowing she must. If not now, certainly later. She was terrified if she let him go she'd wake up and this would all be just a dream.

The thought was so painful, she let out a soft cry.

He kissed her hard, reassuring her that this was all very real. "Get below," he ordered in a hoarse rumble, depositing her feet on the top stair. "Hurry."

She almost slipped down the ladder but Alex's strong hands caught her and he swung her down, following two treads at a time to keep up. They both landed at the bottom and grabbed for each other. Kissing mindlessly, they backed up along a narrow path through the salon, then he lifted her feet over the high transom leading to the tiny stateroom. As soon as they touched the floor again, the backs of her knees hit something soft and firm.

The bed.

The FBI T-shirt she'd changed into from her ruined suit flew over her head. Followed closely by her bra. She gasped. His fingers scraped over the sensitive fronts of her hip bones, making her gasp again as he jerked her jeans and panties down over them. Before she had time to blink—or think—he pushed her back onto the bed, drew off her sneaks and jeans, and threw them aside.

She reached for him, already missing the touch of his hands, the warmth of his mouth, and the scrape of his formidable body against hers. But he just stood there, his chest heaving, his golden hair spiky from her fingers, his stormy eyes fastened on her nude body like twin blue lasers.

"Alex?" she whispered between panting breaths. "Is something wrong?"

He swallowed heavily. "Are you real?" he asked, his voice as thick and hard as the arousal under his jeans. "Please tell me you're fucking real this time."

"Language, Zane," she breathed, wondering if he was still here with her, or if he'd somehow stumbled into one of his nightmarish flashbacks.

But the language admonishment caused the corners of his lips to curve. "Close enough," he said, and threw off his own T-shirt. He kicked aside his shoes.

Her heart caught in her throat at the sight of his body.

So beautiful. Or it had been, before his terrorist guards had used his flesh as a palette for their sadistic amusement.

But no, he was still by far the most gorgeous man she had ever known. His blue eyes were clear and bright, his blond hair like spun sunshine. The hours he'd spent outdoors swimming laps had restored the muscles of his wide shoulders, corded biceps, and six-pack abs, and tinted his skin with a wash of golden spring tan. Before his capture, Alex had been as big and broad and dangerous-looking as a Viking warrior, but now, even with the many scars marring his arms and chest, he looked more like a handsome faerie king hero from some fantasy kingdom.

"Do they disgust you?" he asked softly, brushing his hand over the worst of his scars.

"No," she said, and melted a little at the vulnerability in his eyes. "Nothing about you could ever disgust me, Alex."

Still wearing his jeans, he crawled on top of her and pulled her up the narrow bunk with him until they lay in the middle. "You haven't seen all of me yet," he murmured and touched her cheek with his fingertips.

"Actually, I have."

He paused. "Oh?"

"Mm-hmm. Every"—she reached up and slowly trailed her finger down his chest and abdomen to the waistband resting low on his hips—"last"—she punctuated the word by flicking open the top button—"inch of you." She slid her fingers into his hair and pulled his head down, whispering in his ear, "By the way, I like your . . . tattoo."

He snatched her wrist away from dangerous territory, and slipped his knee between her legs. "And how, exactly, did you happen to be looking at my . . . tattoo?"

She blushed at the memory of her blatant curiosity. His tattoo was an intricate circle of ink around the shaft of his cock, just under the head. As liaison to ZU, she'd heard the rumor that every member of Zero Unit bore one, with a pattern unique to the individual man. A rite of initiation, a way to tell friend from foe . . . and an object lesson in the endurance of pain.

"At Haven Oaks," she confessed, parting her knees for him. "You were sedated. A nurse was giving you a bath so I peeked. I wanted to see it."

He knelt between her thighs, his lips curved. "My prick or the tattoo?"

"Both," she admitted with a naughty smile.

He grasped her behind the knees, lifted them, and spread her legs wide. "Hmm. Isn't that sexual harassment?"

"I wanted to know if reality lived up to my fantasies." Her face heated from the candid confession. And from his casual positioning of her body. It felt strangely arousing to be completely naked and exposed while he was still half dressed, touching her like he had every right to. And talking about his male anatomy.

"And do I?" he asked, his eyes going dark and slumberous. "Live up to your fantasies?"

She licked her lips. "No," she whispered, giving her head a minute shake. At his raised brow, she said truthfully, "You're so much better."

"Good answer," he murmured, looking smug as only a man very confident of his masculinity could. He ran the backs of his hands erotically down her body and the insides of her thighs, spilling a trail of spine-tingling sensation and gooseflesh in its wake. "Because, angel, so are you."

His thumbs brushed intimately along her moist folds. She sucked down a gasped moan.

"No, don't hold back on me, baby," he told her. "No hiding. I want to hear your moans and feel your shivers. I want it all when you come for me."

"I want to see you," she told him, and reached for his waistband.

She thought he might stop her, but after a slight hesitation, he allowed her to unbutton his jeans and spread open the fly. He sprang out, thick and long.

He was bigger now than he'd been at Haven Oaks. A lot bigger.

The infamous ZU tattoo circled the neck of his penis, exotic and intriguing. Unconsciously, her tongue peeked out and moistened her lips. She wanted to take him in her mouth and run her tongue around that band of blue to taste it. To taste *him*.

As if reading her thoughts, he smiled. "Later." And he spread her thighs wider. "Me, first."

His mouth came down on her, hot and wet. He groaned, and his tongue slicked over her, drawing out a sharp cry of pleasure from deep within her. He teased her and played her with his tongue and teeth, bringing her expertly to a crest, backing off just before she tumbled over, then starting all over again.

Desperate to touch him, she reached for him, buried her fingers in his hair. Thrashed and bowed as he pleasured her.

All the years of pent-up feelings poured out from her heart and washed through her, lighting her up from within. This was Alex! She was making love with *Alex*! She could scarcely believe it.

Her body wept as his tongue ravished her. "Please," she begged, writhing in exquisite agony. "Please!"

His mouth covered her and he sucked, his teeth clamping around her just hard enough to send her into the stratosphere. She shattered in a thousand, million pieces and cried out, her body convulsing with the power of her release. She rode it out, drowning in the pleasure of his unrelenting tongue.

Long moments later, when at last she could open her eyes again, he was kneeling above her, watching her with an intensity that might have scared her had she been able to feel anything at all but stunningly good.

"More," she managed, and reached for his jeans. "You now."

She pushed them down his hips. He let her, rolling onto his back to help shuck them off his feet when she didn't have the strength.

When he lay down again, she canted over him. *Oh, yes.* And took him in her mouth.

He shot up like a cannon. "Whoa!" He grabbed her and

pulled her off him. "Jesus *wept*, woman," he groaned. "You can't do that to a man who hasn't had sex in two years. I won't last three seconds." He let out a long, long breath. "Let's save that for next time, yeah?"

Next time? But—

Suddenly she was under him again, and he was between her thighs, pushing them apart with his knees. Pinioning her with his eyes. Fisting his cock, he fitted it to her center. Her breath caught. *How long had she waited for this?* Slowly, he levered his body down over her. His lips met hers and she could taste her desire on them. He kissed her, deep and long, then lifted and gave her that look again. Intense. Hungry. *Dangerous.* A vein beat wildly in his neck, pulsing in unison with the head of his penis as it pushed against her entry.

"What's my name?" he asked, his voice rough like the tear of raw silk.

She looked at him, confused. "What?"

"My name," he demanded forcefully. "What is it?"

Then she realized what he needed to hear.

He'd had amnesia the whole time he was a prisoner, hadn't known his real name. In his dreams, she would use a different name for him every night. But never the right one.

"It's Alex," she said with a moan as the tip of his cock slid past her slick opening. "Christopher Alexander Zane."

When she breathed his name, low and needy like a prayer, it was like something broke free within him. His shoulders notched down and he let out a half-growl, half-laugh. "Thank God, it *is* you. Jesus, Rebel, I've waited so long for this. For you."

With that, he scythed into her, thrusting all the way to the hilt.

She bowed up, crying out his name once more, wrapping her legs around his waist and meeting his driving thrust with her own. He was thick and hard and filled her completely.

Stars burst across her vision. She gasped, close to coming apart again.

And *that's* when she realized why he felt so amazingly, sinfully good. She grabbed his arms, tried to stop him. And herself. "Alex! Wait," she panted.

He pulled out nearly all the way. Opened his eyes to narrow slits, fighting with the effort of control. He hung there for an endless moment as he drilled her with a look, conflict running through every straining muscle. With a muttered curse, he said, "Don't worry, baby. It's okay. You'll be all right."

She teetered on the edge, wondering what he meant, why he suddenly looked so angry. "But—"

"Will *I*?" he asked.

She gasped a nod, knowing he must mean Wade. "I've . . . a-always been careful." *Until now*. "But, Alex—"

His whole body shook as he pistoned into her again, heavy and deep. She felt the jolt of pleasure clear to her toes.

"Please. Just trust me, angel," he rasped out.

She was so close, so needy for him. And knew he had a clean bill of health from Haven Oaks. What could she do but as he asked? So she let herself go. Surrendered to the feelings and sensations that swept over her, giving herself over to the rushing climax that claimed her body a second time as he rammed into her again.

And again. And one last time.

With a strangled roar, he followed her, shooting his hot seed deep into her body.

Unprotected.

Dear lord. What had she done?

EIGHT

BASED on a bit of inside info from his confidential informant Tommy Cantor, Gregg was seated at the counter of a greasy spoon diner located just a block from a midtown NYPD precinct, waiting for his 1:30 meeting to show. The place was filthy with blue uniforms and men in ill-fitting suits with bulges under their armpits. But what the hell, Gregg needed more excitement in his life.

He'd come prepared, though, wearing an NYPD baseball cap and navy blue Windbreaker with POLICE stenciled in big gold letters across the back, worn over his untraceable but standard police-issue Beretta under *his* armpit. Yep, just another one of the boys. Hell, what were they going to do, throw him in the slammer for impersonating a police officer? He should be so fucking lucky.

Still, one thing about cops, they tried their damndest not to shoot innocent people. That could work to Gregg's advantage today. This was the safest place he could think of for an encounter with Colonel Frank Blair.

Yeah, call him crazy, but it was high time the two of them had another little tête-à-tête.

Gregg was pretty sure the man was involved up to his steel-gray eyebrows in Gina's kidnapping and Gregg's own frame-up. So Tommy had arranged this meet-and-greet, under the pretext of Blair meeting with a snitch who was willing to give up Gregg's whereabouts for a price.

The old bastard was nothing if not punctual. At 1:30 p.m. on the dot, the colonel walked into the diner. Or rather, marched in. Naturally, Blair didn't see him at first. Which gave Gregg the opportunity to study his adversary in the mirror above the wait-station.

His former commanding officer hadn't changed one iota in the seven months Gregg had been AWOL. No shocker there. The bastard hadn't changed in the entire dozen-plus years Gregg had been with CIA covert ops. Ex-uniformed army officer and fanatically conservative, Blair was the kind of old-school, piss-and-iron, by-the-book commander that the brass loved and the grunts hated. Blair despised anything that smacked of weakness, and severely punished those who displayed it. You had to respect the old man's vast experience as a leader, but few in ZU actually liked him.

Gregg's cell buzzed. He tapped his earpiece. "Yeah."

"You're good. He's alone," Tommy said, and the line clicked off.

Arrogant SOB. Blair *would* think he could take a young whippersnapper like Gregg with his hands tied behind his back.

Then again, that's what Gregg was counting on.

He saw the instant in which Blair recognized him; the colonel's back went up like a ramrod. But a quick glance around at the diner full of cops convinced the other man not to reach for the weapon Gregg was sure he carried under his green Vietnam-era army field jacket.

Blair marched up, looked at the stool Gregg had deliberately held vacant for him, and sat down with a disgusted sneer.

"You've got some fucking nerve, soldier. I'll give you that."

"I'll take that as a compliment, coming from you," Gregg returned evenly.

"What do you want this time, van Halen?" Straight to the point as always. "To turn yourself in? Tired of running like a coward?"

He decided to do the same. "I want to know why you're working for al Sayika."

"Same old tune, eh?" The old man's face betrayed nothing, a perfect slab of cement. "Told you last time. I work for the President of the United States," Blair said disdainfully. "Not terrorists."

"Bullshit," Gregg growled. "You're the one who ordered me to bring Dr. Cappozi to ZU-NE the day she was kidnapped there, then sent me out of the country so fast I wouldn't notice. You're also the one who made damned sure I was blamed for it."

"That's because you're guilty. A goddamn traitor," Blair growled back.

They glared at each other. It was déjà vu.

Several cops close to them turned to see what the fuss was about, so they both spun away from each other and stared straight ahead. The air around them pulsed with animosity.

Gregg had to admit, Blair was pretty damn convincing, now as before. But then, he would be. He'd worked black ops and told lies for CIA since way back in Cambodia in the '60s. Probably couldn't even tell the difference between truth and lies anymore.

But the big question was, why would he be helping terrorists?

Had Gina been right? Was it simply for money? A slice of the millions' worth of blood diamonds Gina had accused Gregg himself of taking from al Sayika? Gregg had a hard time believing greed would motivate a man like Colonel Blair any more than it did him. But what else would? That's what he needed to find out.

"What say we take a walk," he suggested. "Outside."

Blair didn't object. Wordlessly, he stood and marched for the door. Yeah, definitely arrogant.

"Around the corner in the alley," Gregg directed him when they hit the sidewalk. Blair didn't object to that either. By the time they rounded the corner of the building, Gregg had his Beretta out. He pressed the barrel into the base of the man's skull.

Blair just laughed. "Put your weapon down, soldier. You're not going to kill me and we both know it."

"I'm wanted for treason," Gregg said. "The way I see it, I've got nothing to lose."

"Not if you're guilty," Blair pointed out with uncanny intelligence. Gregg may have underestimated the fucker. "Besides, you pull the trigger and every cop in that diner will be out here in under three seconds."

"Just walk," Gregg ordered, pushing the cold steel into Blair's cervical vertebra, steering him deeper into the alley past where Gregg had parked his Harley. "Okay, hold it. Now talk."

Blair turned. "I've got nothing to say."

"No?" Gregg pulled a silencer out of his Windbreaker pocket and began screwing it onto the Beretta.

Blair's eyes narrowed and he drilled him a penetrating look. "You really gonna play it this way?"

"I really am." Gregg aimed the silenced pistol at the colonel's kneecap.

Blair pushed out a breath. "I told you. You're barking

up the wrong tree, Captain. Those orders came straight from Washington."

At last, something new. "Which orders?"

Blair gestured impatiently. "The ones to bring in Dr. Cappozi to identify the body of her friend, *and* for your mission to Kurdistan."

"Please. There was no body. Rainie Martin wasn't dead," Gregg said impatiently. "Even I knew that." His assignment had been to stop Gina from asking questions about Rainie's disappearance because it involved a sensitive and highly covert CIA mission. A simple honeypot operation—with Gregg as the honey. At least that's what he'd thought at the time. Since when had he gotten so dumb?

Blair bristled, almost convincingly. "I was told she'd died in a plane crash."

Gregg was getting mighty tired of all the lies. He adjusted his aim and started to pull the trigger.

"Wait!"

Gregg halted and met the man's eyes. To the old man's credit, he didn't look the least frightened. What he looked was even more impatient than Gregg. "I'm listening," he prompted.

"I don't know what you're playing at, van Halen, but if you really insist on going through this absurd charade, contact Washington yourself. Confirm that the orders were sent."

"I need a name."

He rattled one off. "He's at the Pentagon."

Anger swept through Gregg so thoroughly he nearly pulled the trigger just on reflex. "You really expect me to believe someone at the *Pentagon* is involved in a treasonous conspiracy to abduct and torture a U.S. citizen and set off biological weapons on American soil?" His voice grew hotter and louder with each syllable. With a jerk, he shifted the aim of the Beretta up to Blair's heart. "How fucking stupid do you think I am?"

Blair stood his ground. "No more stupid than you thinking I'm buying any of this innocence crap. *You* were the only other person who knew Dr. Cappozi would be at ZUNE that day." He leaned over the gun and into Gregg's face. "*You're* the one who set her up, Captain. And you're the one who'll hang for it." He emphasized the word *hang*.

The indictment echoed down the alley like a shot. Gregg clamped his jaw. He should have known this would be a fucking waste of time. He waved the gun at Blair. "Get the hell out of here."

With that, he managed to surprise the other man, whose face registered a millisecond of shock before it went stony again. Then he turned on a boot and marched out of the alley.

The fucking Pentagon. Jesus fucking Christ. And for this he broke cover?

Shit. He should have shot the delusional bastard while he had the chance. God knew, this lapse of judgment would surely come back to bite him in the ass.

GINA paced back and forth across the thick Berber carpet in Gregg's apartment. Where *was* he? It had been nearly four hours since he'd left. Her mind waffled madly between being anxious for him to come back and immense relief that he hadn't.

God, was she messed up.

But he would be back. There was little hope of him leaving her here to starve to death. Miraculously, he'd managed to convince her he wasn't going to kill her—which made sense, when she thought about it. She wasn't valuable to him. But she *was* to the terrorists he was helping.

He'd said it himself . . . maybe one of them thought she could identify him. Or they wanted revenge for her foiling their plans to wreak mass destruction on this country. Gregg could be out there at this very moment, negotiating with al Sayika to return her to them. So *they* could kill her.

Oh, God.

How much would they pay him for her this time around? The price on her head was half a million in illegal diamonds. Maybe they'd tack on a nice bonus if he did the deed for them and just brought them proof she was dead? Or worse, did they want her to finish the perverse bioweapon project that she'd sabotaged during her captivity?

She slapped her hands over her mouth, convulsively swallowing a cry of despair. How had this happened? She'd trained so damned hard with her knife. She'd been so *ready* for him. Ready to rid the world of the bastard for good.

Or so she'd thought.

Visions of the bloodbath on the sidewalk this morning rushed through her mind, pushing out every other rational thought. The strangled cry that was stuck in her throat emerged as a low wail.

"Oh, God!" She doubled over in anguish, her eyes filling with hot tears for the dozenth time that day. "God, help me."

As she was leaning over, she spotted the silver heart peeking out from below her sweatpant leg. *The anklet.* Anger surged through her. A *gift*? A tracker for her own protection? Who was he trying to kid? She didn't want his damned protection. Or the reminder of him, however pretty. Didn't want his jewelry touching her body. She ran into the narrow kitchen and yanked open drawer after drawer searching for something she could use to cut it off. She found a pair of sturdy shears. The kind they showed on TV cutting through pennies. Those would do. She knelt down and grabbed the pretty little heart and pulled it away from her skin, jamming the scissors around the chain to clip it in two.

Suddenly, there was a scratching noise behind her. She spun, and the shears clattered to the floor. Gregg was back!

But it wasn't him. The noise wasn't coming from the door at all. It came from the opposite end of the narrow galley kitchen.

It sounded again. Scratching. Like someone at a window, trying to get in. What was he doing? Or was it the terrorists who'd come for her?

Her heart pounded out of control. Frantically, she looked around for a weapon. She picked up the shears. Dropped them again. Too blunt.

She jumped up and leapt for the counter. Grabbing the coffeepot from the drip machine, she raised the glass to smash it to a razor-sharp edge.

Then all at once she saw who was at the window. Or rather, what. She stopped in mid-motion. And let out a hysterical sob of relief.

"Omigod."

Sitting on the outside windowsill was a little tabby with fluffy, copper-colored fur. It meowed, blinking at her with big, amber kitty eyes.

She hiccupped, and lowered her makeshift weapon. How in the world had it gotten this high up, *outside* the apartment?

As it turned out, there was a metal fire escape running down the side of the apartment building right next to the window—the window with metal bars over it.

The cat meowed again. On the counter, Gina suddenly spotted a small double bowl and a short stack of canned cat food.

"You can't be serious," she murmured incredulously.

Captain Terrifying had a cat? That sounded totally unlike

the control freak she knew Gregg to be. The man always had a carefully thought-out plan for everything, which was then always meticulously executed. His closet and dresser could pass boot camp inspection, and she'd once caught him ironing his T-shirts, for crying out loud. When they used to make love he'd insisted on complete control over her; more often than not he'd handcuff her wrists to the headboard so she couldn't take charge.

Not cat person behavior. Gregg van Halen was most definitely a dog person through and through.

Gina was the cat person. She loved the independence of cats, and their feline discrimination. Unpredictable, moody, proud, they were indomitable. Masters of their universe. Woe betide the human who tried to tame a cat's spirit.

And yet, here was hard evidence staring back at her plain as day, not just from the window, but also from the kitchen counter. The cat was Gregg's. Or rather, he was the cat's.

She walked over and slid the casement up enough to let him in.

Make that let *her* in. Yeah, *that* figured.

"Hey, catnik," she said with a smile when the cat bounded in onto the tiny kitchen table, and stretched up to greet her in that furry, rubby, archy way cats had. After a few neck scratches, it meowed, decided that was enough affection, and jumped from the table onto the counter, sitting pointedly in front of the can opener with tail twitching.

Gina laughed out loud. The unfamiliar sound startled the hell out of her. She stared in wonder at the cat. She hadn't laughed aloud in eight months.

Stepping over to the counter, she gathered up the tabby in her arms and gave it a long hug, which in its infinite cat wisdom, it sank into, giving her cheek a tiny lick with its little sandpapery tongue.

Gina's heart swelled. It was so nice to feel a soft, warm

body against hers. One she knew intended her no harm. Since her rescue, other than hugs from her nurse and best friend, Rainie, she hadn't let anyone else close enough to touch anything but her hand.

The kitty finally pulled away, and she opened a can of fish-flavored food and scooped it out into the bowl. She could swear the feline smiled at her before digging in.

Seeing the animal eat reminded Gina that she probably should, too. Not that she was hungry. She'd lost her appetite eight months ago and hadn't gotten it back. She opened the fridge. Good thing. There wasn't much in it. Mostly water and beer. A variety of condiments, including three types of salsa. Eggs. A few cartons of leftover takeout. A bag of salad. Milk. Gregg liked cereal for breakfast, she recalled. And eggs for dinner. With salsa. But only if he didn't want to take the time to go out to eat. Mainly when they were in bed and rumbling stomachs disrupted the flow of whatever they were doing, making them laugh.

Stifling the too-potent memory of that long-ago laughter, she found a bunch of bananas on the counter, broke one off, and ate it while stroking the cat's soft fur as it licked the bowl clean then had a long drink of water. After giving her fingers another tiny lick, it bounded off to the main room, jumped up on the fat arm of an easy chair sitting next to a small round table with a lamp on it. There was no TV in the apartment, but a book lay facedown on the table, next to a coaster. Gregg's favorite spot to sit and relax . . . when he wasn't in bed.

The cat looked at her expectantly.

She shook her head slowly. "What on earth do you see in him?" she whispered.

But she couldn't resist the draw of the cozy picture. Almost against her will she went over and lowered herself gingerly into the chair. *His* chair. A lingering hint of his cologne perfumed the cushions. Surprisingly, the scent didn't bother her. It was almost . . . comforting. She leaned back experimentally. She could see why it was his favorite spot; the chair was super comfy. With a sigh as close to relaxed as she'd felt in a long, long time, she pulled the lever to recline, brought up the footrest, and burrowed into the yielding depths of the easy chair. Immediately the cat jumped into her lap, curled up on her tummy, and started to purr. It felt warm and soft, and its purr was a soothing rumble of contentedness.

Gina smiled and closed her eyes.

Moments later, she was asleep.

Which was why she never heard the door cautiously open, nor the stealthy footsteps that treaded lightly across the carpet toward her . . .

NINE

SARAH barely made it through the autopsy without tossing her cookies. It was depressing, really. Time was, she could observe one impartially, without her stomach heaving like a ship caught in a typhoon. But that had changed recently. When she'd gotten far too personally involved in a case. As in trying to help a mother and daughter, victims of domestic abuse, who had come to the station wanting to stop the terrible cycle of broken bones and insincere apologies by a lying SOB husband before it was too late. Sarah had told them to leave the bastard, and given them the phone number of a shelter specializing in such things.

They'd left the bastard.

But he hadn't liked Sarah's interference. He'd tracked the wife down through a teacher the little girl had tearfully confided in. The results had been horrific.

Sarah would never, ever forget that double autopsy. As long as she lived, the images of mother and daughter lying on those cold steel tables would haunt her.

But as these things went, the autopsy she was attending today—the woman from the alley—was fairly routine, and the woman's face, with its pale skin and blue-tinted lips, was strangely beautiful in death. Which only made Sarah's stomach feel worse. Asha Mahmood had been fed a high dose of the date rape drug Rohypnol, sexually assaulted, then smothered to death—most likely with a pillow.

Hell of a way to go. Still, technically it looked like your fairly standard Friday-night-date-gone-terribly-wrong. Well, other than the fact that Asha Mahmood had died on a Wednesday. And the address listed on Mahmood's fake driver's license didn't exist. Sarah had wondered if the name was fake, too, but a phone call just before the autopsy from an NYPD detective had put that doubt to rest. Apparently Asha Mahmood's cousin had been killed this morning in a bloodbath in New York City during the commission of a bizarre kidnapping.

Talk about your weird coincidence.

Not—especially in light of SAC Dreamy Blue Eyes's keen interest in the case. A connection? Ya think?

Wade Montana was after something other than dinner and a quick roll in the hay.

Which was just interesting enough of a distraction that Sarah didn't hurl all over the autopsy table. Small favors.

"You know you can wait in the hall," Dr. Stroud—she'd never get used to calling him Johnny—kindly said, glancing at her through his full-face shield with a sympathetic expression. He'd been the examiner on that awful double autopsy and knew the real reason for her newfound squeamishness. "I'll come out and fill you in after I'm done."

She met his eyes, grateful for the rare solidarity. "Thanks. But I'll stay. Climbing back in the saddle again and all that."

He nodded, and went back to work on the entrails.

"Jonesy threw up once," he said conversationally. "All over the vic."

Sarah grinned. "Yeah?"

"The body'd been stuffed into an oil barrel and left for two months. In the middle of summer."

She winced. "God, I remember that one."

"It was a real challenge trying to separate the fluids."

She wrinkled her nose. "Oh. Yuck."

"I'm just saying. You're not the only one who gets bothered. And it's especially bad when a person is emotionally involved. Hell, even I have to leave the room sometimes."

Something uncoiled in her stomach and she suddenly felt less queasy. "I know you're lying, but you're sweet for saying so. Thanks."

"You're a good cop, Sarah. Don't let anyone make you feel less than, just because you care."

She gave him an embarrassed smile, her face heating at the unexpected praise. "Damn, Doc. Your bedside manner is totally wasted on your patients."

He winked as he dumped the liver onto a scale. "Maybe we could—"

Just then her phone rang. Thank *God* she'd never know what he was about to suggest they could—

"McPhee."

"Detective McPhee," drawled a smooth male voice that belonged well south of the Mason-Dixon line. "This is Commander Bobby Lee Quinn calling from Strategic Technical Operations and Rescue Missions Corporation. I wonder if you have a moment?"

She had no clue who this guy or Strategical Techinque whats-its were, but she'd take the interruption. "Um, sure," she said, gesturing to Stroud that she had to take the call, and headed into the hall. "Who did you say you're with,

Commander Quinn?" she asked after making her escape. She pulled out her notebook and a pen.

"STORM Corps. I'm calling regarding a death you're investigating. Asha Mahmood?"

This was getting positively intriguing. "STORM Corps?" she said, noting his name, the time, and the acronym. "What exactly is that?"

"A PMC. We do private special ops work. Detective, are you aware that your victim's cousin was killed this morning in New York City?"

"Yes, I am." She shut up and waited, pondering exactly what kind of special ops work private military contractors did. Wasn't that just a nicer term for mercenaries? Or maybe whackos? She clamped the phone between her ear and her shoulder and jotted a big, fat question mark in her notebook after the organization. She'd have to Google it.

After a brief pause he said, "Have you had a chance to search her apartment yet?"

"Why do you want to know?" Sarah asked carefully.

Again there was a pause. "Would you be open to a little negotiation, Detective McPhee?"

Her brows shot up. Seemed to be the day for it. "What kind of negotiation, Commander Quinn?" she went along.

"You don't have your vic's real address, do you? No, don't bother to deny it. Here's the deal I'm offering. I'll share her address with you if you'll share with us what you find there."

Okay. "Have you ever heard of a thing called obstruction of justice, Commander Quinn?" she asked pointedly. Who *was* this guy?

His laugh was smooth as molasses. "How about if I say pretty please?"

And why did they *al*ways think boyish charm could

win over any female? "I'm afraid I can't reveal information on an ongoing case to unauthorized—"

"Oh, we're authorized," Quinn drawled. "All the way from the top. You're welcome to call Department of Homeland Security and check on us." He repeated his creds and rattled off a couple of DHS names, which she scribbled down while those internal red flags of hers started waving madly again. This case was getting seriously out of hand.

"What is DHS's interest in Asha Mahmood?" she asked. First the FBI and now the DH freaking S!

"The cousin who was killed? His name was Ouda Mahmood, and he was a suspected terrorist. Al Sayika. A woman was kidnapped during the incident. She is a client of ours."

Sarah winced. "Sucks to be you," she offered, not without sympathy.

Quinn's laugh turned dour. "Oh, we know who's got her. Trust me, it will suck *far* worse to be him."

A rash of goose bumps sifted down her arms at the quiet deadliness in the man's voice. "If you know who took her, why do you need my help? And what does Asha Mahmood have to do with it?"

"We know who. We don't know where."

Ah. "So you're hoping something in my vic's apartment will tell you? Seems like a long shot."

"We're following every possible lead. We want her back. Before he kills her."

Sarah sobered, digesting the conversation. He sounded legit. Naturally, she'd check out his references before giving him any information. But in the meantime, why not do a little probing herself? "Tell me, Commander Quinn, do you know an FBI agent by the name of SAC Wade Montana?"

There was an eloquent silence on the other end.

Her eyes narrowed. Un-freaking-believable. The feeb was *so* damn busted.

"What's Montana's interest in this?" she asked.

"He's approached you?"

"Oh, yeah."

"SAC Montana is the kidnapped woman's ex-fiancé."

What? Her jaw dropped. "Are you *kid*ding me? And they're letting him work the case?"

"Not exactly. It's complicated."

She just bet it was. "All right, Commander Quinn. You've been straight with me and I appreciate that. If you check out, you've got yourself a deal."

"Excellent." He gave her Asha Mahmood's address and his own contact information. He must be pretty damn sure of himself.

"I'll be in touch," she told him and hung up the phone. For a long moment, she contemplated her own reflection in the covered window of the morgue's viewing room.

Wow. Things were *definitely* getting interesting.

And she had the distinct feeling that tonight, things would get even more interesting.

Wade Montana hadn't exactly lied to her. But he hadn't told the truth, either. Friend or foe? Either way, the man was trying to play her. Too bad she was so damn attracted to him. Too attracted for her own good. This one could hurt her. In more ways than one.

THE evening sun was hovering like a big red-orange ball above the glittering water of the Chesapeake Bay. Alex checked over the pile of diving gear he'd pulled from the storage benches on the *Stormy Lady*. He was trying like hell to forget about the naked woman dozing below in his bunk.

No time for spinning fantasies. There was work to do. Gear to check. Dive plans to compose.

He forced himself to look at the inspection stickers on

the air tanks and note the dates. But *fuck.* All he wanted to do was go back down to the cabin and keep right on doing what they'd been doing for the past half-dozen hours.

They'd lost the entire afternoon. When Quinn called, as he no doubt would at any minute, to ask if they had located the *Allah's Paradise* and had he found the trigger yet, what the fuck was he going to say? *Sorry, boss. Spent the whole day fucking the woman I've been dreaming about fucking for the last hundred years?*

Quinn would understand.

Uh-huh. Sure he would.

Fuck.

Alex pulled two octopus-shaped regulators and BCD vests from the pile and checked them over. Hell, Alex wasn't sure he understood it himself. Okay, yeah, he understood why *he* had done it. He just wasn't sure why *she* had.

He stood the tanks up and just stared at them.

She hadn't wanted to. At least her mind hadn't. She'd made that crystal clear. But he'd been able to coax her body until it silenced her mind's objections. Made her forget any whatever-commitment to Wade Montana she had, as well as her firm conviction that if she did this, Alex would end up hurting her even more than he already had. Which he no doubt would, if he let their relationship grow to anything beyond just sex.

Which he wouldn't. Couldn't.

All right, fine. He already had. The woman loved him and he damn well knew it. She was already far past just sex.

He was a goddamn bastard, and that was a fact.

But did he regret making love to Rebel? Not for a single second. How fucking selfish was *that*?

"Whatcha doin'?" came her soft enquiry from behind him, startling him out of his litany of self-recrimination. He swung around, knocking the heavy tank over in his haste. It started rolling toward the edge of the deck.

"Shit," he muttered and went after it, grabbing it before it smacked into the low bulwark and did damage.

"Language," she said with a wince. "Sorry. Didn't mean to scare you."

He gave her a withering look he hoped was convincing. *Big, mean spec ops guys did not get scared.*

Yeah, and then there was him.

He dropped his gaze to her outfit. White short-shorts and a snug, light blue hoodie. The halter of a metallic-blue bathing suit peeked out from under it. His mouth watered. "Damn, woman, you can sneak up behind me anytime." He smiled, but her return smile was slow in coming.

"I thought you were going to stop swearing."

"What, me? What gave you that idea?" The thought was ludicrous. His salty vocabulary had been part of his personal vernacular since sitting on his sailor daddy's knee. He wouldn't know how to communicate without it.

"You said you'd stop swearing when I started . . . um . . ." She bit her lip.

He opened his mouth, then shut it. *Oh, hell.* He'd forgotten about that. And she had definitely fucked him. Boy, howdy, had she ever. "I never thought— Hell, baby, you know I wasn't serious."

"I was."

No damn kidding. Her expression was an uneasy truce between desire and doubt.

Jeez, were they still talking about swearing, here?

She obviously had something on her mind. One guess what. His inexcusably weak and imprudent behavior in bed—not using protection.

Shit. He did *not* want to have this conversation right now. He opened his arms, hoping to deflect it. "Come here, you."

She hesitated a beat, then came to him with a reluctance that sent him straight back to full-scale self-recrimination.

"Alex—" she started.

Damn. What was he going to do now? Lie? Or tell the truth and lose her forever? He knew how she felt about having kids.

Despite his assurances, the fact that she'd made love to him unprotected told him louder than words how she felt about him . . . and their future. Which made this conversation completely unavoidable. Hell, maybe it was just as well to get it over with so she'd know where things stood. Temporary pleasure. No future.

"I'm sterile," he said tightly. "Shooting blanks. Can never have kids. That's why we don't need protection."

He felt her go perfectly still.

For his part, he'd long ago resigned himself to his deficiency. As a young man he'd foolishly thought if a woman really loved him, it wouldn't matter to her. He'd been wrong, and had the breakups to prove it. It was one reason he'd ultimately gotten involved with Helena. She'd seen his defect as inconsequential.

But Rebel wouldn't feel that way. She'd often talked about wanting children. Had gotten that soft, dreamy look in her eyes a woman gets when contemplating her ideal future. One filled with a loving husband who came home at night to his wife and a houseful of kids. The kind of future a spec operator could never give her. A future *he* could never give her, even if he quit his job. Because he could never give her children. Which was why this thing between them could go no further than a sexual liaison.

Not that *that* would be any kind of problem, judging by the look on her face.

Her shocked gaze sought his. He wanted to turn away, but manned up and met it. "When I was a kid I got really sick. High fever for a week. That's all it took."

"Oh, Alex. I . . . I'm so sorry." She looked more than sorry. She looked devastated.

He shrugged, going for nonchalant, and gathered her

up in his arms, lifting her into a hug. "Don't be. No biggie. I don't want kids anyway."

He felt more than heard her stunned intake of breath. "Oh."

That lone syllable, more than any words she might have spoken, betrayed her hopes and dreams for them. *Fuck.*

"Because of the job, you know," he tossed out, nuzzling her hair as though the subject were totally irrelevant. "Always gone. Death, injury, and capture looming over every horizon. Wouldn't be fair to a kid. Or a wife, either," he said without thinking. Because it was absolutely true.

"But . . . But what about Helena?"

Oh, hell. "She knew what she was getting into," he quickly prevaricated. "She actually preferred things this way. Gave her more freedom."

"But . . . doesn't she want children?" Rebel asked.

He shook his head. "No." Not with him, anyway.

Rebel's body went even more still, and he realized too late that it must hurt to find out he'd told Helena about his deficiency and not her. They'd told each other everything, or so she'd thought.

If only she knew.

Shit, shit, shit.

He shifted his gaze to the horizon, where the glowing orb of the sun was slowly sinking, painting pale streaks of amber and purple in the sky. He took a deep, steadying breath.

"But enough about my failure as a man," he cheerfully quipped, desperately wanting to end the whole fucking conversation. "We should get *some*thing done this afternoon. How about a quick recert dive?"

She gazed up at him, her breaking heart in her eyes. He wanted to shake her. Banish the guileless disappointment and wistful adoration pooled in them.

"You're not a failure, Alex," she said softly, and kissed him.

His heart squeezed, and he let himself be kissed, even though this was dangerous territory. He was accepting feelings from her from which he should be firmly distancing himself. For her sake.

But she felt too good. And he was too needy of her warm human touch. Of her selfless love and her openhearted passions.

He could never give her what she needed. But he could take what *he* wanted.

He sank into the kiss, pouring himself into the shelter of her tenderness. For an endless moment, he floated in the sensation, soaking up the amazing feel of her body and the certain knowledge of her caring. But then it all became too much to bear. Because that would end all too quickly, now that she knew the truth about him.

With swift motions, he stripped down her shorts and flung off her hoodie. Peeled off her bathing suit. She shivered in the chilly evening air as he wrapped his arms around her and lowered her to the deck, pulling off his own shorts.

"Alex—"

"Don't talk," he growled as he spread her legs and drove his cock deep into her.

Hours of being joined had attuned her body to his; it instantly conformed to his contours, to his manner of thrusting, to his rhythm and his roughly whispered commands. And he had learned hers—what made her moan and shiver, what caused goose bumps to blossom on her satin skin, what wicked words in her ear made her juices flow hotter.

Together, their bodies were a perfect conflagration of pleasure. He scythed into her, and the *Stormy Lady* rocked, the waves of the bay slapping hard against the boat's sides as they plunged mindlessly toward the oblivion of release.

And for a short time he forgot. The tortures of the past

and the uncertainty of the future were lost in the forgetfulness of the present overwhelming pleasure of driving into her again and again and again.

She moaned and held him tight, her gasps a low staccato chant to the primitive mating of their bodies. Her red hair clung to his sweat-slick skin as he buried his face in it, wanting to block out the world around them so only he and she existed.

She cried out and arched her back, her inner muscles tightening around his cock as release pulsed through her. He held back as long as he could, holding back, holding back, until finally he exploded after her in a mind-numbing burst of primal pleasure.

He groaned at the amazing sensation. He groaned at the respite of a mind for once drained of all thought.

And he groaned when the thoughts began slowly to trickle back, and he knew that this amazing, beautiful woman could never truly be his.

TEN

REBEL did great on her recertification dives, as Alex had known she would. He had no problem phoning Quinn afterward to have him fax down a certificate, in case the local authorities asked to see their dive creds.

But to his surprise, Commander Quinn had left New York City for Washington, D.C.

"Really?" he asked Darcy, who'd answered at the penthouse, where his call was forwarded from Quinn's cell phone. He must be on the plane. "What the fuck?"

"A female cousin of one of our terrorists was murdered down there this morning." Darcy briefly described the situation. "Quinn thinks there has to be a connection. He took Tara Reeves with him," she added, doing her best to sound unconcerned, but failing miserably.

Uh-oh. Alex pitied Bobby Lee Quinn if he thought he could pass *that* by his spirited fiancée without paying a steep toll. Darcy Zimmerman was definitely not the kind of woman you wanted pissed off at you, especially over another woman.

"Marc must be thrilled about that," he cleverly observed. Marc Lafayette and Tara Reeves had been inseparable since hooking up on the Louisiana op and subsequently marrying. As had Bobby Lee and Darcy, for that matter. This was probably the first time apart for both couples.

"Apparently the lead detective is a woman," Darcy said, sounding put out. "He thought Tara was the best one to deal with her."

"No doubt true," Alex agreed. Tara had been a Louisiana state trooper before joining STORM. "What's he hoping to find in D.C.?"

"Who knows what Quinn is ever thinking?" she muttered.

Alex chuckled. "You're cute when you're jealous," he said, raising Rebel's eyebrows across the narrow galley, where she was preparing supper for them. Alex winked at her. "I take it Quinn has no idea what he's in for when he gets back."

"Oblivious as always," Darcy confirmed testily.

"But his instincts are good," Alex said. "I'm sure he's onto something in D.C. And trust me, Darce, the way he looks at you, he's probably totally forgotten Tara is even a woman."

Darcy let out an unladylike snort, but when she continued, her voice was somewhat mollified. "Anyway. What can I do for you, Zane?"

He explained about the diving cert for Rebel, who'd gone back to banging pots.

"No problem," Darcy said. "I'll fax it right away. So . . . how's everything *else* going down there?"

It seemed everyone in the universe knew about his thing for Rebel.

"Good," he said. But something in his voice must have clued her to his inner turmoil.

She laughed. "Hmm. Somehow, I think not. Record time, Zane. What did you do to her?"

Incredibly, he felt his cheeks warm. "Not a thing," he said, turning so Rebel couldn't see his face.

"She's standing right there, isn't she?" Amusement danced in Darcy's voice.

"Yes. But I really don't—"

"Oh, my freaking gawd," she exclaimed. "You've *slept* with her! *Already?* It's been, what, three hours since you got there?"

"Nine, for chrissake. And—"

"What about this Montana character she's been dating? Are they going to find his body in some back alley?"

"Fuck, no! Jesus, Darce!" How the hell did everyone know *all* the gory details of his love life? Goddamn it! The body in that back alley was going to be *Kick's*. "I have to go now."

"Rainie always said you two belonged together," she said with a certain perverse glee. "Apparently Commander Bridger thinks so, too. Your Rebel must have made quite an impression on him when they met on the Louisiana op."

Alex's jaw dropped. Commander Bridger was a legend, with a reputation for knowing everything about every single operator employed by STORM. Obviously well-earned.

Darcy continued, "When Bridger heard you'd been sent to Norfolk, he wanted you to ask Special Agent Haywood if she'd consider quitting the FBI and joining us. He's looking for a new head of Victim Family Services."

Alex's eyes went to Rebel, where she was fussing with something on the cooktop. "Is that so," he choked out. WTF. Did the Commander have the hots for his woman, too?

"Take my advice, Zane," Darcy said. "Don't fight the inevitable. Just go with it."

The phone clicked off and he was left staring in consternation at Rebel's back. Was it just him, or had everyone gone completely off their meds?

"Interesting conversation," Rebel ventured from the stove.

His gaze snapped up. She'd turned around and was leaning her butt against the counter, regarding him with crossed arms.

"Fucking in*sane* conversation," he corrected.

"About . . . ?"

He choked again on a swallow. "You, actually."

Her mouth thinned. "Oh?"

"STORM Command wants me to recruit you."

Her lips parted in surprise. "Me?"

With difficulty, he gathered his wits. "You."

"And you find that insane?"

"Damn straight." At the scowl that crossed her face, he backpedaled. "I mean, you'd be great, but I know how much you love the Bureau. You wouldn't want to quit." She didn't say anything to that. "Would you . . . ?"

She turned back to whatever she was cooking. "Of course not. You're right. I can't ever imagine leaving the FBI."

He got the distinct feeling he was missing something here. But he was still too flustered over what Darcy had suggested, and couldn't think about it right now.

Rising from the table, he took the two strides over to Rebel. He gently pushed aside her mane of copper hair and kissed her neck. "Mmm. You smell good."

"It's the stir-fry."

It wasn't, but his stomach seized that moment to rumble loudly. "What can I do?" he asked, peering over her head at the preparations for supper.

"Nothing," she said, and ducked out from his arms to reach for the plates. "Just pour the wine and enjoy the meal."

It might have been his massively guilty conscience, but

he imagined just a shade of "Eat, drink, and be merry, for tomorrow we shall die," about her muttered order.

"Angel—"

She thrust the plates into his hands. "Okay. Set the table, then." She turned away to dish up the rice.

He did as she asked. Then swiped a hand over his mouth and wondered just what the hell he was going to do about the colossal mess he'd made of this whole affair, not to mention his whole damned life, in—yes, fuck it, Darcy was right—fucking record time.

GINA came awake with a gasp. She stiffened in alarm.

Where was she?

She realized she was lying on her side, in a cozy bed. The fleecy fabric of sweatpants caressed her legs and a soft T-shirt hugged her chest. Along with . . . a body. She cracked open an eyelid. And met the enquiring gaze of a pair of golden cat eyes. Gregg's ginger tabby was curled up in her arms, tucked against her breasts, its furry head resting on the pillow just below her chin. She sagged in relief. The sleepy cat reached up and gave her jaw a lick, started purring, then closed its eyes and went back to sleep in mid-purr.

Gina smiled and stroked her fingers through its silky fur, loving the sensation of having her arms around the soft, warm, living creature.

Which was when she noticed the other warm living creature in the bed. Not so soft.

An impossibly large male body was spooned against her back, one arm slung casually over her waist, his leg between her knees, pinning her to the bed.

She went rigid.

"Relax," he murmured. "You'll annoy Penny." When she didn't move a muscle, he said, "The cat."

She licked her lips and swallowed. "What are you doing, Gregg?"

"Getting some much-needed sleep," he returned. "I suggest you do the same."

A noise of incredulity made it past her fear-tightened throat.

"You know, this is getting pretty old," he said, sounding worn out. "Like I've said about a hundred times, if I were going to hurt you, don't you think I'd have done it by now?"

"No. You like to torment me," she squeezed out. "You always have."

He sighed. The heat of his breath stirred the hairs on the top of her head. "Only sexually. And you used to like it when I did."

She didn't want to be reminded of their sex games. He had an obsession about controlling her. And yes, she'd enjoyed it. *Then.* But now . . . An involuntary shudder racked through her. "The thought disgusts me."

"I know." His fingertips started to brush over her abdomen, then halted. "I get it. After what they did to you—"

"Shut up!" she cried, startling the cat so badly it jumped up and scampered off the bed. "Don't you *dare* talk to me about that!" She didn't want his sympathy. Or his pity. She didn't want *anything* from him, including his touch. She moved to follow the cat off the bed.

His arm clamped tighter around her. "We both need sleep, Gina. There's only one bed. I need you to stay."

She tried to pull away. "I don't want to. I'll sleep in the chair."

"No. You have to get over your fear of me. I'm not going to hurt you. We've been through this. I thought you believed me."

Her gaze lighted on the small, incongruous bouquet of yellow roses and forget-me-nots sitting in a vase on the dresser—the flowers she'd bought with him in mind—which he'd plucked from the sidewalk after killing the men who'd intended to abduct her. A part of her wanted to, but . . .

"I don't know what to believe," she confessed, and stopped struggling against his hold. Tears welled in her eyes. He'd always been so damn bossy. And she was so tired of fighting. Fighting him, fighting her fears, fighting to stay alive. Fighting the guilt that had consumed her every day since she'd consented to do her terrorist captors' bidding in order to stay alive.

"Hush, it's okay," his deep voice soothed.

Just as that other deep voice had once done. The Voice had helped her through the worst day of her captivity. She wanted so badly to believe there was someone else who wanted to help her, too. Was it possible?

His big hand brushed over her arm. "I swear to you, Gina, I'm going to get whoever did this to you. To us." She felt the whisper of a kiss behind her ear. "Trust me. For God's sake, please, just trust me."

His plea touched some small, carefully guarded, boarded-up place in her heart. Either that, or on some level she understood she could never win against him. Against her will, the steel coil of tension within her slowly unwound and she sagged back against his solid frame. But she still couldn't let it go completely. "I trusted you before, and look where it got me."

His nose burrowed deeper in her hair. "Me, as well. But they messed with the wrong man if they think they'll get away with it. Work with me, sweet thing. Help me find the real traitor. It would be so much easier to do this together."

The feel of his firm, muscular body pressed up head-to-toe against hers must have been short-circuiting her brain, because she was actually starting to believe him.

Besides, it wasn't like he'd let her leave. At this point, what did she have to lose?

"I'm probably insane," she said with a sigh. "But all right. I'll go along with you. I'll help."

"Thank God." He pressed his body a fraction closer.

"For now. But when this is over, I never want to see you again. Understood?"

He went still for a long moment. Then he said, "Okay. If that's how you want it."

"It is," she assured him.

"All right," he said, and if she didn't know better, she would swear he sounded . . . hurt.

But of course, that was impossible. Men like Gregg van Halen didn't get hurt. They only hurt others.

She had to remember that. In case she was ever tempted to feel anything for the man again. Anything other than hate and mistrust.

SARAH glanced at her watch then checked herself in the mirror one last time. She'd put on one of her best dresses for her "date" with Wade Montana, a knee-length, scoop-necked number in clingy teal with cap sleeves. She'd taken extra care with her makeup so her hazel eyes popped green, and fluffed her hair into a sexy, just-out-of-bed disarray that hopefully made one overlook its ordinary brown color.

Pretty darn hot for an old broad, she thought with a wry smile.

Not that forty-five was old. Some days she felt ancient, but everyone said forty-five was the new thirty-three. Who was she to argue?

The doorbell rang and she opened it to find Wade leaning negligently against one of the pillars that held up the townhouse's portico roof. He held a wine bottle–shaped paper bag in his hand, which he started to lift with a smile, then stopped at the sight of her and whistled approvingly.

"Damn, Detective, you look dynamite."

She looked over his latest-style black suit with black shirt and tie, and grinned back at him. Seemed the aliens only came out at night. "And you look very Men in Black. Do we have time for a glass of whatever that is?" She indicated the bag and swung the door wide for him to come in.

"Absolutely." He sauntered in, brushing a kiss on her cheek as he passed.

She led him to the living room wet bar and handed him a bottle opener while she got out two crystal glasses. He poured a splash in each while she studied him. His brown hair was short but stylish; his ski-tan gave him an athletic, all-American look, as did his square jaw and clear blue eyes. No doubt about it: Wade Montana sure didn't *look* like a lying jerk. He looked like the kind of man every woman dreamed of taking home to mama.

"Did I miss a spot of shaving cream?" he asked, his eyes sparkling knowingly.

"Not that I can see. But I could be persuaded to take a closer look," she said, accepting the wineglass. "I *am* a detective, you know."

The corner of his lip curved. "Please. By all means."

Holding his gaze, she lifted her hand and slowly ran the backs of her fingers over the smooth hollow of his cheek and along his jaw, then trailed them across his chin and above his upper lip. She drew their tips down over his mouth, picking up moisture from his bottom lip as they caught on it.

He let out a soft groan. "Are you trying to seduce me, Detective?"

She gave him a little smile as she lowered her hand and sipped her wine. "Is it working?"

His gaze followed the movement. "Take a wild guess."

She let her own gaze drift down to the front of his pants. Her smile widened. An unbidden thrill spun through her. "I guess it is."

He took a step toward her. But anticipating the move, she turned and strolled to the center of the room. Instead of following, he went over to the bookshelves, tucking his free hand into his trouser pocket. She had to give him points for being a gentleman. Or maybe he just enjoyed the chase as much as she did.

He perused the spines of her books, sipping his wine. He pulled one out, examined the cover, and raised an enquiring brow as he turned the book for her to see. It was an erotic romance novel. Two men and a woman, all nude, were sharing a moment on the cover.

She smiled. "What can I say. Every woman's fantasy."

"Really."

"You've never fantasized about being with two women?"

He replaced the book. "God forbid," he said turning back with a wicked grin. "It's hard enough to please one woman, let alone two."

"You're a terrible liar," she told him with a laugh.

He strolled up to her. "And you're sexy as hell. I may have to do something about that."

"What, before dinner?"

She could see he was torn—the man in him that wanted sex versus the agent that wanted information. Who would win?

"You're right. The night is young," he said, brimming with just the right touch of amused frustration.

Poor baby.

She finished her wine, then reached out to cup his jaw. And kissed him. A measured, open-mouthed kiss, delivered with an edge of need she couldn't quite disguise. A low groan rumbled from his throat. She pulled away before he could step into her and deepen the kiss.

He tossed his wine down in a gulp, set aside the glass, and followed her to the front door, where she grabbed her purse.

He touched her chin with his thumb, pulling it down so her mouth opened a fraction. "You," he said huskily, "are going to be the death of me."

She just smiled. Oh, he had no idea.

ELEVEN

"I have something to confess," Wade said.

Sarah took another spoonful of chocolate mousse. He'd brought her to a very nice restaurant on K Street, which boasted gourmet food and a subdued, romantic atmosphere. They'd eaten a leisurely dinner, talking about everything from rock music to zorbing; everything except why they were really there.

She regarded him with open curiosity as she slowly licked her spoon. *Here it comes*, she thought. At last.

He was momentarily distracted by her tongue painting up the silver dip of the spoon. They'd also been flirting all evening; a slow, delicious buildup to after-dinner possibilities.

"A confession?" she prompted. "Sounds ominous."

He cleared his throat, dragged his gaze to hers. "Yeah, well. I haven't been entirely honest with you," he said.

Wow. *That* was unexpected. Just in case, she pretended

she was only interested in relationship stuff. "Let me guess. You're married."

He blinked. "What? No. God, no. Not married. Not engaged or anything." He paused. "But I used to be. Engaged."

Double wow. This must be the kidnapped ex-fiancée Quinn had mentioned. Sarah couldn't believe Wade was actually coming clean. "What happened?" she asked.

"She left me."

Sarah tilted her head, decided to stick to the same tack. It seemed to be working. She gave him a sexy smile. "I'd say I'm sorry, but I'm really not."

He returned her meaningful smile but it faltered. "She was everything to me. I was pretty angry and devastated for a while. A good long while." He toyed with the stem of his wineglass. "Then I met someone else. Turned out she was married. The wife of a congressman, of all things." He shook his head. "Obviously it didn't work out. But I finally realized life goes on. If it kicks you in the balls, you can't sit around and cry. You've got to kick back."

Sarah nodded. "Moving on is a good thing," she said. God knew, she'd done it often enough.

"I just wanted you to know that, before I tell you the rest."

O-*kay*. "What rest?"

He sat back in his seat. "My ex-fiancée was . . . is . . . a genetic research scientist, a doctor, involved in developing a new type of pediatric immunization, delivered via aerosol. So a kid can just get a spray up the nose instead of a shot in the arm."

Sarah took another bite of her chocolate mousse—which was amazingly delicious—wondering what that had to do with anything. "Sounds great. I hate getting shots."

"Unfortunately, the same spray mechanism can also be

used to weaponize biological agents that are harmful to people."

She frowned, starting to get an inkling of a bad feeling. Hadn't Quinn said Asha Mahmood's cousin was a suspected terrorist? "You mean like biological warfare?"

"Exactly. Last year Gina was kidnapped by al Sayika."

Sarah set her spoon down with a clatter. "Al Sayika the terrorist organization? Seriously?" She'd heard plenty about the fanatical group. Though smaller than al Qaeda, they were just as malevolent, and a whole lot smarter. "What did they do to her?" Sarah asked. She couldn't even begin to imagine.

Fury flashed across his face. "They held her for three months, tortured her, and forced her to weaponize a hideous virus designed to kill millions of people—a hybrid of anthrax and avian flu."

Jesus. "That's horrible. She . . . succeeded?"

He blew out a breath. "Yes and no. She did, but thankfully she's incredibly smart. She was able to imbed a nonreplicator gene into the virus so when it was ultimately sprayed in a crowded sports arena, the disease wasn't spread by the infected people to anyone else. And thank goodness, everyone survived because they got help right away."

"Good lord! You're talking about that incident last year in Louisiana? But they said on the news it was a lone crazy who did that. That they were never able to link it to terrorists."

"The members of the al Sayika cell were all caught or killed. The two men still in detention have never admitted to anything, never said a word, and the only witness has been in hiding, unable to testify up until now. So the information was never released to the public."

Sarah had worked in Washington, D.C., long enough to know such things happened all the time. Ostensibly to protect the public and prevent panic. "What happened to your ex? Was she . . ."

He shook his head, obviously relieved when he said, "DHS, along with an agency called STORM Corps, located where the terrorists were holding her, and mounted a rescue. They also retrieved all the virus canisters so it's no longer a threat."

"Thank God," she breathed. At the mention of Commander Quinn's outfit, her attention spiked. She'd checked online and found the Strategic Technical Operations and Rescue Missions Corporation website, which had been impressive. But anyone could put up a website; that didn't mean STORM was legit. However, she had called his references at DHS and they'd also checked out. Quinn had been telling her the truth and this confirmed it further. "I'm glad she's okay. You said her name is Gina?"

"Gina Cappozi. Except she isn't okay. Al Sayika is out for revenge because of the failure of the virus attack. Or possibly they want to finish what they started. Or some other totally irrational reason, because this morning she was kidnapped again."

The true horror of the situation hit Sarah hard. No wonder he was defying orders to investigate this.

"Oh, Wade. I'm so sorry."

"Yeah." He looked down at his half-eaten plate of food and took a deep breath, looking shaken. Sarah's heart went out to him. "It's somewhat complicated," he continued, "but this morning when she was taken, three of her four attackers were killed. And here's the thing: one of the dead men was a cousin of your vic from the alley yesterday."

Quinn had already told her that. "Asha Mahmood."

He nodded. "They've found evidence that the cousin, Ouda Mahmood, is connected to al Sayika. I'd like to know if Asha is, too."

Sarah held his gaze, wrapping her mind around all he'd

said. Damn. This was way bigger than she'd ever imagined. "Jesus, Wade. Why didn't you tell me right off? Naturally the Metro Police Department would cooperate."

He sighed, closed his eyes for a second, then gave her a weak smile. "Here's the part where I throw myself on your mercy. I'd really like access to everything you find out. But you should know, I'm not officially on this case."

Wow, he really *was* confessing. "And the FBI wants you nowhere near it," she completed for him, an uncomfortable mix of relief and pique running through her. "Because of your personal involvement."

He nodded. "I was reprimanded for involving myself in the original case without disclosing it, so if they find out I'm doing this, it'll either mean my job, or I'll find myself SAC of the Nome, Alaska, field office, and living in an igloo."

They both chuckled, but she felt his pain. She knew what it was like when emotions trumped one's good sense.

Like now, for instance.

She picked up her wine and took a swallow. The cab was full-bodied and strong, just how she liked it. She'd drunk just enough to feel relaxed, but that was probably not a good excuse for what she said next. Chalk *that* up to good old-fashioned disappointment. Even though she knew better. God, hope was such a wretched thing. "So, you decided to seduce the lead detective in order to gain access to the investigation through the back door," she said, more regretful than angry. "Thank God I was a woman," she drawled.

Surprisingly, instead of looking guilty, his smile tilted rakishly. "Yes, but hell, no. I decided to seduce you for entirely different reasons. Which is why I'm telling you all this. So you won't think I have ulterior motives."

She couldn't help herself. She smiled. Either he was a remarkable liar—a distinct possibility, considering his occupation—or he really meant it. Against her better judgment, the hope in her heart reared its pathetic head again. "You realize we'd *both* be in deep shit, not just you," she ventured, "if anyone found out."

"You already know I'm willing to risk it. What about you?"

She laughed. God, she was such a goner. "Are you always this direct, SAC Montana?"

"Only when there's something I want, Detective McPhee." The glitter in his eyes sent a shiver deep inside her. She was so insanely tempted just to say "yes" to him and "screw you" to the color guard doing a frantic routine in her head.

But there was one last thing she needed to know. "Why do you care so much?" she asked. "She's your *ex*. And you've been ordered away from the case in no uncertain terms."

The glitter dimmed perceptibly. He didn't answer right away, but spun his wineglass by the stem. At length he said, "I guess I feel partly responsible. It's a long story, but the short version is Gina called me last year when a friend went missing overseas in some monumental CIA snafu. I'm sorry to say, I didn't go out of my way to help her. She ended up being subverted and used by a CIA covert operative who turned out to be a traitor to his country. He's the one who gave her to the terrorists. And my money's on him being the one who has her now. I couldn't live with myself if he . . ."

Sarah's mouth dropped open. "Surely, you can't blame yourself for any of that, Wade! It isn't *your* fault the man is a traitor."

"I know. But that doesn't make me feel any better. And Gina's already been through so much. I need to find her, Sarah. And I need to get the man who did this to her and see he's put away for good. If only to ease my conscience."

She could understand that. "Of course I'll help however I can." She made a snap decision. "Look. I'm going to Mahmood's apartment tomorrow morning. Why don't you come with me?"

He reached across the table, put his hand over hers, and gave it a squeeze. "Thanks. I really mean that. I know you could get in big trouble for this."

"So what's new?" she said dryly.

His smile changed character as he turned her hand over, and with his other forefinger slowly traced the lifeline down her palm. His touch tingled, zinging awareness through her body. "A troublemaker, eh?" he murmured.

"Can't help myself." And wasn't *that* the truth.

He lightly caressed her hand. "I do like the sound of that." He met her gaze. "You never answered my question." The feel of his fingertips on her skin, stroking the sensitive nerves in her palm, made her insides coil with desire.

"Which question is that?"

"Are you willing to risk sleeping with me?"

She wet her lips. There he went, being direct again. Normally a man didn't ask permission to take things too far. But she had to admit, it had a certain charm. And hell, she *had* worn her best black lace underwear.

She leaned in over their twined hands; a wash of arousal shimmered through her. "Are you any good?" she asked with a naughty smile. Still unsure. But boy, was he tempting.

He closed the scant inches between their faces and brushed a kiss over her mouth, touching his tongue to the seam of her lips. "I guess you'll just have to try me and find out."

GINA had fantasized about Gregg van Halen ever since the day they met. Hot, thrilling fantasies of kinky sex and breathtaking submission. Oh, yes. She'd been thoroughly and completely under his masculine spell from his first audacious kiss, mere hours after meeting. The man oozed primitive, carnal power, and she'd been instantly captivated. She had given herself to him without reservation, in ways she'd never before dared imagine, lying under his bold, muscular body as he turned her inside out with pleasure.

She'd dreamed of him unceasingly, to her waking consternation. When they were together; when she was a captive; after her rescue. Even while she hated him with a burning passion, convinced without a doubt that he'd been responsible for all her pain and suffering, she'd still welcomed him into her dreams so he could bind her to his sturdy iron bed and have his wicked, wicked way with her.

Which was the only possible explanation for what she did as they lay spooned together that night.

She mixed up dreams with reality.

She'd been dreaming of being in his arms, so when she found herself there, bathed in the darkness of his bedroom, she didn't think twice about it, she did what she'd done a thousand times before in the middle of the night, both awake and in dreams. She reached up, put her lips to his, and kissed him.

He must have been fast asleep, because his reaction was slow. He didn't move at first. Only after she teased his mouth with her tongue did he respond with a soft groan deep in his throat. And opened to her.

A spill of desire zinged through her at the familiar, heady taste of him, so arousingly male. Tonight, so much more vivid and earthy than usual. Oh, how she had missed that sensual flavor . . .

She couldn't see his features in the dark, but his fingers tightened just a little on her waist and in the long tangle of her hair, letting her know he wanted her to continue. He let her kiss him, let her use her tongue to explore the soft warmth of his inner mouth. How unlike him to lie back and receive instead of being the aggressor, the dominant partner. She was delighted.

"Gina," he whispered, sliding his hand over her hip. "Sweet baby."

She kissed him and kissed him, until her body hummed hotly with pent-up passion. And still he urged her to take the lead. So she did.

She shoved aside the covers, wanting to feel his bare torso, to smell the dusky essence of his skin up close. She tugged up on his T-shirt and he pulled it over his head for her. But he didn't reach for hers. She did it for him. Tossing it aside, she pillowed her naked breasts provocatively against his chest. As one, they moaned at the mutual burst of pleasure from the contact. She rubbed up against him, his curly hairs tickling her, bringing her nipples to rigid attention.

He groaned her name. And she could feel his cock come to rigid attention, as well. She reached down, slid her hand under his sweatpants. And touched him. His body bowed up and he gave a strangled growl, then twisted and fell onto his back, taking her with him.

It was the jolt from the fall that jerked her fully awake.

She came hurtling out of the twilight dream, sprawled on top of him, her lips to his chest and her fingers around his rampant cock.

She gasped and shot up, scrambling away to the edge of the bed. There she knelt, shaking, with her arms wrapped around herself, panting with the sudden cold and the shock of what she'd done . . .

And from breathless arousal.

She stared at him in the dimness of the bedroom, mute with confusion.

But there was no accusing him of anything. He'd been the reticent one. *She'd* been the one kissing him. Touching him. Seducing him.

In the shafts of moonlight shining through the window she could see his arms stretched over his head. His hands gripped the iron bars of the headboard. His eyes were squeezed tightly shut. Moonbeams danced over his body like fairies.

He didn't say anything. Didn't look. Didn't move.

The silence stretched.

Her shoulders notched down a little, but she was still shaking like a leaf. Her fingers touched the warm silver heart clasped around her ankle. She remembered his promise. To always be there. As her protector.

But who would protect *him* . . . ?

"I'm sorry," she said in a whisper.

He swallowed, his Adam's apple a shadow of movement on his pale throat. "I'm not."

Hearing his deep, gritty voice, goose bumps shimmered down her arms. *Oh, God.* How could she possibly still want this man? And with a searing need that shook her to the core?

She crept a few inches toward him on the mattress. As it dipped, he opened his eyes and looked at her. The intensity of that look almost sent her scurrying away into the next room.

But she didn't. She moved closer. Warily. Like you'd approach a wild beast. She lifted her hand to—

"Gina . . ." he warned, unfurling his fingers from the headboard and lowering his arms. "Don't."

Her heartbeat sped. Her nipples ached. And she made a stunning realization. She *needed* this. Desperately needed the intimate contact. Needed the physical confirmation of life.

It didn't matter that she didn't trust him a hundred percent. Wouldn't matter if she still hated him. He was her lover. And she badly needed him to show her she was really alive. That she had survived all the horror of the past eight months. *That she was still a woman worthy of loving . . . if only by a man like him.*

"I want to," she told him, her voice quavering but insistent.

"You'll regret it." His voice was flat.

"I don't care."

She slipped off her sweatpants and crawled to him. Then pulled the covers up over her back and lay down, canting her body over his.

All the while he watched her, his hard blue eyes filled with an emotion she couldn't begin to name.

"You know me," he warned her. "It's been a long time. I'll want to be rough with you. I'll want to crush you under me. I'll want to tie you up and spank you. I'll want to make you beg . . . but you'll be begging for real and I won't know it. I'll hurt you."

She shivered, knowing it was all true—all except the last part. "You've never hurt me, Gregg," though it pained her to admit it. "Not in bed."

"But it's different now," he said, his words hoarse with need. "*You're* different. You need someone gentle now. I don't know if I can stop myself from doing those things. It's who I am."

"Then let *me* be in control," she said. "Let me tie you up. That way you won't—"

"No!" His fingers dug into her with his firm denial. "No. I can't—" His words broke off with a choke.

And suddenly she had another blinding insight. *Somewhere in the distant past, he'd been through as much pain and torture as she had.*

That's what drove his obsessive need for control.

She understood it, because she now had exactly the same need.

A shudder of intense recognition racked through her body. *They were the same, she and Gregg*. Two halves of the same Janus coin.

As though he could read her mind, he tugged her back

to him, enveloping her in his strong embrace. "I can see what you're thinking, Gina. But we're not alike, you and me. Not even close."

He was so wrong.

The heat of his skin felt so good. She tilted her face up and kissed his throat, shivering at the rough scratch of his jaw against her cheek. Feeling her quiver, he pulled away. She pulled him back. And kissed over the pulse point of his jugular and on down to his collarbone. Under her fingers, the discs of his nipples were hard with arousal. As was the part of him she wanted most, pushing against her thighs.

She kissed her way down to his concave belly, licking at the dip of his navel, toying with the arrow of curly dark hair that disappeared under the waistband of his sweats.

"Help me," she urged, hooking her fingers under the elastic.

In a swift motion he lifted, and they were gone. She heard the open and shut of the nightstand drawer. A small packet pressed onto her palm. She curled her fingers around it . . . and her other hand around his thick erection.

She could wait no longer. She scooted down, and shivered in recognition of the ornate tattooed band that marked his organ as the only one that would ever satisfy her. She took him in her mouth.

A groan burst from him. She tasted his salty essence as his cock wept with desire.

"No," he growled, and lifted her up with corded arms, dragging her up his body until she spanned his shoulders. Then he moved down so his mouth was on her, between her thighs. She grabbed the bars of the headboard. And rode his tongue.

She echoed his low groan. She'd forgotten how utterly amazing sex felt. Real sex, with a real man. With *this* man.

By the time he'd finished with her, she'd forgotten her name. She was boneless from an endless orgasm, limp with pleasure. At that point he could have done anything to her, taken her in any way he wished; she couldn't have stopped him. Wouldn't have, even if she could.

But for some reason it didn't surprise her when he just picked her back up, and with absolute control lowered her down onto his waiting cock. Her on top. He was long and hard, and slid up into her with a firm thrust. Gritting his teeth, he stopped, and waited for her to move.

"You do it," she told him, kissing his mouth. "I have no strength left." Her muscles were like Jell-O.

"You're sure?"

"Very."

She kissed him again. And he began to move his hips, scything up so the tip of his arousal kissed the base of her womb. God, it felt so incredibly good.

"Ah, woman, I've missed you so much," he said on a strangled groan.

She'd missed him, too. Missed this. Missed being so close to another human . . . in pleasure instead of pain. Missed having a man inside her, *this man*, his flesh one with hers, completing her. *Loving her*.

He gripped her behind the neck, holding her mouth down to his for a drowning kiss as he continued to pump up into her. She wrapped her arms around him. And surrendered.

"You're safe with me, Gina," he whispered roughly. "I swear to you, no one will ever hurt you again. Not as long as I'm still breathing."

The promise was delivered with such searing, gut-wrenching conviction, it would be impossible to fake. And that's when she knew. With complete certainty. *He'd been telling the truth*. This whole time she'd been blaming and hating the wrong man. Because there was no way this man in bed with her was capable of hurting her in any way, in or out of bed.

So just as he reached his peak and groaned out his pleasure, she whispered back, "I believe you. Oh, God, Gregg, I do believe you."

TWELVE

SARAH and Wade made it as far as her front door before Wade's cell phone rang. They'd been kissing all the way from the parking garage like a couple of teenagers. She still hadn't decided if she'd go all the way, but she just couldn't stop kissing the man. He was that good.

"God*damn* it," he growled, reluctantly untangling himself from her to dig his buzzing PDA out of his jacket pocket. "I *told* them not to call me unless it's a emergency."

"Don't worry about it. Go ahead." She flung her back against the door of her townhome to catch her breath.

Damn, he was an amazing kisser. *Really* amazing.

"SAC Montana."

She raked through her purse for her keys, found them, and swung the door open. She practically stumbled through it as she heard him say, "Commander Quinn. What can I do for you?" He took a step toward her, then halted at the threshold. "You are?" He glanced at his watch, brows shooting up. "Now?"

What the—?

Wade's gaze darted to her. "Yes, as a matter of fact, I'm with her now. Discussing the case."

Her stomach sank. Okay, so much for it being *her* decision.

After a few seconds he said, "Sure, uh . . . listen, hang on a sec," and pressed a key on his phone, looking guarded. "You talked with Bobby Lee Quinn from STORM Corps earlier today?"

She nodded, jiggling the key out of the lock. "Briefly. He wanted to know if I'd searched Asha Mahmood's apartment yet."

"What did you tell him?"

"That I didn't know where she lived. He gave me the address in return for letting him know what I find."

Wade frowned. "Is that legal?"

Her lips curved. "This coming from you?"

His jaw clenched and unclenched. "Why didn't you tell me you'd spoken to him?"

Wow. He did *not* look happy. "It didn't come up. Why?"

"Quinn's in D.C. And he wants to know what my interest is in Asha Mahmood."

"So tell him."

"Sarah, this is not a polite enquiry. This is STORM trying to shut me out of the case."

Was he *kid*ding? "Why would they do that? Other than the obvious?"

His expression darkened. "I told you. It's complicated."

Her turn to frown.

Jetting out a breath, he punched the button on the phone again. "Look, Quinn. We both want the same thing. Let's make a deal. I'll stay out of your way if you stay out of mine." He listened impassively for a few seconds, then pushed the off button and slid the PDA back into his jacket pocket. "You told him I'd contacted you."

"Hello? Before I knew who you were. I don't normally get this much outside interest in a routine murder case. I wanted to cover my bases. Look, why don't you come in? We can talk about it inside."

He stuffed his hands in his pockets and she knew the night was over. Disappointment spiraled through her.

"He knows we're together now. Which means we're being watched."

"Why on earth would they be watching *us*?" she asked incredulously.

A muscle worked in his jaw and he glanced away for a moment. "Anyway, it's late and I need to go into the office before we meet in the morning. We should both get some sleep."

And so much for being willing to risk it.

"Sure, no problem," she said, resolutely telling herself she'd dodged a bullet rather than getting the shaft. Ha. "Well, thanks for dinner. I really enjoyed it." Except for the part where he turned into a paranoid wuss.

He stepped forward, clearly intending to give her a peck on the cheek. As *if*. She stepped backward. "Goodnight, SAC Montana," she said and firmly shut the door.

Oh, well. She hadn't really wanted to sleep with him anyway.

Honest.

THE rising dawn was chilly on the Chesapeake.

Rebel poured herself a mug of strong coffee and carried it up to the deck of the *Stormy Lady* to watch the sunrise while Alex showered in the teensy stall, and the blueberry muffins she'd thrown together baked in the oven. A layer of gray clouds wrapped the bay in a shroud of thick silence and blocked the rays of the sun.

How appropriate.

She took a long, fortifying sip of coffee. Who would have thought the morning after the first time ever sleeping with the man she'd loved for years and years could be so depressing?

Okay, so not actually depressing. But a touch of sadness marred what should have been the happiest dawn of her life.

Yes, the sex had been incredible. Phenomenal. Making love with Alex had been everything she'd ever dreamed, and so much more. It was the part *after*ward that had put a damper on her total bliss. The part where he'd pretty much come out and told her they had no real future together. He had no interest in marrying her.

Yeah, that had hurt.

As had the crushing news of his inability to have children. Not that it made any difference in her feelings for him. It just took a bit of mental adjusting, that's all. Except he didn't want her. Not as a wife.

And yet, he'd been all too willing to marry Helena. Why not her?

A slash of pain razored through her heart, nearly bringing her to her knees. It was just as she'd feared. Great sex or no, she really was his second choice.

Too distant a second ever to be his wife.

And that *was* depressing.

She swallowed down the urge to scream at the top of her lungs about the unfairness of it all, and took another sip of coffee. Ah, well. She'd known all along she'd come in second. She'd even told him she wouldn't fall into bed with him because of it. Yeah. And just see how long *that* had lasted. About nine seconds.

"There you are," Alex said, popping his head up from below. He came up the ladder, coffee mug in one hand, two muffins in the other. "The timer went off, so I took them out of the oven. These are awesomely delicious, and you"—he leaned down and gave her a kiss—"are amazing. Coffee *and* muffins for breakfast? You spoil me."

Basking in the light of his brilliant smile, she laughed, all her sadness vanishing in a flash. The pleasure in his eyes was too genuine to resist. At least he wanted her for *some*thing. Which was far better than the alternative.

"What, didn't Helena make breakfast for you?" she couldn't stop herself from asking.

"We never spent the night together, so breakfast wasn't an issue," he responded, handing her a muffin.

He'd told her once before that he and Helena had never had sex. Helena's choice. Which was something Rebel still didn't understand, because Helena was not particularly religious, nor did she have any strong moral convictions against premarital sex. She and Alex had been engaged—*engaged*—for more than a year before he was taken hostage by terrorists. And Helena had remained true to his memory the entire time he'd been presumed dead, never once going out with another man. With a love like that, it seemed strange *not* to sleep with him.

Selfishly, Rebel was jubilant. This was a part of Alex that she possessed and her rival didn't. An important part.

Did it shed a certain light on that insanity about Helena ditching him at the altar? Maybe the sex thing should have been a clue.

"Her loss," Rebel said, and leaned in for another kiss. He tasted like blueberries and coffee and cream. "And you're pretty awesomely amazing, yourself," she added, nibbling on his earlobe.

He gave a gravelly hum. "You are too tempting by half, woman. But Quinn will have my hide if we don't produce some results for him by the time he shows up."

"You think he will?"

"Oh, yeah. D.C. isn't that far. Once he's finished with whatever he's doing up there, he'll fly down here for sure."

"I guess we'd better get going, then," she agreed, somewhat reluctantly. "Though how I'm going to manage this dive, I have no idea. My leg muscles are toast."

He grinned. "Too much sex?"

She grinned back. "Is that possible?"

"Hell, no. Guess I'll just have to massage them later." His eyebrows waggled.

She chuckled, finished off her muffin, and headed for the storage bins to fetch their dive gear. "You are so bad."

"Not what you said last night," he called teasingly after her.

After they got their gear assembled, he unzipped a black duffel that bore the distinctive silver STORM emblem. From it, he pulled an instrument that looked a bit like a handheld video game unit, with an LCD screen between two handles covered in buttons.

"What's that?" she asked.

"It's an infrared-enhanced sonar detector. Hopefully it'll be able to locate what's left of *Allah's Paradise* from the surface. That way we'll know the depth and can plan our dives."

"Cool."

He showed her how it worked, then said, "Okay, let's get going."

They suited up, threw out the dive flag buoy, and jumped into the frigid water. "Good grief, it's freezing!" she exclaimed. "Thank goodness for full-body wet suits."

"Wimp," he declared—though he had donned a wet suit, too, she noted—and after hesitating long enough to take a deep breath and grimace at the water below, he disappeared under the murky surface, only his snorkel and tank visible. The man swam like a fish. She'd often wondered why he hadn't joined the Navy SEALs out of college, instead of CIA's Zero Unit.

She stuck out her tongue at his wake, laughed, and

paddled around, adjusting her buoyancy and getting used to the bulky gear while Alex swam concentric circles around the marked area with his gadget.

Five minutes later, he popped his head up with a staccato exhale. "Okay, got it mapped."

Seriously? That was easy.

"Ready?" he asked after quickly punching some numbers into the dive computer strapped to his wrist. He swam over and looked like he wanted to kiss her, but they couldn't manage it because their masks were in the way. Instead, he touched her cheek with his glove. "I'm going to tether us together, okay?" He held up a nylon rope with clips at each end, one of which was attached to his BCD. "Visibility down there is nil, and I want to know where you are at all times."

She nodded. "Works for me." She wasn't ashamed to admit she was a bit nervous about this dive. Until yesterday, it had been several years since she'd been in full dive gear, and a lot longer than that since she'd dived in conditions that weren't clear enough to see beyond your fingertips. On the surface, the Chesapeake Bay was beautiful, but underwater it was a brown, murky mess.

Clipping the tether to her vest, he gave her an uneasy look. "Be careful down there," he said.

"Always."

"If anything happens . . ." he began, then shook his head.

Her smile faded. "Alex?"

"Never mind," he said. "Let's go."

ALEX ignored a growing sense of foreboding and led Rebel down into the Stygian depths of the bay. Jesus, he could hardly see the end of his nose. Even under normal conditions he hated diving in crap like this. Thank God for the sonar, otherwise they'd be down there for days reading the bottom of the bay like Braille for bits of the wreck. It was spread out in an oblong pattern along the silty seabed at least a half-mile long. Luckily, the dive depth was child's play, only about twenty-five feet down. They'd have plenty of time for a thorough search before they had to come up.

The good news was that the bomb had blown a hole straight through the bottom hull of the yacht, which had ignited the fuel tank, which in turn had exploded upward so tightly it had taken just part of the deck and the wheelhouse with it. The rest of the yacht was still largely intact. The bad news? It would all be dangerously unstable. The whole vessel was sitting at a crazy angle, nose up; it could topple over any moment if the current hit it the wrong way.

Hell. He hated taking Rebel with him into this kind of underwater minefield, but there were strict rules against diving alone. He'd just have to clip her to the anchor or something while he explored what remained of the inside of the vessel.

That was the plan, anyway.

The Chesapeake was pretty useless as a dive spot, even at the best of times. If the tides were running, the currents could be downright wicked. The bottom was muddy and there was no interesting fish or plant life to speak of, unless you were mad for oysters and striped bass. Even seaweed refused to grow, since the water was brackish . . . and polluted from three hundred years of industry and farming along the many rivers that fed into it. He was definitely using antibacterial soap for his après-dive shower. He didn't even want to *think* about what the tasty Maryland blue crabs he was planning for dinner tonight had been feeding on all their lives. Well, what the hell. He'd survived sixteen months at Club Torture; herbicides and mercury in his blood were small potatoes.

What he *wouldn't* survive was anything happening to

Rebel on his watch. His chest tightened at the mere thought, and he listened for her bubbles, his muscles easing only when he was certain of her steady rhythmic breathing next to him.

Using the sonar, he guided them down to the main part of the wreck, then passed the instrument over to Rebel and dug out a powerful spotlight from the dive bag he'd brought with things they might need. Switching on the light, visibility didn't improve much, but when they got close, it was enough to make out the vague outlines of the intact bits of the vessel, along with a couple of cruising bass. The spotlight sparked off their striped scales and flashed back from one unblinking eye as they turned on a dime and swam away.

Like the first memorable glimpse of the wreck of the *Titanic*, the yacht's deck railing loomed into view as they approached. High-pitched squeals and creaking bangs of metal grinding on metal punctuated the muffled stillness of the underwater gloom. The whole thing made his hair stand on end.

He motioned to Rebel that he intended to clip her onto the rail and go in on his own. She shook her head and gave the signal for no.

He nodded more firmly, and pulled the rope toward the rail. She pulled it back, swam up in his face, and shook her head again. Even through her mask he could see she had that stubborn set to her eyes. If he insisted on clipping her, she'd just wait until he swam away, then unclip herself and follow him in. And probably lose herself in the liquid muck. God*damn* it.

Suddenly, a long serpentine shape uncoiled itself from the railing and slithered right past them. Rebel squeaked and flipped away, grabbing onto his arm. Her eyes widened at him. *Oops*. Had he forgotten to mention the abundance of brown eels in the bay? Rebel was not a fan of snakes or snakelike creatures of any variety. Her gloved fingers dug into him as she steadied herself. Then, with a firm finality he couldn't miss, she snapped the clip back onto his vest.

He exhaled a long stream of bubbles. He *so* did not want to go in there with Rebel in tow. But he knew a losing battle when he saw one.

Against his better judgment, he guided them to the wheelhouse and ran the spotlight over what was left of it. The remains projected out from the upwardly angled deck like a ghostly cable car going up a mountainside. Most of it had been blown away, and anything it might have contained was now scattered along the bottom. They'd deal with all that on a later dive.

He then led her over to the gaping opening of the main salon and stopped to assess.

Amid the sounds of grinding metal, the carcass of the yacht rocked eerily back and forth, pushed by the strength of the current. The salon doors, along with strips of the hull that had exploded loose, flapped slowly up and down, like skeletons waving at them in slow motion.

Every instinct screamed at him not to go in. *Fuck.* He took several calming breaths and tried to relax. But it was no use. He could feel his heart rate kick up several notches.

Using his hands to show Rebel what he wanted, he jockeyed himself above her so they'd enter the main body of the wreck as a unit. It would get tricky if there were any shallow hatches to go through inside, but he'd just have to stay alert.

They swam in.

Their mostly-by-feel inspection of the large salon revealed that much of the upper structure was still intact. They also found a dozen or so weapons spilling helter-skelter from a cabinet: Kalashnikovs, PKs, even a handheld RPG. Not necessarily hard evidence of terrorism, but not items your average tourist yacht would have onboard. He felt they were definitely on the right track.

Gingerly, so as not to disturb the delicate balance of the wreck, they gathered everything into a couple of large net bags attached by a line to the *Stormy Lady* above, which they'd brought along to haul up evidence in. The guns went in one; several notebooks from a shelf and some disintegrating papers and files from a drawer went in the other. Everything they thought might contain clues to the terrorists' plans and associates was going to the surface with them.

But they found nothing that remotely resembled a trigger. At least, not in the salon.

Rebel tugged on their tether to get his attention. She pointed questioningly to the galley-way leading down to the lower level—presumably the bedrooms. A likely spot for a safe to be hidden, possibly containing the terrorists' orders from what was left of the organization's leadership, notes on the planned D.C. attack, information on their al Sayika contacts, and with any luck a laptop or other computer that might contain all of the above.

Shit.

Alex knew they had to go down there. But the sight of the tight, impossibly dark, cell-like stairway made his nerves jangle like electrodes on a frog. *Or on human flesh.* He battled back his reaction and slammed a lid on it. *Jesus.* This was not the time for that baby-ass PTSD bullshit.

He gave a curt nod and led the way. *Down into the abyss.*

Rebel stayed close. He could feel the tension in her hands as she clung to his thigh and they swam, squeezing down the narrow passage together.

Halfway down, the wreck groaned like a banshee and suddenly shifted.

Rebel yelped and they both tried to brace themselves,

but were swept downward, tumbling and rolling in a hard surge of water that rushed down through the stairwell. The flashlight was torn from Alex's hand. It went spinning away, banged against something solid, and instantly snapped off. They plunged into total darkness.

All at once he felt a tangle of long, slithering bodies dart over his head and around his shoulders, seeking to escape the turbulence. Rebel let out a bubbly scream. She jerked away from him, batting at the fat knot of eels with her hands, twisting and churning madly with her flippers to get away. But she was still tethered to him, so he was yanked along after her. She slammed into a wall. He slammed into her. The wreck rocked violently. She screamed again, but this time it was strangled, like she was choking. He couldn't hear her bubbles anymore. *Fuck!*

He reached out and grabbed for her. She fought him. Banged into the opposite wall. He followed, knocking the wind out of himself. The boat tipped the other way, gaining momentum in its fall. She twisted, grabbed in panic at his air tank, searching blindly for his spare regulator. He caught her around the waist and ripped off his mouthpiece, fed her precious air. She gulped at it greedily, her body shaking like a Chihuahua.

As he pulled the regulator back to his own mouth, the vessel shuddered violently. The sickening grind of metal and the *snap-crackle-pop* of fiberglass breaking up confirmed the worst. The boat was going end over end.

The water in the passageway churned and roiled. Like ragdolls they were thrown into a small, enclosed space. Before he could react, a door slammed shut on them. He felt the walls close in, pinning them inside what felt like a storage bin. *Or a coffin.* His pulse skyrocketed. A sudden violent shudder of claustrophobia froze the breath in his lungs. His mind screamed.

Oh, Jesus God. No!

The shrieks of metal around him morphed into the desperate cries of his dying Zero Unit comrades.

Not now! Not. Now! He had to help Rebel!

But the unrelenting panic overtook him in an avalanche of dread. And once again he was surrounded by the hot, suffocating air of a desert filled with nothing but pain and agony. He lashed out, groping.

Where was his angel?

He tried to call to her. But for some reason he couldn't get any air. He was choking . . . And the villagers were grabbing at him. Seizing his arms and clawing at his ankles. He fought them. Tried to twist away. But it was no use. Someone had him around the neck.

Oh, fuck. He was a dead man!

TUMBLING head over heels in the low storage closet they'd somehow landed in, Rebel struggled not to suck down any more putrid bay water as she warded off Alex's panicked blows.

She needed air! And so did he. She couldn't hear any bubbles at all in the churning darkness. Just the rush of water past her ears, the battering of their limbs against the walls . . . and the loud thundering of her heart.

With a bone-jarring thud, the prow of the boat crashed to the muddy bottom of the bay and bounced.

Please, lord, help me, she prayed.

Yesterday on her recertification dives, retrieving her lost regulator had been so easy. *Tilt and sweep*—the standard safety maneuver every diver had to learn and practice. And there it had always been, in her hand, as it was supposed to be. But now all she'd gotten were handfuls of Alex's arms or legs or neck. Which had turned him into a wild man, kicking and flailing and bringing them both to the brink of drowning, since they were still tethered together. He was obviously in the throes of one of his PTSD episodes and had no idea of the mortal danger he was putting them both in.

Please, God, don't let us die.

The yacht crashed down on the bottom with a final booming *thwack.* Rebel spun around in their tight space and tried again. *For the last time*, if she didn't get air in the next few seconds. Lungs burning and on the verge of bursting, she tipped sideways and focused every cell in her body on locating the floating tentacles of the regulator's octopus.

There!

Her fingertips grazed the illusive air tube. Desperately, she closed her fingers around it, scrabbled up to the end, and mashed the regulator into her mouth. She sucked in deep, beautiful lungfuls of air. And almost passed out from every kind of relief.

Behind her, Alex started to choke. She spun back to him, took another deep breath and stuck the apparatus through the darkness toward the sound, praying his long-honed diver's instincts would kick in despite his mind being on a different—dry—continent. She was rewarded. He seized the regulator greedily and put it to his mouth, oblivious to her need for it. Which was how she knew he was still lost in the grips of the flashback. Lucid, he would let himself die before putting her in jeopardy.

She decided not to fight him over it. She'd lose. Now that he was relatively calm, she reached over his shoulder and, careful not to grab him, felt for the octopus atop his tank. This time she easily found it, brought the apparatus to his lips, and gently switched it for her own. Being tethered to a man in the middle of a psychotic break was not ideal. But at least they were both breathing. And she hadn't died of a heart attack. Yet.

But now what?

Alex had squeezed himself back into a corner of the box and drawn himself into a ball, nursing the air like a baby at his mother's breast. During the time Alex had been recovering at Haven Oaks, she'd seen him go through some awful flashbacks, and learned from Rainie not to touch him then for her own safety. Firmly repeating his name would usually snap him out of it. Eventually. But underwater, that was not an option. She'd just have to wait it out, until he emerged on his own.

Meanwhile . . . She wasn't about to sit cowering in a closet waiting for her man to rescue her. Maybe she should continue the search on her own.

Gingerly, she felt along the sides of the storage area until she found the hatch. Luckily the latch worked from both directions. Popping open the door, she held very still and listened intently. No eerie creaks or groans. No grinding metal. If anything, the wreck sounded more stable than before. Of course, it was hard to tell for sure in total darkness. There was only one way to find out.

She unhooked the line that tethered her to Alex, gathered her courage, and swam out into the black void.

THIRTEEN

THE scent of sex perfumed the bed like peach blossom nectar. Memories of making love with Gina last night filled Gregg's mind as he woke.

Had it really happened? It must have. The proof was curled naked in his arms, clinging to him in her sleep like she was afraid he'd disappear.

She'd said she believed him. A complete turnaround. What had changed her mind? What had made her surrender her fear and come back to him?

He had no clue. But damn, was he glad. Not only because she believed in his innocence—though that was huge—but . . . as much as he was a lone wolf, he really liked being with Gina. He felt better around her. More . . . complete, or happy, or . . . accepted. That was it. He liked her unreserved acceptance of him, despite his many flaws. Although he knew his job was important and necessary, and made the world a much better place, sometimes it felt like he was fighting a hopeless battle all by himself. The fact that Gina trusted him, and believed in him, made all the difference. Like he mattered.

It was a strange feeling, and one he didn't entirely trust. But for now, it felt . . . good. He'd wanted it back. More desperately than he wanted to admit, even to himself.

He was also grateful for the turnaround for an entirely different reason. There were important things that needed doing, and it would be impossible to bring an unwilling woman along with him to do them. This way was a lot easier. Hell, maybe she'd even help him.

Gina stirred, burrowing deeper into his embrace. "Don't go," she murmured against his chest, as though she knew what he was thinking.

His body quickened fiercely as her soft curves pressed into him. "I'm not going anywhere," he assured her, gritting his teeth against the urge to turn her over and take her. It was so hard not to do what came so naturally to him. Not to revert to their old patterns—back before she'd been tortured and beaten to within an inch of her life. Back when she was attracted to the kind of raw, edgy power sex that was so much a part of him.

She wouldn't want that now. She'd freak out and shut down. And he couldn't blame her. *He* was the one who was twisted, who because of his background had an unnatural need to dominate his partner. It was *his* needs that were out of line, not hers.

"It's okay. You can take me," she said, feeling his body's craving and knowing him so well. "If you want to."

"You know I want you, sweet thing. But we've finally gotten to a good place, and I don't want to scare you away again."

She lifted her head and peered up at him. "I'm not afraid of you, Gregg. Not anymore. I know you're not out to kill me. I had it all wrong about you. I'm so sorry."

He pulled her up for a kiss, gazing into her beautiful brown eyes, so full of hurt and vulnerability. "No. I'm the one who's sorry. I got fooled by the bad guys, and you almost died because of it. I'll never forgive myself for that."

She was quiet for a moment, then said, "You couldn't have known what they were planning, Gregg. You don't even know who was behind the kidnapping. Do you?"

He shook his head. "I thought I did. I'm just not so sure anymore."

He told her about what had happened with Colonel Blair, and the dubious assertion his former commander had made about who was involved.

By the time he'd finished, Gina's jaw had dropped nearly to her feet. "He wants you to believe the *U.S. government* helped foreign terrorists mount an attack on our own country? The *Pentagon*? My God. The old man's senile, or on drugs."

"Agreed. That sort of thing only happens in Kiefer Sutherland flicks. Still . . ."

Her jaw dropped even farther. "You *can't* be taking this seriously."

He pushed out a breath. "No, not directly. But . . ." He rubbed a hand over the short spikes of his hair.

"But what?"

"Baby, right now it's our only lead. We know the traitor helping al Sayika has to be someone either in Zero Unit or well-connected on the chain of command. And like it or not, that chain of command ultimately leads to Washington, D.C., and the Pentagon. What if the impossible really is true?"

She uncurled herself and sat up, looking at him with an incredulous expression. "You really want me to believe my own government conspired with terrorists to have me kidnapped?"

He lifted her fingers and kissed her knuckles. "Baby, that's exactly what you thought happened when your friend Rainie disappeared last year. Remember? It's why you kept calling CIA and threatening to give the story to the newspapers."

She looked pained and took a deep, shuddering breath. "You're right. And maybe if I'd done it, if I'd stood up to them, I wouldn't have been kidnapped and tortured for three months."

Damn. This was not where he'd meant to take this conversation.

He sat up, too, and put his hands on either side of her face. "Then they'd just have kidnapped someone else. Someone who might not have survived, who maybe wasn't as smart as you so they couldn't engineer that non-replicator gene into the virus, and millions of people might be dead. But instead, they're still alive today thanks to your strength, your intelligence, and your amazing presence of mind."

As he spoke, her eyes filled with tears. Her chin trembled. "Or maybe that person wouldn't have been as weak as I am, and committed suicide rather than do what those animals wanted."

"No. Gina, no." He gathered her in his arms. "I know a thing or two about blaming yourself for others' actions. You can't think that way. Thanks to you, not a single person died in that attack, or afterward. Baby, you are a goddamn hero and don't you ever forget it."

She glanced away and tears trickled down her cheeks. "I really wish I could believe that," she whispered.

"Believe it." He fingered a lock of her hair. "And sweet thing, I don't know what I would have done if they'd killed you, but it wouldn't have been pretty."

"Oh, Gregg." She threw her arms around him and broke down. Her big, wet tears trailed down his shoulder straight to his heart. "You really have been watching over me this whole time," she said with a shuddering sob. "God, how could I ever have thought—"

"Hush, now. Never mind. You were in very good company."

She clutched him harder. "It's all my fault. I told anyone who'd listen it was you who's the traitor. I should call STORM. Let everyone know—"

"No!" He gripped her arms. Pulling her back, he drilled her with a look. "Contact *no one*, Gina. Not STORM, not the FBI. No one. Not until we figure out who the real traitor is."

"But—"

"I can't take the chance. If they catch me, they'll lock me up in some top secret, high-security prison and throw away the key. Trust me; I'll never see daylight again."

"But if I tell them it wasn't you, if I explain—"

"I've been framed good and solid, Gina. Everyone will think I've gotten to you. Used your old feelings for me to influence your opinion." Her expression fell, and he knew she saw he was right. "Baby, if I'm put away, no one will be looking for the real bad guy. And you'll be in even worse danger than now because I won't be there to protect you."

"What about Alex and Kick? I know for a fact they are just as serious about finding this al Sayika mole as we are. Not to mention Marc Lafayette, who killed the bastard who kidnapped me. They'll believe me if I tell them it's not you."

"Don't even think about it. Even if they do believe you, who's to say there isn't an informant inside STORM, too?"

"But—"

"No buts, Gina. I mean it. We're on our own in this. Okay?"

She reluctantly nodded. "I still think it's a mistake not to trust Alex and Kick."

Gregg drew her into his arms. "Baby, you don't stay alive working as an operator for as long as I have without following your gut instincts. And right now my instincts are telling me one thing loud and clear."

"What's that?"

"Don't trust anyone."

ALEX came to with a start. It was pitch dark, but one thing was totally obvious. He was underwater. In full dive gear.

WTF?

His body came uncoiled and his flippers and hands hit walls all around as he attempted to right himself. He was in a confined space no higher in any direction than his outstretched hand. His mind scrambled for an explanation.

Suddenly, he remembered. T*he unstable yacht. Crashing over. The vortex of water sucking them into the small storage area. Rebel panicking. No air. And then the flashback.*

His thoughts screeched to a halt. *Rebel!*

Where was she?

He did a quick roll, searching the corners of the space by touch. She wasn't there.

Jesus. What had happened to her?

He patted down his BCD, groping for the tether that had bound them together. He found the ends. Both karabiners were intact. Had she unhooked herself? Just left him there?

Not that he blamed her. He would have left himself behind, too. Because right when she'd needed him most, he'd failed her. Turned into a whimpering baby, trapped in his own pathetic mind. He'd put her life in mortal danger. Hell, she could be out there drowning, *or dead*, because of his weakness.

He grabbed for the hatch and wrenched it open. He

needed to find her. He'd tear the goddamn wreck apart if he had to.

A beam of light whipped over him as he surged through the opening. A bubbly exclamation sounded through the darkness, then the light was moving rapidly toward him until Rebel burst into view. She looked unhurt.

Thank God.

He pulled her into his arms and hugged her tight, then motioned upward for them to get the hell out of there.

She signaled for him to wait, disappeared into the gloom for a moment, then returned carrying one of the net evidence bags. It contained several file folders spilling papers. And a black velvet pouch of the kind used for precious gems. Holy fucking crap.

"Diamonds?" he mouthed.

She nodded.

He looked at her in humbled amazement.

While he'd been passed out, cowering in his own traumatized imagination, *she'd* been doing his job for him.

She grabbed the tether and snapped the free end onto her BCD. Then she led him confidently through the remains of the stateroom and up the narrow stairway to the deck, where they checked that the other two net bags were still secured to the line anchored to the *Stormy Lady* above. They added the third bag, then made the ascent up to the surface.

He'd never been so glad to see blue sky in his life.

And had never been so achingly unhappy.

Because in his heart, he knew what he had to do. He'd thought he could go back to work. He'd thought he was ready.

But he wasn't. Not by a mile. He was a danger to himself and all those around him, to those he loved, those who depended on him. It was only a matter of time before he accidentally killed someone.

He couldn't live with that. Couldn't handle being the reason someone he loved got hurt.

He had no choice.

He had to quit STORM. Along with something that was far, far worse.

He had to leave Rebel.

"SAC Montana," Sarah greeted Wade coolly in the lobby of the apartment building where Asha Mahmood had resided. It was in the Dupont Circle area of Washington, D.C. Pricey neighborhood, she mentally observed, instead of noticing how nice Wade looked in his blue suit this morning.

"Please don't let's do this, Sarah," he said when she didn't let herself smile at him. "I'm really sorry about last night. I was an idiot."

Ya think? She glanced around the building's lavishly decorated reception area, complete with security guard, and ignored Wade's surprisingly convincing attempt at a regretful demeanor. She was so over it. And him.

"Whatever you say."

"Look, Sarah, can we—" Wade began.

She was also not going to discuss her personal life in front of others.

"This must be Commander Quinn now," she interrupted, turning to the front door, where an incredibly tall, good-looking man was holding it open for a pretty woman wearing soft woolen trousers and a pastel turtleneck. The man was dressed casually in a black suit jacket over faded blue jeans, but there was no mistaking his military bearing. Quinn had said he'd have another STORM agent with him. Must be them.

"Detective McPhee, good to meet you. Bobby Lee Quinn," the man drawled in that unmistakable good-old-boy accent that was so contrary to the powerful aura of authority that surrounded him both in person and on the phone. He shook her hand. "This is my associate Tara Reeves."

They exchanged hellos while Quinn acknowledged Wade with a frown. "Didn't expect you to be here, Montana."

"Just an observer," he said. "At Detective McPhee's invitation. Just like you."

Not exactly. This morning Sarah had received a personal call from a deputy director at the Department of Homeland Security, who had politely asked her to extend every courtesy to STORM Corps in general, and Commander Quinn in particular. Politely, as in, cooperate or we'll come down on D.C. Metro with a world of hurt. STORM's investigation concerned a matter of national security, he'd said, and her case seemed to tie in with it. Score one for Quinn, zero for Montana.

Not that she was keeping score. Not after last night.

"Shall we?" She grabbed her gear, and the security guard took them up in the elevator to Mahmood's floor.

When they got to the apartment, the door stood slightly ajar.

Sarah cursed, drawing her weapon. "Everyone stay outside while I clear the place."

"No way," Wade said, pulling his automatic from under his jacket. "I'm coming in with you."

So much for being strictly an observer. She would have argued, but Quinn had already slipped through the front door with Tara Reeves covering him from behind.

"Oh, for chrissakes," Sarah muttered under her breath, held up her hand to the security guy to stay put, and hurried in after the STORM agents. Once inside, she halted in her tracks, just as they had.

The apartment was totally trashed.

Quinn and Reeves were poised just beyond the foyer, listening for intruders. After a lengthy pause, Quinn shook his head, and with military hand signals directed Wade and her to go left into the kitchen, while he and Reeves went right into the hallway that presumably led to the bedroom area.

Sarah ground her jaw. This was *her* case and *her* goddamn victim's apartment. *She* should be giving the orders here.

Yeah, good luck with that. Between Quinn and Wade, the cloud of testosterone filling the air was nearly lethal.

Though both men were striving to be professional, she got the distinct feeling there was some bad blood between them. She wondered what that was all about. A woman, perhaps? Gina Cappozi, for instance? Had they been in conflict during her rescue for some reason? Or was it more personal . . . ?

Not her business, she reminded herself, and doused the annoying spark of jealousy that appeared at the thought of Wade Montana fighting over another woman.

How stupid was that?

"Thanks for the help, Commander," she said tetchily when they'd cleared the apartment. "I can take it from here."

"Sorry," he said with a lazy grin. He shrugged. "No disrespect intended, ma'am. Sometimes the training just takes over and I forget myself."

Sure he did. However, it was only thanks to Quinn's largess she was here at all, so she smiled back. "Not a problem."

Tara Reeves pulled a video camera from her shoulder bag. "Mind if I shoot some video, Detective? Naturally we'll supply you with a copy."

"Please, go ahead," she said, grateful she wouldn't have to delay the search until a CSI could get there to do it. She figured if STORM's creds were good enough for DHS, they were good enough for D.C. Metro.

Reeves turned on the camera and they all took a moment to study the mess.

The contents of the upscale apartment were thrown everywhere: bookshelves were swept bare and the expensive-looking decorative items smashed, furniture slashed open so their stuffing poured from the gashes, cushions were ripped, drawers emptied onto the floor; even the food from the refrigerator and freezer were heaped melting and festering on the kitchen floor. In the bedroom, the mattress had been savaged and the closet emptied of clothes, which now lay scattered about in tatters. Holes had been punched in the walls.

"Jesus," Quinn said with a low whistle. "The bastards were certainly thorough."

"Wonder what they were looking for?" Tara Reeves said, slowly panning the room with the video camera for a master shot.

"Same as us, I'd wager," Wade said grimly. "Incriminating evidence."

"Whatever it was, the good news is, it doesn't look like they found it," Sarah ventured.

Wade nodded. "Or they would have stopped searching."

"Unless they weren't exactly sure *what* they were looking for," Tara suggested. "Or didn't want to inadvertently miss anything."

True. "Let's hope they *did* miss something," Sarah said, and called Lieutenant Harding to inform him of the development. He said he'd send CSI, and Jonesy, who was back on duty because his court case had been delayed.

"Metro is sending Crime Scene to check for prints and trace," she reported after hanging up. "My priority is still the murder case, but Commander Quinn, once the rooms have been videotaped, you and Miss Reeves have been okayed to do a visual search for evidence of the cousin. However, anything you find stays with Metro until I get orders otherwise."

"Understood," Quinn said. "And Montana?"

She turned reluctantly to Wade, irritated that she *still* felt an attraction to him. And it didn't help that he was acting so damn contrite. "I guess I could use an extra set of eyes, if you want to come with me."

"Thank you," he told her quietly as they gloved and booted up. "I appreciate you letting me stay."

She glanced at Quinn and Tara, who were going into the kitchen, then leveled him a look. "I keep my promises."

His mouth thinned at the unspoken rebuke. "Sarah—"

"Forget it." She turned away, but he caught her by the arm.

"Honey, your talking to Quinn yesterday took me by surprise, that's all. Being overly suspicious is an occupational hazard. Trust me, I didn't sleep a wink thinking about what a complete ass I was."

Despite herself, she half smiled. "At least we have something in common."

He stepped in closer and murmured, "But an ass who's crazy about you. Forgive me?"

She sighed, even *more* irritated that she was entertaining the notion of giving in to his dubious charm. But there you go. She wanted him. Simple as that.

However, she refused to let him off so easily. It was one thing to know she was weak, another entirely to show her weakness to others. Just look where that had gotten her in the past. "I'll think about it," she said, and took back her arm.

He got the hint. "Okay. I'll try to be patient." And they went to work.

For being so lavish, the apartment was amazingly devoid of personal items. No letters, no bills, no diary, not even a scribbled inscription in Mahmood's few books. But oh. My. God. What they *did* find was an eyebrow-raising collection of sex toys scattered amongst the ruins of the bedroom.

At least Sarah was pretty sure that's what they were. Most of the items she recognized, but some of them . . . Okay, just . . . yikes.

"A call girl?" Wade ventured.

She glanced at him. "Why do you say that?"

"Fairly standard assortment for someone in that profession," he stated, cataloging them with a practiced eye.

A bit too practiced.

"Is that so."

He looked up, realized what she was thinking, and made a face. "I worked on an international prostitution trafficking case for three years, thank you."

"Picked up some interesting educational tidbits, I take it."

"Oh, yeah." The corner of his lip flicked up. "I'll gladly teach you everything I know."

To her chagrin, her face heated. "I haven't forgiven you yet."

"Oh, you've forgiven me."

"And you know this how?"

"You keep staring at my mouth."

She jerked her gaze up. *Damn.* Her cheeks blazed hotter.

Just then Quinn poked his head into the bedroom. "Any luck in here?"

Wade kept his eyes on her as he said, "As a matter of fact"—he casually glanced away, down to a large square metal object he'd been excavating from under a pile of linen—"I found this." He gingerly lifted it up. It was a shredder. He raised the lid for them to see. It was filled with confettied paper.

Quinn walked over and peered into the container. He smiled. "Oh, yeah. Touchdown, baby."

"What?" Sarah asked, following the two of them into the kitchen, where Wade set the machine on the table.

"Some of the strips of paper are badly wrinkled," Quinn explained as he reached into his inside jacket pocket and brought out a square leather case. "Which means the thing jams. Maybe we'll get lucky."

The case contained a dozen shiny metal tools, like a cat burglar's kit. Two minutes later, Quinn had the machine taken apart. With two latex-gloved fingers he extracted a torn quarter page of paper that had gotten stuck between the blades. He grinned triumphantly at it, then handed it to her.

"I'll be damned," she murmured, giving the paper a quick study. Her eyes halted in mid-scan. "It appears you were right about the connection with the cousin."

"What is it?" Wade asked, looking over her shoulder.

"It's a printout of a statement from an online bank account—in the names of both Asha and Ouda Mahmood."

Tara made a noise over Sarah's other shoulder. "The balance is over seven hundred thousand dollars!"

Sarah slid the paper into a plastic protective folder and passed it over to Quinn, who said, "The statement is dated six months ago."

"Six months?" Tara repeated.

Wade snapped to attention. "That's during the time Gina was being held hostage."

"Too bad the rest of it's gone," Tara said, pursing her lips.

Wade flipped out his phone. "Read me the account number. I'll have the Bureau subpoena the bank records."

Sarah shook her head. "FBI's not involved in this case, remember?" she reminded him. "Not unless I request their help."

"Damn it, Sarah!" he said and angrily snapped the phone closed again. "Then fucking request it!" He quickly added, "*Please.*"

"You really want some other FBI agent looking up your ass on this?" Quinn interjected.

Wade did not look pleased at the reminder that his presence was anything but official. He glared at Quinn, then backed down. "Point taken."

"I understand you're anxious for answers," Sarah said to him, breaking the tension and reaching into her pocket for her cell phone. "I can just as easily—"

Commander Quinn put a hand on her arm. "As it turns out, you have no jurisdiction."

She frowned. "What?"

"This is a foreign bank," he pointed out. "Cayman Islands. Let me make a call. I have a friend there. And I'll be happy to share."

She got the distinct feeling it didn't matter what she said, he'd make that call anyway. She might as well see the results. "All right. Have them e-mail me the account records, if you can get them."

"I can get them."

Meanwhile, Tara had been studying the bank statement through the protective plastic. A scowl suddenly swept across her face. "Look at this!"

"What?" Quinn asked.

She pointed to a line on the statement. "This check was made out to an American political campaign." Tara looked ready to spit nails. "Twenty-five thousand dollars' worth!"

"That'll buy you a bit of influence inside the beltway," Sarah said disgustedly.

Tara glanced at Quinn. "And you'll never guess whose campaign fund."

Quinn had gone deadly still. "Whose?"

"The Committee to Reelect Lester Altos. The congressman from *Louisiana*."

At that, Wade's eyes flashed wide. But just as quickly,

his face went completely blank. If Sarah hadn't been looking right at him, she'd have missed it.

Hmmm. What was going on *there*? "And that's significant why?"

Quinn turned to her, his voice cold as steel. "Louisiana is where the al Sayika terrorists maintained their sleeper cell. It's where they held Dr. Cappozi for three months, and tested the bioweapon they forced her to perfect."

What he was hinting at hit Sarah like a blow. My God! A *congressman*? No, she must have misunderstood. "So, what exactly are you saying . . . ?"

"I'm saying it's one hell of a coincidence, don't you think? And I do not like coincidences. Not one little bit."

FOURTEEN

GINA snuggled into the buttery leather seat of the Mercedes Roadster that Gregg had somehow acquired—she'd deliberately not asked how—and wrapped the cashmere sweater he'd bought for her more tightly around her midriff. It was a gorgeous magenta color and looked beautiful with the soft gray skirt and black leather knee boots he'd gotten to go with it. Not to mention the silver necklace and earrings that matched the heart anklet he'd given her. The man had wonderful taste.

"Gotta learn about style when you live undercover," he'd said, looking embarrassed when she'd told him so. "Can't get the details wrong."

"I s'ppose not," she agreed.

"Besides," he'd added, reaching over from the driver's seat to touch her thigh, "I like you in that color."

And she knew why. She owned a set of sexy lingerie in nearly the exact same shade. They'd been his favorite, back before . . .

Once again, involuntary memories of her captivity shivered through her. Would they never stop? She gripped the armrest with white knuckles, fending off her thoughts. The painful images always hit her at the most inappropriate, random moments, and she was never prepared for the onslaught. She hated it.

Gregg's fingers tightened on her thigh. "You okay?"

"Yeah." She turned to gaze at the passing landscape.

They were traveling south on I-95, making the four-hour trip to Washington, D.C. She could scarcely believe in two short days she had changed her mind so thoroughly about Gregg that she had stood silently by as he called the kid next door to take care of Penny the cat—apparently a standing arrangement between them—and come willingly along on this crazy D.C. expedition. Had offered to help him in his search for a traitor who was starting to seem more phantom than real. She prayed she'd made the right decision to trust him.

"Tell me your plan," she said, turning back to him.

He glanced at her from checking the rearview mirror. If her question surprised him, he didn't show it. "I was able to persuade Frank Blair to give me contact information for his Pentagon source. I'll start there. Meet with the guy. See what he has to say."

"Blair?" Alarm zinged up her spine. "But it could be a trap!"

"Which is why you're staying at the hotel. In case something goes wrong."

"And if it does, what am I supposed to do? Call the D.C. police?"

"Hell, no." He moved his hand from her thigh to the steering wheel. "You hightail it back up to Haven Oaks Sanatorium and lock yourself in until you hear from me, or until the traitor is exposed."

She frowned in vague surprise. "But STORM runs Haven Oaks. I thought you didn't trust them."

"I don't trust *any*one. But the security at Haven Oaks is good. You'll be safer there than anywhere else."

She pondered that for a moment. "But *you* got inside."

"Baby, I could get into Fort Knox if I wanted to. But Haven Oaks will do fine to protect you. I've decided the man we're looking for is probably not a professional operator. He's most likely a damn paper-pusher."

That seemed a leap. "How do you figure?"

"Because al Sayika is doing all the dirty work. They're running him, not the other way around. He's a coward. Just sitting back and reaping the rewards of his treachery."

"You think he's doing this for money? The blood diamonds everyone keeps talking about?"

"Let's hope so. Because if he's betraying his own country out of some twisted moral conviction, it's a whole other ball game."

She thought about that, and about everything she'd suffered at the hands of her captors. If it was all because of simple greed . . .

Emotions she'd kept carefully locked away for months suddenly cracked loose and a bone-deep fury swept through her, bubbling and roiling in her chest. It had been easier when she'd thought Gregg was the villain. She'd been able to focus all her negative energy on him. But now, the rage grew inside her, like an ugly, festering cancer, wanting to explode.

"We'll get him," Gregg said, bringing her fingers to his lips. "I swear to you, Gina. We'll get the bastard."

"That's not enough," she said with a hatred that went deep, to her very soul. "I want him dead."

"That can be arranged," he said evenly.

And she knew he would.

Despite her hatred, a chill went up the back of her scalp. "I don't know how can you do this," she said. "Be involved in such terrible things, with such brutal people, day after day, year after year."

He kissed her fingers again, then let them go, his gaze on the road ahead. "Someone has to."

"But why you? What makes you want to do it?"

He let out a long sigh. "You don't want to know."

Except she did. She wanted to know everything about him. What made him tick. Why he could be the way he was and still attract her, inside and out, as no other man ever had.

"Something happened to you," she said, and watched his handsome face cloud over to a grim blank. "Maybe when you were a child . . ." She remembered his statement about being thrown into a foreign prison. "Or maybe you were imprisoned somewhere awful?"

"Gina, leave it alone."

"No," she said. "You're asking me to trust you. I deserve the same trust from you." His mouth thinned, but he still didn't say anything. "I just want to understand you, Gregg."

He shifted in the driver's seat, stretching out his arms and gripping the steering wheel rigidly. "There's nothing to understand," he said, his voice gritty with long-suppressed anger. "I'm fucked up because my mom made me hide in the closet while my father beat her. I tried helping her once and he put me in the hospital. When I was five she died, and we moved. Dad found another woman, then another. I tried to warn them." He shrugged, but unconvincingly. "I finally took off."

Jesus. "How old were you?"

"Ten."

"My God, who took care of you? Did you have relatives?"

He just looked at her, then back at the road. "I got by okay," he said. He uncurled his fingers from the steering wheel and stretched them out. "A couple years later I got hired on as a farmhand up in Indiana. The place was owned by a Vietnam special forces vet. He told me stories, taught me how to hunt, and take care of myself. When he lost the farm, I figured the military was as good a place to be as any. He forged me papers and I joined up."

"Oh, Gregg, I'm so sorry. No child should have to go through that."

"Don't be. I'm fine."

His advice earlier about not blaming oneself for others' actions echoed in her mind. He *wasn't* fine. Who would be? But now she understood his need for complete control—because he'd had none as a child and awful things had happened as a result. She also understood his need for justice from the dark forces of the world who inflicted evil on the innocent.

Her heart went out to him completely.

At first sight, Gina had fallen in love with Gregg van Halen because of his physical beauty and his sexy demeanor. She'd fallen even harder when she'd experienced his edgy, exciting lovemaking. But it went so much deeper than that. Even back then, she'd sensed a vulnerable soul within the man that he worked hard to keep well hidden from everyone around him. But he had responded to her love with a mirrored need and a loyalty that had taken her breath away. They still did.

She leaned across the center console and placed a tender kiss on his cheek. "You're a good man, Gregg."

She wanted to show him there was someone in the world he could always count on being there for him. She would love him, and listen to him, and let him save her.

Then maybe he would stop blaming himself for not being able to save the others.

"I need to talk to you," Alex told Bobby Lee Quinn as soon as he stepped aboard the *Stormy Lady* from the small speedboat the STORM commander had arrived on.

Quinn's eyebrows hiked. "Okay. But I have some pretty important information to relay and I don't have a lot of time. So make it quick."

"Not a problem," Alex said, folding his arms over his chest. "I quit."

Quinn's brows shot even higher. At the same time, a soft gasp sounded behind them. Alex turned to see Rebel standing there, her expression bleeding hurt and disbelief. "What are you talking about?" she asked, her voice cracking.

Fuck. She was supposed to be below making coffee. He hadn't wanted her to hear he was leaving. Not yet.

Cowardly? Yeah, so what else was new?

"You can't quit," Quinn said, yanking him back to the conversation. "You're in the middle of an op."

"All the more reason," Alex returned. "I'm having flashbacks. Screaming, black-outing, striking-out-at-anything-that-moves flashbacks. I'm a danger to myself and everyone around me."

Quinn dropped a duffel bag to the deck. "I'll be the judge of that, Zane." He turned and smiled at Rebel. "Special Agent Haywood. Hope my man here has been treating you well. Is that coffee I smell?"

Alex winced as she jerked her gaze away from him. "Yes," she said to Quinn. "Please, come below and have some."

"Thank you, ma'am. Believe I will."

Down in the small salon, Alex bit his tongue until they'd gathered around the table. It was shaped like a horseshoe booth at a diner. Quinn slid in first, and Alex took the spot opposite while Rebel brought out some sandwiches she'd made and poured mugs of coffee. She then sat down next to Quinn. Her expression told Alex the choice of seats had not been accidental.

"I'm serious about quitting," he persisted despite the

shitstorm coming from the other side of the table, and told Quinn in detail about the diving incident this morning, as well as the episode in the car while on surveillance. "I'm unreliable," he said. "Hell, I'm just plain dangerous."

"I hear you," Quinn said, and turned toward Rebel. "What's your opinion, Agent Haywood?"

She'd been toying with her sandwich the whole time Alex was speaking. She didn't look up. "Zane's right," she shocked him by saying. "He shouldn't be allowed in a position where he could hurt someone."

Inwardly, he sighed. Hell, she was not talking about flashbacks, *that* was for damn sure. Probably even Quinn knew that, judging by his narrowed eyes as his gaze slashed from one to the other.

"All right," the commander said briskly. "Here's what's going to happen. I discovered some things this morning about—" Just then his cell phone rang. He plucked it from his pocket. "Quinn."

Alex waited impatiently for the conversation to end. It didn't take long. Mostly Quinn just listened and cursed repeatedly under his breath, shooting apologetic glances at Rebel each time. Alex wanted to strangle the man for his fucking good manners. Jesus. Southerners!

Finally Quinn hung up, motioned for Rebel to exit the booth, and scooted after her. He grabbed his sandwich on the way out. "Gibran Allawi Bakreen, your suspect from the yacht? He was just murdered in the D.C. hospital where he was being treated for his gunshot wound. We're oscar mike, people."

"Wait!" Alex protested the order. "Damn it, Quinn, I—"

"Murdered how, sir?" Rebel interrupted, passing the commander a Ziploc bag for his sandwich.

"Someone swapped his antibiotic IV drip for a lethal dose of tranquilizers." Quinn took the stairs up to the deck two at a time. "You can damn well forget about quitting," he said over his shoulder as Alex followed. "Aside from anything else, you signed a contract and have a legal obligation to STORM Corps. I'll put you with Darcy on tech if you want out of the field."

"But—"

"And if you feel unable to fulfill *any* duties, Mr. Zane, report the hell back to Haven Oaks and let the psychs finish their job."

"Jesus, that's not—"

"Fuck, man, there isn't an operator I know doesn't have flashbacks. We have options now. Deal with it." Quinn shot him a backward glare. "And here's a piece of free, hard-earned advice. Relationship distractions are far more lethal in this business than anything the enemy can throw at us. Get your dick screwed on right, Zane, and do it now."

Alex's mouth dropped open. He had no response for that. *Je*sus. Was it all so freaking obvious?

Rebel made a choking noise.

"Sorry 'bout the French, ma'am," Quinn said.

She had turned bright red, but soldiered on. "About the evidence we found on the *Allah's Paradise*, sir. Should I send it to Quantico for analysis?"

Quinn shook his head. "Because of the time factor, DHS has authorized STORM to process whatever we find." He paused as he straddled the ladder down to his speedboat. "Since despite everything, y'all were able to conduct a fairly extensive search of *Allah's Paradise* today, I'm going to turn the rest of the search over to the Coast Guard. I want you both up in D.C. immediately," he instructed them. "I'll send the jet back for you."

"Me, too?" Rebel asked in surprise.

Alex's stomach knotted in consternation. Fucking *great*.

The fucking *last* place on earth he wanted Rebel anywhere near was fucking Washington, D.C.

"I still need an FBI liaison," Quinn said, making Alex's

head nearly explode. *Shit.* "Tara's setting up our D.C. headquarters as we speak," Quinn continued. "Pack the collected evidence with care and bring it with you, okay?"

"What about the diamonds we found?"

"Those, too."

Alex's mind was too busy planning the untimely and permanent disappearance of Wade Montana to respond, so Rebel said, "All right, sir."

Quinn grunted, grabbed his duffel bag, and was gone. Seconds later a fantail of water sprayed over them as he gunned the speedboat and headed back toward the distant skyline of Norfolk.

Alex let out an angry, pent-up breath. "Bastard," he growled, debating inwardly whether he meant Quinn or Montana. It was a toss-up.

Wordlessly, Rebel turned on a toe, stalked back to the ladder, and disappeared below. He darted his gaze after her. And rewound back to their present issue.

Fuck.

Fuck, fuck, *fuck.*

"Rebel!" he called, hurrying in pursuit. "Hey! My quitting has nothing to do with you . . . with us. I'm worried, is all. I don't want anything to happen to you because I'm not right in the head."

"Too late," she shot back, striding into their small stateroom and yanking her overnight bag out of the mini-closet.

Ouch.

He halted at the door and watched her furiously pack her things, warring with himself over what to do about it. If he had half a brain, he'd just let her go. For her own good. He should let her stay mad at him. Break off this doomed affair right here and now.

How did he ever think he could just sleep with her and not want more? And yet, more was impossible. He knew that as viscerally as he knew his own glaring deficiencies.

No woman as vibrant and alive as Rebel would want a man who could only disappoint her. Painful as it was, he should just let her go. That was the honorable thing to do. Even if it hurt her now. In the long run, a clean break was best. For them both.

Swallowing down the need to explain all that, ruthlessly suppressing the need to hold her one last time, he forced himself to turn away from her, and went back up on deck.

Throwing out the buoys to mark the wreck of the *Allah's Paradise* felt all too depressingly like marking the abandoned wreck of his own heart. Hell, of his whole damned life.

Christ. Things had been so much easier with Helena. Straightforward. Unemotional. No pain. No indecision.

Of course, he hadn't been in love with Helena.

Blackness swamped over his mood. Obviously that was a *good* thing. Maybe he should call Helena and beg her to take him back. Plead with her to reconsider, and solve both their problems for good—as was their original plan. *That* would put an end to this agony of hurt once and for all.

Along with any chance ever to make things right with Rebel. Which was an even better thing.

It *was.*

He turned over the engine and started the boat forward with a lurch.

Call Helena. Yeah. That should solve *all* his problems.

Sure it would.

FIFTEEN

"YOU called *Helena*?" Rebel could hear the disbelief and pain in her own voice. She'd thought her heart couldn't hurt any more than when Alex had announced to Quinn this morning he wanted to quit the mission. But, wow. Seriously?

Yeah. She'd seen right through *that* one. It hadn't been the mission he'd wanted to quit. It was *her*. And if there'd been any doubt in her mind before now, this announcement proved it.

And she'd *slept* with him, the two-faced, deceiving jerk. She'd actually started fantasizing that he really cared for her! That he wanted to be with her—if not forever, then at least for more than a single night.

How could she have *been* such a fool?

During the whole trip returning the *Stormy Lady* to the marina, she'd been so angry she hadn't exchanged more than five words with him. In Norfolk they'd split up, he checking in with the Coast Guard detail that was to take over the search of the sunken yacht, and she checking in with her boss to make sure her absence was authorized. Unfortunately, it was. Once they got to D.C., she was supposed to go to the hotel where STORM had set up headquarters, then join Commander Quinn at Walter Reed Army Medical Center to help investigate the murder of Gibran Bakreen, the suspect from *Allah's Paradise*. Before going to the airport, she'd also stopped by her apartment for some different clothes to bring along. She was now dressed in a subdued but elegant slate-blue business suit and heels.

She carried an overnight bag, which Alex insisted on taking from her as they stood waiting for the private STORM jet Quinn had sent back to fetch them to taxi up to the gate. That's when, straight-backed, eyes front, duffel over his shoulder, Alex had calmly sprung it on her that he'd spoken with his ex-fiancée.

The morning after they'd made love for the first time ever.

She wanted to kick him with her pointed shoe. Hard. Where it counted.

"I was just returning her call," he said, still without looking at her.

Oh. And that made it *so* much better. "I see."

Not.

Rebel fumed as they climbed up the steep stairs to the door of the jet when it opened. The wind whipped through her hair and she had to hold her skirt down so she didn't pull a complete Marilyn Monroe. Naturally, he was five steps below her, looking up. But his sense of self-preservation was well-honed enough at least to pretend not to notice.

She had never been on a private jet before, and for a moment she halted on the threshold in awe. The STORM Hawker eight-seat jet was the epitome of pure masculine luxury. Decorated in the company's black and silver signature colors against a fuselage of storm-cloud gray, the main cabin seats were full-swivel recliners in soft leather, complete with footrests, an abundance of suede pillows, and warm fur throws. It even smelled masculine; a low note of sandalwood scented the air. She looked longingly as she walked past an oversized sofa that turned into a bed. Not that there was time for a nap. It was a short flight, just over half an hour.

She and Alex were the only passengers. Wonderful.

After takeoff, the cute stew poured them glasses of French champagne and set out a delicious spread of cheese and crackers on the low walnut coffee table between their two seats.

Too bad Rebel was in no mood to enjoy any of it.

All she wanted to do was close her eyes, drink herself into oblivion, and forget about the man sitting across from her.

She proceeded to try.

But apparently he had different plans. Yep. The one time in the history of the *planet* when a man actually wanted to talk, and of course it just *had* to be this man. And only now, after the damage had already been done.

She *so* did not want to hear about his phone call to his ex-fiancée. Or anything else he had to say. Not after this morning.

However, as soon as the attendant disappeared up front with the pilot, he continued his announcement. "Helena wanted to know how we're getting along," he stated.

Sure, she did. So, how had the other woman found out they'd been together to begin with? And why would she care? Unless . . .

Rebel tapped a sharp tattoo on her champagne glass with a fingernail. "What did you tell her?"

He must have picked up on her inner cynicism. "Not that we're fucking," he ground out, "if that's what you're worried about."

Her foot actually twitched.

"*Lang*uage, Zane," she gritted out before taking a big sip of champagne and saying, "Well, that's good, because we're *not*."

"Not what?" he asked, feigning not to understand.

She gave him a death-ray glare. He didn't flinch. Probably didn't even notice. He was too busy examining the untouched Gouda.

"She also wanted to apologize for leaving me at the altar," he added.

"Better late than never," Rebel drawled.

He sighed. "Helena's not a bad person. She just has . . . pressures."

So generous of him to forgive her. "I'm sure you'll be very happy together."

"Angel, we're not—"

"And *enough* with the angel stuff, Zane. You got what you wanted from me. Now please allow me the dignity of not continuing with that whole 'you saved my life in captivity' naked dream farce. I can't be*lieve* I ever fell for that story."

"It's the truth," he said, hurt that she'd think he lied about something so viscerally and elementally real. Or that he'd used those awful memories to . . . what? Seduce her? "And you obviously have no fucking idea what I want, Rebel. *That's* a damn fact."

"Oh?" She turned away from him. "And what could that possibly be?" she spat out. "Because I think you've made it *very* clear what you want. And it's not me. Except to—" Her knuckles blanched white around the stem of her glass.

He snapped his mouth shut. Regrouped. "Listen, I know you're angry with me—"

"Ya think?" she muttered, taking another gulp of champagne and setting down her glass with a loud *clink*. "No, actually, I'm mystified, Alex. Tell me. Why *did* you sleep with me, if you're just going back to her? I really don't understand."

"I'm *not* going back to her," he insisted.

Like she believed that. He *still* wouldn't look at her.

"What. Ever."

"Actually, she's been trying to call and tell you something important, but you won't answer, and you won't call her back." He drained his flute and set it aside. "Boy, does *that* sound familiar."

She snorted. "Yeah, *you're* the wounded parties here."

He sighed again, leaned forward in his seat, and took her hand between his. She *so* wanted to pull it away, but he brushed his lips over her knuckles and she couldn't make herself do it. The pain in her heart needed soothing too badly.

He studied her fingers intently. "I know you're hurting. But please, let me explain. It's not what you think."

No, she was pretty sure it was. But did she really want to know? "Is this going to make things better or worse?" she asked. Already guessing the answer from his posture.

"Honestly? I have no idea," he said, and kissed her hand again. He finally looked up, his gaze filled with misery. "But it's something I've been wanting to tell you for years."

Years? Her distrust slowly deflated as last night's shocking revelation from him arced through her mind. She took a giant mental step back.

Okay. She wasn't being fair. He had to be feeling vulnerable, too.

What could possibly make a man feel worse than not being able to have children? She was still too stunned herself to think rationally about all the implications. She could only imagine what he must have felt. Must still be feeling.

She really didn't want to deal with anything else right

now. Certainly not if it was just one more reason they couldn't be together. But he seemed determined to tell her.

She braced herself for yet another blow. "All right. What is it?"

For a moment he gathered his thoughts. "It's about Helena," he said. "She finally gave me permission to share this with you. But you have to swear not to tell a soul. Especially not her parents."

Rebel blinked. Okay. This was not what she'd expected. She'd expected something about his job. That he'd killed people. Or about the torture he'd endured. Maybe even some awful, fatal disease, God forbid. But . . . "Helena? What about her?"

"Swear you won't tell."

"Yes. I promise."

He took a deep breath. Let it out. "Helena's gay."

Wait. *What?* Astonishment whooshed through her. "Ex*cuse* me?"

"Yeah. Your friend, my ex-fiancée, is a lesbian."

As soon as he said it, a wave of relief flooded across his face. It seemed as though a huge weight had suddenly lifted from his broad shoulders.

Rebel just stared at him in disbelief. "Really?" Not that it would normally be any big deal. But . . .

"Really. And thank *God* it's all out in the open now. Well. Between the three of us, anyway. You can't imagine how good it feels to finally tell you," he said. "I've been pleading with her for years."

"She's *gay*?" she repeated, filled with bewildered incomprehension. This was *crazy*.

"Technically, lesbian," he confirmed with a nod.

A million questions burst through her mind. But one stood out clearly above all others. She cut to the chase. "Alex. If you've known that all this time, why on *earth* would you want to *marry* her?"

How would he even contemplate something like that? What could possibly be his explanation?

The whine of the jet engines pitched higher, filling several long moments. She could relate.

At length he said, "Baby, I get that this might be hard for you to understand."

An understatement if ever she'd heard one. She fought not to feel even more hurt by this than she already felt about everything else this man had heaped on her over the past twenty-four hours. Make that the past several years.

"Believe me, at the time, it seemed like an ideal solution," he said. "For both me and Helena. Me with my overly dangerous job, and my . . . physical inadequacies. Helena with her ridiculously conservative parents and their unbending social expectations for her. Marrying each other would let her keep her family . . . and it would keep me from wanting one."

Taken aback, Rebel reeled as though he'd struck her physically.

His eyes softened, his expression filling with remorse. Then he said the one thing that turned her world completely upside down. "And it would also keep me out of your bed."

GINA and Gregg checked into the Watergate Hotel. The property had a great view of the Potomac and was fairly close to the Pentagon. Despite a recent major renovation, the place felt familiar to Gina. And safe. She'd stayed there on the few occasions she'd come to D.C. for a conference or a government funding interview and her ex-fiancé, Wade, had been off on assignment or a case. But she'd always been on an expense account before. Her eyes popped when she saw the nightly rate on the bill.

"Don't worry about it," Gregg said when she suggested

staying somewhere cheaper. "I want to stay. I like the irony. Of the name," he added when she shot him a startled look. She definitely hadn't pegged Gregg as the political type.

She remembered learning about the infamous old scandal when President Nixon's henchmen had broken into his opponent's Watergate campaign headquarters disguised as maintenance men. "Okay," she said with a chuckle. "But from which point of view? The victims or the plumbers?"

He just winked, requested a suite on the top floor, and signed in as Mr. and Mrs. G. Gordon Paisley. She rolled her eyes. Like they hadn't seen *that* before.

The view from the private balcony was indeed magnificent, and opulent didn't begin to describe the room itself. Marble floors, antique furniture, deep feather canopy bed, spa tub. It even had a fifteen-bottle wine cooler, fully stocked. Naturally.

She turned back from the French doors and let her gaze travel over the luxurious appointments to where Gregg was bending over the minibar checking imported beer labels. He was dressed in black, as was his habit. Snug black T-shirt, low-slung black leather pants, black boots. He'd taken off his black leather motorcycle jacket—the one with the silver chains looped artistically across the front—and slung it on the sofa. Therefore she couldn't miss the black shoulder holster strapped across his broad back with his platinum SIG Sauer tucked under his arm.

He always wore the SIG. She'd seen him with it a hundred times before, if not in its holster then stuck into the front of his waistband where he could always reach it. But for some reason, a shiver now ran down her spine at the sight of the powerful weapon . . . which she knew could just as easily turn on her as protect her.

And suddenly once again she wondered, *was she wrong about him*? What if his remorse was false? What if all those feelings she was experiencing about him were just her needing someone, *anyone*, to protect her? What if the drowningly good sex between them had blinded her—for the second time—to his intent? If he were innocent, shouldn't he have signed the Watergate register as a permutation of the *good* guys rather than the infamous plumbers? Had he made her trust him, spun lies about his childhood, only to lower her defenses and lure her here to another big, anonymous city, away from her home and her STORM bodyguards, far from where anyone was searching for her, in order to—

No. She had to stop thinking like this. He *was* on her side. They *were* after the same thing: to find the traitor who had betrayed them both, so they could get on with it and go back to their normal lives.

Whatever normal was.

"Gina?"

She started badly.

He was watching her closely. "Something wrong?"

She banished the chill from her heart. "No. I'm okay. I just . . ." She shook her head again. "No, it's nothing. So. What do we do now?"

He glanced at his watch. "It's one-thirty. I need to set up a few things, then I want to pay a call on our Pentagon guy."

"What about me?"

He came over and enfolded her in his arms. After a brief hesitation he said, "Damn, girl. You're tense as an itchy trigger finger. Why don't you order up some room service, light some candles, and take a nice relaxing bath?"

Right. Like she could ever relax again. "Why can't I come with you?"

"We already talked about this, sweet thing. I need to know you're safe. That means here. In this room. Talking to no one."

She nibbled on her lip, and made herself ask the simple

question that would tell her if she really should fear him, or if her unease was only the PTSD talking. "Gregg?"

"Yeah, babe."

"What happens afterward?" Her heart thudded painfully against her chest. *Did she really want to know?* Did she really want to admit to herself that she had fallen in love with him completely? Let alone admit it to him . . . "What happens after it's all over?"

His body stiffened almost imperceptibly. "How do you mean?"

"With us. You and me. After we catch the traitor." Her pulse sped when he didn't answer right away. She told herself it didn't matter.

"Gina . . ." He slowly let out a taut breath. "You know what I am. What I do. There's no way you want to be with a man like me. If that's what you're getting at."

Her heart pounded erratically. "You don't love me? Not at all?"

His fingers dug into her arms, then eased up. "Sweetheart, if I ever knew what love is, I've forgotten a long time ago. And I've got no interest in remembering. I'm sorry."

Her chest squeezed. "So you don't want me."

"God, I didn't say that." He wrapped his hand around her jaw and lifted her face to his, drilling her with a look so intense it made her insides quiver. "Woman, I want you like crazy. And I hope like hell you want me, too, and that whenever I'm INCONUS you'll let me come to you."

It was the right answer . . . in the sense that she believed what he was saying. Her jittery recurring paranoia about him was just that. She was safe with him, just as he kept saying. Just as her heart knew.

So why was that same heart crying out that he'd given her exactly the *wrong* answer?

Why did she suddenly feel devastated inside?

Yes, she loved him. At least she thought she did. But

surely, *surely*, she didn't want him to love her back? This man, this macho, controlling, emotionally unavailable mess of a man who was everything any sane woman would avoid? Okay, she needed him right now, needed his warm, safe body next to her at night. Craved the blissful moments of forgetfulness she found in his arms. Even appreciated the fleeting seconds of terror when he became rough, only to remember and force himself to be gentle with her, so she was slowly learning once more to trust a man's sexual aggression.

But what would happen when the bad guys were caught and she no longer needed his physical presence in the same way? Could she be with a man like Gregg for the long term, one who could take a life without blinking? How could she reconcile her deep-seated beliefs as a doctor with what he did for a living? And how could she ever look at him without being deluged with memories of the worst days of her life?

Would she still love him then? Or was he right, and once the danger had passed she would see him for what he truly was, and being with each other would just be a painful reminder . . . ?

There was only one way to know for sure.

"Okay," she said, taking a cleansing breath. "INCONUS. That works for me."

For now.

Gregg searched her eyes and his fingers tightened on her jaw for a millisecond.

"Good," he said, then dropped his hand and stepped away. "I better go. Lock the door after me and don't answer it for anyone."

Gina swallowed. Tried not to let the panic take her. She'd be fine. It wasn't like this was the first time she'd been left alone. And Gregg would be back soon. He would. He'd promised.

"What about that room service?" she asked him.

After a brief hesitation, he bent and pulled a small Beretta from his ankle holster. "Take this. Put your robe on and keep it hidden in the pocket. Aim it at the waiter the entire time he's here and do not hesitate to shoot if he acts the least bit wonky."

Her lips parted on a small quiver of fright. "I suddenly don't think I'm hungry anymore."

"You need to eat, Gina. It's okay. No one knows we're here in D.C. Just stay alert and keep that gun in your hand."

Like an unruly weed, the quiver flared fast and out of control. She reached for him, scared. "Please don't go."

He gave her a reassuring squeeze. "I have to. But swear to me you won't leave the room."

"I won't," she said, breathing deeply to reign in the irrational panic. "I promise."

He kissed her. "I'll be back as soon as I can." Then he let her go and strode out the door. "Lock it," he called sternly from the other side.

She jerked herself out of her immobility and slid the dead bolt home, putting the flats of her palms to the cold wooden panels as she listened for his receding footsteps. She heard nothing. But when she put her eye to the peephole, he was gone.

"Oh, God," she whispered, turned, and leaned her back against the door for support. "Please help me be strong."

She stood like that for a full minute before mustering herself and fetching the fluffy robe from the closet. She put it on and slipped the Beretta into the pocket as Gregg had instructed. Her stomach growled, reminding her she hadn't eaten since early this morning.

She ordered lunch and when it came she held the gun tightly in her pocket while a bellman with a name tag that read "Raj" set the meal out on a small table and chatted away in a Bollywood accent, oblivious to her tension. He ended by holding up a bottle of champagne with a flourish.

"Compliments of the management," Raj said with a bow.

If she hadn't stayed there before, she would instantly have been suspicious, but she knew the gift was de rigueur. The hotel was generous with its top-floor guests. "Thank you," she said, and managed to tip him without shooting either of them in the knee.

As soon as he was gone, she put the gun aside on the sideboard with a shiver. She'd carried a knife but that was different. Less . . . random. A knife was all about the person, where a gun was all about the killing. And despite recent evidence to the contrary, she knew her bloodthirsty craving for revenge was not who she really was. Before she was kidnapped, she'd never in a million years have thought about taking a life. She was a doctor. She *saved* lives. Wanting to kill her attacker the other day weighed heavily on her mind. That she'd very nearly done it . . . well, it was a side of herself that horrified her. The fact that she'd thought it was Gregg, that she'd deliberately set out to see him dead, horrified her even more. What if she'd actually succeeded? She'd have killed the very man trying to protect her. The thought was so horrendous she didn't even want to contemplate it.

He was right about one thing: what she needed was a warm, relaxing bath surrounded by scented candles. She went in and turned on the waterfall tap, which poured into the deep, luxurious spa tub, and started to take off her clothes. At the last minute she remembered the champagne, and went back out to fetch it.

But the ice in the bucket had melted. *Damn.* In the steamy sauna of the bathroom, the wine would soon be warm. Nothing worse than warm champagne. She needed more ice. She stared in indecision at the bucket.

Gregg's warning rang in her ears as clearly as if he were there: *Don't leave the room.*

But the ice machine was just a quick jog down the hall. She'd be there and back in thirty seconds. What could possibly happen?

She turned off the water in the tub, grabbed her room key and the ice bucket. Cautiously, she opened the entry door, and peeked out. The coast was clear. Not a sound could be heard. Not a soul in sight.

She slipped out of the room. And ran for the ice machine.

SIXTEEN

THE STORM jet landed in Washington, D.C., and Rebel exited the plane in a mental fog. Hurt still cascaded through her every few seconds, despite her best attempts to stop it. To stop herself from thinking about why Alex would want to avoid her so badly he'd marry a woman he could never be with. But she couldn't.

They climbed into the waiting limo while the chauffeur loaded their bags into the trunk. Giving her her space, Alex kept up a staccato conversation with the man for the short drive to the hotel where Tara Reeves had set up the STORM operation headquarters.

But as they were about to get out of the limo, Rebel could no longer hold the question inside. "Why?" she asked him. Her voice came out small, like when she was a little girl and a mean uncle had told her the Easter Bunny didn't really leave the chocolate eggs in the bright pink basket by her door each year. "Didn't you want me? You had to know how I felt—" She turned away from him again. "Oh, no. I've made a huge mistake . . ."

"Rebel. Ah, angel. Come here."

He reached for her, but she backed away. She couldn't let him touch her. If he did, she might break down completely. Without waiting for an answer, she shoved open the limo door and almost threw herself out of the vehicle. Straightening her spine, she strode quickly to the hotel reception desk, where they checked in.

As soon as they were alone and the elevator doors closed on them, he dropped their bags and grasped her arms. "Baby, you have to know from the moment I met you, I wanted you crazy bad. Day and night I thought about you, and what it would be like to hold you. *That's* why I agreed to Helena's proposal."

Her jaw dropped. "You can't be serious."

The elevator dinged at the top floor and the doors whooshed open. She swooped out ahead of him. She could not deal with this.

She heard him hurry after her, saying her name.

Nearby, the sound of an ice machine drowned out the unhappy chaos of her thoughts.

She halted, and whirled to face him. "Alex. That makes no sense!"

"It does," he insisted. "Because I knew damn well you wanted children and a normal husband who comes home to you every night. One who shares your life in all ways. I could never give you that. I still can't. Not any part of it."

At that passionate declaration, her heart shattered in her chest. Because she knew it was true. She spun back around and blindly walked down the hallway. She glanced at the key card in her shaking hand to check her room number, but it swam out of focus.

Which is why she didn't see the woman come out of the alcove with her filled ice bucket. Lost in her own roiling emotions, Rebel ran right into her. She gasped, taken by complete surprise.

Ice flew everywhere, ricocheting off the walls and the metal of the ice machine like gunshots. The sound shattered through her thoughts, hurtling her back to reality with a crash.

Instantly, Alex whipped out his weapon and pointed it at the woman. "Stay where you are! Don't move!"

Falling backward into the alcove, the frightened woman scrabbled frantically at her robe, groping for the pockets. Long black hair tumbled over her shoulders, hiding her face.

"Wait!" Rebel exclaimed, grasping Alex's arm. The woman wasn't a threat—she was obviously terrified that they meant to harm *her*.

Seeing the gun, the other woman gave a desperate cry and started to lunge at Alex's chest with her bare fists. "No! I won't let you—"

"Stop!" he commanded, raising his weapon to fire.

"Alex, *no*!" Rebel cried, and shoved his arm to one side.

"Hey!"

The woman slammed into Alex, knocking them both down to the plush carpet. Black hair flew in a flurry as she struggled to get away from him.

"It's okay! We're not going to hurt you!" Rebel assured her loudly, trying to figure out how to stop them without being drawn into the brawl herself. "I promise!"

The woman came to an abrupt halt and looked up, her gaze going from Rebel to Alex and back again. Her eyes widened and she let out a stuttering gasp. "Oh, G-God. A-Alex? R-*Rebel*?"

Sweet goodnight. Disbelief and recognition slammed

into her in equal measures. It wasn't possible . . . But oh, lord! It *was*!

"*Gina?* Is that you?"

DR. Stroud's welcoming smile almost made up for the fact that Sarah was standing in her least favorite spot on earth: the autopsy room.

"Come on in. What a nice surprise!"

Twice in two days. Yikes. A record. One she hoped never to repeat.

"Hello, Dr. Stroud." At his admonishing mock frown, she amended, "Johnny."

"What's up? Lieutenant on the warpath again?"

Sarah laughed nervously, trying to block out the nauseating smell of death and disinfectant. "Not this time. Just came by for the autopsy report on Asha Mahmood." Stroud had left a phone message, but she wanted the whole file. You never knew what it would inadvertently reveal. Thus forcing her to brave her personal nightmare yet again. "Sorry, I got busy yesterday and couldn't return your call." She glanced at the sheet-covered body on the table and swallowed down a lump of queasiness. "That yesterday's vic?"

"Yep." Stroud grinned sympathetically. "But I'm afraid you've missed all the exciting stuff."

"I'm crushed." She tried not to appear too elated. "But I thought the autopsy wasn't until later this afternoon."

"Inexplicably, I find myself ahead of schedule. Must be the anticipation."

The good doctor appeared almost giddy. "Of?" she dutifully prompted, angling away from the remains.

"This," he said proudly, "is my last day as an assistant. Landed myself a new job. Full-fledged medical examiner for the island of Kauai."

"*Hawaii?* Wow." She was impressed. "Damn. I'm jealous. How did you manage that coup?"

"My razor-sharp intelligence and charming personality, of course." The boyish grin widened as he snapped the collar of his lab coat artfully. "And my impeccable style."

She chuckled, but it faded into consternation as she realized— "Hell. That means another new assistant M.E. here." She gave a genuine sigh. "Just when you were getting nicely broken in. Any idea who your replacement will be?"

"No clue. Don't worry, I'll brief them that you're one of the good guys."

"You'd better." She tipped her head at the body on the table. "Speaking of which, if this one's done, do you have a cause of death?"

"Yep. Report's right here; Asha Mahmood's, too." As Stroud walked over to his desk and picked up the files, he asked, "Find out who he is yet?"

"Yeah." She accepted the files and flipped open the top one. "Prints came back to a Raul Chavez. Limo driver. And you'll never guess who his last pickup was." She scanned the autopsy report. Her heartbeat kicked up. "Okay, maybe you would."

"Asha Mahmood."

"Bingo. Mahmood was smothered and Chavez drowned, but it seems they both had an identical dose of Rohypnol in their blood, administered before death."

"Coincidence?"

"I hardly think so. What are the odds they were killed at the same time by the same person?"

"Pretty good, I'd say. TOD fits."

Excitement swirled through her. She couldn't wait to grab a cup of coffee and compare the rest of the two files, then get onto nailing down a solid connection. "Okay, then." She gratefully headed for the door. "Anything else I should know?"

Stroud perched on the corner of his desk, so impossibly young and handsome, and so full of life and possibilities that it almost hurt to look at him. "Just that I'll miss you."

She paused at the door. "I'll miss you, too, Johnny. You take care."

"Kauai. Standing invitation."

"Thanks, Doc. And thanks for the reports." She saluted him with the files and exchanged a warm smile. Damn. She really would miss him.

Feeling a bit wistful . . . and far too old . . . she made her way to the parking lot.

And there, leaning his tight backside against her plainclothes sedan, blue eyes glittering with a whole different kind of anticipation, was the perfect antidote to her blues.

One thing about the man, he was flatteringly persistent.

"Hi," Wade said.

"Hi," she answered, walking up to him.

"Forgive me yet?" he asked, running an impudent finger down her throat.

A trill of desire sang through her breasts. "Maybe."

With no further invitation, he slid his hand around the back of her neck and pulled her mouth to his. For about two nanoseconds she thought about protesting. Then his tongue slid past her lips and she gave up the notion entirely.

He drew her closer. Angled his mouth tighter. A moan eased through her. *Lord*, he tasted good.

"When do you get off?" he murmured between kisses.

Please, God, sometime tonight.

Oops. She pulled away. Cleared her throat. "Um." She retrieved her lost wits. "I may be late. Things are starting to come together on the Mahmood case."

He was watching her lips as she talked. It made them tingle. "Yeah?" But before she could say more, he leaned in and kissed her again. *Damn*.

"Mmm." How could she resist? But she must. She finally turned her head aside, but didn't step back.

He sighed. "Okay. I get the hint. How's the case coming together?"

"The vic from yesterday . . ." She told him what she'd learned from Dr. Stroud. It felt a little strange talking business to an FBI agent with her head on his shoulder and his arms around her . . . but not in a bad way. She could get used to it.

"What's your theory?" he asked. "How does this tie in with Gina's kidnapping, do you suppose?"

"Not sure. I want to compare the autopsies a bit closer. Do a background on the limo driver. Interview his family and co-workers. See if he's involved with the terrorists or just an innocent bystander."

"His name suggests the latter."

"But the Rohypnol suggests the former. There are faster ways of killing bystanders than drowning."

"An accident? He drank something intended for Mahmood?"

"It's possible." But she doubted it. "Maybe I should call Quinn. Get his take."

Wade's muscles stiffened at the mention of the STORM commander. "Don't want mine?"

"Of course I want your opinion, Wade. This isn't a competition. I just want to solve the case."

He relaxed marginally. "I know. There I go again. Sorry."

"Anyway." She stepped out of his arms. "Want to help me go over the autopsy reports? I'm dying for a cup of coffee."

"Sure." He reached for her hand and tugged her back to him. "So. What about later?"

Her breasts zinged again. The man was *so* damn tempting when he was trying to seduce her. "Dinner?"

His lips crooked. "And after that?"

The rest of her zinged. “A movie?”

“You’re killing me here.” She smiled and stepped away again. He held up his hands. “I know, I know. I deserve a sound rejection.”

“You do.” She headed around to the driver’s side of her sedan. “But I did enjoy the kiss.”

“I want you,” he called after her.

There was something irresistibly sexy in the bold challenge of his declaration. Something that made her want to throw aside all her reservations and accept. After all, she’d been thinking the same thing ever since the first time she’d heard his sexy voice over the phone.

“I know,” she said with a smile as he swung open his vehicle’s door. “Follow me?”

“For now.” He pointed a finger at her over the BMW’s roof. “But I’m giving you fair warning.”

“Of what, SAC Montana?”

He sent her a bone-shivering, half-lidded look. “My bed, Detective McPhee. Naked. Tonight.”

WELL, *that* was a complete waste of time.

Gregg stepped up onto a city bus along with a clutch of Pentagon commuters and took a seat on the aisle. As usual, he’d deliberately chosen a bus going in the wrong direction from where he really wanted to go.

Disguising his frustration, he raised the copy of the *Washington Post* he’d grabbed at a newsstand, slid on the pair of thick, black-framed glasses he’d bought earlier at a thrift store in Arlington along with a briefcase and the nondescript brown suit and loafers he was wearing, and pretended to read without a care in the world.

He’d picked up a tail, of course.

No big shock there. After the meeting he’d just left with Frank Blair’s Pentagon contact, he would have been insulted *not* to have acquired one. It would have meant the bad guys didn't take Gregg seriously. As it was, the presence of his tail confirmed three things: 1) the Pentagon guy's involvement in treason on some level, however peripheral or unaware, therefore, 2) that Blair had been telling the truth—about this, anyway, and 3) that either Gregg's credentials when they were scanned or the Pentagon computer files they'd just pulled up during the meeting were being monitored for activity—by someone other than Tommy Cantor, his inside man. Yeah. *Everyone who thinks it's the bad guys doing the watching, raise your hand.*

Okay. So maybe not a *total* waste of time.

However, one thing was pretty clear: Pentagon Guy was not the head honcho traitor. He'd been far too forthcoming. After Gregg had shown him his CIA Zero Unit credentials—which Tommy had managed to keep active on the pretext of tracking the movements of a dangerous rogue operator—and explained he was just fact-checking a report on a completed mission, Blair's contact had willingly logged into the archive database and opened the "person of interest" file on Gina Cappozi and shown Gregg what was in it. Which, shock of shocks, was practically nothing. Other than the fact that the written order to bring her in to ZU-NE last August to identify Rainie Martin's body had *not* originated in the Pentagon. In fact, a search revealed that the archives did not contain a file on Rainie Martin. Not even a mention. Blair's contact had insisted defensively he'd just sent the order on to Zero Unit. He didn't know who they'd come down from. Only that the paperwork had followed regulations and the protocols were correct. Gregg believed the officious twit.

On a hunch, he'd asked if there was a file on Kick Jackson. One came up, all right. With sizeable bandwidth. But it was flagged for level one, passworded clearance—

which neither Gregg nor the other man was authorized to access. Same thing for Alex Zane's file.

The existence of the files was not terribly surprising, given the men's profession. But level one clearance required to view them? *That* was interesting. What was so top secret about what they did for ZU? It could be legit and completely unrelated to the al Sayika connection. Of necessity, military intelligence files on Zero Unit operators tended to be thin and vague—which made these large files unusual. Unusual enough that even Pentagon Guy commented. Though his explanation was that Zane and Jackson must be involved in a critical, long-term ZU op. Gregg knew that wasn't true. They'd both resigned from the unit months ago. He figured those files being pass-coded was far less benign than some op.

And he noticed one other detail as their headers flashed past. *The flag codes for files were the same as the source code listed on the orders to bring in Gina to Zero Unit headquarters.*

Hell yeah, he'd memorized it. Not that it would do him any good. Without the password, Gregg had zero chance of finding out where the written orders and file lock-downs originated—which might have led him straight to the traitor. Unfortunately, computer hacking—especially the goddamn *Pentagon* system—was so far out of Gregg's wheelhouse he had a better chance of being elected President.

He'd just have to find a different way to get the source of those codes.

Which brought him back to his present tail.

The guy was a typical jarhead dressed in khaki who would have blended in perfectly except he kept letting his eyes flick over to Gregg every time he moved his newspaper. *Rookie.*

Gregg briefly considered luring the dimwit into a trap

and forcing him to spill who he was working for. But that would be a useless exercise, without doubt. The jarhead wouldn't know any more than Pentagon Guy had about who was behind his orders. The al Sayika mole was smart. A classic man-behind-the-curtain, pulling strings from afar, with none of his puppets being any the wiser.

Except Gregg.

His cell phone rang. He was surprised to see it was Tommy. "Yeah."

"You've got company."

"No shit," Gregg drawled. Then frowned. "Wait. Where are you?" As far as he knew, Tommy was still up at ZU-NE, not in D.C. He glanced around.

"I meant company at the hotel."

Ah. Gregg came to attention. His first thought was of Gina. "What's going on?"

"Raj called." Raj was the Watergate bellman he'd paid handsomely to keep an eye on the room and Gina, and to call Tommy with hourly updates on who checked into the hotel and who was hanging around that shouldn't be. Tommy continued, "Raj said last night someone booked three doubles and a suite on the top floor. An hour ago, four people and a bunch of equipment arrived."

Gregg let out a curse. "STORM?"

"Judging by the descriptions."

Stunned by the obvious implication, Gregg cursed again and hung up. *Fucking hell.*

The little bitch had sold him out.

He felt gutshot. She'd said she *believed* him. Had sworn she trusted him. He'd put his fucking life in her hands by leaving her alone with a phone and no restraints. But god-*damn* it, as soon as his back was turned, she'd gone running straight back to her so-called protectors. The ones who'd almost gotten her killed. Why did women never, ever, listen to him?

Barely containing his anger, Gregg got up at the Crystal City stop and stalked off the bus. Too late, he remembered his tail. *Fuck.* He needed to get his head back in the game. Leading the man a few blocks, he ducked behind a building and as soon as Mr. Jarhead rounded the corner, he jammed his SIG into the side of the man's neck.

"Get lost," he growled. "Or I'll paint the wall with your brains."

His tail wisely turned and ran.

One problem solved.

Now, what to do about the other, more pressing matter?

He rode the Metro across the river to D.C. and got off at Foggy Bottom. No sense disguising his movements any longer. He was already blown seven ways from Sunday.

He could, of course, bail on the whole damned situation. Disappear into the shadows somewhere in the world and never be heard from again. There were a million places where he could go to ground. He knew how to do it, and he'd stashed enough money in various numbered accounts around the globe that he could live comfortably without working another day for the rest of his life. More than comfortably.

The thing that stopped him was, what would he *do* for the rest of his life?

Without his job he had nothing. He *was* nothing. Gregg van Halen was a shadow, a chameleon, a ghostlike entity moving unseen through the darkest elements of humanity, tasked with luring out evil from where it lay festering and spreading, and eliminating it. Without that single–minded purpose driving him, he would simply be absorbed into his solitary existence and disappear to nothingness. In his world, when a tree fell in the forest, it had never really been there.

Last year, for a few brief weeks, he thought he'd found something more to live for. A reason to try and loosen up on the strict control that had ruled his dark environs for as long as he could remember. A reason to expose himself to the light and linger in the sunshine, for a while at least. A reason to listen to his heart, for once, and let himself feel those emotions so long denied.

Gina.

She was everything he'd ever dreamed of finding. Sweetness. Light. Love. And everything he knew he couldn't keep. *Shouldn't* keep. Because of who he was and what he did. But he'd wanted her so badly. He'd been captivated by her inner strength and her amazing loyalty, by her dizzying sensuality and her sweet submission to his raw ways.

But he should have listened to himself. Not let himself be swayed by fickle, fleeting emotions, or by false feelings of tenderness. Not let himself dream of the impossible.

She had just proven he'd been absolutely right not to trust any of those things. Not to trust *her*. He needed to step back into the shadows where he belonged. He needed to return to his true purpose.

But to do that, he needed to clear his name and get his job back.

Which meant he had to go to the Watergate and somehow try to convince the STORM operators who were hunting him that he was not the traitor they sought. That they should trust him to find out who it really was.

And he needed to look Gina Cappozi in the eye and tell her that if she could do this to him, he was finished being her protector. Through being her lover.

And done being her fool.

SEVENTEEN

BY the time Gregg had ridden up in the Watergate elevator without seeing a single guard or lookout, he figured he knew what was coming.

What the hell. It wasn't the first time he'd walked into the middle of a nest of vipers.

Before exiting at the top floor, he pulled out the SIG and chambered a round in case things got really nasty, then tucked it in the front of his waistband. If you got shoved to the ground on your face, you had a lot better chance of getting to your weapon there than at the small of your back.

Too bad he'd given up the Beretta to the woman. That would teach him.

He walked nonchalantly down the hallway, resisting the temptation to wave to the surveillance camera—just to keep them guessing. At the suite he inserted his key card. The lock snicked green. He took a deep breath, pushed open the door, and stepped into the brightly lit marble foyer.

To his mild surprise he wasn't jumped, or slammed against a wall. Or the floor. In his peripheral vision, he saw Alex Zane standing with his arms crossed like a bouncer on one side of the foyer, and mirroring him on the other was the female FBI agent who'd sat with Gina for hours up at Haven Oaks after her rescue. Though, they'd rarely talked about business. Mostly it was personal stuff. He'd learned more about the two women's love lives than any man had a right to know. And way too much information about how Gina felt about him and his betrayal . . . Maybe now he could return the favor.

When he took another step in, the two melted behind him and shut the door, boxing him in. They were both packing weapons, but neither made a move for them. Well, well. This might actually be civilized.

Straight ahead, the man he recognized as Bobby Lee Quinn, the STORM team leader for Gina's rescue last December, lounged casually in one of the sitting room's leather wing chairs, facing him. His fingers toyed with a bucket of ice sitting on a side table. Gregg put his hands on his hips and just stood there.

Bobby Lee Quinn cocked an eyebrow. "No fight?"

Gregg shrugged. "What's the point? I'm outnumbered."

Quinn puffed out a laugh. "Like that would stop you."

"I could ask the same thing," he pointed out. "I expected major bruises and handcuffs. At the very least, a little saber rattling."

It was Quinn's turn to shrug. "We could do that if you prefer."

Gregg strolled in, tossed the briefcase containing his other clothes onto the sofa, and quickly scanned the sitting room. No one else visible. But the door to the bedroom was closed. Reinforcements? Or Gina? "Or," he said, "you could go fuck yourself."

Quinn's eyes narrowed. Zane took two steps out of the

foyer toward him, and the woman clamped a restraining hand onto his shoulder, then dropped it as soon as Zane glanced at her. Instead of meeting the other man's gaze, she stared unblinkingly at the SIG in Gregg's waistband. He could almost taste the tension arcing between her and Zane. Trouble in the ranks?

Gregg flopped down on the sofa, slung an arm across the back of it, and propped his feet up on the coffee table. Then he pulled the SIG.

Instantly their two automatics were aimed at him. He ignored them. "Let's get one thing straight," he said. "I'm not giving myself up here. And believe me, there's no way in hell I'm going anywhere with any of you. Not without somebody getting real dead real fast. So you may as well listen to what I have to say."

Quinn's expression didn't change. "Don't bother," he returned. "Dr. Cappozi has already given us the whole spiel. You're innocent. *Blah, blah, blah*. Personally, I think she's suffering from PTSD delusions. But she's the *only* reason you're still breathing. So how 'bout I talk and *you* listen."

"Where is she?" Gregg was unable to stop himself from asking. Not that he actually gave a flying fuck.

"She's safe," Quinn said. His jaw flexed. "What happened in New York won't happen again."

"That's for *damn* sure," Gregg muttered. Next time he wouldn't be around to save her ass.

"I suggest you listen carefully. This is how it's going to work," Quinn said. "You're going to answer our questions and tell us everything we want to know, starting with who you just met with and what you talked about. Then we're going to put you under guard while we check out your story. And after that we're going to take a vote. If you pass, you live."

Gregg snorted. An empty threat and they both knew it. Even if they didn't believe him, STORM wouldn't be authorized to execute him. Both CIA and DHS would want to interrogate him before anything like that happened. He was more worried about the traitor piling up additional evidence against him in the meantime, so he wouldn't get the chance to prove himself before being carted off to Siberia or Mogadishu. The best way to prevent that, and to get his job back, was to cooperate. And pray like hell STORM wasn't compromised.

"Fine," he acceded. Besides, at this point he had fuck all to lose. "I just have one condition."

"What's that?" Quinn asked.

"Gina Cappozi," he said. "Two minutes with her. Alone."

"I say we waste the bastard while we still can."

Rarely had Rebel seen Alex in such a foul mood. He didn't want to be here, that was pretty obvious. She wasn't exactly sure if it was because of her presence, or that of his former Zero Unit compatriot, Gregg van Halen. Alex obviously didn't care for the guy. He was convinced van Halen was working for al Sayika, and had killed Dez Johnson yesterday in the attack on Gina. No amount of explanation or pleading by the unhappy Dr. Cappozi that Greg was being framed would persuade him otherwise. The fact that van Halen's own story corroborated everything Gina said, and also matched the forensic evidence from the scene, made no difference.

Alex was out for blood.

Projecting? Just a little, Rebel thought. The violent suggestion was just his raw emotions talking. Not that she exactly blamed him. Not for this, anyway. The man really had suffered at the hands of these terrorists. And if she thought there was a chance van Halen was working for them, she'd be just as hostile to him as Alex. However, she didn't.

"I thought you wanted justice," she responded. "Not retribution."

"In this case they're one and the same," he shot back, undaunted. "Van Halen's guilty as hell. Someone should pay for what happened to Gina and Dez."

And you, she silently added. And Kick, and Tara. And all the others who'd been so badly hurt by these barbaric terrorists. "But we have to be sure it's the *right* person," she argued. "I for one am not convinced Gregg's the traitor."

"Me, neither," interjected Tara, from where she stood at the open French doors to the balcony sipping a Coke. Behind her, the sun was setting over the Potomac, casting a reddish glow over her winter-white turtleneck like a transparent superhero cape. She still looked thin and fragile from her month-long hospital stay after nearly dying during the Louisiana op. If anyone had reason to want retribution, it was Tara. That she also doubted van Halen's guilt spoke volumes, in Rebel's opinion.

"No one's wasting anyone," Commander Quinn stated flatly.

"Then let's turn the fucker over to DHS and let *them* deal with him," Alex said emphatically. "We found him. Our job here's done."

"I'm not so sure," Quinn said. "Have to admit, his story has the ring of truth to it."

"Jesus! Not you, too! Secret codes and government conspiracy for fuck's sake? Come *on*!"

"It's not that far-fetched," Tara said quietly. Tara's mother had died of cancer due to an EPA cover-up of a toxic chemical leak back in the days when the government turned a blind eye to such things. Oh, wait. They still did.

"She's right," Rebel said. "We owe it to their victims to find out the truth."

"Not to mention all the future victims of whatever al

Sayika is planning for Washington, D.C., if we don't stop them," Quinn reminded them. "Gotta say, van Halen looked genuinely outraged when we questioned him about that."

Alex scowled. "What was he supposed to say? 'Oh, yeah, I forgot to tell you about the nuclear trigger I helped smuggle into the country?' Bad guys lie, Quinn. It's what they do."

"I can usually tell when a man's lying to me," Quinn returned evenly. "In any case, we're not making any decisions until Kick, Marc, and Darcy arrive later tonight. We need everyone's input before acting on this. It's too important."

"But DHS—"

"Has already made up its mind. It would take them months to process and clear him. If van Halen's story checks out, we need him free and working with us now, immediately."

"*Working* with us? Are you fucking nuts?" Alex exclaimed.

With a dismissive sigh, the commander turned to Rebel. "Special Agent Haywood—" Quinn began.

"Rebel, please."

He inclined his head. "Okay, Rebel. Our murder investigation of the *Allah's Paradise* suspect has been left hanging long enough. The D.C. Metro police have the lead on this, but I'd like you to get down to Walter Reed and see what you can dig up for us."

She eased out a silent breath of relief. There was nothing she wanted more than to escape Alex's bad mood and stubborn insistence on ignoring her completely—unless he was snapping at her, of course. Which seemed to be his new way of dealing with the hurt he'd caused her. Yeah, *that* made sense.

"Yes, sir," she said.

"And take Zane with you," Quinn added, jerking a thumb in his direction. "He needs cooling down."

Whoa, wait. "But, sir," she protested. "I really—"

"That's an order. And don't come back until you both can be in the same room without wanting to strangle each other." He Frisbee'd a key card to Alex. "Your room's three doors down. I suggest you use it. Otherwise I'll call SAC Montana to come take her off your hands."

Alex's face actually turned purple. He started to sputter.

Quinn rose to his feet and all six-foot-four of him leaned over the table and drilled them both with a meaningful glare. "But first find out who murdered Gibran Bakreen and how they managed it. I'll expect a report in two hours. Now get the hell out of here."

Rebel exhaled sharply, turned, and headed for the door. She didn't wait to see if Alex followed. To paraphrase her childhood idol, frankly, she didn't give a sweet goodnight.

Okay, she did. Quinn was right. If she was never in the same room with Alex Zane again it would be too soon. Well. At least until she'd sorted through the dizzying array of gutting revelations he'd sprung on her since last night. And *that* might take a lifetime of therapy.

She'd made it halfway down the hall before he caught up with her.

"Why don't you follow Quinn's advice and use that room key right now?" she strongly suggested. "I can do the investigation myself. I don't need your—"

"No."

"Seriously? Take the out, Alex. You've made it pretty clear you don't want to work with me. Or anything else with me, for that matter."

"You're wrong."

"Oh? Let's see. What part of 'I want to quit the mission' didn't I understand correctly?"

"I keep telling you. It's because my flashbacks put you in danger. But we're going to a hospital. I think you'll be okay."

A derisive snort escaped. Yeah, she'd be okay. *When she saw his backside for the last time and got over him completely*. Like maybe in, say, oh, *never*.

She slapped her forehead. "Your flashbacks. Right. Yeah, *they* made you want to marry a lesbian rather than be with me."

He swore, and all at once he grabbed her arm from behind. He spun her, slamming her up against a door so hard it rattled. Instinctively, she blocked him with a self-defense move and jerked her knee up to hit him where it would hurt the most. But he'd been working out every day for eight months and he was too fast and far too strong for her. He pinned her to the door.

Her pulse skyrocketed, unsure if he'd suddenly plunged into one of his violent flashbacks and would unconsciously hurt her.

But he didn't move. Just held her there, suspended, her feet scrabbling for purchase two inches above the floor. A moment ticked by. One high heel toppled to the floor. Followed by the other.

"Fuck you," he said. "*Fuck* you."

"Right back at you mister," she retorted furiously.

And then he kissed her. Hard. Savagely. Giving her no quarter to resist.

She struggled, fighting her own desires as much as she wanted to fight him. But she couldn't. Her heart just wouldn't stop wanting him. So with a final halfhearted punch to his shoulder, she caved.

She opened to him, moaning her surrender. She slid her hands up the defined muscles of his biceps and wrapped her arms around his neck.

"Ah, Rebel," he groaned, low and rough. "Angel."

There was a click, and the door behind her suddenly swung open. He held her trapped against him and surged into the room, shoving her up to the wall inside. He kicked the door shut behind them with a *bang*.

Then his lips softened. His hands went from overpowering to persuasive. "Baby, God, it was *always* you I wanted. Always."

Tears filled her eyes. *This was so unfair*. "Liar!"

"I'll show you if you don't believe me."

Her bare feet hit the carpet as his hands drove up under her skirt. In one powerful motion, he ripped off her panties. She gasped, and instantly his tongue swept into her mouth, cutting off the sound. His belt rattled. A second later she was lifted up again. His powerful grip splayed her thighs apart. He kissed her like a man on fire.

The hot, blunt tip of him pushed up against her swollen flesh. She was slick with want and in an agony of need. For one potent, pregnant instant, his eyes met hers.

"*Yes,*" she answered the question burning in them.

And then he was in her. Thrusting up inside her to the very hilt.

She cried out and he captured her moan with his kiss, holding on to her, grinding into her, swallowing her up with his powerful body like she would disappear entirely. She *wanted* to disappear entirely. Wanted to belong to this man so utterly, so completely, there would be no way to separate them ever again.

Tears blinded her, because she knew very well he was taking her in wounded frustration, not because he wanted those same things. But she'd take it. She'd take *him*. For now. Because she was hurt and frustrated, too.

He drove into her. Again and again. Mindless oblivion took over, and forgetting everything else, she gave herself over to the raw physical pleasure of the act. He was rough, he was demanding. He was giving and fulfilling. Most of all, he was *hers*.

For now.

Climax burst over them like a train wreck, sudden, unexpected, total annihilation of the mind and senses.

And when it was over, he leaned heavily into her, against the wall, so neither of them would collapse onto the floor. But it was a near thing.

"Jesus, Rebel," Alex groaned. "Jesus fuck."

She didn't have the energy to admonish his language. But that's when it hit her what she'd done. Add one more layer to the annihilation of her heart. Why did she keep *doing* this to herself?

She swallowed a half sob and dashed at the moisture that trickled onto her cheeks.

He pulled back to look at her. "Are you crying?"

"No." She turned her face away but couldn't disguise the tears in her voice.

"Angel, there's no crying in sex. Unless— God, did I hurt you?"

Men could be so incredibly clueless. "No," she ground out and pushed at his chest. But he was still inside her. He didn't budge.

"Baby . . ." He caught her face in his hand and covered her mouth with his, kissing her deeply. Intensely. But by the end, almost . . . bleakly.

"My beautiful angel," he whispered when he finally lifted his lips. The words were a soft lament. The mood had shifted.

Pain squeezed her heart even as echoes of pleasure pulsed through her center and the taste of him saturated her mouth.

"I don't be*lieve* it. You really are leaving me, aren't you?"

"I'm sorry," he said. "I'm so fucking sorry."

"Why, Alex? Why are you doing this to me?" she asked, nearly suffocating with anguished confusion.

He looked away. "I'm a selfish bastard, Rebel. I had no fucking business touching you. The flashback reminded me of that. That I needed to let you go before . . ."

"Before what?"

He took a deep breath. "Before I couldn't do it. I don't want to give you up." He slid out of her, leaving her cold and empty inside. "But I have to."

She stared at him, a numbing disbelief settling over her. "Surely not *Helena*?"

He closed his eyes and shook his head. "No. That insanity is over. She met someone a while ago, and—" He cursed. "It was such a boneheaded idea to begin with. Why I ever thought it would solve anything . . ."

She let go of his shoulders, where she'd been clinging to him. Gently, he let her slide down the wall to touch the floor, then stepped backward, away from her. Her suit skirt fell back into place. Like nothing had ever happened.

His eyes were shadowed, full of pain. He shut them, blocking her from reading his emotions. "I need to just walk away from you. Face the truth and be a man about it."

"*What* truth?" she asked. "What is this really about, Alex? And I swear if you say it's your stupid job I'll shoot you myself!"

"But it is!" He glanced away, then back. "Partly, anyway. Do you not remember I almost killed you this morning?"

"That wasn't your fault."

"It wouldn't make you any less dead." He shook his head. "Besides, I know you, Rebel. Don't forget, you were my best friend for five years. I *know* what kind of life, what kind of future you want. The kind of man you want. And I'm not it."

Her heart went out to him. "Don't say that. You'll get better. How can you even *think* that? You're all I've *ever* wanted!"

He grasped her by the upper arms, his fingers digging into her flesh. "No, that's not true. And what about a family? Tell me truthfully that you don't want my children just as much as you want me. Go ahead. Tell me, Rebel."

Her lips parted but no words would come out. She couldn't tell him what wasn't true. Because she *did* want his children. Desperately.

"You see? I'm right."

"Maybe there's something they can do about it," she quickly said. "Have you seen a doctor? There've been so many advances in medicine—"

He dropped her arms and his beautiful mouth set itself in a cruel parody of a smile. "There. That's what I mean. It's been less than twenty-four hours and already you're trying to change reality. Imagine how you'll feel in ten years when your biological clock is running out and you finally realize it's not going to happen?"

They stared at each other for a long moment, each coming to the most painful conclusion possible.

"I am what I am, angel. Nothing's going to change that part of me."

"But—"

"No buts." He ran his fingertips over her cheek. "That look in your eyes is exactly the reason I can't stay. Watching that love and hope turn to hate and sorrow will kill me. I can't do it. And you shouldn't have to. You *don't* have to."

She felt sick to her stomach. He pressed a deliberate kiss to her forehead.

"Forget about me, Rebel. Find someone else who can give you that beautiful life you want. Hell, go back to Montana. Even he'd be a better choice than me."

Then he opened the door and waited for her to go out. She was too shell-shocked to protest. Shell-shocked, because she had just learned an ugly truth about herself: he could well be right about her. She didn't want to think so. But she was just uncertain enough about the depth of her desire, that the painful future he foresaw could happen, that she swallowed her fervent denials and walked out of the room without another word.

And *that* was the worst truth of all.

EIGHTEEN

SARAH got a call from Lieutenant Harding to join him at Walter Reed Army Medical Center just as she and Wade had ordered coffee at a nearby Cosi, and spread out Asha Mahmood's and Raul Chavez's autopsy files on a table way in the back.

"Damn," she muttered. "I have to go. The murder of a suspect in federal custody this morning at Walter Reed seems to be linked to the Mahmood case."

Wade glanced up sharply. "You mean Gibran Allawi Bakreen?"

"You know about the case?"

"Suspected terrorist, believed connected to al Sayika. Possibly to Gina's kidnapping. He was shot while being arrested yesterday during a joint FBI/Coast Guard/DHS operation in Norfolk. Somehow he got sent to the army hospital when his wound reopened during transport to his interrogation here in D.C. It's a freaking jurisdictional nightmare."

She rolled her eyes and started to gather up the files.

"So they called in D.C. Metro in order to keep the peace between the alphabets?"

He grimaced. "Something like that. You getting assigned to it?"

"God, I hope not. Right now the lieutenant just needs to know what I've learned about Mahmood. Want to tag along?" She smiled. "Since the Bureau's part of the nightmare, and all."

He looked torn. "Hell, you know I shouldn't be seen with you."

She winked. "So wait five minutes before walking in."

"Devious." His body brushed intimately against hers as they rose. He kissed her ear and whispered, "I knew there was a reason I like you so much."

When they got to the hospital, they split up.

"I'm going to stop by security," he said. "See what I can find out there."

Sarah went up to the third floor, where the lieutenant was waiting for her. Walking into the ward reception area, she ran into a tangle of arguing G-men with every possible three-letter combination emblazoned on hats and Windbreakers. Good grief.

She held up her creds to a Metro officer checking them, and elbowed her way to the lieutenant, who was speaking to a willowy redhead in a slate blue suit nodding and taking notes. Directly behind the woman a seriously tall, grim-faced, blond man stood with his arms crossed, his eyes traveling the room like he wanted to kill something. He saw Sarah approach and his body rippled to alertness. The woman looked like a feeb. He didn't.

"Ah. Here she is now," Lieutenant Harding said, raising a hand to beckon Sarah into the conversation. "Detective McPhee, this is Special Agent Haywood, FBI. I was just filling her in on the Asha Mahmood case."

Sarah shook hands with the other woman, waiting for

an introduction to the man behind her. When none was given, she tipped her head toward him. "And he is?"

"Not here," Agent Haywood said crisply, and continued to ignore the man.

Instead of objecting, he just sized Sarah up, apparently decided she was harmless, and went back to scanning the waiting room like a wolf looking for prey.

Ho-kay, then.

"What would you like to know?" she asked Haywood.

"What have you got?" the FBI agent answered with a smile, pen poised.

At the LT's nod, Sarah gave her a rundown on all the relevant information, omitting sources in case she needed a bargaining chip later. But she omitted nothing important—this was terrorists they were talking about, right here on American soil.

When she got to the part about Raul Chavez and the autopsy results, Special Agent Haywood glanced up, startled, then wrote like crazy. Even Mr. Wolf looked Sarah's way and frowned.

"Have you established a definite connection between my two murders and this one?" Sarah asked.

"This is the first I've heard of your second victim. But we believe—" She halted in mid-sentence, looking over Sarah's shoulder. Her eyes widened slightly and twin banners of red streaked across her cheeks.

The wolf's blue eyes cut like lasers in the same direction, practically singeing the air with their intensity. His muscles bunched as though he were getting ready to pounce and rip something to shreds.

Curiosity firmly captured, Sarah turned to see what unlucky soul was about to become mincemeat. She blinked.

It was *Wade*.

Halfway through the room he had stopped in mid-stride, visibly taken aback.

She blinked again. Wow. No history *here* or anything.

She debated whether to be jealous or not. Decided against it. The wolf looked jealous enough for both of them.

Special Agent Haywood recovered first. She turned to Lieutenant Harding. "Did you request the D.C. field office?" she asked.

"No," he assured her. "I thought Norfolk was handling this case."

"You?" she asked Sarah.

"Don't look at me," Sarah said. Well, she *hadn't* called them.

Wade walked up. "Hello, Rebel."

"What's going on, Wade? Has something happened?" Agent Haywood asked him.

"Didn't know you were in town," he said pleasantly enough, but his tight lips betrayed him. "You should have called."

The banners intensified. "We just got in a few hours ago. Sorry. I've been busy."

"So I see." He glanced to the wolf. Nodded stiffly. "Zane." *Zane, huh?* Wade ignored the rabid-dog looks the other man gave him, and said to Sarah, "Detective McPhee, good to see you again."

She was grateful he was playing it professional and distant. No way was she getting dragged into *this* dogfight. Nor did she want her boss to witness any possible fallout.

"SAC Montana," she acknowledged, then observed neutrally to her boss, "Gee, Lieutenant, you'd never know D.C. Metro was lead on this case. Seems to be some confusion."

Harding grunted, then looked around as though seeing the chaos for the first time. "Damn straight. Time I did something about it, too." He strode off, bristling.

"You'll have to teach me how to do that someday," Special Agent Haywood mumbled. She sketched a mystical half circle in the air with her fingers, and said, "Those aren't the droids you want," in a Jedi voice, then flashed Rebel a wry smile.

Sarah chuckled and decided she liked the pretty redhead, despite the male posturing going on over her.

But as soon as the lieutenant was gone, Wade's demeanor changed on a dime. He turned angrily on Zane. "What the hell is STORM doing in D.C.?" he demanded. "Why aren't you out looking for Gina Cappozi?"

STORM? Sarah did a double-take at Zane. *Ah.* That explained it.

"Because we've found her," Zane shot back with equal force.

"What?"

"Keep your voices down," Agent Haywood admonished the men sharply. People around them were starting to stare.

"Is she all right? Why wasn't I informed?" Wade ground out.

Zane got in his face. "Because *you* have no goddamn business—"

"Shut *up*, Alex," Special Agent Haywood said. "You, too, Wade." She turned to Sarah apologetically. "Sorry, Detective McPhee. I think maybe I'd better take these boys outside."

"Uh, sure," she said.

Agent Haywood started to herd the two men toward the stairs, then turned back to her. "Do you have a card? So I can get in touch with you later?"

Sarah produced one. "Call anytime."

The other woman tucked it into her jacket pocket. "Thanks. I'll be in touch." Then she hurried after Wade and Zane, who were moving through the crowd like two beasts stalking each other.

"Yeah. Good luck," Sarah mumbled after her.

What the hell was *that* all about?

Like she had to ask. Nothing got men's competitive hackles up faster than a beautiful woman.

Maybe *this* was the relationship Wade had mentioned. The one after Gina that hadn't worked out. She could certainly see the stunning Agent Haywood with him. But no, he'd said it was some congressman's wife. Still. There was definitely something going on between them. And where did the feral Mr. Zane fit into the picture?

Ah, well. Not her concern.

She felt a pang of regret. Obviously the whole *my bed, naked* thing with Wade was not happening. Yet again. Which was just as well. SAC Montana was smart, successful, and sexy as all get-out, but the man came with hidden baggage that seemed to catapult out of nowhere with surprising regularity. No doubt it was a stroke of luck that something always stopped her just before making that irreversible decision to jump into bed with him.

Though he *was* an amazing kisser. She could only imagine what he'd be like in—

Forget it, Sarah. That was just not meant to be.

"McPhee!"

Lieutenant Harding was summoning her from the nurses' station. She put all thoughts of Wade and kissing and getting naked from her mind. Anyhow, tonight she'd be otherwise occupied.

It was time to put this *case* to bed.

"QUINN warned us you might show up here, sniffing at Detective McPhee as a way to worm yourself into this investigation, too." Alex was so furious he practically growled the words at Wade Montana. "Do you really think she's that stupid?"

Montana didn't respond.

Alex was pacing back and forth in a deserted courtyard

outside the hospital cafeteria where Rebel had dragged them. Montana sat at one of the rusting metal tables that dotted the cement patio, the accompanying chairs squeaking in gusts of a cold wind that had picked up. Rebel had admonished them to keep it down for heaven's sake, and gone for coffee. Alex wanted something stronger. A *lot* stronger.

"You still in therapy for your PTSD?" Montana asked. Alex spun and glared at him. "I'm just saying. Your temper could use some work."

He held on to his knee-jerk response. The fact that the fuckwad was right just made it even more infuriating. Though in this particular case, his mercurial temper had nothing to do with it. It was the thought of *his* woman ending up with Montana that had him seeing red. That he'd actually suggested it was beyond comprehension.

He forced himself to calm down. They were not talking about Rebel, but about Gina's case. "You were warned by your own people to stay away from this investigation, Montana. Gina's fine. She doesn't need your help."

"Hell, Gina's not what this is about and we both know it," Montana volleyed back. "Admit it. You're jealous of my involvement with Rebel."

"You are *not* involved with her," Alex said through gritted teeth.

Montana shot him a smug look. "Says who?"

"She does."

"It must be true then." This with a casual shrug.

The bastard was just baiting him. He knew that. *Fuck.* It was working.

But Alex had no right to be jealous. No authority to tell this asshole where he could shove his fucking bogus involvement. Alex had let Rebel go, and he meant to stick by that. It was the right thing to do. It *was.*

No matter how much it would tear him up inside.

Funny . . . sixteen months of torture, sickness, and degradation had not managed to kill him or diminish his inner spirit. But leaving Rebel behind just might.

"Doesn't matter either way," Alex told Montana now. "But you stay the fuck *away* from this investigation."

"Not until I talk to Gina. I want to see for myself that she's safe."

"And then you'll walk away?"

"From the case."

Alex's fingers curled into fists. He wanted to hammer the bastard into the pavement.

But he had no right.

"Fine," he said. "We'll arrange a phone call."

Montana shook his head. "No way. In person."

"In person what?" Rebel walked up briskly, carrying a cardboard tray that held three large cups of coffee. She handed one each to him and Montana. "I hope you realize I *don't* fetch coffee," she groused. "I only did it to get away from you two morons."

Alex held the hot cup in his hand and breathed in. But it wasn't the coffee he smelled. It was Rebel. Standing this close to her, he caught a slight drift of her fragrance. And a hint of sex. *Their* sex, the lingering scent of their mingled essence. He could smell it—the barest suggestion—on her skirt and her skin. Was it crass to hope Montana could, too?

He didn't care. He wanted the other man to know Rebel belonged to *him*. That his body had been deep inside her just a few short minutes ago. That he had claimed her as his. *His* lover. *His* woman. *His*.

Except . . . she wasn't. Could never be.

Fuck.

"Alex?"

He looked up and realized he had squeezed the coffee cup so hard the lid had popped off and the scalding liquid was cascading down his hand. But the pain he felt had nothing to do with coffee.

"Shit," he said, unable to stand the torture any longer. "You want me gone?" He threw the crumpled cup into a trash can. "I'm already there." He pretended he didn't see the hurt that flashed through her expressive green eyes. "You win, Montana. She's all yours. I've got somewhere else to be."

And then he stalked determinedly out of the courtyard, and out of Rebel's life.

For good.

"THE man's a goddamn fool and that's a fact," Wade said when the dust had settled.

Rebel clamped down mercilessly on the feelings of despair that burst through her at Alex's abrupt departure, and gave Wade as brave a smile as she could muster.

"C'est la vie," she said and lifted a shoulder, but must not have pulled it off with the proper sangfroid, because Wade put down his cup, rose, and held out his arms to her.

"Come here. You need a hug, sweetheart."

She hesitated for a second. Then stepped into his embrace. "Oh, Wade," she lamented softly. "What am I going to do?"

He kissed her forehead. "You finally slept with him, didn't you." It wasn't a question.

She fought hard not to break down. "Yeah."

"I can smell him on you. The fucking bastard."

There wasn't much she could say to that other than, "Language, Wade."

"Was the asshole any good, at least?"

She choked out a half laugh, half sob.

From anyone else, the question would have been crude and insulting. But their relationship had centered around sex, and it had been a good one as far as that sort of relationship went. They'd broken rules together, climaxed together, and been able to do and talk about pretty much anything having to do with sex together. It was all the other stuff she'd had trouble with. Because she was in love with someone else. He'd known that. Hoped he could change her mind. And when he couldn't, he'd graciously let her go. But still tried to provoke Alex at every opportunity. She suspected more out of loyalty to her than any real jealousy . . .

"That good, eh," he observed.

Which only made her want to laugh and cry harder. "I am such an idiot," she moaned.

"No. He is. A certified, class-A, clueless, obtuse dolt. What is his goddamn problem?"

"He has . . . issues." She sighed.

"No fucking kidding." Wade's voice was gratifyingly aggravated.

"He insists we can't be together."

"So what the hell does he call fucking you? An accidental slip of the cock? Jesus, Rebel, if you want him dead, I swear to God, I'll arrange it."

"No!" She knew, of course, he wasn't serious. But it felt really good to have someone on her side. "As tempting as the offer is, he's not worth going to jail. I'll get over him. I always do."

"So I've noticed," he drawled.

"Hey." She punched his chest. But felt a little better.

He chuckled. "Go on, blame it on me."

At least her world wasn't coming to an end. Quite.

"Speaking of . . . um, slipping," she ventured. "Are you hitting on that pretty detective? The one upstairs?"

His lips crooked wickedly. "I don't know what you mean."

She looked up at him. "Don't play dumb with me, SAC Montana. I know how you operate."

"Do you, now?"

"Yeah. You'll do anything to stay involved in Gina's case. Including seducing a police detective . . . or a Bureau subordinate," she added pointedly.

He kissed her temple. "Honey, you know it may have started that way, but—"

"I know." She gave him a smile of understanding. "But what Alex said is true. We've found Gina. She's with STORM and safe now, I promise. So there's no reason to go breaking the heart of some innocent police detective."

"I'm wounded," he protested. "What gave you the idea I'd break her heart?"

"I saw the way she looked at you. Wondering why you were fighting with Alex over me."

"I wasn't fighting over you." He sighed. "Okay, fine, I was. I can't help that the man pushes my buttons. He doesn't deserve you."

"Now she thinks you don't deserve *her*."

"All this from one look?" He made a face. "Damn. Anyone ever tell you you're far too good at your job, Haywood?"

She smiled. "You did once."

"Very funny." He sighed into her hair. "For the record, Detective McPhee is a very sexy lady. I like her a lot."

"But you love Gina," she said gently. "Anyone with eyes can see you still haven't gotten over her."

For the briefest of seconds, his mouth turned down. He shook his head. "Don't be ridiculous," he returned. "I've told you. Gina moved on a long time ago. And so have I."

"Yeah," she said. "I get that. Just like me and Alex."

GINA stood before the door of the bedroom where Gregg was being confined and tried to work up the courage to go in. Quinn had said he wanted to see her. Alone. For two minutes.

Two minutes?

Not two hours. Which would be enough time to make love. Or two days. Which would be enough time to make love *and* talk about their future. But two minutes. That wasn't enough time for anything . . . except to say goodbye.

With Gregg, the future had always been a big question mark. Or rather, the length of their time together had been a big question mark. The future? They had none, other than the occasional physical rendezvous. He'd made that plain as day. But she'd thought they would have a bit more of a present. To figure things out. At least until the traitor was found.

But it seemed two minutes was all she would get of him.

Why? What had changed his mind about her?

No mystery there. *Her own irresponsible actions.*

The knowledge sent shards of regret stinging through her veins. He'd counted on her and she'd let him down. If only she hadn't gone out for ice. None of this would be happening. Quite so soon, at any rate.

She closed her eyes and reached deep inside for her strength. She knew it was in there somewhere. It used to flow so freely within her body and her soul. Before . . .

But it *was* still there. She'd felt brief flashes of her old self, strong and capable, over the past few days. *Since being with Gregg*. It was as if being with him was slowly healing the part of her that had been so thoroughly broken by her terrorist captors. Maybe it was his own awesome strength that somehow melded into her while making love. Maybe it was that he always made her feel so physically safe that she had time to work on other things. Maybe it was the profound relief that the man she had once loved *hadn't* betrayed her, as she'd believed for all those months.

Whatever it was, her inner will to be strong was slowly returning—all because of Gregg.

She swallowed heavily. What would she do when she no longer had his sure, steady power to draw from? She didn't think she was ready to stand on her own. She was afraid she'd fall apart.

She couldn't lose him.

Not yet.

Without letting herself think, she raised her hand and knocked at the door. No sound came from the bedroom. No *Come in*. Not even a *Go away*. From a nearby chair, Quinn nodded encouragingly at her. So she boldly opened the bedroom door and went in.

Gregg lay stretched out on the bed, ankles crossed, one arm under his head, the other alongside it. His wrists were handcuffed together. Seeing him bound like that made her want to throw up.

His eyes were closed. "Gregg?" she asked softly, in case he was asleep.

His lids cracked and he looked at her. He didn't smile. Or answer. His only other movement was a tight bunching of his cheek muscles. *Oh, God*. He was furious.

Her heartbeat kicked up. *She had to do this*.

Coming in, she closed the door behind her and took a few steps toward the bed. "Gregg, I'm so—"

"Don't," he growled.

Her lips parted. "But I—"

"I don't want to hear it. I don't want to hear anything you have to say. I just want you to stand there and listen."

Before . . . *before,* she would have stalked over, wagging her finger and given him an earful for not listening to her apology. But now she just stood there, cut to the quick and shocked by the palpable waves of anger coming off him.

"I took responsibility for what happened to you last year and tried to make up for it, Gina. I watched over you. I protected you. I saved your life more than once. I didn't ask you to like me. Definitely didn't ask you to make love to me. All I asked in return was for you to trust me."

"I did. I do!"

But he didn't seem to hear her declaration. He kept right on talking. "You prefer STORM? Great. They're in charge now. But whatever happens, know one thing, Gina, and believe it with everything in you: I'm not working for al Sayika. It's not me who's the bad guy here."

"I know that," she said.

"Good. That's it, then. We're done," he said, and closed his eyes.

Dismay seeped through her. She yearned for a kind word from him. One that would tell her everything would be all right. That they'd find the real traitor. Together. That they'd get through this somehow. Together.

"That's it?" she whispered.

"No. There is one last thing."

Her heart leapt. "Yes?"

"When you leave, Gina? Don't come back. I don't ever want to see you again."

NINETEEN

BEFORE Gina could even begin to react to Gregg's brutal echo of her own cutting words from two days ago, there was a knock at the door and Quinn put his head in. "The others are here, van Halen. You've had your two minutes. Let's go."

With a curt nod, Gregg rose from the bed with his usual catlike grace. But his handcuffs caught on the quilt and he had to stop and disentangle himself.

Gina's stomach clenched. "Are those really necessary?" she asked Quinn. "It's not like he could escape even if he wanted to."

Quinn gave her an oh-how-little-you-know-of-the-man raised eyebrow, but relented nonetheless. He tossed Gregg the key. "Your woman has faith in you, van Halen. Don't fuck it up."

Your woman. Quinn's unexpected verbal coupling of them sent an unbidden spill of hope spinning through her.

Gregg unlocked the cuffs and threw them onto the nightstand. "She's not my woman."

Hope curdled to humiliation. Why was he being so damned hard on her? All she did was go out for ice. She hadn't done this on purpose!

As promised, the whole team was waiting in the sitting room. Gina had already spent time this afternoon with the others, so she now greeted Darcy and Marc warmly, and gave Kick a hug. "How's Rainie?" she asked her best friend's new husband.

"Very relieved we found you unharmed," he said, scrutinizing her to make sure she really *was* unharmed. Rainie had been worried. Satisfied, he added, "I told her you'd call after Darce sets up a secure line."

"No calls," Gregg cut in. Gina looked from him to Kick and back again. "No calls," Gregg repeated in a tone that dared to be disobeyed.

"Okay. No calls," she agreed, disappointed but determined not to increase his ire with her. Rainie would wait until the bad guy was caught. Being married to Kick, she knew the drill.

Quinn clapped his hands. "All right, people, grab a drink, grab a seat, and let's get started. We've got a lot of ground to cover."

Everyone pulled the furniture around to face one another and settled in. A lamp was snapped on at one end of the couch. Gregg took a seat in a straight-backed chair as far as possible from the pool of light. And her.

Visibly uncomfortable at being the center of attention, for the next hour he told his side of the events that had unfolded over the past eight months concerning her and the terrorists. His expression was stark and forbidding, and though his narrative revolved around her, not once did he look at her where she sat on a tapestry love seat next to Rebel.

Half the team had already heard his story, half hadn't. But everyone paid close attention and asked questions trying to trip him up. No one could. By the end, even Alex had grudgingly come around.

During the exchange, Gina had been truly humbled hearing of the efforts every person in the room had made to help rescue and protect her from the al Sayika terrorists who had targeted her. She knew Alex felt the same way. By killing her captors, the team had avenged him, as well. They both owed these people their lives.

Listening to Gregg talk, it was more than obvious he shared their hatred of the fanatical terrorists, and would do anything in his power to bring down whoever was helping them—and framing him to take the blame for their atrocities.

When the interrogation was over, Quinn called for a vote. This time, not a single hand was raised in favor of turning Gregg over to Homeland Security.

"Welcome to the team, van Halen," Kick said, unpropping himself from his spot against the fireplace to walk over and shake his hand.

The gesture seemed to break the dam of tension in the room, and everyone relaxed in a spate of welcomes, drink-fetching, and an outburst of relieved chatter.

Only Gina remained silent, still fighting her inner misery over Gregg's categorical rejection. Although relieved at their decision not to turn him over to DHS, it was clear he was not pleased at having his hand forced to join the team. He blamed *her* for that. And rightly so. It *was* her fault. If only he'd let her tell him how sorry she was.

After a few agonizing minutes of self-recrimination, she was grateful when Quinn brought the group back to order. "Okay, sit rep, people. The whole damn thing. Let's go around the room and see where we are. Kick, you're up."

Kick nodded. "Let's see. After the attack on Gina two

days ago in New York, Marc, Miles, and I checked out the three attackers who were killed. Two of them had entered the country illegally, no visas. NYPD found fake Saudi passports at the flophouse in Astoria where the two were living. That was pretty much all."

"Where are the passports?" Darcy asked. "Our lab has a pretty good database of active forgers. They may be able to trace where they were made." She was sitting in an easy chair with Quinn perched on its arm, his hand draped over her shoulder . . . the posture of a man in love and not afraid to show it. Gina sighed.

"NYPD has them," Kick said. "DHS has requested they be turned over, but it could be days. You know government red tape."

"Amen to that," Rebel muttered. Everyone chuckled.

Gina wondered briefly how the FBI agent had managed to be included on the team. Not only was she an outsider and a fed—and everyone agreed the traitor most likely worked for the government—but it was common knowledge she'd had—was still having?—an affair with Gina's own ex-fiancé, Wade—not that Gina minded terribly about that part. *And* that she'd been in love for years—unrequited until recently—with Alex Zane, with whom she seemed to be having some sort of explosion brewing at the moment, judging by the tension arcing between them like downed power lines.

"What about Ouda Mahmood?" Rebel asked Kick.

"Confirmed close ties to al Sayika, which we already knew," Kick said. "Thanks to Darcy's quick work with the fingerprints, Marc and I got to his apartment before NYPD and were able to search it thoroughly. We photographed everything, scanned his mail and documents before we had to bail."

"No laptop?" Darcy asked.

Kick shook his head. "They must have been using a library or Internet café. Miles stayed in New York to continue looking."

"They must have," Tara put in, "because when Bobby Lee and I searched the cousin's place here in D.C.—Asha Mahmood, the woman killed two days ago?—we found shredded evidence of online communication between them."

"Please tell me you found her computer," Kick said.

Tara shook her head. "I'll bet that's what the break-in was all about. Getting their hands on Asha's computer or laptop, and destroying evidence that could link our traitor to her and al Sayika."

"Did you find anything at all?"

"As a matter of fact," Quinn said, "a statement turned up for an offshore account owned jointly by Asha and Ouda. They'd written a $25,000 check to the reelection committee of a certain Louisiana congressman."

"Which one?" Gregg interjected, frowning.

"Lester Altos," Quinn said.

Alex glanced up sharply. "Altos?"

"What is it?" Quinn asked.

"Altos was one of the politicians who sat in when the Pentagon debriefed me after my stay at Club Torture." He looked over at Gina. "What about you?"

She tried to think back. That awful time was all just a blur. She'd been so out of it with the pain and the medication and the horror of it all . . . "I don't know. Maybe. There were a few politicians from Louisiana. He could have been one of them."

"I'll try and find out through the Bureau," Rebel said, writing his name down. "There should be records."

"As soon as I get the mainframe computer station up and running here, I'll dig up everything I can on the good congressman," Darcy said.

"If he's our guy, we'll need to move quickly," Kick said.

Darcy nodded. "But we can't go after a U.S. congressman half-cocked. It would be a bad mistake if we're wrong. We need to be very sure of his complicity first."

"I'm still waiting to hear from my contact in the Caymans," Quinn added, "to see if that's the only large payout the Mahmoods made, and if they had any other accounts at the bank there. Altos could just be a smoke screen," he cautioned. "Or laundering money into his campaign fund any way he can."

Curled up on one end of the sofa, Tara glanced down at Marc, who was lounging on the floor at her feet. "Did you find any financial-type paperwork in Ouda Mahmood's apartment?" she asked.

"There may have been," Marc said. "I seem to recall seeing a bank statement or two."

"I'll look through your scans and check," she volunteered, then exchanged a smile with her husband. Their expressions were filled with so much love that Gina's heart literally ached.

Tara's and Marc's were the first faces she'd seen when STORM had burst through the door in Louisiana, guns blazing, to rescue her. Gina had been devastated when Tara nearly died from the hideous virus the terrorists had forced her to perfect. And was convinced it was Marc's deep love and unflagging presence by Tara's side during her tug-of-war with death that had pulled her through in the end. The couple would always have a special place in Gina's heart.

How she longed to have a love as strong and true as theirs!

"Okay, what else?" Quinn asked.

Alex straightened from where he stood bookends at the fireplace with Kick, and outlined the search he and Rebel had done on *Allah's Paradise*. "Haven't heard back yet from forensics on most of the evidence we brought up from the wreck. Hopefully tomorrow."

As Alex spoke, Rebel shifted restlessly on the love seat next to her, brushing nonexistent lint from her skirt. *They* weren't looking at each other, either.

"But aside from the million dollars' worth of diamonds Rebel found, I did notice one other interesting item: a preliminary agenda for a Military Defense Subcommittee meeting of the House Appropriations Committee, scheduled for this Saturday."

Everyone sat up straight.

"Where's it being held?" Quinn quickly asked.

"The Capitol."

"Could that be the terrorists' possible target in D.C.? The Capitol Building?" Tara asked, alarmed. She unconsciously reached for Marc's hand.

"Unlikely," Gregg said from his place in the shadows. "Security there is too strict. They'd never get any kind of weapon through."

"Unless it was biological," Tara reminded them.

There was a brief silence as they all remembered Louisiana, and how close a call it had been for every one of them.

"I'll alert DHS," Quinn said. "But I agree with van Halen. If they go to the considerable risk of penetrating such a secure target, why not release the weapon on the full congress? Why a small subcommittee meeting?"

"A statement?" Darcy suggested. "It *is* the Defense subcommittee."

"Aren't they about to announce a new program to fight terrorism within the country?" Tara said.

"Not al Sayika's style," Kick said. "Their targets have all been high profile. And what about the nuclear trigger we've been looking for? Doesn't fit." He shook his head. "Van Halen's right. This isn't it."

"Speaking of which, any sign of the nuclear trigger that was supposed to be onboard the yacht?" Darcy asked Alex.

"Nothing," he responded. "The good news is there was no indication of any nuclear material ever being onboard. Radiation levels registered zip."

"Are we sure it was *Allah's Paradise* bringing this trigger into the country?" Tara asked.

Sitting back in the shadows, Gregg was still frowning. "You keep mentioning a nuclear trigger. What's that all about?"

Quinn leafed through a file and walked a paper over to him. "NSA intercepted this e-mail several days ago."

Gregg read aloud, his deep voice resonating through the room, "'Zero hour approaches! The garden of paradise beckons. The trigger will arrive tomorrow. Praise God and do His will!'" He studied the e-mail for a moment. "What makes you think this means a nuclear trigger?" he finally asked.

Rebel responded, "Chatter regarding an al Sayika attack on D.C. has been intercepted from multiple sources lately. They've used dirty bombs before, in Europe and Indonesia. A triggering device is always the most difficult part to get hold of, and it would have to be brought here from overseas. It just makes sense."

Gregg nodded thoughtfully and passed the e-mail back to Quinn. "I assume from the discussion you don't have anything on the attack plans?"

"We've got a whole lot of conjecture," Alex said disgustedly.

"But there is definitely something going on in D.C.," Rebel said. "There have been three murders here over the past forty-eight hours, all linked to al Sayika. I think if we . . ."

Gina should have been listening, she really should. But she felt in imminent danger of overload . . . from more than one direction. She lost the thread of the discussion completely and melted into the background, trying her best to pull her gaze away from Gregg. But it wasn't possible.

Bathed in shadows, he was the dark enigma in the room, an unmoving chiaroscuro portrait who watched the intense team discussion from his cocoon of uncompromising distance. He spoke cordially when spoken to, contributing sharp insight when asked, but volunteered nothing without prompting. He soaked up the circling activity like a black hole in their midst, a powerful, magnetic force, pulling in and gathering, but drawing awareness only through his very invisibility. You knew he was there, saw the void of his shape, but not the actual man who filled it. Not really. And only if you paid attention . . .

She shivered at the analogy. At his dark beauty. At the force of his attraction over her flesh. She wanted to throw herself into the black vortex of his power and let herself be carried deep inside him, to his very soul, and banish the pain behind his shadows.

So when his midnight blue eyes slowly turned and sought her out, snakelike in their sinister focus, her pulse took off in flight. Was he finally going to acknowledge her presence? For an endless moment, his gaze bored into her.

He cleared his throat. As though at a signal, all conversation stopped.

He looked away from her. "About this trigger thing."

"You have an idea?" Quinn asked.

"Maybe. What if it's *not* a nuclear-triggering device?"

Tara's face paled. "You mean it's a trigger for some other kind of weapon?"

"What if it's not a device at all?" he suggested. "What if it's a person?" He looked over at Kick. So did everyone else.

Gina suddenly realized what he was saying. *Kick was the team's sniper.*

Kick nodded. "Yup, the thought crossed my mind when

I read the message, too. Sometimes they called me 'the trigger' in my old unit."

Quinn, Marc, and Alex nodded along with him. They were all spec operators from way back. "So rather than a bomb," Quinn said thoughtfully, "you're talking a Day of the Jackal scenario."

Gina swallowed. The assassination of the president of the United States. A terrible thought.

"You mean the trigger is some kind of hired gun? A political assassin?" Tara asked doubtfully.

"Sweet goodnight!" Rebel said, shooting straight up on the love seat. "The man that got away!"

"I actually think they got Bruce Willis in the end," Alex drawled.

"No!" Rebel exclaimed. "I mean, on *Allah's Paradise*. Don't you remember I told you I may have seen another person onboard? While I was talking on the phone to—" She stopped abruptly. Jerked her attention to Quinn. "Someone may have jumped overboard, just before the yacht exploded. I can't be certain. It was just a quick flash in my peripheral vision. I put it in my report, thinking he may have taken the trigger with him. But I never thought about him actually *being* the trigger."

"*Merde,*" Marc swore.

"To take a successful shot at POTUS—the President—and survive," Kick ventured, shaking his head, "this assassin would need mad skills."

"Maybe he doesn't intend to survive," Marc said somberly.

"Or," Gregg said into the pool of ensuing silence, "maybe POTUS isn't the target."

"Who else could it be?" Rebel asked.

He slowly turned to Gina. And pointed. "Her."

TWENTY

GREGG sat back as everyone turned to Gina and stared. Mouths dropped open in bewilderment.

"I hope you're not serious," Gina choked out.

"Explain," Quinn ordered.

But how did you explain a feeling? A feeling he'd had ever since listening via the bug he'd planted in her room at Haven Oaks to every debrief she'd been put through by STORM after her rescue? A feeling only intensified by finding that Pentagon file on her this morning—with a source code matching those on Zane's and Jackson's level one secure files. It had to have been the traitor responsible for all three attempts on their lives. Nothing else made sense.

Gregg spread his hands. "You think al Sayika is out to kill Gina in revenge for her escaping and sabotaging their Armageddon virus, right?"

"Not like there's any doubt," Kick said. "There's a price on her head," he reminded him. "Just like there is on mine and Alex's."

"And about a thousand other people they consider enemies," Gregg agreed. "But how many of those revenge targets have they actually killed?"

"Lots," Alex said, and ticked off on his fingers. "The Saudi princess, the French police commander, the attempt on the Swedish minister of justice . . ." He ran out of steam with a frown.

"You prove my point. None of those were for revenge. They were *primary* targets, high-profile public figures already in the media spotlight, killed to garner attention to al Sayika's twisted cause. Gina is a university research scientist working behind the scenes with kids' vaccines. Her kidnapping was never even released to the public."

"But they *did* try to assassinate her," Tara said. "You were there."

"What if it wasn't al Sayika behind the attempt?"

"Who else would it be?" Darcy asked. "The attackers had proven ties to the organization."

"Yes, but they also had ties elsewhere."

"You mean D.C.," Quinn said, getting to his feet. Gregg could see the wheels turning. The commander was actually listening.

Gina blinked. "I don't understand." She looked spooked and confused.

But Gregg refused to feel sorry for her. He refused to feel *anything* for her. She'd lied to him. She'd sworn that he could trust her, then deliberately betrayed that trust. He could be sitting behind bars right now, his life over, because of her. He still might—if there was an al Sayika mole hidden among these people.

He reluctantly turned to her. But he couldn't make himself meet those frightened eyes. He spoke to her lips. "What if there's someone else with an actual motive to kill you specifically?"

She paled. “Like who?” But he got the distinct feeling she’d really wanted to say, “Like *you*?”

Her lips started to quiver, a trembling so subtle you had to be looking right at them to see it. He knew that quiver. Intimately. When he’d had her tied to the bed, helpless, and was about to do something that both thrilled and terrified her in equal measure, he’d learned to worship that tiny quiver of excitement.

But now it just meant terror.

With good reason.

He suddenly realized everyone was staring at him, waiting for his answer.

“Wade Montana,” Alex Zane suddenly blurted out, pacing away from the fireplace where he’d been leaning with a scowl on his face. “The ex-fiancé lives in D.C., and he can’t stay away from this case.”

“Don’t be absurd,” the redheaded FBI agent countered hotly before Gregg could open his mouth. “It’s not Wade.”

Zane jabbed his finger angrily at her. “*You* suspected him yourself, back in December, before you got so damn friendly with him. The jilted lover is always at the top of your list of murder suspects, your very words.”

At the phrase *jilted lover*, Gina’s eyes widened and slid to Gregg. This time he met her gaze, his mouth pressed thin. A frisson of tense awareness passed between them.

“You can’t possibly think Wade is involved with al Sayika,” she said hoarsely to him.

“His behavior is suspicious,” Gregg said. “But no, that’s not who I meant.”

“Then who?”

“Think, Gina. Back to when you were being held captive. You saw something you shouldn’t have. Some*one* you shouldn’t have.”

She turned inward, thinking, shaking her head slowly back and forth. “But they’re all dead. Or in prison.”

"Not all of them," he said. Urging her to remember.

And then she did. She sucked in a soft breath. He could see the awful memory of her life's worst moments swirl through her whole body like a whiff of poison gas. And then came the pain of realizing that the one good, kind part of that memory was in fact the most evil thing of all.

"Oh, God," she whispered. "The Voice. The man who helped me. Comforted me. *He's the traitor.*"

DETECTIVE Jonas Loudon poked his head around the side of Sarah's cubicle. "Something interesting came up in the Raul Chavez interviews. Thought you might want to hear," he boomed.

Wincing, Sarah saved the report she was writing, glanced at the time on her computer, and looked up. "Jesus, Jonesy. It's ten o'clock on a Friday night. Don't you have a hot date or something?"

"This coming from Detective frickin' Lonelyheart."

"I'll have you know I *had* a date lined up for tonight. Told the guy to stuff it." *More or less.* Surely, not returning three phone messages and two texts qualified?

"Let me guess. He didn't ask you for dinner and a movie first."

"Nah." She waved her hand in mock disgust. "He *did.* Who's got time for all that foreplay?"

Jonesy guffawed loudly. "And me, I got the opposite problem. All the dames my age wanna play frickin' bingo for six hours before lettin' a man score."

She tsked. "Getting old sucks the big one."

"I wish," Jonesy said in a snickering lament.

"*Any*way," she groaned, rolling her eyes. "The Chavez interviews?"

"Oh, yeah. So I went down to the limo service garage

this evening. Caught a lot of the drivers waxin' and lubin' in anticipation of the big night, bein' the weekend an' all. Got 'em talking about Raul. Seems he was pretty well liked by the clients. Easygoin', knew how to keep his mouth shut about things. Like what? I asks. That's when they get all twitchy."

Sarah leaned back in her office chair and swiveled it back and forth. "About?"

"Took me a while to get it out of them, but it seems Chavez drove Asha Mahmood around quite a bit. But she's not the one who hired him." He paused for dramatic effect.

She bit. "Okay. So who did?"

"Her sugar daddy."

Sarah recalled vividly the embarrassing abundance of sex toys they'd found at Mahmood's trashed apartment. It fit.

"Her *married* sugar daddy," Jonesy continued before she could comment. "Who's supposedly some bigwig—wait for it—up on the Hill."

She stopped swiveling. "The Hill? As in Capitol Hill? A *congressman*?"

He shrugged expansively. "Or a senator, or aide, or hell, the vice president. No one knew for sure. Could be the frickin' janitor, for all the conjecture. Except—"

Excitement began to buzz through her. "Except janitors don't have the kind of cash it takes to hire limos for their mistresses."

"*Cash* being the operative word."

Her excitement deflated. "Damn. No credit card receipts?"

Jonesy shook his head. "No paper trail at all. The man has obviously done this before. Or—"

"Or . . ." Sarah suddenly recalled the very large campaign contribution from the Mahmood cousins' joint account to a certain Louisiana congressman. *Oh, yeah. Gotcha.* "Or the bastard has a lot more to hide than just a cheating dick."

"I hope you don't mind sharing a room," Rebel asked, glancing over at Gina, who was arranging her few things in a dresser drawer in their room at the Watergate.

The other woman looked up and smiled. "Not at all. It'll be great to catch up. I haven't seen you since . . . um, you moved down to Norfolk."

Rebel's mouth curved. Gina should be a diplomat. "You mean since I grew a pair and finally left Alex, only to sabotage myself by hooking up with Wade?"

Gina had been in bad shape when she was brought to Haven Oaks, but not bad enough that all the love triangle dramas revolving around Rebel had escaped her notice. The miracle was that they'd become friends anyway. Rebel had desperately needed the distraction, and had sat for hours with the rescued hostage, distracting her in turn from her recurring nightmares by talking nonstop about Alex, and Helena, and even Wade—after Gina convinced her she'd left him ages ago and had no interest in reuniting.

"Oh, Wade's not such a bad guy," Gina said now, closing the drawer. "You could have done worse."

"Other than the fact that he was my boss and emotionally unavailable? Do you *see* a pattern here?"

Gina laughed and went to curl up on one of the beds. "Alex isn't your boss," she pointed out.

"Technically, he is. Or maybe it's Quinn now. Whatever. Either way, he *was* my first official assignment as an FBI agent. My Zero Unit liaison." An embarrassingly appropriate term. Or rather, not . . . "Though to be fair, I suppose I was even more unavailable than Wade was."

Gina gave her a wry look. "Ain't love grand. Always there to mess a woman up when she least needs it."

Rebel flopped onto the other bed like a snow angel. "Amen to that."

"So what's going on between you and Alex? Something's changed. I can tell."

Pain razored through Rebel's heart for the hundredth time that day, just as powerful as the first ninety-nine. "I slept with him last night. Finally, after all these years. And this morning, he decided he can't be with me." She battled back the urge to roll into a ball and cry.

"Oh, sweetie. I'm so sorry. How did *that* happen?"

The infertility was too personal an issue to discuss without his permission. But she could share his worry about his job and the PTSD. "It was so good," she said. "I was happy." *For the most part.* "He seemed happy, too. Then he had that flashback while we were diving, and it all kind of fell apart from there."

"Ah. I understand."

Rebel glanced over. Her friend's focus had turned inward, her expression bleak, raw. Rebel had seen Alex with that same expression on his face. It was the memories rearing up.

"I dealt with it," Rebel continued. "I tried to be strong for him . . . help him through it." She sighed. "But I think I remind him too much of . . ." *The memories.* "He told me he dreamed of me, you know. Over there, while he was a prisoner."

Gina came back from wherever she'd been. "He did?"

Rebel nodded. "All the time, he said."

Gina smiled. "That proves he loves you."

Right. "Not enough to deal with the problems keeping us apart. He just wants to run away."

"Maybe he's afraid to face them. I'm sure he's feeling weak and vulnerable right now. He could be afraid you won't love him anymore, now that you've seen his weakness displayed so vividly. Seen him completely helpless. Men like to think they're strong, invincible. Especially men in Alex's profession."

Rebel rolled to her stomach, resting her chin in her hand. It made a lot of sense. Even for the sterility thing. Although Alex had never been the caveman macho type. But the heirs to a man's name—or lack thereof—could be an explosive issue. Wars had been fought over it.

"You told me once you dreamed of Gregg while you were . . . captive. How did you feel when you saw him again?"

"Not exactly the same situation," Gina said dryly. "I wanted to kill him. Literally."

"Maybe you could give me lessons." They laughed. "Though I take it Gregg didn't play along. What happened? You two sort of skipped over that part in your stories earlier."

Gina's smile gradually faded as she answered. "He convinced me I was wrong about him. He's actually helped me a lot. Psychologically. I feel better around him. Safe."

"Hardly surprising," Rebel observed. "That man's got to be the scariest human being I've ever met in my life. Those eyes. Like he can read every thought in your head." She shivered.

"He can," Gina said, almost sadly. She toyed with a silver chain around her ankle. A small heart hung from it. "Every thought."

"So . . . if you don't mind me asking . . . why are you sharing a room with *me*?"

Gina pulled a pillow to her middle and curled around it. "He's angry with me. He wanted to find the traitor on his own and he blames me for being forced to work with STORM."

Rebel could hear a world of hurt in those words. Obviously her deep feelings for the man had returned with a vengeance now that he'd been absolved of betraying her. "But it's not your fault we ran into you in the corridor. Not that I'm sorry we did . . . But seriously, what were the odds?"

"That's the problem. Gregg doesn't believe in coincidences. I'm sure he thinks I called Alex or Kick. Sold him out."

"But you didn't! You should tell him that."

"I tried. He won't listen."

Rebel sat up on the bed. "Then, girl, you need to march yourself over there and *make* him listen. This is ridiculous! You love him. At least *one* of us should have a happy ending."

Gina hugged her pillow harder. Her brown eyes swam with misery. "Then I guess it's up to you, girlfriend. Because it doesn't matter how I feel. The one thing I know about Gregg van Halen is, the man does not believe in love. There's not going to be any happy ending for Gregg and me."

If Rebel didn't already feel completely heartbroken for herself, her heart would have broken all over for her friend.

How did two such intelligent, sensitive, and giving women end up in this lonely, painful position? *Men!* She wanted to send the entire male population to some other galaxy and leave them there forever. See how they'd do without women in their lives.

She jumped up and stalked into the bathroom to get ready for bed. The pathetic part? They'd probably do just *fine* without women. In fact, the obtuse jerks probably wouldn't even *notice* anything was missing. Well. Except late at night, of course. Probably the only time female presence would be missed.

When she came out again, Gina was asleep, clinging to her pillow like she wished it were Mr. Tall-Dark-and-Scary hugging her back.

Rebel turned off the light and crawled under the covers. And wished she had the courage to march over to Alex's room and make *him* listen.

Tell him how she felt about him. How desperately she loved him. That he was making the biggest mistake of his life by shutting her out.

But was that really true? Or was he right? In years to come, when she hadn't felt the amazing joy of giving birth, and knew she would never look into the eyes of a child and see the man she loved . . . would she resent him? Would their happiness slowly fall apart because she could never accept the crushing finality of his condition?

Honestly, she could not see that happening. She loved him too much. And there were other options available. Good options.

But could she convince him to give her a chance to plead her case? And if he did . . . even then, he may not trust her promise.

Because Gregg van Halen might not believe in love, but it was pretty obvious . . . Alex Zane did not believe in *her*.

And in the end, wasn't that what love was all about?

THE night was dark, and cold, and went on forever.

Tossing and turning and freezing, no matter how many blankets she piled on, Gina could not get warm. But the problem wasn't with the room's temperature, or the blankets. It was with her.

She missed Gregg.

She missed his heat. She missed his protective arms around her. She missed his steady heartbeat at her back, reminding her with its even rhythm that if she woke from another nightmare he'd be there to kiss her brow and soothe her fears.

Which was why, before she realized what she was doing, she once again found herself standing in the middle of their old suite, working up the courage to go into the bedroom and confront him.

She'd been vaguely surprised her key card still worked; he must have forgotten to have it reprogrammed. Around her, the sitting room was dark and still, only the low hum of the minibar fridge broke the silence. He'd left the French door curtains open, and through them the indigo sky of the city night basked in the glow of the moon and a smattering of pale stars.

On bare feet, wearing nothing but the plush hotel robe—a girl could dream, couldn't she?—she padded to his bedroom door. And quietly opened it.

The room was a gaping maw of total blackness, so quiet she could hear her own blood sussing through her veins. But she could smell him, the subtle scent of her lover beckoning to her body like a whispered command. She took a step in.

And another.

It was so dark she couldn't see the bed. Or the door to the bathroom, or even her own hand when she raised it to feel her way through the pitch blackness.

"Gregg?" she whispered.

Right behind her came the metallic *snick* of a gun slide unracking.

She whirled, almost tripping, clutching the robe to her breasts. The bedroom door had closed. She sensed the specter of a figure standing in front of it. Her heartbeat stalled. For a second, terror held her mute, and unable to move. Then her body started to tremble.

"What are you doing here, Gina?" Gregg's voice asked from the darkness.

Relief jellied her limbs. She wanted to run to him, to

fling her shaking body into his arms. But God knew what he'd do.

"I came to talk to you," she managed.

"Not interested," he said brusquely and brushed past her.

"Why are you doing this?" Her voice cracked on the desperate question. "Being so cold?"

His gun clattered onto the nightstand. "You really have to ask that?"

She listened carefully, trying to follow his movements. But it was no use. He moved like a ghost. "Working with STORM isn't a bad thing, Gregg. They know you're innocent. They want to help us."

"This doesn't have anything to do with STORM," he bit out.

She drew in a calming breath. "Look, I'm sorry I left the suite this morning. I'm sorry I—"

Suddenly he was looming over her. "You *betrayed* me, Gina. You called them when I told you not to."

"No! I—" She stumbled backward, panic searing through her at his palpable anger. His huge body crowded over hers.

"Revenge, sweet thing? For me bringing you to ZU-NE? Is that what what your artful seduction was all about? To convince me I could trust you, so you could—"

"No!" Her breath lodged hard in her lungs when he grasped her shoulders and yanked her up against his chest.

"You want to try again?" he growled. "I crave you enough it just might work."

She was quaking so hard her teeth started to chatter. He didn't under*stand*. She had to make him understand.

His mouth crashed down on hers. Brutal. Bruising. His tongue slashed over hers, punishing. She'd never known him like this before. So out of control. It terrified her.

She tore her lips from his and wrenched her face away.

"S-stop!" she stammered, digging her fingers into his biceps. "G-Gregg, s-s-stop!"

He ground to a halt. His breath came fast and hard, his whole body coiled tight as a sailor's knot. "No? Not into it? Too bad."

"Listen to me," she pleaded hoarsely.

"You've done enough talking." He tried to pull away, but she grabbed him and clung. "Let go of me, Gina."

"I didn't call STORM!" she cried, finding her voice. "Didn't Quinn tell you?"

"You really think I bought that story?"

"But it's true! I just went out for ice. I ran into Alex and Rebel in the hall. It was a total accident, Gregg, I swear it's the truth."

He went still.

She slid her arms around his rigid torso. "I'm sorry. Yes, I broke my promise and left the room. But I just wanted some ice. I never . . . Not in a million years did I think . . . I'm *so* sorry, Gregg. But I did not call them. Please, don't be angry with me."

He stood silent for a long time. She could feel his rapid pulse where her breasts pressed into his chest. Her own heart beat wildly.

"You're really trying to tell me," he finally said, "that STORM being at the same hotel as us was nothing more than a coincidence."

"Yes! They checked in last night. Before we even left New York. How could they know?" He didn't answer. "Call the front desk if you don't believe me!"

Finally he moved. Set her away. Swore under his breath.

This time she let him go. He paced to the window, whipped open the curtains and stood rigidly, his dark form silhouetted against the bright silver ribbon of the moonlit Potomac River and the twinkling lights of Virginia beyond.

At length he turned and looked at her. "Okay. I believe you."

"Thank God," she whispered, relief a living thing.

He held out his hands to her. "Come here."

She rushed into his arms. "Oh, Gregg, I really am sorry."

After a moment he said, "I'm sorry, too. I was wrong. I shouldn't have leapt to conclusions. Shouldn't have shut down your explanation. I let my emotions rule my head. God knows, I should know better."

Emotions? Did that mean he actually felt something for her? Something more than simple lust?

"Emotions aren't always a bad thing," she said softly, burrowing into his embrace. Letting the panic ebb away and the comfort of his physical presence wash over her. Maybe she had a chance with him, after all.

"They're always bad for a man like me," he refuted. "My job, my life, all depend on keeping a clear head and being able to make rational decisions. Emotions will kill you every time."

Or so he thought. Because he'd learned long ago that love meant only pain, betrayal, and death. She understood that was why he always had to be in control, master of everything around him. Never trusting his emotions enough to let go and just feel.

"You're wrong," she said with an aching heart as he leaned down to kiss her . . . a soft, melding, seductive kiss. She wanted so badly to be the one to show him that it didn't have to be that way. That emotions and letting go could sometimes be a *good* thing. So very good. She dissolved into him with a sigh. "Oh, Gregg. Please. Let me show you how wrong you are."

TWENTY-ONE

GREGG knew by making love to Gina again he was just digging himself a deeper emotional grave, but he wanted her too badly to resist. He *needed* her too badly.

"My sweet Gina," he whispered. "How I wish it were true."

He slid the robe from her shoulders. If there'd been any chance of being able to back away, it vanished when he realized she was naked under it. With a groan, he swept her into his arms and carried her to his bed.

"How do you see in this darkness?" she murmured when he pulled off his sweatpants and followed her down onto the feather-soft quilt.

"Instinct," he murmured, and used it now to sense what she wanted most from him. She made it too easy. She put her arms around him and drew him down on top of her, guiding his lips to hers with a hand on his cheek.

"What are your instincts telling you?" she whispered.

"To kiss you," he said, and covered her mouth with his. The taste of her poured through him, drowning him in a torrent of desire. He angled in deeper. He didn't know what it was about this woman, but he could never get enough of her. Never taste her enough, never touch her enough. It was frightening how much he wanted her. The craving to own her completely, to control her every move, was a powerful, living thing within him.

When he'd drunk himself dizzy, he lifted to trail kisses over her cheeks and eyes. He settled his body between her thighs, and she spread them wider, inviting him in.

"What are they telling you now?" she asked.

It had been too damned long. And those instincts were telling him she was ready. He reached over to the night-stand and picked up the handcuffs he'd tossed there earlier. He removed the key and tucked it under the pillow.

"This." He trailed them down her arm, letting her feel the cold metal against her skin.

Her breath sucked in. "Gregg . . ."

"It's okay, baby. You trust me, don't you?"

He felt her heartbeat start to race. "Yes, but—"

"With your life?"

"Of course, but I—"

"Remember all the times we've done this before?" He wanted it back. Needed her to be okay with it. With him. The way he really was. Not just this kinder, gentler version. He felt her nod reluctantly. "Did I ever hurt you?"

"No," she whispered. Her body undulated under his, pressing his cock against her crease. She'd started to tremble. "Can't we just—"

"I want you to know absolutely you have nothing to fear from me. I want to get back what we had before. Complete and utter trust between us."

He heard her swallow heavily. For an endless moment

they lay there, almost but not quite joined, their bodies hot and pulsing with need for each other. "Okay," she finally whispered.

A thrill of anticipation sang through him. He tamped it back down. He must be gentle with her. He kissed her as he slid one cuff around her wrist and locked it. She let out a soft whimper as it snapped shut.

"Listen to your instincts, sweetheart. What are they telling you?" he murmured into her mouth.

"To trust you."

"Trust them," he whispered. "Trust me." He raised her arms above her head and threaded the free cuff around one of the wooden spindles of the antique four-poster bed, then put it around her other wrist. "Okay?"

"Yes," she managed.

Her whole body was shaking now. From excitement? Or fear? Impossible to tell.

His fingers sought her breasts. Her nipples were hard little knots, spiraling tighter at his touch. *Excitement*. He groaned and put his lips to one of them, sucking hard.

She gasped. But it was definitely the good kind. A gasp of pleasure.

He couldn't wait any longer. He pulled back and slid into her with a single thrust. The slick, wet heat of her surrounded him, pulling twin groans from deep within them. He gathered her in his arms, holding her body tight and close under him. He withdrew and thrust home again. The handcuffs jingled.

"Good?" he asked.

"More," she gasped out. *Thank God*.

He almost lost it. He had to slow things down.

"But first, this," he said, swiftly pulling out. He shifted himself downward to give her an even more intimate kiss. She gasped low when his tongue circled and flicked, her slim form bowing up under him, letting him know his instincts were exactly right. She was so ready for him. For all of this.

He filled his senses with her entirely, stoking his own excitement with her passionate response. She moaned his name, and an urgent spill of possessiveness shimmered through his blood. She was his completely.

His.

He lost himself in her delicious surrender to the mastery of his lips and tongue. He loved doing this to her, loved the stark sensuality of the act, loved the total submission it always brought her to. He could tease, incite, withhold, reward, all with lethal precision, to give her more pleasure than she could stand. With this, he ruled her body completely. And in doing so, his own pleasure increased tenfold.

He finally let her come, riding the shuddering crest of her explosive release until she lay limp and helplessly spent beneath him.

He quickly sheathed himself and levered back onto her. He kissed the lingering moan from her lips and thrust his cock deep into her. She hummed and lifted her legs, wrapping them around his waist, the way she knew he liked it.

He enjoyed rough power sex, but this moment of acceptance was what he loved best of all. When he had conquered her completely, and she was warm and soft and open, helpless in the palm of his hand, all tied up and utterly his for the taking.

He pushed his cock deeper, as far into her as he could go. And then he held himself perfectly still for a handful of pounding heartbeats. Enjoying the pure throbbing pleasure of her acquiescence. She reached up and kissed him, an openmouthed kiss of breathtaking adoration.

"What are your instincts telling you now?" she whispered against his tongue.

That he loved her.

The thought was so quick and devastating that his breath sucked in in an implosion of denial.

No! He didn't love her. He couldn't. He didn't know how to love. Wasn't even sure what it was.

He shoved aside the impossible thought and whispered, "That I'm very glad you're mine."

The darkness wrapped them in a blanket of comfort, isolating them from the harsh reality of the outside world. He wished he could stay here with her forever, just like this.

"I *am* yours," she whispered. "I love you."

The words hit him like a shotgun blast in the chest, crashing him from his warm fantasy. She'd said it before. On that first day. Except then it had been in the past tense, and shouted at him like a curse. *I loved you!* she had cried, *Why did you betray me?* But he'd thought she was lying, using emotions to try and get to him.

"Don't," he quietly begged her now. "I can't be what you want me to be, Gina. I've already told you that."

"I know," she said. "I don't expect you to love me back. I just needed to say it once. To let you know how I feel. I do love you, Gregg. So much."

A thread of panic wound around his heart. God, could she really mean it?

"You're killing me, baby. I really wish—"

"Shhh, it's okay," she gently said. Her body moved under his. Tempting. Seducing. Hot and willing. "Do you trust your instincts, Gregg?"

The panic hummed through him. *Did* he love her? How could he know?

"I mean really trust them?" she pressed. "About me?"

He felt her body under his, joined with his, so warm and accepting, so full of life, and love, and trust. Even handcuffed and completely under his control, and after all she'd been through, she was still so fucking strong and true it filled him with awe. Love? Who knew? But one thing he did know.

"I do trust them," he whispered. "And you."

He felt her lips smile against his skin. "That's all I want. It's enough for me."

But it wasn't enough for him. He wanted to do more. He needed to prove his trust to her. As she had, time and again, for him.

As frightening as it was, he knew how he could do it. How he *must* do it. To show her in actions what he couldn't put into words.

Reaching under the pillow for the key, he unlocked the handcuffs that bound her to the headboard. He lowered her arms, and pressed the cuffs into her hands. Then he rolled off her, out of her, going onto his back.

"Me," he said. The panic wound around his heart like a greedy monster, nearly robbing him of his willpower.

He sensed her profound hesitation. But he needed to do this. To prove to himself that he could.

"Quickly," he ordered. "Do it!" He beat back the inner demons that threatened to make him rip the cuffs from her hands and throw them across the room.

"Are you sure?" she whispered. "It's okay, really, you don't—"

"But I do," he said. He didn't know why, but doing this was suddenly more important than anything he'd ever done before in his life. For her. But mostly for himself. "I trust you."

He heard her swallow. "All right."

With trembling fingers, she found one of his wrists and snapped the cuff around it. He gritted his teeth. The fact that she was so reluctant helped. The urge to spin her on her back and resume the dominant position was urgent and powerful. It would be so damn easy. But he resisted with everything in him. He had to know if he could do this.

She slid the open cuff around a spindle and reached for his other wrist. He fisted his hand reflexively. She sucked in a breath.

He took a deep breath. Forced himself to relax his hand. "Go on. Don't be afraid," he told her. And she snapped the other cuff home.

His heartbeat took off. He yanked at the metal bracelets. He was well and truly caught. *Jesus!* What was he doing? She could—

She canted over him. And whispered, "Now I can do anything I want to you."

His pulse doubled. But as her hands touched his body, a strange thing happened. Instead of panic, his body felt an electric jolt of pleasure. Then she kissed him. And all at once he didn't know whether to be terrified or excited beyond belief.

"Gina . . ." he choked out.

But she didn't listen. She climbed onto his body, pressed her beautiful breasts against him, and put her clever mouth to his skin, and proceeded to tear his world order to pieces. He groaned as she touched him in places he never allowed anyone to touch, shivered as she licked his flesh into a frenzy of desire, and shook with infinite pleasure as she took his rampant cock in her mouth, and tortured him with her tongue.

"Gina, please," he begged, and once again he felt her smile.

"I think I like you helpless," she murmured.

God help him!

"Don't get used to it," he returned through a clenched jaw. He was so over his panic. Now he was just ravenous. Explosive. He wanted her *now*. He tugged at the handcuffs. They just got tighter. "Let me loose!"

"No."

"I want to be inside you when I come," he ground out, teetering on the very edge of losing control.

Something in his tone must have clued her to his sincerity. She hesitated. He heard a soft moan of agreement. She reached under the pillow for the key.

Fuck that.

"Hurry," he said. "Slide up on top of me."

She did so, and before he could draw a shaky breath, he was deep inside her. Wet and hot, she felt *so* fucking good. But handcuffs or no, he wanted her under him. Two decades of hand-to-hand combat took over and, handcuffs and all, in the blink of an eye he'd spun their bodies and pinned her under him.

"That's better," he murmured, gripping the spindles of the headboard. Taking over.

"Not fair," she protested breathlessly as he drove into her. But she wrapped her legs around his waist. He'd proven his trust. Now she just wanted him.

He kissed her deep and long, and started to move. More and more urgently. Filling her and worshiping her flesh with his. Showing her with his body and soul what his rational mind still refused to acknowledge.

That he *wanted* her to love him. Desperately. Longingly. Deep inside, he yearned for her to fill the dark, empty place that had been his heart for as long as he could remember. A heart he'd deliberately allowed no one to enter.

Until now.

She gasped as he pounded into her. Clung to him as he rode her toward oblivion. Both of them cried out in a single explosion of pleasure and emotion, the unexpected power of their combined climax blowing them away completely.

"Oh, Gregg," she sighed breathlessly when their pulses

returned from the stratosphere and they floated back to earth.

"I'm here," he told her, holding her close after she finally brought out the key and released him. "I'm not going anywhere."

And for the first time ever, he really wished he didn't have to leave.

BUT he did.

As soon as Gina fell asleep, Gregg slipped from the bed and padded quietly to the bathroom. He quickly dressed, then went into the sitting room and closed the bedroom door silently behind him.

He lifted the phone and asked for Rebel Haywood's room.

"Hello?" came the groggy answer before the first ring ended.

"Sorry for waking you, Special Agent Haywood. This is Gregg van Halen."

"Oh?" There was a micro-pause. "*Oh*. Hang on. Gina's right—" There was a muffled cry. "Oh, no! She's not—"

"Gina's with me," he cut in. "Sleeping. She's fine.

"Oh. Thank God," the FBI agent breathed. "Give me a heart attack."

"I have a favor to ask. Can you come over and stay with her? I have something I need to do, and don't want to leave her alone."

There was a rustling of bedcovers. "Uh, sure. Just give me five minutes."

When she arrived, dressed and armed, Agent Haywood didn't ask where he was going or for how long. But when he opened the door to leave the suite, she did say, "You're coming back, aren't you?"

"Yes," he assured her. "Just keep her safe until I do."

She smiled. "I will."

He closed the door behind him, and wondered what Alex Zane's problem was. The woman was smart, beautiful, and loyal, and obviously had it bad for the dimwit. Was the guy fucking blind?

Whatever. Not his business.

He retrieved the Mercedes and pointed it toward McLean, Virginia, the pricy suburb where Lester Altos maintained his D.C. residence. After setting up her computers, STORM's comp spec Darcy Zimmerman had been able to ferret out the address, along with a few other interesting tidbits about the congressman from Louisiana. Principal among which was that Altos sat on the Military Defense Subcommittee of the mega-influential House Appropriations Committee. The *same* subcommittee for which Zane had found a meeting agenda on the terrorists' sunken yacht.

Hello? Was there any doubt they'd found their guy?

Quinn was right to call STORM to assign another team to follow through on the nuclear trigger theory with the Coast Guard, just in case this new angle was wrong. But Gregg was sure this was the right direction. Everything was falling into place.

He had argued for going in fast and hard and apologizing later if they were wrong. Marc Lafayette had agreed, outraged that his beloved home state might be represented by a slimy traitor.

Quinn, however, would not be rushed. He wanted hard evidence, so any charges against Altos would be iron-clad. He wanted the bastard behind bars for the rest of his life, or better yet, at the end of a hangman's noose. He had a point.

But Gregg had his doubts Altos would ever see a trial, judging by the look on Kick Jackson's face. The man was on a serious crusade for revenge. Something about a massacre in Afghanistan, or was it the Sudan . . . Of course,

Kick would have to get in line behind Gregg. The image of Gina being carried off the plane after her rescue, battered, bruised, and bloody, drugged because she was so traumatized she could barely function, was forever burned in Gregg's brain. Someone would pay for that. If it was the last thing he did.

In any case, the team had argued back and forth until Darcy had finally shooed everyone to their own rooms to get some shut-eye. They would come up with a plan in the morning.

Gregg had other ideas.

Gina showing up at his door had caused a delay, but not changed his mind. If anything, it had strengthened his resolve. She loved him. He would *not* let her down.

ALTOS'S three-story colonial mansion was tucked into a wide, azalea-filled lot on a tree-lined lane. Gregg drove past, wanting to get a feel for the neighborhood and decide where he would set up his surveillance. Easy. A tall, slotted topiary hedge ran between two houses directly across the street. On his second pass, he saw movement. For an instant, the very edge of a man-shaped shadow scudded along the perimeter, paused, then retreated back into it. Just enough of a glimpse for a trained eye to spot.

Jackson. Gregg had to smile. The guy must want company.

What the hell. He was part of a team now.

He parked the Mercedes a mile or so away, strapped on his fanny pack entry kit, zipped up his black hoodie, and slipped back through the darkness. Approaching the hedge, he gave a low bird call. A dove coo answered. He slid through one of the manicured breaks.

"What up," Jackson greeted him in a low voice, leaning with his back against a brick wall behind the hedge. He was holding a pair of night vision goggles in one hand, a sniper rifle slung over his shoulder.

"Great minds," Gregg returned with a bump of his fist and a jerk of his chin across at the Altos place. "So. Anything going on?"

"Not yet."

"Yet?"

"Had a look-see earlier. One car missing from the garage. No one seems to be home."

"Just one? Wife in town?"

"Yup."

Frowning, Gregg consulted his watch. Well past three a.m. "Hot date?" Altos's trophy wife was considerably younger.

Kick looked skeptical. "How long have they been married?"

"Ten years." Long enough for the honeymoon to be over. "Shit."

"Could he be running? Spooked by the flag your Pentagon files search triggered?"

"Possibly." Gregg debated. Decided if the team was compromised, no way was Jackson the mole. "Or maybe he was warned."

The other man's gaze sharpened. When he answered, his voice was quiet but forceful. "If someone warned him, it wasn't by anyone in STORM. I know these people. I would trust my life to every one of them."

Gregg was pretty good at reading people. Jackson meant every word.

"It remains to be seen," the other man went on, "whether or not we can trust *you*."

Gregg didn't bother to be offended. Kick had been one of the first to vote in his favor this afternoon. But suspicion kept a man alive. "Fair enough," Gregg said. "So, what's the plan?"

"My plan was to watch and wait. But I could be persuaded."

Gregg smiled. "Fancy a little B&E?"

"That's taking a bit of a risk, isn't it?"

"No business for the faint of heart. How 'bout if I enter and you watch my back?"

Kick's brows rose. "You trust me?"

"Like I have a choice?"

"Yeah, you do."

He shrugged. "Whatever. I'm going in. Alarms?"

"Ancient."

Gregg rattled off his cell phone number and set it to vibrate. "Text me if company arrives."

"Will do."

He closed his eyes for a moment and tested the mood of the street. All felt tranquil. So, with a nod to Jackson, he melted into the shadows.

GREGG made quick work of getting inside the house. The security system was child's play, which told him either a) Altos had nothing to hide, or b) the congressman felt totally safe with his secrets.

Innocent? Or overconfident?

Just in case, Gregg checked carefully for more sophisticated security measures. Hidden cameras. Pressure triggers. Silent alarms. There was nothing.

He checked the bedroom. No signs of hurried packing. Two suitcases stood unused in the walk-in closet. No empty hangers. Two electric toothbrushes sat charging on the bathroom counter. So, Altos hadn't taken off.

Next he located the home office. Lester Altos had been a politician for more than half his life, of which over a dozen years had been as a Louisiana congressman. One wall contained a shoulder-height bank of cabinets that held more files and documents than Gregg could search through in a month. He took one look, and went to the desk to turn on the computer instead. His hacker skills were novice at best, but one thing he had learned long ago was to interrupt the boot-up bios before the OS started, and have the computer make a call to mama. Mama, in this case, being Darcy Zimmerman's STORM mainframe computer station, the ISP for which he'd obtained from her earlier. Once the two computers had talked to each other, Darcy could find her way back in.

As he waited for the scroll of code across the screen that signaled docking was complete, he skimmed his gaze around the rest of Altos's highly polished desk. Other than a picture of his young wife and a goldfish bowl containing one bright red Siamese fighting fish and a handful of bright white gravel, the surface was clear.

The drawers were filled with a completely normal and boring assortment of office supplies. He found nothing whatsoever of interest.

After shutting down the computer again, he went to the file cabinet and started riffling through the drawers. Going specifically after bank info, he retrieved several folders filled with statements, photographed them with his PDA for account numbers, and forwarded the pix to Darcy, along with a few other bits and pieces. Then he sent it all to Tommy, too, because you just never knew.

Finally, he hit the folders with all the logical names: Gina Cappozi, both Mahmoods, all the dead suspects from New York and *Allah's Paradise*, Alex, Kick, and himself. Came up empty.

Ah, well. That had been a long shot. They'd already established the traitor was not a moron. Keeping hard-copy links to bad guys would have been extremely stupid.

No, any real evidence would be hidden in the computer. Hopefully Darcy would have better luck.

His phone buzzed and he checked the screen.

Hds up. Cmpny.

Time to go? Gregg listened, watching the fish swim round and round its bowl on the desk, its scales flashing red and silver against the glittering gravel. After a full minute there was still no distinctive rumble of the garage door opening.

He made his way to the front of the house and peeked out through a curtained window. A dark blue luxury sedan had pulled to the curb at the head of the home's brick walkway. A man and a woman sat in front talking, the man in the driver's seat.

Gregg lifted a pair of binoculars from his kit and zoomed in on the woman. Her earrings glinted back at him in the moonlight like the fish's scales. The trophy wife. He moved his focus to the man. But from this angle, he could only see up to the guy's shoulders. Damn.

After making a quick stop back in the office, he took the stairs down. Shifting the goldfish bowl he'd just grabbed under his arm, he paused to peer out through the curtains again. This time he had a better view. The two people in the car didn't seem to be in any hurry. They started to argue. A few minutes later, the man gestured angrily, slashing a hand through his hair. The wife's door jerked open. She made one parting shot, then jumped out of the sedan. The man bent over to the passenger side, calling after her.

Gregg should be oscar mike. He was about to turn away. But what he saw made him stop in his tracks. The man's face as he leaned over was clearly illuminated by a pool of moonlight. For a second Gregg just stared. What the fucking hell.

Well, well, well. Wasn't *that* interesting.

Maybe ol' Alex Zane wasn't so crazy after all. Because Gregg recognized the man at once.

And damned if it wasn't SAC Wade Montana.

TWENTY-TWO

"MONTANA and the wife?"

"It's a theory."

"It wouldn't be the first time a wife intercepted classified intel from a husband working for the government and used it for profit," Quinn said.

"Or a government official blackmailing her into doing it," Darcy suggested.

The team erupted in heated discussion. They'd all been summoned to the STORM suite for a sunrise breakfast, where Kick and van Halen had just finished telling of their nocturnal adventures. Marc had already been dispatched to watch the Altos house until a strategy could be decided.

Alex took another bite of toast and gracefully refrained from saying "I told you so." But inside he was doing the Snoopy dance. He'd been right about the bastard all along.

He glanced at Rebel. His beautiful angel looked more like the angel of death. Furious that her lover—*former* lover, he corrected himself—had been called into question. Yet again.

"I'm telling you, you're wrong," she insisted for the dozenth time. "He would never hurt Gina. He just wants to be sure she's safe. He feels partly responsible for what's happening to her."

Gina was sitting on the sofa next to van Halen. *She* looked like she wanted to sink right through the floor and disappear. But she didn't defend Montana, Alex noted.

He gritted his teeth. Only Rebel was doing that. Along with shooting him dagger looks. What? Could he help it the man was a traitor? At least she wasn't still sleeping with the bastard.

He hoped.

Bad enough he'd thought for one electrically evil moment that she'd spent the night with van Halen. He'd caught her coming out of the other man's hotel suite this morning in blatant dishabille, as his mama used to say. Thankfully, Gina had followed close behind and saved his ass the embarrassment of a very ugly scene. Hearing Gregg's story over breakfast, and seeing the way he now held Gina close to his side, explained Rebel's presence in his suite, which Alex had not been able to bring himself to ask her about at the time. Not after she'd politely nodded good morning to him without a damn *hint* in her demeanor that just the day before they'd been agonizing over not having children together. No doubt he had Montana to thank for that, too. Had she actually *taken* his ill-conceived advice?

Jesus.

"So what are we going to do about this goddamn goat-fuck?" he asked now. Meaning the Altos thing.

Rebel skewered him with another death-ray glare. Language? Probably not.

Her phone rang and with an angry stab she shut it off.

Okay, then.

"They had an affair," Gina said into the momentary blip of awkward silence. "Wade and Erika Altos. A few months after he and I broke up. He told me about it at the time. Probably thought it would make me jealous and go back to him."

Darcy snorted. "Yeah, because taking up with another woman is *al*ways the best way to endear yourself to the one you love," she muttered, pouring coffee into two fresh mugs and handing one to Quinn. "Typical."

Rebel continued to glare at Alex.

What?

"You hear what they were arguing about?" Quinn asked.

Kick shook his head. "The car windows were closed."

"We have to assume he told her about us finding the 25K al Sayika contribution to her husband's campaign at Mahmood's apartment," Tara observed.

"If the wife didn't already know."

"So if she tries to blow town, she's guilty and we pick her up," Kick said, checking his cell phone for texts. So far, no movement reported from Marc.

"And if Congressman Altos packs his bags, he's the guilty party," Quinn said, "and we have the evidence we need to put the thumb screws on him about our Trigger theory. I feel like we're running out of time. If we're right and it is a presidential assassination they're planning, we need to notify POTUS. But I'd like a little more evidence than pure conjecture." He looked to Darcy. "Still nothing from Altos's home computer?"

"Not a blessed thing. No hidden files, no suspicious e-mails. Not even any porn. The man's freaking Mr. Clean," she said, visibly frustrated as she headed back to the conference table where, judging by the dirty cups and empty snack bags, she'd already been working at her computer array for hours.

"Did he ever return home last night?" Tara asked.

"About half an hour after the wife came home," van Halen confirmed. Alex watched as one of his fingers unconsciously stirred the water in the fish bowl he'd stolen from Altos's desk last night, making its lone inhabitant dart nervously back and forth. Seriously? The man might be an ace operator, but he was truly certifiable.

"Either way the chips fall," Alex said, "Montana is guilty of aiding and abetting, and DHS arrests his ass for breach of national security."

"That's not fair." Rebel looked ready to explode. "We need to question him first. I'm sure he has a good explanation."

"No doubt," Alex drawled. "And I for one would love to hear it."

"Good," Quinn said, getting to his feet. "Because I want you to go get SAC Montana and bring him here. Whatever he knows about this whole mess, I mean to find out, one way or another. Take Rebel with you, Zane, and tell him we've decided to let him see Gina, since he asked yesterday. If he's innocent, he's got nothing to worry about." He turned to Rebel. "That fair enough for you?"

"Yes, sir," she said, getting to her feet. "Right away."

"Hey," Alex protested, holding up his toast. "I haven't finished eating yet."

"Tough," she said, and strode out the door.

"Fuck me," he muttered, and got up to follow.

"And Zane," Quinn said testily, tossing him the keys to one of the team's SUVs, "I ordered you to *fix* that situation."

Alex grabbed his jacket and shoulder-holster, which were draped over his chair, and on his way to the door threw them on. "I did, Commander," he returned over one shoulder. "Can't you tell?"

A fingerprint had come back from the murder scene at Walter Reed. Bleary-eyed, Sarah stared at the name on the

ID. It had taken quite a bit of digging, but she'd finally found the bastard in the OPM government employee database.

Gregg van Halen. A former CIA agent gone rogue.

She frowned. Hadn't Wade mentioned a CIA covert operative who'd turned traitor? The man he thought kidnapped his ex-fiancée a few days ago?

She looked at van Halen's face on the computer monitor. Short-cropped sandy hair, angular jaw, shadowed cheekbones. Brutally handsome, as the song went. Like he could kill a man and not even blink. Which he obviously had at Walter Reed. She just prayed he hadn't killed Wade's ex-fiancée, Gina, too.

With a yawn, she hit the button on the computer to print out a hard copy.

She'd worked all night and was dog tired. She'd managed to get a warrant for the limo service's call records, and had tracked down every single incoming phone number listed. There'd been thirteen numbers for offices up on the Hill, which she planned to narrow down this morning by hook or by crook.

As soon as she got herself another cup of coffee.

And phoned Wade.

She'd been ducking his calls since yesterday afternoon, and regardless of how big of a jerk she thought he was for engaging in a dogfight over another woman right in front of her face, he deserved to know about van Halen.

She also wanted to find out if her newest murder suspect was the same man Wade suspected of abducting his ex-fiancée. It made sense, but she needed to know for sure.

She should call Commander Quinn, as well. Although, he did have other sources. The wolf guarding Wade's redheaded FBI agent at the hospital had been from STORM, and had no doubt given Quinn a full report. Still. The commander had been as good as his word, so Sarah wanted to return the favor. And who knew, maybe he'd dug up something she hadn't.

But first, coffee.

Okay. And maybe a ten-minute nap.

AFTER the breakfast meeting, Gina was feeling a little shell-shocked by everything that had come to light. Either that, or the exhaustion was finally catching up with her.

Kick and Tara had gone back to McLean to join Marc surveilling the Altos house, watching to see whether the husband or the wife would make the first move.

Quinn had finally gotten a call from his contact in the Cayman Islands, along with an e-mailed packet of bank statements from him. He'd been plenty excited about whatever was in it. He and Gregg were about to leave for the Capitol for a meeting with Congressman Altos's chief of staff. It was Saturday, but the man was in the office preparing last-minute details for a subcommittee meeting of the House Appropriations Committee, which the congressman was scheduled to attend that afternoon.

Gina still found it hard to believe a member of congress would betray his country. And for what? Pure greed, if Gregg was right about the al Sayika blood diamonds being his motive. It would almost be more palatable if the other theory was correct, that the terrorists themselves were planning to set off a dirty bomb. As terrifying as that was, the motive would be ideological, not simple avarice. She was glad Quinn had put three other men on tracking down the nuclear trigger possibility. But her money was on greed.

"You'll be okay?" Gregg asked, putting his arms around her. He was wearing the brown suit again. He looked strangely at home in it. Like a real businessman. If only. But after last night she knew this man would never be tamed. Even in handcuffs, he took total charge.

"I'm fine. Really," she said. "Go. Just hurry back."

"I will." He kissed her. "Stay with Darcy. She'll keep you safe while I'm gone. I hear the woman knows seven kinds of marshal arts, all black belts."

She smiled, glancing over at Darcy, who rolled her eyes with a grin, then went back to her computers.

"And don't even think about—"

"I know, I know. No going out for ice."

He kissed the tip of her nose. "For *any* reason. Not without Darcy."

"I promise."

"We'll be back soon. Hopefully before Alex and Rebel bring in Montana."

With a final kiss, he followed Quinn out the door. It closed behind them.

"Hold on to that one, girlfriend," Darcy said without taking her eyes off her computer screen. "He's definitely a keeper."

"Yeah," Gina said with a stab of hopeless longing. "If only he felt the same way." She couldn't help feeling she was living a temporary reprieve. When she'd awakened this morning to find him gone . . .

Darcy spun her chair around and regarded her. "Gina. The man is head over heels. Anyone can see that."

"Maybe. And maybe in a parallel universe he'd do something about it. But not in this one." His life was his job. There was no room for her in it.

"Really? What's his problem?" The monitor beeped twice, and she spun back to type furiously on the keyboard for a few seconds, then twirled around again, looking at her expectantly.

Gina wandered over to the easy chair and sat on the fat arm. "He had a rough time as a kid. He's shut himself off. Refuses to acknowledge his emotions. Doesn't think he's capable of love."

Darcy's brows went up. "Jeez. Someone should hand him a mirror when he looks at you."

Gina smiled wistfully. "I'm such a wreck, I'm terrified I'll drive him away just through my neediness. He's the only thing keeping me sane through all of this. I'm so tired I'm about to fall over, but I can't even sleep without him there."

Darcy gave her a worried look. "You should try anyway. Curl up on the sofa until the guys get back. Who knows, maybe you'll drift off."

Gina looked around the sitting room, ablaze with sunlight pouring through the windows and French doors, and alive with the techy noises from Darcy's computers. No way. She sighed, and thought longingly of the bed she just left . . .

Well, why not?

"Maybe I will try," she said, getting up. "But not here. Our suite is right across the hall. I'll be able to smell him in the bed. With the drapes pulled, I can pretend he's there, sleeping next to me. It could work."

Darcy crossed her arms. "You heard what he said. No leaving the suite. *This* one."

"Without you, he said." Gina spread her hands in appeal. "You can walk me across the hall and watch me go in and close the door. I swear I won't open it for anyone, and I'll call you when I want to come back. I even have a gun. Gregg gave me his Beretta yesterday."

Darcy started to shake her head. "I don't—"

"Please?" Gina said. "I've been terrified nonstop for a week. I could really use the rest, before . . ."

She didn't complete the sentence, but she could tell that Darcy understood. Having narrowed down Altos or his wife as the traitor, events were starting to come to a head. But if the Trigger was still out there somewhere, and Gina had an awful feeling he was, things would get a lot worse before they got better. She didn't want to be cross-eyed from exhaustion when all hell broke loose.

"I shouldn't," Darcy said, breaking down. "But I do get the man-smell thing. I'm the same way about Bobby Lee. So I'll go along with this. But I swear, if you step foot outside that room without calling me I'll shoot you myself. I'm serious."

"I won't. Cross my heart," Gina said, and on impulse gave the other woman a hug.

With a start, she realized Darcy was the first person she'd willingly touched since her abduction, other than Rainie and Gregg. A milestone? Oh, yes. A happy one.

Darcy insisted on clearing the other suite first, of course. With weapon drawn, she searched every nook and cranny before giving Gina the okay to come farther than one step inside the door.

"Is that the Beretta?" Darcy asked, and pointed to the gun that still sat where Gina had left it on the sideboard yesterday.

She nodded.

"Keep it with you. Put it under your pillow while you sleep."

"I will. And thanks," Gina said, preparing to close the door after Darcy as she left. "I'll call."

"*No ice*," the other woman warned with a wag of her finger, walking across the hall again. "And no room service, either!"

Gina laughed and waved, and closed the door as Darcy watched like a hawk. "Don't worry," she assured her firmly. "Not a chance in hell."

"YES, I'm Bruce Hearn. What can I do for you gentlemen?"

Altos's chief of staff sized up Gregg and Quinn in a

heartbeat. He did not ask them to sit, did not offer them a beverage. Maybe it was the thrift shop suits. Hearn's own attire was strictly Brooks Brothers. Or maybe even tailor-made.

Quinn, however, was not taking no for an answer. He gave the man his best lazy Southern smile and ambled farther into the office. Gregg took up a position closer to the door. He could play dumb muscle when called for.

"You, Mr. Hearn," Quinn drawled with calm confidence, "are in very big trouble, sir."

The other man straightened and marched straight to the desk, where he lifted the phone. "I'm calling security."

Quinn tipped a photo of Asha Mahmood onto the desktop, where it skidded to a stop directly in front of Hearn. "I wouldn't do that, if I were you."

Hearn stopped abruptly. Slowly, he set the receiver down. His eyes jerked up from the photo. "Who is that? What's this all about?"

"Oh, I think you know who she is," Quinn said. "*And* what this is all about."

The chief of staff looked from Quinn to the photo and back again. Oddly, he didn't seem the least bit rattled. "Who are you people?" he demanded.

"Someone who just might be able to keep your butt out of prison. But only if you cooperate and answer my questions."

One gray-tinged brow went up. "About what?" Quinn pointed to the photo. Hearn hesitated for a moment, then said archly, "She's a . . . friend of the congressman."

Quinn continued to quiz the man while Gregg observed. On the downside of fifty, Altos's chief of staff appeared to be the epitome of a Washington insider: groomed, wealthy, entitled. For someone being threatened, Bruce Hearn was also remarkably composed. He didn't even glance in Gregg's direction. Blythe ignorance? Gregg didn't think so. On the contrary, Hearn had the look of a man who'd been around the block a time or three but knew how to conceal it well. But then, so did everyone working inside the beltway.

Gregg decided to take a stroll around the office. Hearn began to protest, but was cut off by Quinn. Gregg was careful not to touch. Just look. Everything appeared completely normal. The door to the private office presumably used by Congressman Altos stood partially open, so he ducked inside for a look-see.

He smiled. On the desk stood a pristinely kept goldfish bowl identical to the one he'd taken from the Altos mansion last night, except the fish was blue, and the gravel was red and white arranged in neat stripes. How patriotic.

Placed exactly below the glass bowl was an agenda for a meeting of the Defense subcommittee that Congressman Altos would be attending at two o'clock. The subject: the final vote on a recommendation for tougher laws on terrorism. Talk about ironic.

Gregg checked his watch. It was just after eleven. He quickly read over the agenda. And saw something that he hadn't on the one Zane found on *Allah's Paradise*. Something scheduled for right after the meeting.

Oh, *shit*.

Quinn finished up his interview, and just before they left, Gregg turned back to Hearn. "Nice betta."

The chief of staff met his gaze directly. "What?"

"The Siamese fighting fish. In Altos's office."

"Oh. Yes."

"Who takes care of it?"

He lifted a shoulder. "Some pet store sends a person. I'm not sure."

They exited the building and trotted down the impressive front steps of the Capitol.

"Siamese fighting fish?" Quinn asked. "Like the one you liberated from his house?"

"Yep."

There was a brief pause. "The diamonds, you think?"

The man was quick. "Yep."

"Figured," Quinn observed. "Pretty obvious, don't you think?"

"Almost like the guy wants to get caught."

Quinn frowned. "Huh. See anything else?"

"The agenda for this afternoon's meeting."

"And?"

"There's a new item. A press conference scheduled for directly afterward. One guess who'll be attending."

Quinn's gaze collided with his. "Jesus," he cursed. "Tell me it's not—"

"Yep," Gregg said. "POTUS."

TWENTY-THREE

A knock on the door dragged Gina from a deep sleep. Groggily she tried to focus on the bedside clock, but the numbers were just a blur. Reaching under her pillow she grasped the Beretta, then swung her legs unsteadily off the bed.

She shook herself to clear the mental cobwebs. Who could it be? Darcy hadn't called her, and she had most definitely not ordered room service. She gripped the gun harder, debating what to do.

There was another knock. She decided to check the peephole and see who it was. Padding stealthily to the living room, she quietly approached the door and quickly put her eye to the lens.

Crap. It was Wade.

He squinted at the peephole. "Gina?" he mouthed, though she couldn't hear a sound through the thick door.

What the . . . ? She turned and leaned her back against

the cool wood and tried to marshal her thoughts. He didn't look dangerous. He looked tired. As tired as she felt.

She was pretty sure this would be a violation of her agreement with both Gregg and Darcy, but he looked so darned earnest.

She kept the chain on and cracked it open just wide enough to peer at him, gripping the Beretta the whole time. "Wade? What are you doing here?"

He smiled uncertainly. "Is everything okay? Can I come in?"

She stood on tiptoe to look behind him. "Where are Alex and Rebel?"

"Don't know. Haven't seen them." He stood there, looking a tad wistful and abandoned, waiting for her to invite him in.

"How did you find me?" she asked hesitantly.

Wryly, he lifted a shoulder. "I *am* an FBI agent, Gina. I knew STORM had you in protective custody. It wasn't too hard to track down where they were staying. Can we talk?"

Should she risk it?

This was *Wade*, she reminded herself. The man she'd made love with for three years, had been engaged to marry. A man who had risked his career to follow her case so she'd be safe. It would be fine.

"Okay. Just for a minute," she said. She unhooked the chain and stepped backward, and slid the gun into her robe pocket.

He came in and tentatively closed the door. "I can't tell you how relieved I am to see you. I just wanted to be sure you're really okay."

"I am. Thanks."

He took another step in. "Gina, I'm so sorry about everything that's happened. I know it's all my fault, and I—"

"Don't be silly," she countered. "Of course it's not your fault."

He grimaced. "I was the one who put you in touch with CIA back when Rainie disappeared. That's when you met that man, and everything started to—"

"What man?" she interrupted warily.

"The traitor, that rogue agent, Captain van Halen."

She suddenly realized he had no idea Gregg was not a bad guy. He still thought he was working for the terrorists. "No, Wade, he's not a traitor. You don't understand. Gregg is helping me."

Wade's expression shifted to a portrait of incredulity. "Jesus, Gina! He's wanted for *murder*. Van Halen killed those men in New York, and another at Walter Reed Army Medical Center. I'm working with the Metro detective on the case. She knows he's here in D.C., and—"

Panic surged through Gina. "*What?* My God, no! He's *innocent* of all those things they're accusing him of!"

Wade appeared genuinely taken aback. "How can you be so sure?"

"STORM interrogated him. They believed his story enough that they put him on the team hunting the real traitor." She met her ex-fiancé's eyes and held them. "Gregg and I are together, Wade. He'd never hurt me. We're lovers."

Wade slid his hands into his trouser pockets and stared at her for a long moment. "I see. That's . . . um . . . Shit, that's . . ."

She didn't really want to hear his opinion of her choice of lover. It wasn't like Wade had been suffering through a monastic life of deprivation since they broke up. Besides, she couldn't shake the questions the STORM meeting had raised about him.

"There's something I need to ask you," she said.

He blew out a breath. Swiped his hand over his mouth. It looked like he was about to say something else, but changed his mind. "Okay. Sure."

"What were you doing last night with Erika Altos?"

His face drained of color. "Christ. How do you know about that?"

Not a good sign. "The team saw you with her," she said, folding her arms across her middle. "In your car, outside her house. Arguing."

He paced away, visibly agitated. "Oh, Jesus, fuck."

A spiral of alarm began to wend its way through her. Good lord. Could he really be involved? "Tell me what's going on, Wade. Are you mixed up in something you shouldn't be? Please tell me you're not—"

"No! God, no." He turned back to her, his hands on his hips, face ashen. "I just . . . I got things all wrong. Damn it, this wasn't supposed to—"

"What? Talk to me."

He closed his eyes and cursed again silently. Then he took a deep breath and opened them again. "You know Erika and I had a brief affair a few years back."

Gina nodded guardedly. "You told me."

"Well, we've kept in touch." He raised a hand like a stop sign. "Friends. Not romantically. We have lunch. Talk. She's lonely." He shrugged.

Right. "Okay. So . . . ?"

"So when the Mahmood investigation turned up evidence of a huge contribution to her husband's campaign that could be traced directly to a terrorist organization, I thought I should tell her. So she could distance herself from him before the shit hits the fan. Which it will. Soon."

Gina's jaw dropped. Thank God he wasn't involved, but— "My God, Wade. You could get in such trouble for warning her!"

He puffed out a breath. "No shit."

"But why the argument? Didn't she believe you?"

"Oh, she believed me. We argued because she wanted to tell Bruce Hearn, her husband's chief of staff, and warn him, too."

Gina was outraged. "Doesn't she understand what it could do to your career if it came out you leaked that information?" Aside from the fact that it would make him look guilty as hell. Alex Zane already wanted to have him arrested. This would clinch it for sure.

"She didn't care." He slashed a hand through his hair. "Apparently she's now sleeping with this Hearn character."

"Good lord."

"It gets worse," Wade said. "Back when we were seeing each other, somehow Hearn found out." He grimaced. "Apparently there are photos. Ever since then, he's been . . . asking me for favors. In exchange for his silence."

Her eyes widened. "He's *blackmailing* you?"

Wade took a few steps toward her, palms out in appeal. "Nothing terribly sinister. Mostly intel on the congressman's political opponents. A few times he wanted information from Interpol on some foreign nationals. Stuff the FBI has access to that others wouldn't. I went along with it because the information was harmless and Erika begged me not to blow up her marriage."

Gina could just imagine. Wade was a chauvinist son of a bitch, but at times he could be a real softie. "Oh, Wade."

"The thing is . . ." He was standing right in front of her now. "Last year Hearn wanted to know about you."

"Me?" Surprise rendered her speechless.

"The congressman had heard you were making trouble at CIA about your friend Rainie's disappearance. He wanted to know why."

A sick feeling seeped through her stomach. She vividly recalled Gregg's theory that she might be the traitor's actual target. Could it really be Congressman Altos after her? "But why?" she asked. "What did you tell him?"

"The truth. That you were just looking for your friend. I gave Hearn the same phone number I'd given you."

The phone number that had led her straight to Gregg.

She struggled to stay calm. "I don't understand."

"The congressman is on the Military Defense Subcommittee for House Appropriations. Hearn said they were checking into illegal Zero Unit operations for CIA. At the time it sounded legit, like he might actually be able to help you."

"Oh." That didn't sound so bad. But her pulse was still buzzing. *Some*thing didn't add up.

"I didn't think too much about it. Not until that big campaign contribution came to light yesterday. Then I started to wonder . . . could it really be a coincidence that al Sayika was involved in sabotaging the Zero Unit operation *and* donating money to Congressman Altos's campaign? Like everyone else, I was focusing on van Halen. Thinking he was Altos's man inside Zero Unit. The one who sold you out."

"He wasn't!"

"Gina, I believe you. But don't you see?"

She regarded him with growing disquiet. Honest to God, she didn't *want* to see. "What . . . ?"

"During the argument last night I asked Erika if she knew anything about it. If your name had ever come up in *her* conversations with Altos or Hearn. Not about Rainie, but about your genetics research."

A prickling of real foreboding began to trickle through her. "Wade. What are you saying?"

A look of misery crossed his face. "She told me yes, that the subcommittee had been looking for a scientist to consult on bioweapons, and because we'd talked, she knew about your work. *She* was the one who told Altos about you."

Oh, God. A tremble started deep within Gina. "When?"

His face was ashen. "Just before you were captured."

She stumbled to a chair and sat down hard in it, gripping the sides to keep from collapsing to the floor. A noise of disbelief slipped past her quivering lips. "My God," she cried. "It was *you*."

His body sagged. "Sweetheart, I am so sorry. I never meant for any of this to happen. You have to know that."

"*You're* the one who brought me to the attention of terrorists?"

He covered his eyes with a shaking hand. "All along, I had this horrible feeling it was my fault for giving you the damned phone number that put you in touch with van Halen. I was so sure it was him! But all along it was *me* who'd given you to the terrorists. I am *so* fucking sorry!"

He swiped his eyes with his hand and she realized they'd filled with tears.

Like a balloon deflating, all her inner anguish over the randomness and injustice of her terrible ordeal dissolved at the sight of his profound distress. Despite everything she'd suffered, her heart went out to him.

She couldn't stand seeing him so defeated. She rose and went to him, put her arms around him.

"Don't do this to yourself, Wade. You didn't know. How could you? And I survived. I'll be fine."

"Thank God." He held her tight for a long time. "Thank God."

The closure felt good, empathy and understanding surrounding them both in a cocoon of forgiveness. Somehow she knew they'd be able to put the past behind them now. Both of them. He could finally move on and find a new love, without sabotaging the relationship. And she . . .

Well, she could stop jumping at shadows. That was a good start.

Love? She sighed inwardly. Maybe in time Gregg would come around . . .

Wade kissed her lightly, and they gave each other a final squeeze.

"We should tell Quinn," she said, and let him go. "STORM will want to know all this."

"Yeah," he said, straightening his spine. "Erika said Altos is meeting with the Appropriations Committee today." He checked his watch. "It should be starting about now. We could catch him as he comes out."

"The team knows about the meeting. That may already be the plan."

Come to think of it . . . If it was that late, why hadn't Darcy or Gregg woken her already?

As if on cue, there was a knock at the door.

"This is probably them now," she said. "Ready to meet Gregg?"

"What the hell," Wade said philosophically. "May as well get the apology over with."

She smiled as she went to answer the knock. "Don't worry. I'm sure he'll be gentle with you." She swung open the door.

And found herself staring down the barrel of a gun. Held by a stranger.

Shock froze her to the spot. She tried to scream, but her throat had instantly dried to dust.

Behind her, she heard Wade's quick intake of breath and the slide of his shoulder holster. "What the hell are you—"

The gun jammed into her forehead. She squeaked in terror.

"Don't," the stranger ordered, looking past her at Wade. "Throw it down. Over here." Through the rush of blood in her ears, his voice sounded vaguely familiar.

Wade swore, and a second later she heard a thud in the carpet by her feet.

The man's focus shifted back to her. "Walk backward."

She forced herself to move, praying she wouldn't trip. "Who are you?" she asked tightly. He was well dressed, in an expensive suit. Stylish hair, graying at the temples. Had she seen him before? Who knew. He looked and sounded exactly like half a million other men in Washington, D.C. What he *didn't* look like was a terrorist.

He gave her an odd smile, tilting his head. But didn't answer.

Instead, he made Wade cuff his wrists behind his back with his own handcuffs.

She had to do something! Then she remembered . . .

Carefully she slipped her hand into her robe pocket and wrapped it around the Beretta.

"You'll never get away with this, Hearn," Wade gritted out.

Hearn? She swallowed heavily. So Altos's chief of staff *was* involved.

"You're dead wrong, Montana," Hearn said. "We've been getting away with it for years."

We? Was the wife part of it, too? Jesus, Tara had been right!

Hearn held out a water bottle to Gina and jerked the gun at Wade. "Take this and make him drink it."

Wait. *What*? He was going to *poison* them?

Instead of reaching for the bottle, she whipped the Beretta from her pocket. "No!"

But by now her hands were shaking so badly, his struck out and lightning fast he knocked the gun from her grip. To her horror she suddenly saw his sleeve was soaked in blood. "Try that again," he growled harshly, "and I'll shoot you both right here."

She believed him.

She took the bottle. "What's in the water?" Her voice quavered as she uncapped the lid.

"Rohypnol," Hearn said, and turned his gaze to Wade. "Drink it and you'll be unconscious in twenty minutes. You won't feel a thing. Or I can shoot you in the head now. Your choice." The man looked completely unmoved by the monstrous thing he was saying. As though it were a choice between paper or plastic at the grocery store.

Jesus God.

Wade opened his mouth and gestured with his chin for her to pour.

"Please," she begged Hearn. *Please, God.* This could *not* be happening. "Don't do this."

Hearn ignored her plea. "Don't even think about spilling it," he told her as though she hadn't spoken. "That'll just get him a bullet between the eyes."

"Go on," Wade said bravely, and tears blurred her vision. "It'll be okay."

But they both knew it wouldn't.

"I'm so sorry," she whispered threadily. And fed him the water.

TWENTY-FOUR

"WHERE the fucking hell *is* the bastard?"

Montana had dropped off the face of the earth. Alex and Rebel were currently standing in front of the D.C. Metro First District station. They'd thought maybe he was with that lady detective he seemed to like. Admittedly, a long shot.

Alex tried to walk off his frustration by pacing back and forth on the sidewalk, but it was only getting worse. Even Rebel was looking worried. She'd long since given up correcting his language.

She raised her go-cup and took a jerky sip of her second double latte in as many hours. "He must be out working on a case or something."

Right. And Alex's PTSD was completely cured. And oh, yeah, world peace had just been declared.

"We're wasting our time. We should get back to the team," he said disgustedly.

Rebel's expression turned mulish. "Quinn said to bring Wade in. We should keep looking."

Alex ticked off on his fingers. "Montana's not answering any of his phones or pages. He's not at his apartment, and his car is gone. The Washington field office has no clue where he is. Ditto Quantico. He's not here at Metro, or with Detective McPhee. Where would you suggest we check next? The zoo?"

"I don't know!" Exasperation rang in her voice.

"Admit it, your man is involved in treason and has skipped town." It had nothing to do with personal feelings. That was the most logical conclusion.

Rebel's fists clenched. "Wade is not a traitor. And he's *not* my man. I don't *have* a man." This last was delivered with particular venom.

Okay. He deserved that.

He'd broken her heart and crushed her dreams, all after taking ruthless advantage of her feelings for him. He was the worst kind of excuse for a man and he knew it. But when it came to this one woman, he lost all semblance of levelheadedness and rationality.

He knew she'd been holding it together all morning by a thread. It was a tribute to her professionalism that she could be in the same room with him and not fall apart completely. Or pull out her gun and shoot him.

If only she knew how much causing her pain was killing him inside. How much he ached to be a whole man for her. How much he truly loved her. But sterility was not something that might go away someday, like his PTSD. He couldn't ask for that kind of sacrifice from her. He just couldn't.

"Rebel—"

"Not now, Alex."

A siren wailed past on the street. Turning, she walked back toward the lot where they'd parked the SUV. He followed after. The whole way, he battled the urge to grab her and hold her tight and tell her how fucking much he loved her, and that he was doing all this for *her* fucking sake, goddamn it! For her future happiness.

"I'll drive," she said when they got to the SUV.

He started to pass her the keys. But as soon as his fingers touched hers, he couldn't help himself. He captured her hand and tugged her to him.

"Please, Alex, I can't do this," she said, her voice brittle with emotion.

He gathered her into a warm embrace. The frustration was tying him in knots. "I just want you to know—"

"You realize we're standing in a parking lot surrounded by strangers, right?" Nearby, a two-way police radio squawked. A group of cops walked by, giving them looks.

"I honestly don't give a damn." He pressed his cheek to her fragrant red hair. She smelled like sweet dreams and fairy tales. Clean. Flowery. Alluring.

Unattainable.

He put his lips to her temple. Forced himself not to kiss the soft expanse of skin. "I just need you to understand. It's better this way."

"I know you think it is." As he watched, her beautiful green eyes filled. "But when you make love to me, your body is telling me something different."

Another siren whizzed by. "I should never have done that. It was wrong to let you think we had a future when I knew damn well we didn't." He took her face between his hands, his heart going through a meat grinder. "I can't give you the life you deserve."

A tear crept over her lashes. "Isn't that for *me* to decide?" The plea was simple, eloquent. And broke his heart completely.

He said with more sorrow than he ever imagined possible, "I wish to God things could be different."

"But they *can* be," she said. "You *will* get better. And there are other options for children. It doesn't have to end like this."

"Even if—" He shook his head. Firmed his resolve. "No. This was all a mistake. Nothing's changed."

Those sad green eyes regarded him for an endless, heart-rending moment. "You're wrong, Alex," she refuted softly. "*Everything's* changed."

Then she put her mouth to his and kissed him. She opened to him, heart and soul, and he groaned in an agony of need. Every cell of his body yearned for her.

And God help him, he kissed her back.

SARAH cracked her eyes open and lifted her head from the desk, wincing at the crick in her neck. The big black-and-white clock on the wall swam into focus.

Damn it! She'd only meant to sleep for twenty minutes. It had now been nearly four hours! Shit, shit, shit.

She wobbled to her feet, shaking out her sleeping ankle, and limped over to the coffeepot. The black liquid in the bottom would eat through her cup if she didn't drink it fast enough, but that was probably just what she needed. Jeez, she was getting too old for these all-nighters.

Bleary-eyed, she tried to remember what was on top of her to-do list for today.

Oh, yeah. Call Wade Montana.

Not for a date. She was way past *that* childish infatuation. Call it temporary insanity, due to the man's *GQ* good looks. Okay, and his awesome kissing. But the guy had major issues, and the last thing she needed in her life was a man with bigger problems than her own.

Too bad. He really was charming when he wanted to be.

She gulped down the coffee and waited for the buzz

to hit. When it did, she dialed Montana's number. It took several rings for him to answer.

"Hullo?" He sounded groggy. Gee, maybe he'd been taking a nap, too.

"Hi. It's Sarah. Sorry I've been busy and missed your calls."

"Oh. No problem." There was a rustling noise and what sounded like a woman's muffled cry in the background. "Sorry. Um. The televishion."

There was more rustling. Presumably he went to shut it off. Waiting, she riffled through the papers on her desk until she found the printout on the fingerprint ID from the Walter Reed murder.

"I'm gladge you called," he mumbled when he came back. Damn. He must have been pounding them down. Was there a game on or something? "I wanted to 'pologize for my—"

"No need," she cut him off cheerfully. "Really. I actually just called to relay some information that could be linked to your ex-fiancée's case. Are you still—"

"No, that's—" There was a thud in the background. "I mean, yeah. I am. Go 'head."

"Anyway. Forensics found a fingerprint at the murder scene yesterday and I got an ID," she said briskly. "It came back to a Gregg van Halen, who seems to have worked for CIA in some capacity. Details are a bit vague."

"Ahh." He sounded almost disappointed. "Anything elsh?"

For someone who yesterday had been so determined to hunt this guy down, he seemed singularly indifferent today. "Nope. That's it. Just thought you'd be concerned that the man who may have kidnapped your ex-fiancée is a cold-blooded murderer." She did her best to keep the cynicism from her tone. Wow. Maybe she had totally misjudged the situation. And the man.

There was a muffled silence. "Yeah." He cleared his throat. "I found out something that might interesht ya, too."

She sat up. "What?"

There was a waver in Wade's voice. Halen. "He'sh at the Watergate. Top floor."

"Damn, Wade. Are you serious?" She was already pulling her vest from her bottom drawer. "Why didn't you say so right away?

"Shorry, I . . ." It sounded like he drifted off for a second.

"Never mind. Thanks for the tip."

"Sarah?" he blurted loudly, like he'd jerked awake. "Be careful."

"I'll be fine. You just take care of yourself, Montana. Try making a pot of coffee. And I'll let you know what happens with van Halen."

Putting down the phone, she shook her head. Wow. *That* was a crying shame. Not even three o'clock in the afternoon.

Anyway. With any luck, his tip was good. She checked her weapon and slung on her vest. This was exactly the break she needed to boost her career out of the dumper.

She yelled for Jonesy. "Grab your gear, detective! Let's go catch us a killer!"

TWENTY-FIVE

"STORM Mike calling STORM Dog Six, over."

Dog Six was military-speak for commanding officer. Meaning Quinn. It was Marc calling in. He and Kick had followed Altos to the Capitol Building when he'd left his McLean house earlier that morning.

The whole team had gone to headsets, and been briefed on what happened with Bruce Hearn at Altos's office. After spending two hours with the Secret Service wrangling over how best to handle the afternoon press conference, Gregg and Quinn were now speeding back to the hotel. Gregg was behind the wheel of the SUV.

Quinn tapped his comm button. "This is STORM Dog Six actual. Go ahead STORM Mike, over."

"No movement from Altos yet," Marc reported. "The meeting is still in progress, over."

Gregg let out a breath. "We may just pull this thing off," he muttered off-comm.

"Copy that, STORM Mike. Stick with the committee,"

Quinn ordered Marc. "Kilo, the Homies will be on scene shortly." Kilo was Kick. "They'll read you into the plan. We're trying our best to pull POTUS from the press conference, over."

There was a relieved murmur from the whole team. Not one of them wanted to let the President walk into the middle of this powder keg. The potential for a goatfuck was all too real.

"Sure hope he listens to his advisors this time, over," Kick said. The man was notorious for disregarding personal safety. Said he preferred to be a man of the people. Admirable. But foolish.

"You and me both," Quinn said. "Juliet, how's the wife doing, over?" Juliet was Tara Reeves. She'd been left on stakeout at the house in McLean.

"All quiet here, boss, over."

"Good deal. Okay, updates in ten, people. Over and out."

Gregg sped through a yellow, taking a left on two wheels. He was anxious to get back to Gina. They'd been away for nearly four hours. Far too long for comfort. Darcy had said she was sleeping, so she hadn't been on the comm with the others. He needed to see her. His nerves were pricking, which they only did when he sensed something wrong. He couldn't imagine what, but he couldn't shake the feeling.

"What's the plan now?" he asked Quinn, clicking off his headset.

Quinn tapped his, as well. "Get to the hotel. Grab Darcy and the gear and get back to—"

"And Gina."

Quinn shook his head. "Gina's not an operator. She'll be in the way."

Gregg pressed his lips together. "I'm not leaving her alone. Especially not with what's going down. She's still a target."

Quinn hung on as Gregg took another corner. "Every indication is the Trigger is an assassin, and that he's planning to be at that press conference after the subcommittee meeting. He can't be in two places at once."

"I get that, but it's still just an educated guess. What if we're wrong?"

"We're not. But I can bring someone in from STORM to watch Gina. She'll be fine until it's over."

Gregg didn't like it. Not one fucking bit. He needed to have eyes on his woman.

"This is our chance to put an end to this traitor, van Halen. It's also your best chance to get your job back. I thought that's what you wanted."

"It is." He jetted out a breath and pulled into the Watergate. He parked behind a police car in the valet roundabout. "I do. But I made a vow to protect Gina until we catch this bastard and she can go back home to her real life."

Quinn regarded him for a drawn out moment. "You gonna be in it?"

"What?" With a frown at the police cruiser, Gregg told the valet they'd be right back, then said to Quinn, "Darcy would have warned us if something's wrong, yeah?"

In answer Quinn hit the comm. "STORM Zulu, everything okay at home, over?"

"Zulu here, Dog Six. Quiet as a mouse. Been chatting with the Homies. They're briefing Kilo as we speak, over."

"Is Gina awake yet?" Gregg asked, dispensing with protocol since he wasn't sure of her call sign. Or his, for that matter.

"STORM Victor, I presume? I'm about to go wake Charlie, over." So he was Victor and Gina was Charlie.

"Don't bother, Zulu. I'll do it, over," he said.

"ETA one minute," Quinn said, and tapped off the comm again as they stepped into the elevator. They both faced forward in formation, feet spread and arms crossed. "So," Quinn said, "are you going to be?"

Gregg turned his head. "Excuse me?"

"In Gina's life."

He faced forward again. "No."

"Because . . ."

"I'm an operator. I don't do relationships."

Quinn snorted. "Yeah, I can see that," he drawled.

"A comedian? Really?"

"I'm just sayin'. You might want to rethink that whole lone-wolf lifestyle thing. Makes for a very lonely old age, I hear."

"I doubt I'll live that long."

Quinn's lip quirked. "Hell, you're pretty good. It could happen."

Was that a compliment? "Thanks," Gregg said. "I think."

"In fact, so good, after this is over, you want a job you don't have to compromise your values, come see me."

The elevator dinged open, and Quinn strode out. Gregg was so taken aback he almost let the doors close on him. He stuck his hand out at the last second, bounced them open again, and followed.

Work for STORM? Was Quinn crazy?

Gregg knew the acronym stood for Strategic Technical Operations and Rescue Missions. Mainly STORM was hired by private companies and individuals to recover and defend hostages and other assets. But they were also occasionally hired by governments all over the world, to carry out ultra-sensitive or controversial special ops. Sort of like Zero Unit, but without the strict CIA agenda.

The thing was, Gregg liked the CIA agenda. Values? Someone needed to defend this country in the meanest, darkest, dirtiest cesspools of the world with just one mandate: keep America safe using any methods necessary. That's what Zero Unit did. Those values suited Gregg. Because he was dark, mean, and dirty, too. He did not play well with others. His father had seen to that.

"Gina's across the hall," Darcy said when he walked into the suite.

"What? *Alone?*" he burst out, reversing his momentum to double-time over there.

"She begged," Darcy called after him as he went. "I cleared the room myself. She swore she wouldn't—"

The rest was lost as the door slammed. He jabbed his key card into the lock and flung the door open.

"Gina!" he called. "Are you—"

But it wasn't Gina who greeted him inside. It was a female police detective holding up a badge in one hand and a weapon in the other.

"D.C. Metro Police. Freeze!"

Before he could draw his SIG, the muzzle of a gun was jammed in his back. "Don't even think about it, scumbag," a gruff voice advised. A man grabbed his arm from behind and the hard steel of a handcuff slapped around one wrist.

"Gregg van Halen, you are under arrest for—" the woman began.

Screw that. "Gina!" he shouted. But Gina didn't answer. Fear slammed through him.

"—the murder of Gibran Allawi—"

"There's no one else here," the male voice behind Gregg informed him. The muzzle in his back dropped away. His other arm was yanked backward.

"—Bakreen. You have the right to remain silent—"

"What have you done with her?" Gregg growled. "Where's Dr. Cappozi?"

"—but anything you say . . . Are you paying *attention* to me, mister?" the detective demanded.

"No one else is *here*," the man behind him repeated impatiently. The other cuff started to snap home.

No. Fucking. Way.

Instinct took over. Gregg slammed his elbow into the man's face at the same time he kicked the gun from the detective's hand. Surprise flashed across her face. He did a roundhouse and knocked her out cold. He spun. The man was already down, groaning and clutching his bloody nose. Gregg knocked him out, too. That's when he noticed a piece of paper lying on the floor. Chillingly familiar.

Fuck.

He scooped up the man's keys and both of their weapons, and in five seconds was halfway down the emergency stairs. He reached for his comm. He knocked it and it went flying down the concrete stairwell. Before he could swerve to miss, his boot landed on the thin plastic with a firm *crunch.*

Shit!

His phone rang. *Thank God.* "Gina?" he barked. The name bounced like a gun rapport off the narrow cement enclosure.

"What the hell is going on?" came Quinn's voice.

"Cops were waiting for me," he ground out. "Gina's gone."

Quinn swore. Gregg could hear him conferring heatedly with Darcy. "She swears Gina was there—"

Gregg vaulted out of the hotel's front entry. "Save it. He's got her, Quinn. I saw a copy of the subcommittee meeting agenda on the floor. Same as at Altos's office." About as blatant a message as it got. "It has to be the Trigger."

The commander cursed again. "You know this can't change anything, van Halen. The mission takes priority. We have to finish this, regardless."

"You do what you have to do," Gregg said, made a quick decision, and jumped into the cop car. He stabbed the stolen keys into the ignition and gunned it. "I'm not part of your fucking team, and I'm going after Gina. I am *not* letting that bastard kill her."

"But you have no idea where he's taken her!"

"Hell, Quinn, we both know exactly where he's taking her."

"And what about POTUS? If he decides to attend that press conference against our advice? What if this bastard succeeds in assassinating the goddamn *President* because your head is somewhere else entirely? We need every man together on this op. We need you to—"

Gregg took a deep, painful breath. "Sorry, man." And threw the phone out the window.

Fuck.

The woman he loved . . .

Or the President of the United States . . .

How could he possibly choose?

TWENTY-SIX

GOD*DAMN* it!

Sarah came awake on the hotel room floor with a splitting head and furious as hell. She peeled her eyes open and scanned the room. Jonesy was still out. Their suspect was long gone.

God*damn* it!

Her own fault. What a complete freaking idiot! She should have anticipated that van Halen would not come easily. He'd already murdered at least one person, probably three. He'd have nothing to lose by killing two more, even cops. The miracle was that he'd left them alive.

Gritting her teeth against the wash of pain that flashed through her skull, she crawled over to Jonesy. On her way, her hand landed on a piece of paper. She paused a moment, letting the rockets' red glare in her head settle down, then with difficulty focused on the paper. She read over it twice, just to be sure she wasn't hallucinating.

Her anger ratcheted up. Wow. Un-freaking-believable.

But there was a God.

Dragging the paper by one corner, she continued over to Jonesy. She peered at his battered face, wincing. Ouch. That would get ugly before it got better.

"Detective," she said to rouse him, sitting on her heels a healthy distance from his fists. She didn't want to get clocked by friendly fire. "Wakey, wakey."

He moaned and his eyes gradually fluttered open. "Fuckin' A. What the—" His hand went to his bloody nose. "Hell."

"Yeah," she responded, touching the lump rising on the left side of her head. "I'm really gonna love explaining to Lieutenant Harding how we let a murderer escape."

Jonesy closed his eyes again on a groan. "There goes my fuckin' gold watch."

"Or maybe not." She tipped her head. "Can you walk?"

"Maybe." He slitted his eyes and gazed up at her. "Depends on where we're goin'."

She held up the paper and smiled. It was not a nice smile.

"Same place he is."

ALL hell was breaking loose.

Gina was missing. Wade had vanished. Gregg was a fugitive and AWOL. The Trigger was closing in on a presidential assassination, and the rest of the team was scrambling with the Secret Service to put a plan into motion that was really no plan at all.

Now this.

Rebel pulled her FBI cap over her hair and stepped gingerly around the bloody, lifeless body of Erika Altos. It was lying on the hardwood floor of the victim's McLean foyer. The congressman's wife had been stabbed in the back.

The team had been so preoccupied with everything hitting the fan at once, that when Tara reported Mrs. Altos had a visitor and pixed Darcy a photo of the man, it had taken several minutes for her to run the ID. By the time it came back as Bruce Hearn, and Tara had crashed through the front door with weapon drawn, it had been too late. Erika was dead, and Hearn was nowhere to be found.

Rebel had been tasked with helping Tara secure the house until DHS arrived. Alex had dropped her off in McLean and was now on his way to Hearn's apartment to check for evidence of flight, then meet the rest of the team at the Capitol building.

She already missed him.

Funny how a single kiss could turn one's entire world upside down, and make things so crystal clear . . .

She smiled inwardly. Not that there had ever been any doubt. She loved him just as he was. Nothing would change that. Nothing.

"So *Hearn* killed Erika Altos," Kick said, jerking her rudely back to the present. They'd all switched on for a quick strategy meeting.

No time for mushy daydreams.

"When Gregg asked him earlier about the fishbowl," Quinn said, "Hearn must have known the game was up. He came straight here to McLean to eliminate the most dangerous witness against him before he disappeared for good."

"You realize what that means," Darcy said.

"It means we were wrong about the congressman," Marc said angrily. "We figured it was him or the wife. But Hearn had even better access to classified intel than she did. Dead easy for his chief of staff to set him up to look guilty. *Merde*. We should have seen that one coming."

"We did," Alex said. A car horn beeped over his comm. "Well, Gregg did. And the wife was obviously involved, or she wouldn't be dead."

"All three could be in it together," Tara suggested, joining Rebel in the foyer. She'd been examining the kitchen for missing knives. She shook her head. "As equal partners. Illegal conflict diamonds are easy money, tax-free—as long as you don't have a conscience. There was a million bucks' worth on that yacht. Not to mention the fishbowls. At least another mil there. Plenty to go around for three partners."

Rebel gazed at the blood still seeping from the gaping wound in Erika Altos's back. Hearn had been in a hurry. Hadn't wanted to take the time to smother her with a pillow like he'd done Asha Mahmood. Or maybe a knife was just more personal. Had they been sexually involved? Probably.

"I don't think so," Rebel said. "Hearn's your real traitor. This is him cleaning up loose ends. The wife was most likely an accomplice, but I'd be willing to bet the congressman doesn't have a clue about any of this."

"I agree," Marc said. "Hearn must have arranged the attack on Gina in New York, but when it failed, he killed Asha and Ouda Mahmood to cover his tracks. For both the botched hit and the al Sayika campaign contributions he'd been funneling through them to implicate the congressman. There'll no doubt be evidence proving that Asha Mahmood was Altos's mistress and Raul Chavez was hired to set up their illicit meetings. But my money is on the wife being Hearn's bedmate."

"Which would explain how he planted the diamonds in the fishbowl at the Altos home," Rebel said.

"All of which set up Congressman Altos to take the fall for today's assassination, and for being al Sayika's inside man on the Hill," Quinn agreed. "Hearn's one clever bastard."

"But one thing doesn't add up," Darcy said thoughtfully. "Why take Gina with him today? Why not just kill her like he did all the others?"

"We don't know that he *hasn't* killed her," Kick reminded them tersely. "Just taken her somewhere more secluded to do it."

There were several beats of tense silence.

"She could still be alive," Tara said hopefully.

"Are we thinking that Hearn is the Trigger?" Alex asked. Another car horn blared over his comm. He must be driving like a lunatic.

"He doesn't strike me as a professional assassin," Kick said.

"He's not," Darcy said. "I'm looking at Hearn's online credit card statements right now. He has several charges every day for the past two weeks in D.C., so he wasn't ever in Norfolk, or on the *Allah's Paradise*. If Rebel saw the Trigger jumping off that yacht, the Trigger's not Hearn."

"So we may be looking at a nuclear trigger, after all," Quinn said with a curse. "Not an assassin."

"The bomb dogs are already there at the Capitol. If there's a bomb, they'll find it," Darcy said.

"Don't forget Gibran Allawi Bakreen's murder at the hospital," Rebel reminded them. "That murder is definitely part of this. And Hearn was in a meeting at the time of death. Bakreen's killer must be someone else, which means the Trigger has to be a person."

"I agree," Alex said.

"Gregg's fingerprint was found at the scene," Tara reluctantly pointed out. "And he's disappeared now."

"That print was planted," Marc said. "It's easy to do. It fits with the continuing frame job on van Halen, not *Allah's Paradise*, or the e-mail. *Non*, Van Halen's not the Trigger."

"But it is someone with access to his prints."

"Which could be just about anyone. He may have obtained them as far back as Gregg's assignment to distract Gina, when the decision was first made to frame him."

"Okay. So at the very least, we're dealing with two

people," Tara said, summing up. "For sure the traitor is Hearn, who is killing witnesses to cover his tracks so he can disappear, and the Trigger, who presumably has been paid to assassinate the President."

"But the question stands," Darcy said. "Why would either one of them take Gina hostage?"

"Because van Halen was right," Kick said. "She must be able to identify the Trigger."

"Which means if she isn't already dead, she will be soon," Kick said grimly. "Unless van Halen finds her."

"I think the assassin is using her as bait," Quinn said. "To lure van Halen out in the open. They've framed him as tight as they've sewn up Altos. They need him there at the press conference to take the fall for the assassination, and it's pretty obvious how he feels about Gina."

"Shit," Alex said. "One more unknown variable to throw a monkey wrench in the plan. Oh, wait. There *is* no plan," he said sardonically.

Basically their plan was to show up armored in Kevlar and let Hearn continue with *his* plan, and hopefully expose the Trigger for them. Preferably before any shooting started. STORM's ace in the hole was that by now every Secret Service agent on the Capitol Building detail had memorized the whole team's photos, including Gregg's and Gina's, so no one was going to think *they* were bad guys and shoot *them*. Which was no doubt what Hearn and the Trigger were going for, at the very least for Gregg and Gina.

"Thank goodness Secret Service has convinced POTUS to stay away from that press conference," Rebel said gratefully.

"We just have to keep our eyes peeled when they announce he won't be speaking," Quinn said.

Kick cursed softly. "And pray like hell this crazy non-plan works."

TWENTY-SEVEN

"PLEASE don't do this."

Gina had never been so terrified in her life. Not when she'd been captured and beaten by terrorists, not when she'd stared down the barrel of her attacker's gun in New York. Not when Alex had tackled her on the way back from the ice machine. This was a different kind of fear. Not for herself, but for the man she loved.

"There's just one more thing I have to do," Bruce Hearn told her with a fatherly smile as he drove toward Capitol Hill. "Then you can go."

Hearn's expression was completely normal. Like they were just going out for a leisurely stroll on the Mall.

Except he'd put her in handcuffs. And Wade was locked in the trunk.

Oh my God. Hearn was lying through his teeth. He had no intention of letting either of them go.

She wondered how Wade was doing back there. Rohypnol was not usually fatal by itself, but who knew how big a dose Hearn had given him. He must be unconscious by now. They'd been driving a circuit from K Street down to Constitution and back for half an hour now.

She wanted so badly to give in to the trembling. Sink down into the front seat of the car and weep. But she had ruthlessly stopped her body's instinctive panicked reaction this long, and she wasn't about to surrender to it now. She *had* to be strong. Figure this out. For Wade. For Gregg. For herself and the future she wanted.

Think!

"What do you have to do?" she asked Hearn, battling to keep the tremor from mincing her voice to bits.

"I have to save the President. They're going to kill him, you know."

She whipped her head around, unsure if she'd heard him correctly. He kept mumbling.

Alarm slammed through her. "The *President*?" She regarded him with growing horror. So the team was right. Good lord, did they know? She had to stall him. Figure out a way to tell them. "Someone's going to kill the President? Who?"

"You know who." He gave her a look of pity. "Your lover, van Halen. Did no one tell you he's a traitor to his country?"

She scuttled backward, stunned. *Ohgodohgod.* "No! He's not!"

Hearn laughed. "You don't have to worry about that ruthless bastard anymore. I've informed the FBI of his plot. They're ready for him. Snipers on every roof. SWAT waiting to shoot him down at the first sign. Trust me. The President will be fine."

Oh, sweet *Je*sus. Oh, holy Mother of God.

The cops were going to kill Gregg on sight, and ask questions later.

Please say this wasn't happening . . .

But it was.

She had to warn him!

Hearn pulled into a parking spot off Capitol Circle reserved for staffers and slid his pass onto the dashboard. He pointed up to the Capitol steps, where a cluster of microphones awaited, along with a growing crowd of reporters and tourists drawn by the hubbub. The place was crawling with Secret Service.

"Here?" she asked in surprise. It was rare that the President gave such a public press brief and photo op. So rare, in fact, she asked, "How do you know the President will be here?"

He sent her an indulgent look as he got out of the car. "I have access to every secret this country has, sweetheart. I know everything about everyone."

A shiver traveled down her spine and up again. Getting away with his crimes for so long had obviously distorted his self-importance. The man was insane.

He came around to her door and opened it. Before he let her out, he said, "Gina, don't forget your boyfriend in the trunk. If you shout a warning, if you try to attract any attention, if you so much as open your mouth and say a single word to anyone about . . . well, anything . . . I'm serious"—he looked almost apologetic—"I *will* kill you. Then I'll suffocate your friend in the trunk and throw him in the Potomac on my way out of town."

Somehow she already knew that.

"I won't," she promised. Right. *In a parallel universe.*

He extended his hand and helped her out of the car like a gentleman, and checked that her handcuffs were still secure behind her back. Then he took off his suit jacket and draped it over her shoulders to hide the cuffs. It left him in shirtsleeves and tie, but it was a bright, sunny April day and in the sea of casual tourists and workers from the surrounding government buildings, he wouldn't even make a blip on the radar of any law enforcement official who looked at them.

Like, for instance, the female cop hurrying past right now. He actually waved at her. Whistling, he clipped his Capitol staffer ID to his breast pocket.

"What are you planning?" Gina asked nervously as the slimy bastard put his arm carelessly around her shoulder. He steered her toward the crowd on the Capitol steps.

"Me? Nothing at all." When they reached the broad expanse of terraced marble, he breathed in a lungful of fresh air and gazed around like a delighted tourist taking in the sights of his capital city. He turned and gave her a smile. "I'm just here to watch Gregg van Halen die."

TWENTY-EIGHT

REBEL leapt out of the SUV and hurried toward the crush of people that had gathered on the grand staircase rising up the eastern side of the Capitol Building. Two seconds later, Tara was striding along next to her.

This was it. After the President had bowed out, Congressman Altos had been briefed on the threat, and had insisted on holding the press conference as scheduled. He'd been stricken by the news of his wife's death and of his chief of staff's plans to frame him for treason, and wanted to nail both the traitor and his hired henchman. It was incredibly risky, but this could be their one and only chance to identify and catch the al Sayika assassin known as the Trigger. Everything had to look completely normal to lure him out of hiding.

Forcing herself not to run, Rebel kept her FBI badge and face visible at all times so she'd be recognized by the myriad Secret Service and other law enforcement officers spaced every two inches on the newly seeded lawn and watching passersby like hawks. Tara did the same with her DHS creds. The rest of the team had been issued Homeland Security IDs for the op, and all of them had dressed in dark suits over their Kevlar. When in Rome . . .

Rebel tapped her comm. "STORM Hotel and Juliet arriving on scene." For some obscure reason Tara, who didn't have a single *J* in any of her names, went by Juliet, the call sign for *J*. Rebel sensed a story there, but hadn't had time to ask. "STORM Dog Six, do you read?"

"STORM Zulu, here. Hotel and Juliet, please switch to channel 8. We have about a thousand bears onboard, over," said Darcy.

Rebel would have chuckled if she weren't so worried about reaching her assigned position in time. The press conference was set to start any minute. She and Tara dialed to the other channel.

"Anyone get hold of Victor, over?" she asked.

Gregg van Halen was a real concern. She'd been trying to get him to answer his phone since he'd gone off-grid at the Watergate nearly two hours ago, bound and determined to track down his vanished Gina.

"He's still going to voice mail," Darcy came back. "Report any sightings and read him in if at all possible. That goes for everyone, over."

They'd left messages outlining the loose plan they'd hammered out with Secret Service and DHS, but who knew if he'd checked them. Unless he had already found Gina—very doubtful—Gregg would show up at the press conference looking for blood. The man was definitely a wild card in all this. She prayed no one got hurt because of it. She'd pleaded with him to call her, and worn her Bluetooth just in case.

Above her, the Capitol steps rose up in three steep tiers, separated by landings and flanked by square, flat buttresses bearing lampposts, statues, and Secret Service agents. Tara slipped into the throng to the right and started up the first flight. Rebel was supposed to find Alex and help cover the left.

There was a stir at the very top landing and the excited crowd, having heard the rumor of a presidential appearance, surged upward, pulling her along past the chain barrier that had been lowered for the occasion.

Rebel's pulse doubled. *This was it.* But where was Alex?

A group of dignitaries appeared between the two columns at the center of the portico at the very top, and approached the phalanx of microphones that had been set up. The subcommittee had arrived to make their announcement of the new and improved budget on the fight against terrorism. A cacophony of shouts raised up, a score of questions instantly thrown at them. Someone spoke loudly over the mic, trying to quiet down the reporters.

Rebel craned her neck, still looking for Alex. Her cell phone rang.

She tapped the earpiece. "Alex, where are you?"

"Sugar, if you don't know where the man is, *I* surely don't," came the honeyed drawl of the last person on earth Rebel wanted to talk to at the moment. Luckily, she had an excellent excuse not to.

"Right above you by the lamppost." This from Alex over the comm. She'd forgotten everyone could still hear her.

Rebel muted her comm mic as she looked up, searching for him. "Helena. I can't talk now. I'm in—"

"Yes, yes. I know. You're in the middle of something. You always are, sugar."

"Seriously. I have to—"

"Positions, people," came Quinn's command over the comm. "It's showtime."

She spotted Darcy several steps below the portico, standing shoulder-to-shoulder in the solid line of ultra-alert black-suited Secret Service agents who stood guard, preventing the public from reaching the landing. Other than being the only tall, willowy blonde, she blended in perfectly, earpiece and all. But no Alex. What had he said about a lamppost?

"I'm hanging up now," Rebel told Helena and reached for the off button.

"Rebel, you and I need to have a talk," Helena said in that precisely polite way a true Southern aristocrat could command an icicle to stop melting.

Rebel's finger hovered above the Bluetooth. Her heart stuttered. She did *not* need this now.

"We have Alpha at the podium," Darcy said, pulling her attention. *A* for Altos.

Rebel darted her gaze up to the island of microphones where the congressman stood. Arranged behind him in a half circle were five men and a woman, presumably the rest of the subcommittee. Was it her imagination, or did they all look crazy nervous?

"I've got him covered, over," Kick said immediately.

"Lord. The man's either a saint or a coward," she muttered.

"Well, I don't know about that," Helena said in her other ear with just a shade of amusement. "I suppose it depends on your point of view."

What?

Oh, right. "Helena, I really—"

On cue, Rebel's eyes collided with Alex. He raised a hand, beckoning her to him.

For now, or forever . . . ?

She wanted to stop what was happening and fling herself into his arms and tell him how badly she wanted a chance at forever.

And she was certain he did, too. That kiss . . . it had been utterly earth-shattering. He hadn't actually said "I love you," but it had been there in his eyes. And when she'd told him there were other options for a family, he hadn't argued or disagreed. He'd kissed her. Wonderfully. Thoroughly. Expressively. Until Quinn's untimely interruption, calling them back to the fold.

Speaking of which—

She jerked herself out of the joyful memory, lifted her own hand in acknowledgment, and started to blaze a path up through the sea of bodies toward Alex. At the microphone, Congressman Altos stuttered over his statement.

Suddenly she saw a very familiar head bobbing above the spectators, making its way upward as well.

Bruce Hearn. And he had Gina! His arm was tight around her shoulders preventing her from escaping. Rebel mashed the comm excitedly. "This is STORM Hotel. I have eyes on Tango One." *T* for terrorist—the code they'd assigned Hearn. "He's got Charlie with him. First tier, dead center, over."

"I'm there, over," Marc said.

"What are you—" Helena asked in her other ear. "Oh. You really *are* working."

"Yeah, and I have to go."

"Where are you? Norfolk?" Helena asked. "I'll fly down. We do need to talk. About Alex."

Rebel had nearly made it up the steps to him. He was standing like a figurehead on the front edge of the upper buttress, his alert gaze sweeping the crowd. Tall, muscular, confident, his scarred face radiated the kind of beauty that came from a good soul as much as great bone structure.

Their eyes caught.

He sent her a brilliant smile and a bad-boy wink. He was so perfectly gorgeous and desirable it made her throat ache. She loved him *so* much.

Her lips curved. And she said, "No Helena. We don't need to talk. Not about Alex, anyway."

She saw him turn and make his way back along the edge,

then jump over the side onto the landing below. He was coming to her. *Her.*

"Yes, well—" Helena began.

"He told me about your arrangement," Rebel interrupted, watching him jostle down through the crowd to reach her. She felt more alive and certain than she ever had in her life. "And everything else, too."

"Ah."

"There's only one thing left that needs saying." She gathered up all the love in her heart, and said, "Alex is mine. *Mine*, Helena. I honestly don't care if you are gay, and even less that you may need him as a beard for your stodgy parents. Just grow up and tell them, already. Because you can't have him back. So don't even ask."

And then she hung up.

With a smile of personal triumph, she started up the few remaining steps that lay between her and the man who was her destiny.

Above them, Altos continued his speech. Reporters shouted questions. She saw Kick disappear behind one of the pillars. Marc was closing in on Hearn and Gina.

Alex had halted on the steps.

But . . . something was wrong.

Her smile quickly faded. He was wrestling against the press of the crowd, which tried to squeeze around him. She gasped as he flung himself into a ball at the base of the buttress wall and shielded himself from the concerned few who stopped to reach out and help him.

Oh, dear lord.

This was not good.

SCORCHING desert heat was closing in on him fast. Already, Alex could feel sweat drenching his face. His armpits. Far away, the screams started.

Ah, fucking hell. Please, please, *please.* Not now! Not when the whole damn team was depending on him. And Rebel—

"Get a grip, Zane," a commanding male voice growled in his ear. "Pull yourself together, man."

The surprise was just enough to snatch Alex back from the dusty brink of the Afghan village. He blinked. "Van Halen?"

"Get up, brother. Come on. Snap out of it. You can do it."

He fought the panic that had taken over his gut. Peered shakily over his shoulder. The man staring back at him wore a Nationals baseball cap and dark sunglasses. Was it really van Halen? Or was his mind playing even more bizarre tricks than usual, and this just another hallucination?

The screams in his head grew louder. He teetered.

"Gotta save them," he mumbled, teetering, teetering. "Gotta save . . ."

"Gotta save the *President*, Zane." Van Halen looked up toward the portico and swore. "Jesus, didn't you people warn him?"

"The plan . . . POTUS not coming. An ambush . . ."

The screams grew louder. It didn't sound like they were in his head anymore. *It was an ambush!*

"Altos is announcing the President now. *Christ!*" Gregg glanced briefly at Alex. "Wait. POTUS isn't coming?"

"Gotta save . . . Gotta save . . ." He suddenly remembered. "Gina!"

At the name, van Halen's hand shot out and grabbed him. "What about Gina? Have you seen her?"

Just then, the crowd went wild, screaming and jumping up and down at the news that the President would be speaking in a few minutes. Every eye was on the podium. Except Alex's. He squeezed his shut and tried to shake off van Halen.

"Zane!" Gregg demanded. "Have you *seen* Gina?"

Alex fought against the blackness. Saw her face in his mind. And . . . And . . . He pried his eyes open. "Hearn. He's got her . . . They were . . ." He shifted his gaze up the endless upward-marching ranks of marble steps, filled with a riot of cheering people. "Up there."

Somewhere, Rebel's voice called frantically. "Alex! Where are you?"

Good fucking question.

Here? Or off in never-never land?

He blinked up at van Halen. Hanging onto reality with everything in him.

"Here!" the other man shouted, jumping up. And then he was gone, vanishing into the crowd like a mirage.

"Alex!" Rebel's face appeared above him. "Oh, Alex, are you all right?" She knelt and put her arms around him and kissed his sweaty temple.

And the most unexpected thing happened. At her touch, the panic started to ebb away.

"Yeah," he managed. Bit by bit he shook out the blackness and his tense muscles. "I think so."

Rebel hit her comm. "Hotel here. X-ray's good. Just a glitch with his comm, over." She muted hers again and glanced around on the ground. "Alex, your headset. Help me find it."

He was sitting on it, thankfully in one piece. He slid it on. "STORM Dog Six, X-ray back on comm. Sir, Victor's here. In hot pursuit of Tango One, over."

There was a chorus of curses. "Nothing to do about it," Quinn said. "Back on task, people. The Trigger is here somewhere. Let's find the fucker before van Halen takes down Tango One, over."

Alex scrambled to his feet and took Rebel's hand. "Come on."

The Trigger would be as close to the portico as possible. Waiting for the perfect moment to take his shot at the President.

Together they climbed the steps, threading their way through the throng of people that had finally quieted down to hear what Congressman Altos was announcing.

"This is it," came Quinn's quiet admonition.

Everyone was in place. Kick with his sniper rifle among the Secret Service agents behind a pillar on one side of the podium, Quinn mirroring him on the other. Darcy still stood in the human barricade below the portico; Marc covered the center, sneaking up behind Hearn and Gina. Tara was positioned along the right edge of the steps, he and Rebel along the left.

Where the hell had van Halen gone to?

Scanning the crowd for anyone acting suspicious, Alex tuned out the announcement and kept moving upward. Altos had been instructed to draw out the suspense over the President's imminent arrival as long as possible. The moment it was clear he wouldn't be coming was when the Trigger would be most visible. He'd be turning away from the podium. Reassessing. Changing plans. Moving position, either to go to plan B or to get the hell out of there.

"In distant training camps and even in our own cities," Altos boomed, "there are people plotting to take American lives. Neither the President nor anyone else standing here today can say there will not be another terrorist attack on our soil. But we can say with certainty that the President and this committee will do everything in our power to keep the American people safe. And to that end . . ."

The speech went on. Alex fanned inward to join Marc, his gaze darting down the steps to anything that moved.

He spotted a woman wearing a D.C. POLICE Windbreaker climbing steadily up through the middle of the crowd. She looked very determined.

And very familiar.

Suddenly it clicked. She was the detective that Rebel had questioned at the hospital. He frowned. Had she been brought into the loop? Or . . .

Surely, *she* wasn't the—

Holy shit!

"This is X-ray. STORM Mike, you've got a possible hostile approaching your six. STORM Dog, that Metro Detective Sarah McPhee, the one on the Mahmood case. Is she part of this op, over?"

"Hell, no," Quinn came back. "She's the one who arrested Victor earlier." Alex saw him step out from behind the pillar and train a set of binoculars on the area around Marc. "This looks like trouble. Get on her, X-ray. Mike, stay on Tango One and Charlie until we figure out what the hell's going on, over."

Finally Congressman Altos could delay no longer. "I regret to announce that the President was called away to deal with a last-minute emergency," he said, and the crowd let out a collective groan.

That's when Alex saw a man in a Nationals cap slide in between two spectators just above Hearn and Gina. Detective McPhee was right below them.

Oh. Fuck.

"The detective has spotted Victor," he reported, and took off up the steps.

Before he could reach McPhee and stop her, she drew her weapon and pointed it at Gregg.

"Metro Police! Freeze or you're a dead man!"

GREGG froze.

All around him, the metallic din of dozens of guns being locked and loaded ricocheted off the marble. At the podium, the congressman halted as Secret Servicemen surrounded him. The crowd started to scream and run, or drop to the ground and cover their heads.

Gregg looked down at Gina. Her eyes widened as she realized who he was. The scumfucker Hearn had his arm around her, smiling like an idiot. Her own arms she held stiffly behind her back. Handcuffs?

"Get away from him!" Gregg yelled to her.

She shook her head, glancing desperately at Hearn, whose smile turned almost gleeful when he saw Gregg.

The female detective elbowed her way past them, shouting something at him, but there was no way he could hear. And as much as he wanted to, there was also no way he could pull the SIG and shoot Hearn. Not without his actions being grossly misinterpreted by the detective.

Thank God Alex Zane was vaulting up the steps toward them.

Gregg raised his hands above his head to show he was cooperating. Zane would set the detective straight.

Suddenly a shot rang out. Congressman Altos screamed. It quickly turned to a sickening gurgle as he sank to the stone floor of the portico.

Gregg held very still as pandemonium erupted all around. Every fed within a hundred yards wheeled their aim to him, their most logical suspect, then realized he wasn't the shooter.

But who was?

The panicked crowd rushed down the steps, screaming and clawing to escape danger. A man in a vintage green army jacket knocked Hearn off balance and he went tumbling.

Colonel Blair? Damn it! Gregg should have killed him in the alley that day while he had the chance!

Before the fucker could get to her, Gregg lunged for Gina. Found the cold barrel of the female detective's gun stuck in his chest instead.

"Him!" he shouted at Marc and pointed to Blair. Marc reached out and grabbed the colonel.

Gina screamed. Gregg whirled and started toward her.

"Halt!" the cop shouted at him. "Or I'll—"

The rest of the detective's words were lost as Gregg saw a Secret Service agent grab Gina and band an arm around her middle. She struggled in vain.

That was no Secret Service agent.

The man stood behind her like a coward, holding a Beretta to her neck, hiding it under her long black hair.

"Hush, now," the man crooned. "I don't want to hurt you."

Gina's eyes went wide. They met Gregg's, wild with fear. "It's *him*," she mouthed. "The Voice!"

Gregg halted, paralyzed with shock.

Oh, God.

"Tommy?"

The kid's youthful face didn't hold even a shade of remorse. "You're making this way too easy, Cap." He shifted the aim of his hidden Beretta to Gregg.

"What the *hell* . . . ?"

"Sorry, Cap. You always taught me not to leave loose ends."

The detective was still shouting at Gregg, oblivious to the man just behind her who was about to kill him—with a gun identical to her own. By the time forensics proved her innocent, he'd be dead and Tommy would be long gone.

The little shit.

The President had never been the target. The kid was cleaning house, eliminating loose ends. And they'd all shown up, just as he'd planned it all along.

Fuck. Gregg had taught him too well.

"Why?" he asked, fury coiling like a snake in his belly. Not that he needed to ask. Pure fucking greed. Tommy had always craved the finer things in life but never had the skills needed to earn them honestly. Gregg should have seen this coming.

"Why not?" Tommy's shoulder lifted. "Like you always said, I'm not cut out for the military life."

But there was one fatal flaw with the little fuckwad's plan. He'd have to kill Gina, too. No chance in hell Gregg would let that happen.

All around, bedlam reigned. Marc had Blair on the ground, struggling to subdue him. Alex Zane had almost reached them. But Zane still hadn't seen Tommy. He was beelining it straight for the detective. She was coming at Gregg now, brandishing a pair of handcuffs. *Shit.*

Gregg took a deep breath. *Now or never.*

He shoved the detective to the ground.

And pulled the SIG on the bad guy.

Zane's surprised eyes cut to Tommy. He understood in a flash. In one fluid motion, he shifted direction and made a leaping dive at the kid.

Just as Blair shouted. And Tommy pulled the trigger.

The gunshot boomed. Zane went down.

Goddamn it!

Gregg watched in horror. It should have been *him*!

For a nanosecond, Tommy froze in confusion. But it was enough. Gina wrenched away from him, dropped to the steps, and rolled into the retreating crowd. *Safe.*

His shot was clear, but Gregg wasn't willing to risk the lives of innocent bystanders. He lowered the SIG.

And took Tommy's second shot in the chest.

He staggered and grunted. Fucking *hell*, it hurt.

To his surprise, Blair tackled Tommy. Had he misjudged him, too? Blair's tackle was followed by about a hundred Secret Service agents. *Thank God.*

What Gregg didn't expect was to be shot again. This time in the head. By Bruce Hearn.

Fuck. Somehow the goddamn bastard had gotten loose. Blood flew everywhere. Slowly, Gregg fell, dizzy with an intense slam of pain in his skull. He heard Gina cry his name.

The lady detective was on her feet again, looming above him. But she was smarter than he'd given her credit for. She shielded his body and aimed her weapon at Hearn faster than his own head was spinning.

"Go ahead," she growled at the traitor. "Make my day."

Gregg smiled. *You go, girl.*

Then everything went black.

TWENTY-NINE

ALEX lay strapped to a gurney, grimacing against the stabbing pain in his ribs as the ambulance took another corner at high speed. Lights flashed red and white. The siren blared unceasingly.

But it was all over. *Thank you, Jesus.*

The Trigger had been caught, along with the traitor Bruce Hearn. They'd both spend the rest of their lives in prison. Alex, Kick, and Gina could now emerge from hiding and live normal lives.

He smiled up at Rebel as she took his hand between hers. God, she was so fucking beautiful. But her answering expression looked like she was debating whether to kiss him or kill him.

Uh-oh.

"That was a stupid stunt," she scolded. It was the first time they'd had a chance to talk alone since their fateful kiss. "Jumping in front of a gun like that."

"Sorry," he said, but his smile was unrepentant. He was too happy to have any regrets. Hell, he was even glad they'd rescued Wade Montana from Hearn's car trunk before he suffocated to death. Especially when that lady detective had fussed over Wade so much, and he'd kissed her right on the mouth in front of the whole world. Alex got the distinct impression Montana wouldn't be hanging around Rebel anymore.

She rolled her expressive green eyes. They shone in the flashing lights of the ambulance. "Oh, stuff it. You are *so* not sorry."

His grin widened. "What's the matter? Worried about me?"

"You are impossible, you know that? You should be counting your blessings the bullet hit your vest and not your head like Gregg."

He suddenly saw those were *tears* shining in her eyes. She wasn't teasing. She was genuinely upset.

He lifted his free hand and lightly touched his ribs—at least two of which were broken from the impact of the bullet. "Believe me, I *am* counting my blessings. Big-time. But I had no choice taking that bullet for van Halen. I didn't know if he was wearing Kevlar or not. And I owed him."

She put his hand to her cheek. "Your life?"

He tucked a stray hair behind her ear. "Maybe. Who can say what might have happened if that flashback had taken me out? I sure as hell hope he makes it."

She turned to kiss his fingers. "Me, too. Gina is beside herself. Thank God the first shot hit his vest."

"Will someone call and let us know how he is?"

She nodded. Her loving gaze lingered on him, like she had something on her mind. But not Gregg.

"Angel, what?" he asked.

A thousand emotions seemed to scud through her eyes. Happiness. Uncertainty. Hope . . . ?

She shook her head. "Nothing. It'll keep."

Apprehension seeped through him. "Talk to me, baby. What's going on?"

Letting his hands go, she drew in a deep breath. Rather than explaining, she pressed a few buttons on her cell phone and handed it to him. She'd pulled up a text message. From Helena.

Hny, its abt damn time!
Mk him hppy.
Mk him marry u.
PS Pls dnt tell mama & ddy I'm gay.

For a second he just stared. Obviously, the women had talked.

He sighed and handed Rebel back the phone. "Believe me, I wish it were possible. But Angel, I'm a mess, inside and out, you know that. It just wouldn't be fair to you—"

"Which you took it upon yourself to decide for both of us. *That's* what isn't fair."

Pain razored through his heart. "Don't you remember? I gave you the chance to tell me it didn't matter. That you would want me even knowing I couldn't give you children." He glanced away, unable to face her pity. "You couldn't do it."

"Is it too late?" she asked softly.

He stilled. Looked up at her. A bittersweet mix of hope and despair spilled through him. He swallowed. "You can't possibly—"

"But I do."

"Rebel—"

"Yes, I want children. But there are lots of ways to bring a child into one's life, Alex." A lone tear trickled down her cheek; her voice was soft and wavering with emotion. "There's only one you. And you're the one I want."

They were the sweetest words he'd ever heard. "Do you really mean that?" He prayed with everything in him that she truly did.

"With all my heart."

Did he dare believe her? He wanted to. Desperately. He had denied himself this moment for so damn long. All his life, it seemed. He felt like he was jumping off a cliff into the unknown. But at some point, a man had to take a chance or call himself a damn coward.

"I don't know how I got so damn lucky," he said, and another tear trickled down her cheek. Hopefully one of happiness. "But God knows I love you, Rebel Haywood."

"Oh, Alex," she whispered, and leaned down to tenderly kiss him. "I love you, too. So very much."

He held her hands between his. "I've wanted you from the moment I saw you walk into our first meeting with that stupid bun in your gorgeous red hair, and I loved you from the first time I said 'fuck' and you got all flustered and told me a real gentleman doesn't curse."

She gave him a watery smile. "I could be wrong about that."

"It's been killing me not to have you all these years. Staying away, being just friends, because I thought it was best for you. Praying you'd find someone else instead and put me out of my misery. Wanting to die when you did."

She closed her eyes. Opened them. The pure, honest light of love in them took his breath away. "There was never anyone else, Christopher Alexander Zane. Just a poor substitute for the man I really love."

The sound of his name on her lips, so sure, so filled with precious love and promise, gave him the courage he needed. He couldn't go on without her. He didn't even want to try. "Rebel please, for the love of God, will you marry me?"

She smiled. The sexy, mysterious smile his beautiful angel had given him in countless hope-filled dreams. "Yes, oh, yes." She brushed his lips with hers and whispered, "I thought you'd never ask."

THIRTY

THE wedding was a month later.

It was one of those rare days in New York City when the sun was brilliant in an azure blue sky, the temperature was a perfect seventy-five degrees, and the sanitation workers were not on strike. The air on the rooftop terrace of the Park Avenue hotel where the wedding was being held smelled of springtime and champagne, and two hundred fragrant white damask roses sent by STORM.

The entire terrace was festooned with gossamer white sheers, artfully draped, flowing and billowing in the soft breeze.

Gina was the maid of honor.

From her place behind the discreet curtain that had been set up to conceal the bride and her attendants, Gina smoothed her gown and peeked out at the assembled friends and family of the happy couple. Everyone was finding seats on several rows of white padded folding chairs arranged to face the arched bower of flowers where the ceremony would take place.

There were lots of familiar faces: Tara and Marc Lafayette; Bobby Lee Quinn and his fiancée, Darcy Zimmerman; STORM Commander Kurt Bridger and several other STORM operators she recognized. Detective Sarah McPhee had flown up from D.C., and Kick's friend Dr. Nathan Daneby had also arrived at the last minute from somewhere in Africa, where he was setting up his fifth Doctors for Peace refugee camp. Lord, wasn't *he* a handsome devil.

Speaking of which.

Alex walked in from the side to stand nervously in front of the flower-laden arch. Following behind the groom came Kick Jackson, the best man. And damn, didn't they clean up nicely. Both wore dove-gray morning suits, which they carried with surprising ease and panache for men more used to dressing in camouflage.

But neither of them could hold a candle to the third, similarly clad groomsman, who hung back in the shadows, seemingly hesitant to join them.

Gregg van Halen was still the most gorgeously striking man Gina had ever met. It didn't matter if he was wearing motorcycle leathers, cammo fatigues, a Helmut Lang suit, or nothing at all; he never failed to make her pulse race and her knees weak.

How close she had come to losing him! Her heart squeezed just thinking about that awful day.

"Good thing I have such a hard head," Gregg had joked painfully when he'd awakened from his weeklong coma—part of which had been deliberately induced by his doctors to help the swelling in his brain heal more quickly—and learned that by a pure miracle Hearn's bullet had bounced off his skull instead of penetrating it. The bone had been crushed at the point of impact, and he'd suffered a massive contusion. But he'd lived. With no permanent damage. Physically, anyway.

But he was having a hard time adjusting to the end of his career as he knew it. There was no possibility to continue as an undercover operator after his face had been plastered all over every newspaper and newscast in the country as the man who'd brought down a traitor plotting to kill the President.

Gregg was a hero. Along with Alex, Detective McPhee, and Frank Blair—who it turned out really had been hunting the mole in his organization all along.

But Gregg'd had to resign from Zero Unit. It had been a tough blow.

Not to Gina, of course. She'd been secretly thrilled. Maybe he would decide to stay with her. Settle down.

It could happen. Sure, it could.

"Is everyone seated?" Rainie asked from behind her. Rainie was the bridesmaid. "Omigod, Geen, I'm so excited. Everything is so beautiful, isn't it?" Her best friend put her arms around her and gave her a big hug. "You're beautiful, too, BFF."

Gina smiled broadly and hugged her back. "Back at you, girlfriend." They were both wearing Lazaro, as was the bride, compliments of the bride's parents. The gowns were absolutely stunning, Rebel in antique white, Gina and Rainie in pale coral. Mr. and Mrs. Haywood had always loved Alex, and had spared no expense on the wedding, absolutely delighted their daughter had decided to quit the FBI to take Commander Bridger up on his earlier offer to head the Victim Family Services division of STORM. They'd credited it all to Alex.

Little did they know that this new job would take their daughter all over the world, following her soon-to-be husband as he helped rescue hostages and victims of kidnappings. And a few assorted covert missions here and there.

"I just love weddings," Rainie said on a sigh, and gave Gina another hug. "I can't wait for yours."

Gina's gaze strayed to Gregg, who was still standing in the shadows on the periphery, looking uncomfortable that he couldn't simply fade into the background and disappear. He was even wearing dark sunglasses.

"Don't hold your breath," she said with a different sort of sigh. She touched the silver heart necklace that nestled between her breasts. The one he'd bought her to match the anklet. She was wearing both today, along with the earrings. "He hasn't asked. And I doubt he will. Gregg isn't the marrying kind. Remember?"

Up until recently—very recently—neither was Gina. But spending every waking moment by Gregg's side as he fought for his life, holding his hand when he opened his eyes for the first time after regaining consciousness, then curling up next to him during the sleepless nights as he wrestled with the changes being thrust unwillingly into his life . . . she realized how badly she wanted to be part of that life.

What would she do if he left her?

What would she do *when* he left her?

She could feel it, a restlessness buzzing just below his surface. He'd made his decision. Resolved his course of action. And she was so afraid it did not include her.

"We'll see," Rainie said with a kiss on her cheek.

"See what?" Rebel asked, coming up to them with a rustle of silk and a beaming smile. "What are you looking at?" Rebel peeked past the curtain, too.

"Our men," Rainie said with a grin. "What else? My God, what a trio. They're so handsome it almost hurts."

"But it hurts so good," Rebel agreed, her eyes sparkling with happiness.

Gina laughed, too, though she wasn't quite so sure about the good part. Still, she was over the moon for Rebel, and for Rainie, of course. Rainie had just confided last night amid tears of joy that she and Kick were expecting their first child in eight months.

"Come on. Let's make a wedding wish," Rainie said, joining their hands in a tight circle. They bowed their heads together, touching foreheads. Gina felt the teasing scratch of Rebel's bridal veil against her cheek, along with a pang of intense longing in her heart.

She closed her eyes and made a wish.

Please. Just let him love me.

The music swelled, and she took a deep breath, kissed Rebel on the cheek, and stepped out from behind the curtain. To the festive trill of organ music, she started the stately glide down the white runner.

A murmur of admiration rose from the crowd. The dress really *was* dazzling. The STORM guys in the audience ogled her appreciatively. But Gina only had eyes for one man. He gazed back at her from the front of the terrace with a stunned look on his face.

She smiled. Okay, so it wasn't just the dress.

One thing about Rebel's friend Helena—who had also been invited to the wedding along with her partner, Linda—she was a real artist when it came to hair and makeup. Gina had never in her life looked quite this good.

As though transfixed, Gregg stepped out of the shadows. He removed his sunglasses. A passing cloud drifted on, leaving him bathed in a pool of golden sunshine. Her throat tightened at the stark beauty of the man.

As Gina walked slowly down the aisle, he came forward, too, step by hesitant step. Until they met in front of the bower.

She had no idea what he would do. This hadn't been part of the rehearsal. He wasn't even the best man, and therefore not her partner. Technically.

He seemed to awaken, startled to see where he was standing. But as always, Gregg van Halen was master of the moment. He gave her a look she couldn't begin to decipher, and bent to kiss her lightly on the lips.

"You look like a goddess," he whispered.

The crowd ahhhhed.

Then he gallantly escorted her to her place, and returned to his. Bemused, Kick took his cue and did the same for his wife. It was a lovely addition to the ceremony.

And just about melted Gina's heart.

The rest was even lovelier.

And when it was over, and the newlyweds had danced their first dance together, Gregg led Gina out onto the crowded wooden floor that had replaced the rows of seats.

An old rock tune was playing, but he tugged her into his arms and held her cheek-to-cheek.

"I've always hated weddings," he said.

She was still dewy-eyed and sniffling over the beautiful ceremony, so his almost clinical observation came as a cold dash of water. "Oh," she said.

"But then," he continued, "it's never been friends getting married, and I've never been part of it. And before today, I've sure as hell never had the urge to peel the gown off the maid of honor in front of the entire congregation."

"Oh," she said.

He pulled her closer. "You take my breath away," he whispered. "Completely."

"Oh." She sighed, smiled, and put her head on his shoulder. "I'm glad. Because the feeling is mutual."

"Yeah?"

"Yeah."

Just then, Detective McPhee danced by in the arms of Wade Montana. She was totally captivated by something he was saying.

"Who'd have thought," she remarked, eyeing them.

"He's totally into her. It could work." Gregg's gaze slid to the sidelines, to a pair of STORM guys watching the detective with interest as they sipped champagne. "Though it looks like he might have some competition."

Gina regarded Gregg with a raised brow. "You considering taking up matchmaking as your new career?" she teased.

"Very funny." He grinned, but it faded all too quickly.

Damn. She *had* to bring it up.

STORM Corps had officially reiterated Quinn's job offer almost as soon as Gregg had come out of his coma. Not undercover, but as an operator nonetheless. Bridger had shown up at the hospital with Quinn and left details in a big bronze envelope for Gregg to consider at his leisure. He was still considering. But as generous as the offer was—Gina had peeked while he was sleeping—she didn't think he was going to take it. He hadn't said anything, but she just had a feeling.

She didn't know if that was a good thing or a bad thing.

"What *are* you going to do?" she asked, unable to help herself.

"Honestly? I don't know." He brushed his lips over her temple. "Tell you what I'd *like* to do . . ."

"Hmmm?"

"Remember that thing about peeling off the maid of honor's dress?"

His arms were wrapped around her, holding her body close to his. She could feel every inch of his tall, broad, muscular frame under the fine wool of his morning suit and silk shirt. *Every* inch.

"I seem to recall."

"What do you think about the idea?"

They hadn't made love for a month. Not since before he was shot. Doctor's orders. Her nipples tightened at the prospect of the ban being lifted. Or maybe it was all those delicious inches she could feel.

She pretended to be scandalized. "Right here in front of everyone?"

"Hell no. I want you all to myself. Too many lecherous guys giving you the eye here."

A thrill sifted through her at the possessive look he gifted her with.

"What does your doctor say?"

"He says I'm not to overtax myself."

She gave him a moue. "That's no fun."

"For the first three or four times," he amended with a smile, and nuzzled her behind the ear. "The way I'm feeling, I figure we can get that over with in a couple of hours."

She choked out a laugh. "Probably not exactly what he meant."

"I want you. I've been going nuts every night when you snuggle up to me in that hospital bed. Not even a proper kiss goodnight."

She giggled. "Your blood pressure monitor kept going off."

"Not anymore. I'm officially discharged. Let's go back to my place."

"You mean . . . right now?" She glanced around. The reception was just getting started. "Isn't the maid of honor supposed to make a toast later? Help with the bouquet?" *Hopefully catch it . . .*

He made a face. "You're right. It would be rude to leave so soon. We'll wait five more minutes."

Laughing softly together, they continued to dance for a few more bars of music.

Then he said, "Would you like to catch the bouquet?" as though he'd been reading her thoughts earlier.

She felt her face heat. She was not in the habit of throwing herself at a man. She'd never had to. Men had always come to her. Besides, she'd never *needed* a man in her life just for the sake of having one. Even now, after everything that had happened, she knew she'd be fine on her own. She had always been a strong, independent woman. Partly because of the confidence Gregg had given her, she soon would be again.

So it shocked her just a little when she found herself peeking covetously at the bride's bouquet and whispering, "Yes, I believe I would."

He smiled and led her off the dance floor. Putting his arm around her, he steered her over to the edge of the roof terrace.

It was a tall building, and the city of New York was spread out below them in a sweeping panorama of color and movement. Bright. Vibrant. Alive. Like her love for this remarkable man.

He embraced her from behind, his tall frame wrapped around her like a shield. For a long while he just held her. Listening to the music and laughter of the wedding party, gazing out at the incredible view.

"What I've done for most of my life . . ." he said at length. "It hasn't been nice. And it definitely hasn't been pretty."

She nodded, resting her arms over his, loving the feel of his solid bulk at her back. "That's why you understand what I've been through. Those who haven't experienced the worst of humanity themselves can't possibly know what it's like."

He eased out a long breath. His arms tightened around her. "It works both ways."

"Yeah?" she whispered. Hardly daring to hope.

"You get me," he said. "More than anyone on earth ever has. From the beginning, you saw what I was, and it didn't scare you."

"Maybe a little." She smiled. "But in a good way."

"Well, *I'm* sure as hell scared," he said with a wry chuckle. "And not just a little. I've gone up against a dozen armed men with just my bare hands and haven't been half this terrified."

He wasn't the only one scared to death. Her pulse was suddenly racing. "Of me?"

"Of that damned bouquet."

She turned her head to look up at him. "You don't have to be. We don't need a bouquet, Gregg. We can just—"

"No. That's the thing. I *want* to give you one. I want to give you a ring and a dress, and everything that goes with it. I want you to be mine. Forever. I just . . ."

Her heart nearly stopped when he didn't go on.

He took a deep breath. "I'm afraid I don't know how to love you like you deserve to be loved."

Of all the things he might have said . . . "Oh, Gregg." She turned in his arms and put hers around him, moved to tears. "Believe me, you already do."

He brushed his thumb, oh, so tenderly, over her cheek, gathering up the tear. He touched the heart earring he'd given her. "Yeah?"

How could he ever doubt it? "Oh, yes."

He smiled almost shyly. "I'm glad you feel that way. Because I do love you. I didn't think I'd ever know what that feels like. But if this isn't love, I can't imagine what is. It's pretty damn amazing."

Surprised joy bubbled through her. She couldn't believe he'd actually said the words. "I love you, too, Gregg. With all my heart."

He put his arms around her and kissed her. It was the sweetest kiss she'd ever tasted. Bursting with the flavor of unexplored emotions and a future just waiting to be savored.

"So, about that bouquet," he murmured. From somewhere he produced a gorgeous small bunch of yellow roses and blue forget-me-nots. She smiled in recognition. He offered it to her.

"It's perfect," she whispered. She took the beautiful flowers and returned his kiss with all the love she felt in her heart. "And so are you."

"Be mine, Gina," he said. "Be mine for always, and I promise I'll keep you safe and never let you want for anything."

"I will. For always," she said, holding him close. Was it really possible to be this happy? "Oh, Gregg. You're all I'll ever want."

She knew that whatever their tomorrows held, they'd always meet it together, and their hearts would be filled with love.

And then he kissed her. A sweet, loving kiss. A kiss that would last forever.

ALSO FROM

NINA BRUHNS

SHOOT TO THRILL

A sexy black-ops hero and a beautiful ER nurse must fight for their lives—and for a love they never thought possible.

Only former CIA spy Kick Jackson can identify a terrorist and stop a bloodbath—and his conscience won't let him walk away. His enemies send him running into the arms of the one woman with the power to save him: nurse Rainie Martin. Thrown together in a deadly international game, they must battle to stay alive while finding the courage to open their hearts.